# BOND HUNTER

A NOVEL

*by*

KIA W. MCINERNY

BOND HUNTER



ISBN-Paperback: 9780984729418

PUBLISHED IN USA BY:
Size Four Publishing

For questions about the novel or the author, please refer to
*kiawrites.com (Fiction Page)*

Cover art and design: *Drew Stalker, London*



First printing, 2015

## AUTHOR'S NOTE

Between 1924 and 1930, through the U.S. "Dawes Plan" the cash starved Weimar government acquired capital through foreign loans. Backed by gold, and with interest payable in U.S. dollars, the bonds were aggressively sold throughout small-town America, by one of Wall Street's most prestigious banking houses. Shortly after Adolph Hitler's appointment as Chancellor, the Third Reich defaulted on the loans, using the issuing banks to buy back the bonds from panicked investors for pennies on the dollar. Following Hitler's defeat, Germany was pressured to repay all of its debt. Through political sleight-of-hand, Germany did not pay it all back, leaving many U.S. investors unpaid after 80 years. This is the subject of BOND HUNTER. *[Find more history and images on Amazon's Kia McInerny Page.]*

*For and in grateful acknowledgment of ~*

*Gary and Teddy, for their inspiration; and Mick and Mike, for their incisive comments.*

*Special thanks to Jeffrey Weston for encouraging my interest in the German gold bonds.*

## *1*
## *3 October 1994, Manhattan*

Quiet autumn rain was falling in the street outside the brownstone offices of Rand & Rand, Attorneys at Law. Inside, Kenna Rand sat at her grandfather's desk in the ground-floor library they had shared as law partners. A fireplace of pale limestone dominated the high-ceilinged rooms and a low fire had been burning for some time within. Kenna sat in silence, acutely aware of the warmth and comfort, in striking contrast to the terror of the day before.

She took a sip of Barry's tea with milk that she had brewed simply as an excuse for getting out her mother's tea set. She inspected the teacup, saucer, and small plate. The graceful shapes of the Irish-made china gave form to her past.

Her mother had preferred Lapsang Souchong, a strange smoky tea that made Kenna gag and moue up her face. She knew this preference of Moira Rand because she had been told by her grandfather, keeping alive for her some memory of the parents who had died when she was three. But her parents were gone. And now, grandfather too. Gone.

At the first burp of the fax machine, she stood up. She hovered over it, willing herself to wait until the sound stopped completely. Two double-spaced pages reposed in the in-tray. This, then, would be the report of her grandfather's attending physician she had insisted he fax over to her. She skipped the preliminary remarks and turned to page two, ignoring her racing pulse: "Findings:"

*"Deceased expired within four hours of the onset of symptoms: delirium, high fever, rapid heart rate. Cause of death: heart failure. Noted: small amounts of an unknown viral agent of high toxicity in subject's blood... tests inconclusive."*

Bloody cold, she murmured, adopting an expletive of her grandfather's. Bloody damn bleeping chilly account of the death of someone whom she'd never imagined losing.

Seating herself again at the desk, she stared at the words. She had thought the report would galvanize her. Now the question came: galvanize her to do what?

The rain struck the window like the rapping of an insistent stranger. She turned to the darkened glass. In her reflection, the events of yesterday commenced unfolding like a series of movie stills. She was lost in the horror of it once more.

# 2
## *2 October 1994*

Kenna glanced behind her and saw the woman, still twenty yards behind them, advancing with long striding steps. The cruelty of the stranger's face briefly shocked Kenna, the impression etching itself into her unconscious. How could it not? The man's Fedora, shading her cheek line, what little of it remained exposed beyond the frames of the aviator glasses she wore. Leather coat zipped up tight at the woman's throat. Pointy boots.

The woman looked to be in her late forties, with an austere European style. Fashionable again to wear hats, Kenna thought. But mostly among twenty-somethings like herself. The effect was a bit of drama that did not quite fit the morning's Sunday-in-the-park motif.

Kenna resisted the impulse to walk faster. She felt herself frowning, gave the stranger a few seconds more, then shifted her attention to her grandfather, her emotions still uncertain after the contentiousness of half an hour before.

The gray dawn had turned into one of those crisp, brilliant October Sundays the city was known for, when a seductive breeze and dazzling sun drew every child, woman and man to the outdoors. It was understood people would drift outside to sample what paradise must be like. The kind of day, Kenna later thought, with bitterness at Nature's guile, on which John Lennon had been killed.

"'Tis beautiful in New York today," Jack Rand said, lapsing into his native Irish manner of speech. "Ye were right to get us out of the office." He squinted upward. "Sun's fierce this morning. We'll be bronzed into a California tan before noon."

His words were a gracious attempt to dismiss her cloudburst from this morning. She felt the small sense of shame over her remarks and pushed it away.

He studied her silent profile. "Not all about winning, lass. Sometimes pitching the pebble into the water is enough. No need to drain the lake."

"I hope you'll be happy then, with a Pyrrhic victory."

"Are we onto that again?" He cocked his head in mock appraisal. "And do ye know who King Pyrrhus was?"

"Do you?"

"That's my girl."

She decided to meet him half way. "Greek King who lost so many men in his battle with the Romans, he remarked: 'Another such victory and I shall be ruined.'"

"I don't intend to lose this battle." His smile returned. "Anyway, ye cannot say the subject lacks romance. The Weimar bond portfolio hasn't been seen since the 1950s."

"Shouldn't we ask why?"

He linked her arm through his. "What thinks ye about touring the Aran Islands on me way back? Won't be cold in Ireland for another month. Bit of fishing. Golf. On that windswept tundra they call a fairway. Fireside chess over a pint of Guinness and soda bread sandwiches. Ye could meet me in Shannon, lass. Aye, could do with a spit of a holiday – after the Swiss bankers."

So he would make the trip to Basel, in spite of her misgivings. Project still on then. All systems go.

The woman was gaining on them. Or was she pacing them? Was this the kind of person the German government would send to check out her grandfather? As she watched, the figure disappeared behind a man jogging with twin strollers. She felt relieved.

"Remember our trip to Kilgornin – when ye was a kid? Scramblin' over McCarthy Castle with your cousins. Couldn't tear ya' away. Even at the gloom of dusk when the chill clung fierce as death." There was a catch in his voice when he spoke of Ireland.

"It was the Norse broke down our castle, grandfather,' ye said." He lifted his head in a sly smile. "Bloody Norse." His rancor against Ireland's early invaders was a secret jest between them.

"I'd love to go there again," The urgency in her voice was fresh, and surprised her.

Jack Rand paused to adjust his neck scarf, a thinly veiled attempt to hide his shortness of breath. She had been walking too fast for him, a pace that had not been a problem a year ago. Or even last spring.

"How about it, then? Good for one more turn around the park? We'll make ourselves fierce for tea and sausages."

They reached the shortcut path to Tavern on the Green. The eleven o'clock bells rang out pure as a child's laughter, a sudden breeze swept the last scent of blossoms her way. Kenna had to confess she was looking forward to a cup of Earl Grey and plate of sausages and eggs.

"Let's turn down now," she said. "Stake out our table before the brunch-crowd."

As she spoke, her eye caught the stranger behind them. Chill out, why don't you? What the bloody hell is your hurry? Instinctively, she led her grandfather closer to the stone bridge. He smiled into her own green-gray eyes, tucking a dark curl behind her ear. She returned his smile, a small one, and resolved to refrain, at least this morning, from further discussion of the Weimar bonds.

She heard the swish of leather in movement. Felt the pressure of something behind her. The next moment Jack

Rand was clutching his shoulder. His face flinched in pain, his strong features contorted.

"Gramper. Gramps. Are you okay?"

Even as she supported him, she flipped open her cell phone, tapped in the numbers and heard the brisk greeting of the emergency receptionist. "Nine-One-One. Where are you?"

What instinct caused her to look up?

In chocolate Fedora and leather jacket, a woman's back was vanishing among the joggers of Central Park.

"Stop! Please. Help!"

Kenna turned back to her grandfather who had crumpled to the sidewalk.

## 3
## *5 October, 1994 Westport*

The wake for Jack Rand was held in his sister's Connecticut garden, where the accents flew thick and strong. As Irish as the brown ale her guests called 'lovely porter.' As hearty as the soda bread sandwiches of smoked salmon imported from the North Sea, and served by the old-country couple who'd started with Aunt May, fresh off the boat and thankful for employment.

Michael Fein arrived late to the rambling white cottage in Westport. He made his way through the house to the garden, where the mourners were in full enjoyment of the last of autumn's crisp, fair days.

*I'm the only Jew here*, Michael Fein thought as he took in the russet cheeks and cornflower eyes of Jack Rand's relations. But religion wasn't the only thing that distinguished Michael Fein from the other mourners. They believed Jack Rand's death was from natural causes.

Michael accepted a glass of mineral water from a passing tray, scanning the guests until he located Jack's granddaughter, standing apart. He matched this young woman with his memory of an elegant, remote child from the Bronx. She would be in her mid to late twenties now. She was still athletic and reserved. *Too* reserved. It might be more difficult than he'd imagined to break the ice.

Michael enjoyed a talent for appraising women. He was hardly a Casanova, but had long ago given up concealing his admiration for the opposite gender. Still, a woman had to possess something more than mere beauty to compel his interest. Intelligence. An air of mystery. Some quality to excite his curiosity. He studied Kenna Rand with the concentration of an artist about to paint her.

Her dark hair wound itself into an abundance of natural curls secured by combs. Kennedy hair, he thought. What would it be like when it was free, tumbling down? And her eyes, ink blue. She was five feet seven, plus or minus, but so slender in the black linen sheath that she looked taller.

Certainly he had known women who were more beautiful. His former wife for example. But there was an exotic quality about Kenna. An athlete's grace – and something else. A defect really. Her eyes were almond shaped and close together, giving her the gaze of a Sphinx. Not wide-eyed, or conventional. He found the result oddly compelling.

As Michael studied her, he became aware that Kenna was the subject of another's interest. He glimpsed the other man, blond, agile, moving in and out of the dappled light. A handsome man, bold, with a deft charisma, he wore a dark suit and white linen shirt. He wore no tie, and below his trousers, black canvas sneakers with high tops.

Even as Michael watched, the other maneuvered with purpose. Michael decided he was accustomed to moving quickly. A spy, Michael thought fancifully. And he decided it was probably time to do what he had come here to do.

# 4

She was here to observe, not to grieve, Kenna told herself. Grieving was private. She remained apart from the others, surveying her great-aunt's garden, using fierce concentration, an old trick of childhood, to shut back emotion. Today, she would be the watcher. From such an exercise she would use this unhappy event.

A covey of green and black mallards gathered at the near end of the pond under a congress of willows. The air was soft for October, the sky crisp and dazzling. Yet the birds flapped fretfully. Change was near.

*Where are you, grandfather?*

One day in her childhood, she'd hidden under a pile of leaves at this spot. She had grown cold and fallen asleep and, when she awoke, a light snow obscured her view of the house. Trees, swing and gazebo had become intimidating goblins in a Grimm's fairytale. She felt too scared to strike out on her own and it was dark at four o'clock when her grandfather clasped her hard to his chest.

*A wake is no place for grief, lass.*

Scanning the guests, she saw Michael Fein and remembered what she was there for. She had expected someone from JAFA to turn up. How could they stay away? One of them had something to tell her.

Dark, bulky, attractive, he might have been an inch taller than Kenna, but he looked shorter. Broad without flab, too trim to be called fat, not muscular enough to be stout, he was an ample man, exuding a male energy that held the promise of security. His passions, she decided, with an athlete's disapproval, would include fine wine and fois gras, and other luxuries of the senses.

So here was the head of JAFA. The acronym meant nothing to most people. Jack Rand had only recently been retained by the group, a quasi-political entity seeking to address "ownership questions" from the days when the Nazis seized property belonging to Jewish citizens. Her grandfather's skill of refined arm twisting led to the return of large art holdings from galleries as revered as London's Tate and New York's Metropolitan Museum. But success had emboldened JAFA. The trip to Basel, for example. Was it driven by the need to resolve injustices of the past – or political thuggery?

Michael crossed the lawn to the tented table where Kenna stood among the rounds of storytelling and gossip. She took her time meeting his eyes, knowing she could not avoid the interview altogether, but willing herself to hold out as long as she could. No one said she had to be gracious. If Michael Fein himself was here – exalted lawyer for Jewish causes, honorary chair of Columbia Law School, spokesman, author, advocate for Nazi reparations – if he had decided to attend her grandfather's wake in lieu of sending an associate, he must want something. And if he wanted the interview that badly, he could come to her.

The lyrical speech of her Irish relations swirled around her.

"So, Kenna, luv, listen to this. Ye didn't know your grandfather in the early days. Never turn his back on a fight. We was staggerin' home from the pub one night, me being new to Dodge City, when two blackguards shifted us for our wallets. We hadn't more than five bucks between us – nothin' to fight for. But Jack, he gives me a wink that says we'll play it to the end. With naught but drink for courage, he looks the ruffians dead-on in their eyes: 'yer not knowin' who we are, obviously, he says. 'Yer not knowin' who ye got on the other end of the tether.'

"Puffed up tall, and lookin' fierce – always did have the gentleman's posture, did Jack, and with me lookin' on all reverence, as if he were the Pope. 'I'm the limb of the law,' he says in a whisper. 'The limb of the law.'

"What do ye think the scoundrels done then?"

The story teller paused for dramatic effect.

"They throw down our wallets and takes off like two hares from a blue tick hound. And yer grandfather – he roars. Laughed 'til the tears fell, we did."

"Aye. Aye. 'Tis so," a companion piped up. "As I'm standin' here with this lovely brown porter."

Two women exchanged a look and tittered, including Kenna in the joke. "We're here about Jack, Kevin," one said.

"Ah, yes." The sudden transformation into mournful-face was comical. "'Tis sad Jack will never lift another glass of Guinness."

A strange race, she thought, that admires its drink with such passion.

Michael Fein made no outward display of impatience, just stood within earshot, openly enjoying the repartee. Give him that, Kenna decided, when at last he made eye contact with her, and offered a conspiratorial shrug. He knew how to discreetly bide his time.

"You're not Irish," she said.

"But you are."

"Irish-American,"

Kenna studied the man with interest. His beard was closely trimmed, soft, lustrous, and black. Dark hair, slicked back, and quick dark eyes, with an expression of amused observation that said he belonged here.

"The Jews and the Irish," Michael picked up the thread. "In some ways our stories are similar. The British attempted to annihilate the Irish by starving them, and the Nazis – well, we know all that. The difference is the Celts held onto their land. It's taken us two thousand years to reclaim ours. And, by the looks of events in the Middle East, we're still fighting for it."

"Tribes. Hasn't civilization grown beyond that?" She regretted the tone even before the words were out of her mouth. She knew she sounded arch. And rude, given who the man was.

"I suppose we're a tribe of our own," she amended. "Anglo-Americans."

"Your parents were Irish?"

"My mother's family came from Galway. The Aran Islands, if you know where they are. My father was from Kerry in the south."

She looked down at the golden cuff bracelet that circled her wrist. It had a mate in Dublin's Celtic Museum.

"I'm American really. Born and bred." She was aware her accent betrayed her, too soft to be British, too crisp for American.

"I was born right here in Westport," she said. "It's true I have an Irish passport. That was my grandfather's doing." She was speaking too much, out of nervousness.

The man in high-topped sneakers watched them from the pond. Though in his late forties, he appeared fit as a schoolboy with a schoolboy's nonchalance. Not exactly your local choirmaster–she was sure he too had come for something more than to pay his respects.

She turned back to Michael. "The Irish encourage dual citizenship," she continued in a casual tone, already regretting her comment about the passport. The less JAFA knew about her the better.

"It's their way of denying a negative population rate. As a people, you'll find we're comfortable with denial." The casualness was gone now. She made a slight gesture at their surroundings as if to say: "See how we deal with death?"

Michael nodded his understanding. Dancing. Storytelling. Children playing tag through the obstacle course of Sunday-dressed adults. It was only three in the afternoon and the men were already growing blurred with drink, weaving as they stood, or stumbling like toddlers to the bar. And all around them, the murmurs of whispered gossip, secret denunciations, and invocations of the ancient mysticism they called the Church.

"Is all this meant to console me?" she asked.

"I wish I knew you well enough to answer that," he said, with a crooked smile. He hesitated. "I did know your grandfather. It sounds false – every tribute does – but he was an astute lawyer. An individual of high intelligence and strong personal ethics. I thought him an exemplary man. But I can't claim to be completely unbiased – if it weren't for Jack Rand I wouldn't be here today."

"That sounds a bit dramatic."

A quick grin flashed through his beard. "High drama," he agreed. "But true. I wasn't conceived yet when my family fled Germany but I always knew it was your grandfather who arranged our entry into the U.S. It must have been very difficult at that time. An unpopular cause – landing a boat load of Jews at Ellis. That's why I said – "

"I understood you," Kenna replied. "You wouldn't be here today."

Only a subtle tightening of his mouth suggested his impatience. "I would have liked to offer a eulogy. I was traveling when I heard."

"It wouldn't have changed anything for me."

*Ye're gifted more than most, lass. Ye can spare a little charm.*

"We could sit down for a moment," she said.

She led him across the lawn to the gazebo, using the opportunity to check on the man in the black sneakers. He was occupied at the bar for the moment, but hardly fitting in. Good. Why don't you just have a brew and leave?

Michael Fein moved lightly despite his build, in a way that robust people often surprise with their grace. An air of natural confidence as he moved bespoke that all the universe was created for his interest and amusement.

When they reached the pergola by the pond, she chose an iron bench, which said they would not be staying long. He took a seat on the rustic swing across from her and, as if he knew his choice would disarm her, tapped it into motion with his foot.

"Forgive me," he said. "I wouldn't intrude on your grief. But the matter is urgent." He brought the swing to a stop. "I represent JAFA."

"I know." Her thoughts returned to the Sunday before, and the legal brief her grandfather had asked her to review.

Tears threatened to surface. She lowered her eyes to the grass, as if she was absorbed in Michael's words.

"On Friday," he was saying, "thanks in part to your grandfather's lobbying, the German government offered to make good on outstanding bonds tendered through BIS – the Bank for International Settlements. Our portfolio of such bonds is substantial. But the window of opportunity is brief. Our request for an extension has been declined. The bonds must be registered there within two weeks."

She felt the urge to run. Out the gates and up the silent roads. An all-out wild sprint until she limped, hit the wall like every runner does, sooner or later.

"Your grandfather was going to represent us in Basel. Now – " He proffered a shrug that made it seem they were in this together.

So that's it. She was to play youthful Maid Marian to his deliberately disarming Robin Hood. Window-dressing for the organization's attempt to strong-arm blood money for a forgotten cache of old bonds. *Rather the long way around, isn't it?*

"The bonds contain the gold clause," Michael continued, as if she did not know as much or more than he did about the bonds. "JAFA's portfolio is worth billions of dollars in today's terms."

Kenna lifted her brow in skepticism. Well – yes. That could be true. But the German government was struggling to unify the European Union, straining to pump up a stagnant economy and retain its image as Europe's strongman. JAFA's demand on the gold bonds would be staggering. With gold at $400 per ounce and interest accruing at 7% from the 1930s, each $1000 bond could be worth half a million dollars. No–it would not be easy to forge a settlement of such vast sums. She had said as much to her grandfather.

"I know," Michael said quietly. "It's a long shot. Germany has avoided paying for six decades. And the State Department is unlikely to force their hand right now. Claims associated with Israel – not the most popular of U.S. allies. Like you, we have concerns. I've read your law review article."

With her left hand she etched the Celtic torque into her wrist until a red line inflamed her skin. Obviously some vetting of her was done in advance of his visit today. He had armed himself for flattery. An immediate wariness raised the pale hair along her arms.

"The few individuals who've tried to redeem them in the past have met with – accidents," she said. She felt her cheeks turn hot. "Like my grandfather–whom you admire so much."

"You don't really believe there's any connection."

"No?"

"Your grandfather was known for high profile cases. If you have reason to suspect foul play, there's a long list–"

"Right."

"It's been a tedious path," Michael said. "At last the subject of Nazi reparations is on the table. Germany has signaled the financial world it will review the subject of bond repayment. But, as I'm sure you realize, time is against us. Soon the original investors will be dead. Most are in their eighties. Sympathy for their claims will die with them –"

"I'm familiar with the cause." She'd enjoyed doing the bond research for her grandfather. Turning her notes into a law review article didn't hurt her scholastically. Her conclusion, that Germany's recent unification removed a major obstacle to enforcement of the debt, formed the basis for JAFA's demand. Yes. She knew the issues.

"– the claim could be settled in two weeks. Once the demand is submitted to BIS, your role would be finished. We need you in Basel. To add credibility, like your grandfather. Two weeks. Possibly three. After that..." He waited, watching her. "Jack was prepared to leave immediately."

Kenna suppressed an impulse to turn away. "I'm starting a new job," she said.

"Attorney position?"

"Yes."

"Where?"

"Hermann & Kroft."

Michael gave a low whistle. "Very nice. Plum job. John Hermann – former Secretary of State?"

"Yes."

"Nice contacts," he said.

"For helping JAFA, you mean?"

"Yes."

At least he had the good grace not to evade the truth. She slid forward on the chair. "To be perfectly candid, your offer doesn't make any sense. Yes – I know the history of the bonds. I am familiar with your aims. But why hire me? Negotiations of this complexity are never handled by first-year lawyers."

He offered an ironic smile. "Perhaps I was wrong in thinking my reasons are obvious."

"What reasons? Because I'm a woman – or a Gentile? Or do you simply want someone else to take the fall?"

Michael pursed his lips in gentle rebuke. He shrugged. "Nobody knows this obscure area as you do. You're miles ahead of other lawyers we could attach at this point."

She shook off the slimy mantle of expert. "You're a member of the Bar – why don't you handle it?"

"I intend to – with your assistance."

*The gold bonds – they're danger, lass.*

She straightened as if to stand up. For her, the interview was finished. "I'm honored to receive your offer," she said, falling back on another trick of childhood – using formality to distance herself.

He restrained her with his hand. "You're about to say no. Don't insult me by pretending to be flattered. That isn't what this is about."

"Excuse me, I must be slow witted today. What exactly is in it for me?"

"Don't you want to know who killed your grandfather?"

The words hovered between them. In contrast to the delicate terms of his pitch, obviously scripted – his last words had the force of a hammer. Billions of dollars at stake, he had said. Gold reserves. European Union. Political ties to Israel. And JAFA knew. This man knew. *Bloody murderer!*

She dared not speak until she'd got hold of herself. So far, he continued, in his cool, reasonable voice, no one connected Jack Rand's death to JAFA. It was a time for – discretion. It would mean so much right now if she could step into her grandfather's shoes. Assume his role – help to avoid the adverse publicity of a difficult association.

Her mind leapt ahead, scanning for the clincher – the final sympathetic "close" of his appeal. Not difficult at all to lie about her grandfather's death, collude in some official sanitized version. Even give out a press release about a sudden stroke. Heart attack. Bad case of flu. Then take up the baton as if it had been passed in a schoolyard game. You can go to hell, she decided. She wanted to get up and jog to the house, through the front door and outside to the street, leaving him there. But she felt frozen in place. Unable to lift a muscle. She would remain seated like a statue until his last words were out.

"All we're asking is your consideration. This is a turning point for JAFA – and for you."

The seconds passed with his eyes on her. She realized she must have given herself away to a near-stranger. Michael Fein had discerned her deepest fears, played on them, and brilliantly exploited them. She eased forward again. He seemed to be waiting.

A fretful cacophony drew Kenna's eyes to the pond. An unexpected gust of wind swept the last of summer's leaves onto the vast lawn. As she shivered in her sleeveless sheath, the mallards flapped anxiously and tried to fly. She stood up. With reluctance, she felt his extended hand grip hers in a formal parting handshake. "I hope you don't expect me to thank you for coming," she said.

#

The fiddlers were setting up as Michael prepared to leave the wake. He liked Irish music and dancing, and he was almost sorry he could not stay. But his work was done. She hadn't said no. Still, Michael paused, curious. Waiting.

The deft man in the black sneakers approached Kenna and stood close, closer than Michael would have, crowding her, teasing her with his physical encroachment, as if daring her to step back. A spy, Michael thought, with sudden whimsy.

A fleeting sensuality passed over Kenna's features even as she drew back from him. Abruptly the younger man met Michael's eyes. The moment of contact between the two men, though slight, created an almost primal tension between them.

Michael felt the hard seed of disappointment before he turned away. Women were drawn to him. Kenna Rand had been, too. In their brief meeting, he had glimpsed the fierce, self-reliant child he remembered, lonely and furious at being alone. Still, he hadn't come here for romance but for business. And he was forty-seven. The operative, if that was what he was, deserved the field.

The spy, the Celtic princess and the Jewish lawyer, Michael thought, as he claimed the only German car in the driveway.

# 5

The guest who claimed Kenna's attention was a youthful-looking man closer to forty than thirty. Expression tracks crinkled the fair skin around his eyes, suggesting years of squinting into the sea. "The Spy," Michael Fein had named him. "Adventurer," another might have said. And in truth, Nicholas Chariot was both.

"At last we meet," The man said, issuing his name in a clipped manner.

"Chariot," she repeated.

She knew the name, though she had tried to stay aloof from that part of her grandfather's life. The Irish part. Kenna extended her hand automatically, aware of an urgent desire to avoid this interview. This man had been an acquaintance of her grandfather's. What did he want from her?

"I wouldn't have thought you'd attend," she said. She found herself speaking with the crisp formality that came naturally to her in the company of strangers.

Chariot moved farther into her private space. His tone took on a mocking Irishness. "`Tis the Fates have brought us together."

Games. She would not participate – not today of all days.

"Why did you come?" she asked.

"I'm part of Jack's unfinished business."

"How does that concern me?"

"I don't have to spell it out for you." He spoke softly now, with no trace of the accent. "I promised Jack. We go back awhile. A long time, it would seem to you." He paused, selecting carefully his words. "Look – Michael Fein and JAFA will ask you to carry on. They've probably convinced you to go to Basel."

He checked his facts in her eyes. "It's dangerous for you to become involved. We can't always protect you."

"We?" Kenna allowed her voice to convey impatience, though it was fear she struggled to suppress.

"What is it you've come to say, what do you know about my grandfather's death?"

"Murderer, is it? Is that what the lady thinks of me?"

"This is not the time –" And then she knew it *was* the time. "Who should I be looking for? And where should I be looking? At least tell me that. If a debt is owed to my grandfather, pay it to me."

But she was too late. Aunt May approached in the company of Cardinal Leary. Bloody church. What solace could it offer now?

Nicholas Chariot, too, observed Aunt May and the priest bearing down upon them. He drew a card from his pocket and pressed it into Kenna's hand. "You won't always see us," he said, speaking quickly. "But we'll be there."

"What are you talking about?"

"Irish loyalty. A promise to your grandfather. That's all you need to know." The bold man in high-topped sneakers flashed a smile as he moved away.

Kenna studied the engraved name of an organization with a Gaelic name. On the back was a handwritten telephone number with an international prefix.

"Bloody hell," Kenna said softly before greeting the Cardinal.

# 6
## *6 October, 1994*

A thin European drizzle darkened Zurich's Bahnhofstrasse as Klaus Kessel came out of the central railway station and strode the few steps to the Zurich branch of J.Dalton & Company.

The historic building, whose original classical design of 1894 was now famous for a fanciful facade by Espano Rivera added a century later, dominated Zurich's famous banking street like a dowager-queen among courtiers.

Kessel swept through the sea of commuters, a vain, handsome man of five feet eleven inches with salon-bronzed skin and a fringe of cornsilk hair that wisped back from his collar. His brows were so fair they were mere suggestions above the Ray-ban wraparounds that shielded his startling green eyes – the result of intensely-hued contact lenses that covered his own irises of yellow gray.

He was not smiling. His summons to the old-line banking firm had been somewhat peremptory. He had been told to go along, listen to the banker's proposal. Yet he suppressed a nagging suspicion that he was part of the "favor to a friend" syndrome that marred the relationship between American intelligence and big business. To be perfectly blunt, the interview would be a waste of time. He had long ago reached the point of intolerance for such an exercise. Civilians, he thought with disgust. They caused problems every time.

Kessel carried a briefcase of brushed aluminum. His jacket of Spanish leather, khaki trousers, shirt of blue linen, rubber-soled English loafers, and short, biscuit-colored gloves, buttoned snugly at the wrists, imparted a look that was intimidating and all-business.

Indeed the impression was suited to the man. His first career with the Navy Seals had trained him in survival and killing. Two years at Monterey's institute of linguistics gave him a mastery of German, French, and Spanish, while a degree in economics from Geneva's International School, with a minor in computer science, augmented his skills.

Kessel represented the new breed of global executive, equally able to hack into a target's computer files or dispatch him with a silenced Glock magnum. Outwardly at least, he was the ideal choice for his position as European bureau head of economic espionage for the Central Intelligence Agency.

On this patchy autumn morning in the middle of a dull week, Kessel's aluminum briefcase contained only a two-page briefing document. The subject of that treatise was gold – specifically, the historic German gold bonds issued by Wall Street firms during Hitler's rise to power. Kessel was among the few who could predict that the outcome of the German bond issue was crucial not only to the fate of the European Union – but to the economic supremacy of the United States.

## 7

The man who had bidden Kessel to appear at the offices of J.Dalton & Company stood at the window overlooking the Bahnhofstrasse from the 13th floor.

John Hermann was solid as an oak, with a powerful well-shaped head. He could have passed easily for any of the sixty-something men who ruled the corporate dynasties of the late twentieth century. Behind his back – never in his presence – he was called "the Umlaut," a crude sobriquet that attested as much to his aggressive bearing and speech as it implied concerning his savagery in business.

As Hermann watched, Kessel swiftly ascended the steps to the bronze doors of the building. Even pausing outside to snap an answer for security, the CIA man was in motion. Hermann thrust his face close to the glass and pursed his lips in approval. Not to be stopped, the banker thought. Like some predator cat on the plains of Africa.

A few moments later, Kessel was shown into the green and gold conference room. He ignored Hermann's extended hand, seated himself in the middle of the long table and casually crossed his legs. He took in the banker's icy blue eyes and brush-cut, salt-and-pepper hair that stood up from his head like a dense crop of thistles. A chance contact with the crown of his host's head could do serious damage.

"Let us confirm what you have been told," Hermann began. Though naturalized as an American citizen, in his excitement Hermann spoke with a strong Teutonic accent.

Kessel opened the briefcase and removed the document. He scarcely looked at it, however, preferring to offer his account in a terse clipped manner.

"As outside director for the international banking firm of J.Dalton & Company, you are concerned about a large debt issue that the firm floated for the German government in the years that preceded the Third Reich. Over $800 million payable in gold coin and marketed largely to American Jews.

"Hitler ceased interest payments in 1934. His finance minister then offered to repurchase the devalued bonds at depreciated rates, using the same U.S. banks to fleece the bond-holders on the buy-back. I assume your firm profited from the commissions on the way out as on the way in –"

"I resent your use of the word 'fleece' in this context," Hermann grunted. His stainless steel watchband clicked on the glass table in a gesture of irritation. "It was a clever partnership: German thrift, American opportunism."

Kessel continued his businesslike tone. "A large series of bonds remains outstanding. A young woman in New York –" he pretended to consult his notes.

"–Kenna Rand– recently inherited her grandfather's portfolio of gold bonds. That in itself would not be a problem. Germany has avoided payment for decades. But she is a novice lawyer who has become something of an expert on their arcane terms."

His pace quickened. "Rand is known to have published a little known legal paper in which she asserts that J. Dalton, as trustee for the original bond-holders, failed to protect their interests. You suspect she has been approached by JAFA, which possesses the largest holding of outstanding gold bonds in the world. At the current price of Troy gold, JAFA's demand would bankrupt Germany, and turn the fledgling EU into a beggar economy – leaving the bank a singularly attractive 'deep pocket.'"

Kessel drilled Hermann through his Ray-bans, challenging the man to contradict his words. "For reasons that are obvious, you wish to discourage any such demand and, it appears, the State Department supports your goals. Is that about it?"

Hermann got up to close the door, which had drifted open, shutting out the tapping of his secretary's word processing, and the click of her assistant's heels as she moved between printer and desk. Unobserved by Hermann, the two women exchanged a look.

"You see exactly," Hermann said to Kessel. "We have a political problem."

Kessel studied the row of clocks on the damask wall behind his host: Zurich, New York, London, Hong Kong. Master of time zones. How pretentious. As if Hermann had his fingers on the pulse of three continents. As any fool could appreciate, the second hands were not even synchronized. The current time in Hong Kong clicked past – yes, twenty seconds later than in London. He already felt decidedly bored.

"You see what we are facing," Hermann insisted. "Such an event would be catastrophic. At today's value per Troy ounce, each $1,000 bond approaches $400,000. Add interest, penalties . . . I invite you to do the math as they say."

"I see why Germany has been slow to pay its debt," Kessel said, dryly.

"Yes. Yes." Hermann spoke impatiently. "The stakes are enormous. Germany's gold reserves would be reduced to nothing." He swept an arm angrily eastward toward Frankfurt. "We could care less how Germany shoots itself in its penis –"

An interesting metaphor, Kessel thought. He looked at his chronograph. Hermann was now halfway through the thirty minutes Kessel had mentally allotted to the meeting. And still no specific request for Kessel to take back to his superiors. A prickle of apprehension ran along his temple. Was the die already cast—was he to serve the interests of this *banker*?

Hermann continued. "Germany has been pressured by the Volcker Commission and other Jewish advocates to honor these antique instruments. Switzerland has already set a dangerous precedent by recognizing the lost assets of the Jews. Their Holocaust fund grows larger every day. Who knows what Switzerland's 'tainted neutrality' will end up costing the Swiss?" His disdain for the inconvenience of the situation was clear.

"A demand on German gold reserves at this time? If Germany cannot pay – or will not... well, you see the issue."

"Not really."

"Then you are an imbecile."

Kessel could feel an incipient rage building. He was not flattered to be summoned to heel by Hermann, a former Secretary of State. "Former" was, for Kessel, the operative word. Hermann left office in the 1970s in disgrace, having diverted U.S. financial support to certain international banks in which Hermann held controlling interests.

"This is the German Chancellor's problem," Kessel said, keeping his tone airy. "His government has to keep up reserves to remain in the European Union. If Germany pulls out, dreams of European unity are little more than sugar plum tarts in a Eurocrat's brain."

He lazily dropped his head from one side to the other, cracking his neck. "If you actually fear a demand on the bank, I don't see why you don't offer some token payment to the Israelis – for goodwill – and force Germany to pay a compromise sum in cash."

"Ludicrous! Never would it happen that way. In secret meetings among the European banking community, we discuss these things. German officials have confided absolutely – Germany has no intention of paying this debt."

"The bank has a problem," Kessel agreed, conversationally

"Not just the bank," Hermann said.

This nearly brought Kessel over the table. "Why should the U.S. be at risk?"

What arrogance for this civilian to attempt to manipulate the United States. A quick snap of the man's cervical vertebrae would plunge his skull into his collarbone. Kessel savored the vision for a second or two – the Umlaut, collapsed like a lifeless puppet.

He eased back in his chair. "One could take the view that the investors are entitled to the benefit of their contracts," Kessel said, trying now to goad the man. "Why – this lawyer Rand might ask, did they choose a high-risk investment in the first place, if not for your firm's reputation?"

Kessel leaned forward, enjoying himself now. "Where then, Dr. Hermann, do the equities lie? With the Wall Street bankers whose German alliance made them rich or–" He managed to put a tone of delicate derision into his voice, "the investors who were defrauded?"

Kessel had Hermann's full and unblinking attention.

"Such arguments," he continued, "if presented to the World Court at the Hague – in the current political climate, could lead to dire events. A collapse on Wall Street for example. The end of the firm. A fine old war-horse brought down at the end of the twentieth century. I would not be surprised if the bank's corporate suitor – oh, yes, I know about that – were impelled into the arms of Morgan Bank."

"You are not here to speculate," the man said curtly. "The point is… the point is–" He thrust his cranium toward his guest with new aggression. "Will you remove those sunglasses!"

Kessel removed his wraparounds with deliberation, exposing his galactic green stare.

A harsh grunt of surprise issued from the base of the bank director's throat.

"Don't you find your affectation something of a hindrance in your profession?" he demanded.

"To the contrary," Kessel replied. "It's all part of my stock-in-trade."

Kessel continued to regard the man unsmiling through his lizard gaze. And though the director's expression grew, if anything, more malevolent, Kessel did not yield. He could easily have punctured those watery blue eyes with his penknife and watch the blood spout from his fleshy arrogant face.

"You may be right," Hermann said. "In your analysis of fault. But you do not have all the facts in your papers. The U.S. has cause to be concerned. In 1930, a close relationship existed between the bank and certain cabinet members. At the bank's request, the United States Treasury issued letters endorsing the bonds. These letters are in the files of this woman's grandfather, also an attorney. Neither the bank nor the State Department can risk Germany's bad faith. We must remove this contingent liability for once and for all."

Kessel restored his Ray-bans to his face. "How convenient for you that the interests of the United States coincide with saving your firm from extinction," he said coldly." He gathered his files. "Let me warn you, if any conflict arises between U.S. interests and those of J.Dalton & Company…" He regarded the banker meaningfully.

"That is not possible."

"You should also know that I work alone. I am not a 'team player.'"

Hermann rose. "My secretary has your ticket on Lufthansa. Zurich to New York. The flight leaves this evening. Once there, you will coordinate with Andrea Reich-Hermann, director of Foreign Assets for the State Department. She has been briefed on your role in this. You are to observe, and act. All in your discretion."

Kessel glared at the man silently. So that's how it was. All had been decided before he'd even left his apartment this morning. "How far am I authorized to go?"

"I had hoped my message was clear: the bonds, the lawyer, those are the parameters of the problem. The details I leave to you." Hermann gestured his dismissal with the barely concealed ire of a host whose guest has outstayed his welcome.

#

Simple enough, Kessel thought, as he descended into the Bahnhofstrasse. He could steal the bonds and letters of endorsement. That much was easily accomplished. As for Kenna Rand, Hermann clearly thought he was hiring a grunt assassin, one who would snap on a silencer and dispatch the lawyer without thinking. That was surely one way to achieve the objective. But Kessel had another idea in mind. More artful. Less likely to implode. Already a plan was taking shape that would get him to New York and back within the week.

# 8

When it is noon in Zurich, it is six a.m. in New York. At that time of the morning the brownstone interior of Rand & Rand was cool as a cave. The street-floor library and study bore the deep chill of autumn.

Kenna slipped on her cotton pullover and, securing her hair with tortoise-shell combs, she seated herself at her grandfather's desk of Irish oak. She switched on CNN's international report and adjusted the volume to low.

She had completed her five-mile run, showered and breakfasted quickly on oat bran cereal with currants and cinnamon. Preparing enough for two came automatically. When she realized what she had done, she clasped her left hand around the bracelet of her right wrist and shut her eyes briefly, letting the sorrow pass over her. She rinsed her grandfather's portion into the sink, washed and dried the pan, and put it away. Then she made herself a fresh pot of tea and began the task of sorting her grandfather's records.

*Goodbye, Lass.*

Jack Rand had pared down his work to a comfortable gentleman's practice, handling only a few cases of particular interest. Kenna went over the files quickly, dictating a brisk letter to each client on a small hand-held Olympia. Her grandfather's clerk would type them up when he came in on Friday.

A neat stack of correspondence lay in the mahogany tray and she dictated quick responses to these as well. The last item was a small engraved envelope that bore the seal of the State Department. Inside was an invitation from Andrea Reich-Hermann, director of Foreign Assets. Cocktails. Tomorrow night, wasn't it? A hospitality event to welcome would-be trade partners from Europe, Asia, South America. She turned the envelope over expecting some mistake, but the hand- lettered name was correct: *Jack Rand, Esq.*

Kenna started to tap the number of the regrets-only line, then paused. Propping the card against the chrome desk lamp, she regarded it thoughtfully.

The international settlements office in Basel was a European central bank, formed after World War I to resolve claims against Germany. She had not accepted Michael Fein's offer. But if she *were* to accept, a letter of introduction would be – if not essential – extremely helpful. Who better to arrange this than the director of foreign assets?

Kenna turned up the volume of CNN's business report. From Frankfurt, a chunky woman with a coiffure less "styled" than shaken, reported the news from Europe in a snappy delivery that owed much to American slang. "In the markets today, more bobbing and weaving in time to Wall Street – what else is new? Expect more of the same this week as Greenspan ratchets down the so-called exuberance in the U.S. economy. That said, Germany's Bundesbank threw down the glove today for Italy and France. Raise those gold reserves or forget European Union membership in the near term. Germany has surely been eating its spinach lately. With gross national product up sharply over last year, there is much grumbling now that Europe's mighty-man is setting the financial pace. The Italian government, for one, has requested EU limits be lowered, insisting that reserves are artificially high to preserve power in the few. But for now, Brussels and Frankfurt are holding fast – that's the news from Frankfurt. Back to you, Lynn, in New York."

Peppy, bottle-blond New York Lynn was a pale sister to Frankfurt's frumpy yet imposing Sylvia Valtin. Kenna pressed the audio-mute button and swung her chair around to her grandfather's wall safe. Right-left-right to her birth date. From the safe, she removed the stiff brown portfolio containing Jack Rand's collection of gold bonds.

The package was the size of a folded newspaper, tied with a leather strap. On top was a memo in her grandfather's hand: "100 shares, bearer bonds, original value $1,000 each."

She loosened the strap and drew out a stack of crisp certificates printed on their face in three columns of English, German and French. In English, she read:

"Payable in gold coin of the United States of America of the standard of weight and fineness existing as of January 1, 1930… "

Small fortune – or worthless antiques? Kenna leafed through the bonds absently, prolonging the moment when she would dial Michael Fein's number and decline his offer.

Tucked between the pages was a black and white photograph. It was old and creased. Someone had placed it among the stack of certificates to keep it from curling, and then forgotten about it.

In the photo a schoolgirl, not more than nine years old, stood before the iron gates of a handsome residence. Behind her spread a formal garden and broad lawn. The girl's dark curls were held back by barrettes in the style of the 1940s, and her eyes shone with youthful expectancy. Her hands rested against the pleats of a plaid dress with white cuffs and collar. She loosely held the lead of an English spaniel.

Kenna turned the photograph over. The writing was light, made in pencil. She could see it was her grandfather's. The first notation, "Lara D., Berlin 1945." And then, in bolder script, "Where?" the word was underlined twice.

She had never seen the photograph before but the child's tentative smile aroused a faint memory. She searched through the small cache of archived files she had found earlier and put aside for storage. The name was familiar to her. She liked the sound of it. Lara. Romantic and sensible at the same time. An unusual name.

She imagined the little girl's parents choosing the name, feeling pleased with it, as her own parents might have chosen hers. Perhaps it derived from a book heroine or film actress. She studied the photograph again. It revived details of a story she'd learned so long ago it seemed a dark fairytale.

She located the thin file and began reading her grandfather's notes, filling in historical details from films and documentaries she had seen.

It was early in 1945, twilight for Germany's war on Europe. Adolf Hitler was growing ever more desperate, sending boys of twelve and thirteen to their deaths in his futile campaign against the Russians. His resources, financial and human, had run dry.

Against that backdrop, a young woman retained Jack Rand to barter a child's passage from Berlin to the United States. She had left the child in Germany to visit her parents, then feared for her own life if she returned. Jack was then twenty-five, Kenna's age, not long out of training for the bar at Dublin's Trinity College and filled with determination for correcting the wrongs of the world.

In the room's silence, Kenna slivered her eyes against the present and listened, as if her grandfather's client were there on the other side of the desk. *Take these bonds*, the woman pleaded. *Find Lara. Bring her to America.*

It was exactly the kind of challenge Jack Rand would have accepted. He had no use for the bonds his client offered in lieu of fees. His sense of justice would not have allowed him to decline. And he would have used his natural negotiation skills to carry out his charge.

Kenna regarded the bonds with fresh eyes, feeling her grandfather's frustration. What had happened to the child Lara? Had she believed her mother – or sister or aunt – would come for her? Did she feel terror – or worse – abandoned? Mom. Mommy. Mama.

A good faith tender had been forwarded to Berlin. Promises had been given. Arrangements made. And a false confidence imparted to his client by the youthful attorney. Despite pages of hopeful correspondence, it seemed the child had disappeared. The attorney's negotiations with the German government came to nothing. Jack Rand had failed.

Kenna swallowed hard. The tea felt like sand in her throat. It wasn't as if she couldn't spare a week from her life to fly to Basel, to press JAFA's arguments to the bank. Easy, then, to go on to Berlin, where the Allied Command Records were located. Others had solved the war's mysteries there. It was not implausible that a record of her grandfather's inquiries about Lara existed in its files. In the silence, she heard his voice – gentle, well-educated, with the faint lilt of the old country even after all these years:

*When, if not now, lass?*

Promptly at nine o'clock, Kenna dialed JAFA's offices in downtown Manhattan and was immediately put through to Michael Fein. Without prelude, she related the terms under which she would act as JAFA's special counsel in Basel. Agreed, he said, after a silence that was meant to seem reflective.

Almost as an after-thought, she invited him to join her the next evening at Andrea Reich-Hermann's apartment. His tone became cheerful. Expansive. Offering to send a car for her. Or, better yet, pick her up on the way to Andrea's. They could talk in the cab. Time was short, he said. There was planning to be done. Clearly, he assumed he had won her over. That her decision was due to that engaging artfulness he had displayed at the wake.

She politely cut him off. "I have a lot to do, Michael. Let's plan to arrive separately. I'll phone acceptance for us both. See you tomorrow tonight."

Then she dialed the State Department, and asked to be connected to the office of Foreign Assets. The cool British accent of Andrea's assistant came on the line.

"Accepting for tomorrow night? Will Andrea know you?"

"You may tell her," Kenna said, without a trace of uncertainty in her voice. "I represent the largest private holding of German gold bonds in the world."

# 9

Less than three miles from the brownstone where Kenna was seated at her grandfather's desk, a woman paced the carpeted luxury of her sixth floor suite in Manhattan's Carlton Regent Hotel.

Fabia Santiago was not a woman who spent her time in idleness. In silk shell, gold necklace and rings, she did not give the appearance of one awaiting an important business call. Even now she busied herself in preparation for the caller, listening to the playback of a man's voice on a hand held micro-cassette recorder, and flipping the pages of a paperback titled *A History of Modern Europe* that lay open on the desk. Next to the paperback lay the case for the micro-cassette.

The narrator's precise tone dominated the silent room: "*Slovakia is a country the size of Texas. It is bordered by Austria, Poland, Hungary and Czechoslovakia. When German troops invaded Czechoslovakia in 1939, Slovakia formed a Fascist state under Germany's protection. As such, Slovakia borrowed heavily to support Hitler's war on Europe. After the Allied victory in 1945, Slovakia fell to Soviet rule, under which it languished until the failure of Communism in 1989 led to Slovakian independence. But its financial link to Germany remains strong, as it continues to borrow heavily in an effort to modernize.*"

Fabia switched off the tape, lit a cigarette and inhaled deeply. The smoke exited her nostrils in two even streams. She moved slightly to check her image in the wall mirror. Her carefully coiffed cap of yellow hair and tailored suit suggested the perfection of a store mannequin.

She let her thoughts return to the day's modern history lesson. Slovakia's future as a sovereign state depended on solvency. And that depended on Germany's forgiveness of Slovakia's debt next week. If the struggling government could offer, as offset, the German gold bonds…

Given the hotel's double-paned windows, the silence was stifling. She stalked the periphery of the room, meeting the liquid gaze of her Doberman, who posed alert and quivering before a shining domed platter.

The dog inched forward as if to rise.

"Stay!"

He emitted a low growl. The woman locked eyes with the animal. His hostility escalated. Ears shot upward. The tan daggers along his snout crimped. And the sharp incisors the breed was known for bared through his lips. She closed her jeweled fingers slowly into a fist and pounded it once against her thigh.

Seconds passed before the dog's growl ceased. Almost imperceptibly, his haunches relaxed. But he could not conceal the intensity of his interest in the covered plate.

She had been christened Fabia Santiago Bucher by her mother, a large-boned Argentine Jew fifteen years younger than Fabia's father. The first time Fabia had seen her father she had fallen in love with him. He sat smoking with her mother in one of the bars that served the working class neighborhoods of greater Buenos Aires. She could see him now, gesturing with languid effeminacy, mocking Fabia and her brother Miguel with watery blue eyes that glittered with indifference.

Fabia had fallen lovestruck for the coarse gray wool of her father's German soldier's uniform, the alcoholic flush of his baby-soft cheeks and the stain of nicotine upon his pudgy fingers with their chewed nails. At some point that year in the early 1950s, shortly after Fabia turned five, Horst Bucher had married her mother, and the family moved the few miles to central Buenos Aires. There she became known as the 'donkey's daughter,' a crude reference to her father's role assisting the outflow of Germany's elite SS corps into Argentina. That was when she had first seen the crisp imposing currency known as the Weimar bonds.

She narrowed her eyes at the silent phone.

On the first ring, Fabia stubbed out her cigarette, removed her eighteen karat gold frames, folded them carefully before placing them in a velvet-lined eyeglass case.

On the second ring, she seated herself at the desk and clicked open a leather briefcase whose contents included the components of a travel umbrella. The umbrella's tip had been removed and fitted with a needle and syringe. Next to the shaft lay a jeweler's plastic bag, which contained two shiny brown pods from a South American plant common to most tropical gardens. The bag was coated with the residue of a third pod that had recently been encapsulated in the umbrella's tip. A mortar and pestle for grinding spices were also encased in plastic and coated with the same residue.

From the pocket of the briefcase Fabia removed a small leather pad of note paper and nudged it into position. In a careful script, she wrote: "Slovakian commission," lingering over the final word, adding little fluted swirls to the bottom of each "s."

On the fourth ring of the hotel telephone, she lifted the receiver.

"Countess Santiago?"

"Yes."

"You have the bonds?"

"Yes," she lied. "You will pay my price?"

The caller's hesitation was almost imperceptible. "On delivery. We will call back with the meeting place."

She set the phone back on its cradle and twiddled her gloved fingers at the Doberman. The dog rose and cantered to his mistress, nervously flicking his eyes from his mistress to the plate at her feet. She knelt down and raised the cover. The hotel kitchen's best sirloin tartare. At her signal, the dog lunged at the ground flesh.

"Don't get sloppy, Mister A," she said.

# # #

Almost immediately the phone rang again.

"This is Pradeep at reception. Could you join us for a brief conference, Madam?"

"Now?"

"At your convenience."

Despite the inquiring tone, it was statement, not question.

With one hand, she fanned the credit cards in different names that lay in a pile on the desk, and frowned. Her last transaction had precipitated the Isle of Man banking scandal in 1991. For her, the job had proven very successful. But that was three years ago. Other projects had failed, for one reason or another and she had lived on pittances since then. Dissipated, the large account she maintained in Lucerne, lavished on a lifestyle she loved. And now…

Unbearable humiliation.

Her first impulse was to keep the man waiting at least fifteen minutes. Then she thought better of it. She snapped the short lead on Mister A, restored the cards to her belt-purse and took the elevator to the second floor. She descended the stairs to the lobby, well aware of the distraction caused by her companion. She strode with Mr. A to the desk, where the elegant brown-skinned man named Pradeep studied his records with false interest.

"Is there a problem, Pradeep?"

"To be frank," the desk man began in the most sympathetic of voices. "Your credit card was not accepted." He spoke in a whisper. But she was too skilled an actor herself to be deceived by his show of concern for her privacy.

"Ah." She smiled, with a brilliance born of long practice. "I have had this trouble in the past when I leave Argentina. My husband's bank is so vigilant about my security." She removed the Cartier folio from her belt-purse and selected a card. He studied it.

"Madame," (We've progressed to Madame? she thought). "The name on this card is not the same as the registration."

"Is that a problem?"

"Well, we require–"

"You require payment. This card was issued in my unmarried name, before my marriage to Count Santiago. However, it is still active. I'm sure you will find it satisfactory."

"Excuse me." He left the desk, presumably to run the card through the hotel's charge plate. It was then that she saw the man watching her.

Was it the youngish man she had spoken with on the phone less than ten minutes before? Perhaps he had phoned from the lobby. That would have been clever. He could keep an eye on her, ensure that she was alone.

But the adrenaline pumping through her told her this was wrong. He looked – English. He looked, if she consulted past experience, like British intelligence. She had anticipated his arrival. But that did not mean she was ready for it. Just a little too soon.

"Pradeep," she kept her voice low and peremptory. "Pradeep."

"Yes, Madam?"

"Cancel the charge. I prefer to pay cash. A draft is arriving from Lucerne this afternoon. Will it be fine if we settle the account when it comes in?"

"Madam." Pradeep was very serious, very respectful in his assent. But he already knew it was a tactic. Did she imagine he didn't know?

"Please then follow up with me this afternoon, after your draft comes in. And–I will just keep your card, Madam. Just in case."

"Oh? Oh, yes. You can return it to me on checkout. Mr. A needs his morning stroll. I will just..."

"About your dog, Madam. Some of the guests object to the presence of the dog in the elevator. Perhaps you could call the bellman when your dog desires to leave the hotel, and he can take him down the back stairs."

"But my dog has always been welcome here. He doesn't like strangers handling him. This is insulting, Pradeep. What would you have me do?"

"We will help you find a kennel, Madam. Or – another hotel that is not so discerning."

"When?" Her voice betrayed her, showing the pressure and the fear. So close to her goal. One more night. Two days at the most.

"I will take care of it, Madam. I will find another hotel for you as soon as possible."

She must have imagined it, his nod in the direction of the intelligence man. He opened his beautifully manicured brown hands with an air of resignation. "I offer my apologies. The other guests…"

Tightly reining the dog, she addressed the animal: "Andiamo, Mister A." She swept through the lobby and out the glass doors. The surveillance man rose from his chair, put down his copy of the International Tribune and followed her out to the street.

# *10*

At five o'clock that evening, a Lufthansa jumbo jet from Zurich, Switzerland swung over the flat, reedy beaches of Long Island and released its landing gear for arrival at John F. Kennedy International Airport.

Klaus Kessel, already alert in his first-class seat, observed the plane's descent over the Atlantic Ocean. He had felt watched during the entire flight. Someone in business class had followed him on the plane. He felt certain of it. The woman had not diverted her eyes when he stared through her the several times he had forced their eyes to meet.

He ran through a contingency escape plan in the unlikely event the plane plunged into the rolling sea that lay on either side of the runway. He visualized himself arriving first at the front exit, torquing the handle upward, flinging the door inside and activating the slide.

Forget waiting for instructions from cabin personnel. He could be manning one of the rubber floats before the other cretins who were his fellow passengers realized they were down.

Alternatively, if he already faced fire on the exit side, he knew how to open the small service door on the right side of the plane. There would be no slide and no raft. If he had to jump into the freezing sea, so be it. There would be plenty of local water craft within minutes.

Satisfied with his mental preparation, Kessel drew out a contact-lens case and, with the efficiency of long practice, popped the leaf-green lenses into place.

Kessel had not been to New York for some time. Since his appointment to the Zurich office, he had been largely on his own. For one thing, Zurich was no longer fervent with espionage activity. Not of the traditional kind. The Middle East was the Agency's fashion darling of the moment, and he had not been chosen to oversee the hastily-assembled European staff to root out hostile Islamic activity, despite his years of loyalty and experience. He had not been among those lucky veterans whose ho-hum career path had profited from the sudden escalation of America's war on nuclear weapons. No one gave a hot-damn what he accomplished from his one man freedom stronghold in the center of Zurich. No one in the Agency-command, he thought with fresh outrage, really understood what Kessel did.

This line of thought brought him back to the subject of his visit. Nagging doubts remained. The CIA had its own share of bunglers. There had been budget cuts, lost confidence, talk of shutting down the unit altogether. Now things had gotten so bad it seemed, he was being called upon to take orders from a civilian.

Kessel swung through customs and out onto the curb. He hailed a cab and, despite the strain of a six-hour international flight, headed straight for the office of Andrea Reich-Hermann on the 15th floor of the aluminum and glass tower that comprised the Citicorp Building in mid-town Manhattan.

## *11*
## *7 October, 1994*

The brownstone where Kenna and her grandfather had lived most of Kenna's life was a stern but lovely building on a street that looked deserted. Hunched in the portico of a similar structure across the street Klaus Kessel waited.

While the CIA man admired the symmetry of New York's nineteenth century town houses, he was far from dwelling on the architectural details of the one he was about to enter. His thoughts stirred with the sour feeling that had come over him during his fifteen minutes with Andrea Reich-Herman.

The foreign assets secretary was attractive enough, but cold. Fresh from a six-hour flight, he had rushed to midtown Manhattan to catch her before she left for the day. Instead of appreciating the effort, she greeted him with all the civility of a headmistress scolding a truant minor.

According to Andrea, the attorney was expected with other guests at Andrea's apartment at eight o'clock. Kessel arrived at the Rand residence at 7 p.m. to be sure he saw her leave. Don't leave the details to others, Kessel had heard often enough from his military father. And certainly not to civilians.

After ten minutes he grew restless. The gale that had greeted him at Kennedy had increased its velocity. He turned the collar of his jacket up and slipped on his leather gloves against the chill.

Finally, the girl came out. Not at all the scholarly couch-potato of his conjecture. No one had taken the trouble to provide a recent photo of her, and he had entertained himself on the plane by imagining a library rat, with black rimmed glasses and a figure like a cheese ball.

The young woman who scanned the street for a taxi was a graceful athlete in high heels, wearing a slim-fitted sheath under a long woolen coat. Something in her lithe movements reminded him of a woman he had scarcely thought of until now. Gabriela. Briefly, she raised her eyes to his position, as if she knew he was there. He got off a quick series of snapshots before shifting into the shadows.

The cab arrived out of nowhere, sliding along the row of apartment houses until she was hidden from him. Waiting for the driver to pull away from the curb, Kessel realized with a sinking spirit that he did not have the stomach for killing a woman – anymore, that was. He had told himself that he'd recovered from the trauma of Gabriela. And he had, he corrected himself. This young woman reminded him of Gabriela's daughter and thus of Gabriela. That's all it was. A resemblance. Same age, slender build. That blend of youth and gravitas in her expression. He would get over it. In the meantime, there was no question of killing her, if things worked out as he planned.

Murder was a relic of the old days anyway, wasn't it? When every target was deemed dispensable, and the instruction to "eliminate the problem" meant a silencer tucked into the cleft at the base of the target's ear. He thought of his father: "You don't have the F.B. to do the job – do it anyway."

"F.B." He supposed the initials stood for "fucking balls." His father had sneered at him when he asked. Part of his father's extensive personal code, avoiding expletives: "Profanity is the weak man's eloquence," he said.

So be it. Grit. Courage. "Guts" was probably the literal synonym. Even – if it came to that – killing a woman. He'd proved that he had the guts. For male targets. A shiv in Hermann's belly wouldn't trouble his sleep for a second. But since that night, not so long ago, really, and Gabriela… don't go there, he warned himself.

## *12*

A bright moon shone on the discreet numbers of the building's canopy as Kenna emerged from the taxi. The strong breeze that had come up in the afternoon whipped at the sliver of dress under her coat. She compared the address to the paneled card she drew from her evening purse and dismissed the driver.

Andrea Reich Hermann's apartment reposed on the ninth floor of the Sherry-Netherlands cooperative. It was a graceful residence, still traditionally chic, despite a collection of new-money people from California's tech set, who had muscled in to exploit Manhattan's plunge in real estate prices.

Kenna moved through the brass doors to a reception lobby, where she was greeted by Michael Fein.

"Good timing," he said, in a collegial tone.

"Ditto."

She felt a certain ambivalence upon seeing him, having regretted over the afternoon her impulsive act of hijacking an invitation meant for her grandfather. Not to mention arriving with JAFA's bag man in tow.

Michael had already seen to checking her name off the guest list, jotting her name and his own on two coat labels in a quick, aggressive hand. The one he presented to her read: "Kenna Rand, Attorney." No affiliation. Good. Just the facts, ma'am.

She moved with him to the elevator and arrived first at the call-button, surprised at his phantom scowl that said he hated to come in second.

The street door opened behind them, admitting a small, noisy party of lavishly attired couples. Cocktail-circuit veterans, she noted, with printed name tags waiting for them. As the elevator doors burped open in response to her summons, the new arrivals swept past her into the car.

"Show time," Michael announced in a manner that only pretended to be confidential. "Enter New York's A-list."

The remark was not lost on the car's occupants. Every eye seemed to study the pair in the smoky glass of the interior.

Michael appeared relaxed in his evening clothes. But her simple outfit was in sharp contrast to the silk suits and platinum wristwatches around them. Over the sheath she had worn to her grandfather's wake, a bolero jacket with Spanish trim circled her waistline. And her jogger's watch, with its leather strap and night-glow face was a practical, if unfeminine, choice.

"Slightly underdressed," she murmured for Michael's ears only.

"'Youth' is the best designer label you can wear," he replied in his street voice, as if he expected hurrahs all round. Only clipped smiles greeted the remark, and Kenna hoped she was not among those she needed to impress.

After a long and chilly ascent, the doors parted onto a foyer of highly polished parquet. In the main room, a row of crystal chandeliers shone over an island of French carpet, while a school of waiters in shimmering jackets bore trays of smoked salmon and champagne.

As an attendant relieved the guests of their coats, Kenna felt her energy quicken. Even Michael appeared affected by the rich tableaux, his face alive with a mixture of curiosity and bonhomie that said he belonged here.

"Hungry?" He halted a waiter bearing a tray of canapés.

She slipped three quail's eggs and two salmon toasts onto a linen napkin. Interesting venue, she thought. Accomplished people. This was a world Jack Rand had learned to navigate on his own terms. *You will too, lass.*

She made short work of the smoked salmon and caviar, the icy freshness of the salmon still a dim second to the shared brown bread sandwiches of Galway, and got her bearings.

At the far end of the room, their hostess stood in earnest conversation with a regal blond. Andrea had changed her hair since last year when Kenna first met her. Shorter and bouncier now with red highlights. But it was the blonde who was the more arresting figure, even from twenty feet away. Her age was difficult to discern. Could have been thirty-five or a youthful sixty. She wore a full length sable coat and gold rimmed glasses. As Kenna watched, the woman's coat fanned out to reveal a dog, nervous and attentive by her side.

## *13*

As the taxi's tail-lights receded, Kessel rallied himself for the job at hand. He slipped into the foyer of the apartment, removing the stealth-view night goggles from his jacket. Government issue, he'd had to pay for them out of his own pocket. He put them on.

As if he'd known the layout all his life, Kessel moved to the office on the ground floor. He seated himself easily at Jack Rand's desk and studied the programmable safe in the cabinet behind his chair. One of his keys would operate the override system. He turned the key with a penlight clenched between his teeth. No need to risk exposure by turning on a lamp.

Briefly, the LCD flashed a number, confirming the code he had worked out based upon significant dates in Jack Rand's history. Rand's grand-daughter had been born in April, 1970. Not a bad year, Kessel thought. In fact, it was a good year – *before* all the bad years. With a minimum of effort, he soon had the safe opened and the files it contained stacked neatly for his review.

He removed also the slim portfolio containing Jack Rand's small cache of bonds. Payment in lieu of fees no doubt. Letter inside from J. Dalton & Company documented the original purchase transaction in the United States. A written assignment from two families with Jewish surnames confirmed transfer to Jack Rand. With a certified copy of her grandfather's will leaving the bonds to her, the lawyer would have no trouble establishing a valid chain of custody.

Kessel paused, deliberating. If he took the documents right now, the validity of the Rand portfolio would be in question. And if he took the bonds too, so much the better. Unfortunately, Kenna Rand did not appear to be an imbecile. Once the Rand bonds were gone, JAFA would be alerted. He did not want to spoil the surprise he had planned for them.

He drew out the stack of bonds from its folio. He had studied a photocopy in Zurich. But there was a tactile beauty to the originals. The paper was stiff, with the feel of starched linen. The lettering was fine, the German words slightly formal and old-fashioned.

*The German Reich, for value received, hereby promises to pay…*

J. Dalton & Company and Hitler, what a team. Ah, here was something. A list of serial numbers under JAFA's letterhead. The bonds themselves would be kept at JAFA's offices. In the interests of expediency, Kessel strode to the fax machine on a table near the door, placed the pages in the tray, and pressed "copy." He stood in front of it with his coat open to shield the scanning ray from the street. The machine cranked out fifteen pages of JAFA's serial numbers.

Kessel shoved the copies under his jacket. Seating himself again at the desk, he thumbed through the stack of labeled files.

He opened the file marked "Lara D," a thin folder with almost nothing in it.

Jack Rand's January, 1945 letter to Hermann Schacht, Hitler's Minister of Finance, had elicited a curt reply, written in German. Kessel had no trouble translating its brisk message. "We regret we cannot offer assistance… the bonds you offer are worthless. The Reich has issued its pronouncement of default, all payments of interest have ceased. Please immediately deliver all such bonds in your client's possession to the Reichsbank to be cancelled."

Right. He turned to the file on JAFA and flipped through its contents, memorizing names, dates. With a digital camera and strobe-flash, he photographed each item in order. Letters to the Bank for International Settlements. Retainer letter from JAFA. Photograph of Lara, 1945. Notes on a yellow pad.

The name André Lebecque caught his attention as did the address in Valorbé, Switzerland. Kessel recalled the name clearly. He knew it in the context of one of his own files obtained from allied high command records, 1945. The connection concerned him. Things had gone farther than anyone knew.

## *14*

Kenna watched the waiter top off her glass, then took a sip. The champagne had an immediate effect, a pleasant one.

Michael's gaze had focused upon the two women. His narrowed eyes said he did not know them. "Our hostess–how well do you know her?"

"Andrea seemed a sort of mentor once," she said.

The memory brought with it the prick of self-consciousness. She had interviewed the foreign assets secretary in her last year at Columbia, seeking comment for her law review article. Over her grandfather's objection, she had titled the piece to attract controversy– "Weimar Bonds – Fool's Gold or International Shell Game?" –and it did, drawing nervous attention from a few economists and banking experts on Columbia's advance copy list.

Flattered to get an appointment with Andrea, she traveled by subway to the deputy's midtown offices in the Citicorp Tower. Over lunch in the Penthouse dining room, Kenna summarized her bond research. Andrea listened politely enough, frowning slightly at her guest's suggestion that the debt might be enforced, even now. But when Kenna proposed the claim should be immediately tendered to the World Court to determine if it was still viable, Andrea's manner turned cool. She dismissed Kenna's remarks as inflammatory conjecture, with the unsavory potential for creating chaos in international financial markets.

Kenna had hardly touched the chef's signature cassoulet when Andrea snapped her fingers for the check. How quickly she had gone from clever wunderkind to overzealous law student.

"I'm afraid I spent the subway ride back wishing I had shown more diplomacy," she finished.

Michael issued a short bark of amusement. "Ha! Economic self-interest, that's all. Reich-Hermann prefers the buttered side of her bread. You'll get used to it."

She doubted she would. It had felt like a huge blow to her self-esteem.

Michael shrugged. "It's true a mega-demand on Europe's gold reserves is critical right now – given the threat of a common currency with super-parity to the dollar, there are many in the U.S. who would like to put the brakes on Europe's muscle-flexing." He touched her glass with his own. "Imagine the effect JAFA's claim, if recognized, will have on Germany's dominance in Europe. It could bankrupt the German treasury, and plunge the country's credit rating to zed. With Germany on the skids, it would put an end to Euro-phoria on Wall Street."

"Is that your objective?"

"I'm only proposing there are strategic reasons for Andrea to support our claims."

Michael lifted another caviar toast as a waiter floated by. "You haven't been waving a red cape, have you? There's a guy heading our way who looks like he busted the gates of 'La Corrida.' Our illustrious host, I presume?"

Blast and damn. It was John Hermann, all right, crossing the room with his trademark aggressive stride.

"We're in rare company tonight," Michael regarded the older man with curiosity. "Laid low for a few decades, hasn't he? Former Secretary of State, currently a name partner in the powerhouse Wall Street law firm soon to be your employer. Didn't he leave office in disgrace? Conflict of interest charges or something?"

“I don’t know the details.” She hadn’t expected Hermann to be here. Wasn't he scheduled to be in Europe until the fifteenth? She realized too late how her decision to help JAFA would sound. The firm's head of employment had accepted the new start date easily enough but… She should have put Michael off until she had spoken directly with the hiring partner, who at that moment charged toward them.

The erect man with the spikes of white hair reached them in a few steps. He regarded Kenna in a hungry manner as she made the introductions, then turned to Michael.

"Are you in government, Mr. Fein?"

"Not really," Michael said, easily. "I'm an attorney for JAFA – the Jewish American Free Alliance. Our client –" Michael's gesture included Kenna, "is presently pursuing a significant claim against the German government on a portfolio of pre-war bonds. Are you familiar with the Weimar gold bonds?"

Hermann’s style was to ignore polite questions. He turned his attention to Kenna, "You are involved with this?"

She felt her face flush ever so slightly. "Yes, actually. On a consulting basis. A temporary commitment–”

"Does this mean you are rejecting the position we offered you?"

"Not at all. It’s a project begun by Jack Rand, my grandfather. He passed away last week.” She found herself scrambling to regain her poise. “I spoke to Brian Lee in human resources this morning. He agreed to move my start date to December 1st. I’m looking forward to joining you then.”

"You are?" The forced jocularity in Hermann's voice did nothing to lessen the chill. "You were scheduled to start in two weeks. We expect you.”

Kenna flinched from the mixed scent of Scotch, stale breath, and cologne. “My firm is not accustomed to assuming the position of lapdog at the whim of first-year associates. I suggest you revise your plans.”

She realized she was being rebuked. Defensiveness gave way to irritation. If he chose to withdraw the offer that would be one thing. Easily managed in a telephone call – "we have reviewed our needs… circumstances have changed…" But she did not like to be bullied.

"Your decision creates a problem for me," Hermann said. "It confirms the impression I recently obtained from reading your law review article: your sympathies with the Zionist viewpoint."

"What?"

"Your veiled assertion that the London Debt Agreement was a sell-out to avoid yet a third world war over German debt is highly specious. The idea of post-war complicity in a game against the Jews makes your entire position unreliable."

"The facts speak for themselves. I confirmed them with Professor Miron. As you know, he's the recognized expert on the London Accord."

"Precisely. And he is a Zionist. But you will undoubtedly claim you were not aware of his affinity for extremist views."

"I doubt very much Dr. Miron is biased as you suggest. At issue is the integrity of a country's debt obligations. The investors just happen to be largely from the Jewish community." She felt herself to be in shock. "This whole conversation is troubling."

"I agree. You seem to possess a level of naiveté that's astounding given your education. Next you'll tell me that a separate Jewish state is necessary and any and all means to achieve this end are justified. Even, if it comes to that, obviously bogus claims based upon worthless debt instruments." His intensity made her step back.

"What do you know about this organization you've aligned yourself with?"

"Just a minute…" Until now Michael appeared to enjoy the parry and counter-parry. But with Hermann's descent into blatant rudeness, Michael's wry social presence became a dark, defending force.

"It's okay, Michael." She turned to Hermann, meeting his eyes. "We're talking about bearer bonds. Not Zionism. I plan to start your position later than we discussed, that's all, for reasons I've explained to you. One can't anticipate the death of someone close to you."

"Really? *You* appear to have used the event to your advantage."

Kenna's left hand tightened over her bracelet.

"I need to finish my grandfather's affairs. A short delay won't prejudice your firm. He would have wanted–" She had trouble with the words.

"We didn't hire your grandfather," Hermann said. "But maybe we should have. I wonder–" He tilted toward her until the gusts of Scotch-halitosis-aftershave threatened to make her retch. "–whether you consider this appropriate conduct for an attorney."

Michael started to speak. She stopped him with her hand. "I believe our discussion is finished," she said. "I hesitate to say this–after your comments–but I still value the chance to work with you."

"Not enough, apparently, to keep your commitment."

Before she could respond, Hermann clicked his heels and bowed over her hand in a confusing display of chivalry. "Excuse me for now," he said, and left them.

## 15

Still holding the penlight in his teeth, Kessel replaced the files in the safe. He opened a drawer, removed a file of edited pages labeled in script: *Draft: Weimar Bonds: Fool's Gold or International Shell Game.* He began to skim Kenna's research notes.

*Between 1924 and 1930 a number of New York banking and investment houses – notably J. Dalton & Company – flooded the country with German bonds... targeted New York Jews, preying upon their fears for family members left behind in Europe, who now faced a German government growing increasingly anti-Semitic.*

*When Hitler assumed power in 1933... plunged the issue into default, rendering the bonds worthless. The issuing bank, J. Dalton & Co., is said to have repurchased the bonds for pennies on the dollar... repatriated bonds were not canceled and destroyed as required by international law, but re-marketed on the Berlin Bourse and through Swiss exchanges in Zurich and Geneva, at prices substantially higher than those paid to the investors to liquidate their holdings...*

Right. Fraud, then. Hermann had drastically understated the bank's exposure.

Kessel heard a car pull up outside the brownstone and stop with its motor running. A door slammed and the car roared away. He paused, uncertain. Take the bonds? They were large, cumbersome. Do nothing clumsily, his father had told him.

He replaced the portfolio and the files, ever-careful, even in haste, to avoid leaving any clue of his presence. Kenna

Rand's portfolio of bonds and authenticating documents could stay where they were. For now.

He locked the safe behind the desk, moved to a place beside the street door, and removed a folded ski mask from the pocket of his jacket. He stood for several minutes without donning the mask, hoping the subject would enter. Physical surveillance still aroused in him an almost sexual tension–a part of him welcomed the release of an encounter. Time seemed to stand still. But when Kessel studied the frosted glass of the front door, he saw no one.

Sweeping the apartment once more with his night goggles, Kessel folded the mask into his pocket. He knew more than when he arrived. Enough to confirm the lawyer must be prevented from leaving the United States. He removed the goggles and stepped lightly into the street.

# 16

The foreign assets deputy's glamour at close range confirmed to the world at large, or at least New York political society that fifty can be very chic. She wore layers of coral chiffon with matching t-strap sandals, and a manner as bright as her attire.

"My husband greeted you already, I see." Andrea Reich-Hermann's eyes narrowed with unmistakable disdain as her husband crossed the room toward a man in a pea green suit.

Kenna returned Andrea's greeting with a smile and a firm handshake, but she felt shaken. Hermann's vitriole was disturbing. Her words came out with less warmth and more formality than she intended. "Thank you for inviting me tonight."

Andrea regarded Michael with coy curiosity, waiting until Kenna introduced them before extending her hand.

Michael spoke first. "Madam Secretary – what a pleasure. You know me from my position with JAFA. We've been trading phone messages for weeks."

"Don't tell me–" She offered a bland smile. "The Weimar bond claims. As Kenna can tell you, I'm terribly sympathetic. The United States has long supported the goal of Jewish reparations. Sadly, I'm rarely able to help in these matters."

She turned to Kenna, the smile-mask dropping and a freshly compassionate one taking its place. "I am sorry to learn about your grandfather. His loss will be felt by many."

"Thank you."

Kenna dismissed the "many," along with the notion that Andrea could have any idea of the real circumstances of Jack Rand's death. No one did, outside of New York's finest, who had cautiously filed the case a "suspicious death."

"I'm taking over his work with JAFA–temporarily."

"You *are*?" Andrea glanced with mild shock at Michael, then back to Kenna. "I thought you were going to work at my husband's firm."

Here we go again. A pariah already and she'd passed the New York bar less than three months ago. The prospect of asking her hostess for a letter to BIS suddenly seemed as remote as soliciting an invitation to join her in the Hamptons, and about as likely to be granted .

"May I join you?" The stranger's voice, almost a command, claimed their attention. Andrea turned slightly to make way for the arresting woman in her sable coat. She adroitly introduced them. "Countess Fabia Santiago."

The Countess' hard, attractive face had seemed younger at a distance. In her late forties, Kenna would guess, with elaborate makeup and hair piled on her head like a concoction of marzipan. At close range, the full length coat seemed even more excessive in the overheated rooms.

As if reading Kenna's thoughts, the woman shrugged the coat onto her shoulders where it loosened into plumes down her back. Wrapped in her gloved hand was the short, red leash that circled the dog's throat.

The Doberman was smallish and brownish black. A taut and muscular ninety pounds at least. Tan markings from eyes to snout were shaped like daggers, imparting a malevolent presence to the skittish pet.

Don't look down, Kenna counseled herself. No good could come of encouraging the woman's affectations.

"I see you notice my dog," the Countess said, in thickly accented English. "Mister A is not purebred. He is a blend of German and Latin. Like his mistress." She snapped the dog on his snout with the end of his lead. He bared his teeth, inches from Kenna's skirt hem. "Don't get sloppy, Mister A."

"Fabia is from Argentina," Andrea said, a lively ringmaster now. "Italian husbands, notwithstanding." She bestowed a knowing smile on her guests. "But thoroughly American in spirit. Fabia deals in currencies. Only just arrived from Buenos Aires and hasn't suffered a minute's jet lag. Fabia, this young woman is an expert on international finance – or soon will be, after working with my husband. Kenna, please share your fascinating theories with Countess before she collapses."

Andrea linked her arm through Michael's, making him her new favorite. "Let me introduce you to some of the other guests."

He shuttered his surprise, allowing himself to be spirited away in the company of his hostess.

A brief panic passed over Kenna. She would have preferred a few moments in private to reflect on her exchange with John Hermann. Instead, apparently she was to make small talk with the Argentine currencies dealer with Italian husbands. She could not help wondering: Currency–or bonds? Convenient–or just cozy coincidence? She felt again the Doberman's nostrils uncomfortably close to her thigh.

"Don't worry about your outfit. Mister A knows his manners."

"Not fond of the breed," Kenna said. "Jogger."

"Mister A loves to run."

Oh. Good.

The woman snapped the dog on his snout. He bared his teeth. "Six weeks with the best trainer in South America. Cunano of Bolivia. You've heard of him?"

"Should I have?"

"Cunano trains only full-bloods," the Countess announced, as if she were leading a tutorial on the subject. "He made an exception for Mister A. Dreadfully expensive. But he's worth it. All the drug dealers use Cunano. The dogs are savage at guarding the dealers' enclaves, yet they socialize beautifully. Don't you, Mister A? He won't slobber–even if he attack you, pardon my English. No slobbering at all."

"That's reassuring," Kenna said. Even if he attack you. So he wouldn't slobber. Just bite right through the bone like a gentleman. The Countess was playing with her.

"How long have you known Andrea," she asked.

Countess waved her hand to encompass a long-ago and beautiful past. "Andrea's husband visited Buenos Aires many times as Secretary of State. We had a difficult banking climate then. Outrageous. Our valuations rose and fell by the hour. Each day, one had to stand in line at the banks for cash. John–Andrea's husband, helped to stabilize our financial markets. I was often invited to John's villa in Careyes, Mexico. After he left office we remained friends. Mr. A and I still visit there. Twice, three times a year. It's a beautiful place. Perhaps you will be invited sometime."

The prospect was not attractive.

"Now all is changed," Countess continued. "I am sure you know he was disgraced in the occasional witch hunt that accompanies a change in U.S. political parties. Impossible. *Such* a talented man. He must stay in the background, or it will all be dragged out again. And, tragically, my country's peso has collapsed. Once more, my country is destitute."

"Yes. I'm sorry. Your country is suffering." She *was* sorry – for the Argentine people. But wasn't the Countess partly responsible? She would bet all the Countess' funds were in Europe or the Caymans. How could confidence be restored to financial markets, if everyone dabbled in currencies other than their own?

"Are you enjoying this?" The Countess' gaze floated beyond Kenna to the crush of guests.

Sumptuous room, glittering people. Not to mention the astonishing figure of the Countess herself. It was the height of the party. Noise, gaiety, gossip was at its peak. And the champagne went down well. She wasn't much of a drinker, but–yes–she was beginning to enjoy herself.

"Bal-oney," the Countess answered her own question, regarding with contempt two petite matrons in almost matching celadon silk suits. "The beige Armanis are here. *En flotilla.*"

"Armani is bad?"

The Countess brought her gaze back to Kenna.

"Where have you been?"

Kenna did not bother to repress her laughter. This hostile friend of Andrea's had the sting of a scorpion. "I'm hardly an expert in fashion."

"No? Well, I offer you some advice." The Countess parted her coat to display a bouclé-knit sheath of lemon yellow. "Check out Escada. It will suit you. Call Marina at the store on 5th. If you give her my name, she will instruct you." She skirted her eyes over Kenna's frame. "You have to wear names these days, you can't make your clothing yourself."

Ouch. "Thanks for the tip – though I don't think I can afford Escada right now."

"No?" The Countess feigned a perfunctory interest. "What do you do – for John Hermann?"

"I'm an attorney."

"A lawyer." The Countess offered a shrug. "You look like a debutante."

Now Kenna was sure some kind of game was under way. Her interest picked up.

Narrowing her eyes behind the mauve-colored lenses, Countess asked. "Where did you go to school?"

"Columbia."

"Local school."

Clean shot. "I wouldn't expect you to know much about it." She turned the conversation back to the Countess. "Andrea says you deal in currencies. Is that your profession?"

"I am a banker."

"In Buenos Aires?"

"My first husband inherited a bank there. Joe Alvarez. Not Spanish looking at all. Blond and blue-eyed. Spoiled too. When I was awarded the bank at our divorce, what a crying baby he was! Now I am on the board of three banks in Chile and Argentina. They say – it sounds immodest – I am the richest woman in South America. And, thanks to my second husband, I have my title. I need not marry anymore."

Yes? Well, that's not the easiest remark to respond to. Kenna probed for humor in the shaded eyes and sumptuously contoured mouth, but found none.

"I could have been a lawyer," the Countess mused, continuing her soliloquy. "But in the circles I come from, the profession is – well, there's something unsavory about it – isn't there? At least that is what prevented me from pursuing my interest. My family would not have approved."

"Argentine families must have strange ideas," Kenna said mildly. "Law is considered a profession here, like medicine or research. Attorneys are considered well educated. Compared to – bankers, for example."

The blond woman digested this, found it unappealing.

Back to the game, Kenna thought. Why not tug – just a little – on the bait? "What kind of currencies do you handle?"

"Actually, I am collecting international bonds just now. Pre-war."

Oh. So that's where we're going. "My companion represents a large portfolio of German bonds," she said, unable to resist temptation. "From the 1930s. Pre-war, as you said."

"The Weimar bonds?" Too fast.

"Then you know about them."

"That's why Andrea introduces us I suppose." The delivery is laconic, just short of indifference. "I am the expert on such things. Let your friend show them to me, I'll tell him if they are any good."

"Thank you, but there's no need. There's no question of authenticity."

"Ha! The lawyer says so, it must be so. Certainty of youth – maybe that is what John finds attractive."

The Countess issued a throaty gust, more scornful than amused. "I must tell you–" she lowered her voice in a show of confidentiality. "A large collection of gold-backed bonds were stolen from the Reichsbank in May, 1945. They were stored there awaiting cancellation. Over the years, they have turned up in parcels – fifty million dollars or so at a time. Germany will not honor them, and those who have tried to pass them are arrested by Interpol. If your colleague's bonds were among them, they are worthless contraband."

Kenna could barely suppress her impatience with the older woman's patronizing manner. "I know all about Germany's claims."

"Then you know you will need an expert to evaluate your friend's portfolio."

Countess gestured to a waiter bearing a tray of brimming champagne flutes. "Is this Veuve Clicquot reserve?" she demanded.

"I don't know, madam."

The older woman lifted a glass of the pale, exuberant liquid from the tray, studied its color against the ceiling light, and cautiously took a sip before waving the perplexed young man away.

She resumed her arrogant tone. "Germany's 'claims,' as you put it, make your friend's bonds of questionable validity. Even if they were not among those looted, there have been forgeries. New ones surface every day. The German government works very closely with the FBI, I am told, to find looted or forged bonds. They put in prison any criminals who try to pass them. Interpol, the FBI – it is necessary that someone with my knowledge authenticate them for you."

"There are relatively few forgeries," Kenna replied, with the calm of one who has anticipated her opponent's argument. "And they're easily detected. The quality of the paper, the printing – German on one side, English on the other, all are factors that discourage counterfeiting. It's a difficult job for a forger."

"Ah! But you are wrong. Last year in Miami–"

"Forgive me for interrupting you. I read the account you refer to. The FBI seized a portfolio of bonds in an undercover sting, claiming they were forged. But the owner disappeared before they could charge her. The claim was never proved."

"Germany maintains a list of the looted bonds. If the serial numbers are on that list…"

She was aware of Germany's so-called 'Schacht List', named for the Nazi finance minister whose corrupt gamesmanship served to defraud the Reich's creditors. "I've heard such a list exists. Rather self-serving, isn't it? It was years after the war that Germany raised this defense to the bonds. If there is such a list, why do the Germans refuse to let anyone see it?"

"She has the answer for everything it seems–doesn't she, Mister A?"

A short snap of the leash brought the dog to his feet. "I repeat my offer to examine the portfolio. If your colleague wishes to avoid these risks, I will purchase the bonds myself. No questions asked. Of course, their worth may be only antique value."

Kenna cannot help but smile. You want the portfolio, you just don't want to pay for it.

"Antique value is nominal," Kenna said, enunciating clearly as to a child. "The worth of Troy gold has risen many times since 1945. In Basel, full value will be given–"

"She believes in Santa Claus," the Countess informed Mister A, whose ears tensed at his mistress' dangerous tone. "My offer stands."

"Please don't consider you've made an offer. This qualifies as small talk."

"Oh? I see something of the lawyer in you, after all."

The Countess gave Kenna a tight-lipped smile. "But you might heed the warning of someone who has followed these affairs. People have been killed trying to redeem the German gold bonds."

"Excuse me for now," Kenna said, adopting Hermann's departure line. "I hope you enjoy your visit to New York."

# 17

The time had come when most guests were eager to move along to their dinner reservations at Lutece or Four Seasons Grill, and couples mingled in restless conviviality by the elevator.

Michael Fein watched the dwindling party from the foyer. It was easy to avoid the Regency table with pots of chocolate fondue and fresh cream if he remained on the periphery. He felt a curious elation. The evening had aroused in him a marvelous vitality. He was too intelligent and self-aware to deny its source. He accepted a last champagne from a passing tray and raised his glass to the chandelier in a subtle toast. "Jews and Celts," he murmured.

And then he saw him. The short, ugly man in the green European suit. Michael had seen that peculiar dull shade in the lounges at Charles De Gaulle and Heathrow airports. Maybe European unity had a chance--at least they all seemed to be drawn to the same suit. But what the hell was *he* doing here?

# 18

Kenna slipped down the short hallway to the powder room. Without entering, she removed a wand of lip gloss from her purse and touched up her mouth.

The evening's thrust and parry had sapped her energy for the anticipated tete-a-tete with Andrea, her level of confidence dissolving like so much rain over pavement.

In spite of Andrea's coolness this evening, Kenna felt a vexing need for the foreign deputy's approval. Andrea might be a little flashy and ultra-political. But she was sophisticated and accomplished, with interesting and influential friends. Something in Kenna made her long to be among them.

When she returned to the drawing room, Andrea was waiting for her. "There you are. We haven't had a moment together all evening." Linking her arm through Kenna's, Andrea guided her down a long corridor of plush carpeting. "Step into my dressing room with me while we chat."

"Everyone's leaving now," she said. "Michael and I will have to hustle if we want to find a cab." She flicked her eyes to her watch. "I'll call you tomorrow, if I may."

"But you're here now. I want to talk to you about your association with JAFA. Michael Fein can wait a few minutes."

Kenna wondered if the ensuing moments were awkward silence, or merely "pregnant pause." She rummaged around for an introductory phrase to launch the subject of her visit to the settlements bank. Nothing suitable presented itself, and she decided to let Andrea speak first.

Her hostess drew up sharply before a closed door. "Did you hear that? Voices in my study."

She'd heard them. Contralto murmur in answer to John Hermann's baritone. Kenna inclined her head. "Perhaps your husband is meeting with someone."

"Obviously. But he wouldn't be working now. We don't allow guests in there. Off limits." Andrea checked Kenna's face, making her a sudden compatriot. "Shall we investigate?"

What was the childhood phrase – let's not and say we did.

Andrea clasped the study door and turned its handle. When she found it locked her brow went up. "We'll see about this."

Bloody hell–to coin her grandfather's favorite term of outrage. It was okay with her if John Hermann's reputation as a "player" was about to be confirmed, but Andrea would not appreciate being humiliated in front of her protegé.

"I should go."

Andrea's hand lay impatiently on the powder room knob. "Let me deal with this first."

Like a doomed convict, Kenna trailed Andrea into her dressing room, leaving the door open behind her. The room was large and well lit, with mirrored walls above a long makeup counter, and a toilet behind shuttered doors. To her dismay, a pass-through at one end led to the adjacent room.

Andrea strode to the pass-through and rapped twice on the panel door. The murmur of voices stopped. Andrea tapped the door. It sprung open. She stepped into an anteroom with a partially closed door leading to her study.

In the seconds before Andrea entered the study, Kenna felt conscious of the rush of movement in the corridor. She moved instinctively to limit Andrea's view in the mirrors, and caught the figure of the sable-wrapped Countess sweeping toward the foyer, Mister A pacing briskly at her side.

"Oh, it's just you, John," Andrea said to the man seated awkwardly on a sofa arm.

"Who else?"

Andrea threw the door wide open and scanned the room's every corner.

"You're talking to yourself?"

"I needed a private moment."

"When we have guests?"

"I lock the door to keep people out."

"You keep the wrong people in," Andrea said.

Kenna marveled at the control in the older woman's voice. Even from her place near the vanity, she could take in the Countess' perfume. Andrea closed the panel firmly, and Kenna caught the expression of fury before her hostess turned back to her.

"At least we won't be disturbed now," she said, seating herself at the vanity. She regarded Kenna through lowered lids.

"My schedule is terribly full. I'm tired. But I wanted you to know that I'm glad you decided to attend tonight. It isn't difficult to guess what's on your mind." The older woman unlatched a small drawer and drew out lipstick and pencil. She applied the color in quick, tense strokes. "I assume you want my opinion on whether you should become involved with JAFA's claim."

"Not exactly."

Andrea's eyes flicked up to hers in a show of polite interest.

"Actually. I hesitate to impose on you–"

Nothing like the scene she had scripted in her mind. Hadn't she intended to let Andrea initiate the offer? She would have to gut it through now –

"As you've guessed–" she tried for disarming awkwardness "–I've agreed to step in and help JAFA redeem their bonds in Basel. I'm sure you know the tender must be made by the end of next week. My grandfather may have spoken to you about it."

Okay, what's next? You won't have her attention forever. She wet her lips. "Quite frankly, we could use an introduction to the Swiss settlements bank. JAFA would appreciate it. If you could, I mean. I wasn't sure, but I thought – is that something you could help with?"

"It's gone that far, has it?" Andrea's voice was steely.

Kenna remained silent, waiting.

"The State Department avoids disputes between private individuals and foreign nations."

"There's no dispute. We intend simply to tender the bonds. JAFA intends, I mean. The bank will present them for payment. Germany will either approve or decline the tender." Her manner said it was all pro forma – not a big deal really. "A letter or telephone call from you would be extremely helpful to begin the process."

Andrea replaced her lipstick and pencil in the drawer. It shut with a self-lock and she tugged it a little to check it, all the time keeping her attention on Kenna, without giving anything away. "No doubt. Half the people in Manhattan would enjoy using my contacts. But I can't help in private matters."

That word again. "It's not exactly private."

She felt the fire return. Unbidden, came the image of her grandfather clutching his shoulder. And there was Lara's photograph. She was dismayed to feel a sense of passion and impatience surging up. Why shouldn't Andrea write a letter of introduction? Couldn't she make a bloody phone call?

*Hold y'er spirit, lass.*

Kenna relaxed casually against the counter. A friendly discussion between equals, her posture said. Not the time to trot out a romantic history of the bonds. Nothing to do with genocide, murder or betrayal.

"You know this better than I–" The tentative approach. "The bonds were issued under an international agreement between Germany and the U.S. Our Treasury endorsed the investment as a sound one. Germany's default in 1933 created shock waves. Your office should have demanded restitution at that time. But the fate of the German bonds was then, and still is, a State Department matter."

Andrea's eyes narrowed. "I'm aware of your position."

The Deputy stood up, smoothing her skirt with a brisk motion. When she spoke, she'd put on a voice that was patronizing and impatient.

"You've made your point. Now let me share something with you for your own good. Your law review article was creative. I'm sure you can rely on it to open many doors, especially among the investors who collect these bonds. But your ideas are mere conjecture. The events of World War II altered finances in ways that are not for you and me to second-guess. If Germany wants to make good on its debt, that's a matter for its chancellor. We can't get involved in wrangling over dubious antiques.

"There's no question of their being worthless," Kenna said carefully.

"Oh? Even your article spells out hurdles to redemption." She shrugged. "The answer's the same. I can do nothing for you in Basel."

Andrea cast a strange look toward the door leading to her husband's study.

"But perhaps there is one thing I can do, as a personal favor to your grandfather."

Kenna swallowed hard. "I'm grateful for any help you can offer," she said, as if learning her lines for the first time.

"I'll ask Countess to call you."

Kenna drew back without thinking. "What do you mean?"

"The Countess collects antique bonds for her bank portfolios. She expressed interest tonight in buying JAFA's bonds."

"She spoke to you about it?"

"She mentioned her interest in them. I'm willing to arrange a meeting to discuss a sale."

Kenna back-pedaled furiously, straining for tact. "There's no time. We're leaving for Basel this week."

Andrea's smile had grown cool. "I vouch for the Countess, if that's what you're thinking. If you can't rely on my introduction–"

This is not how things were supposed to go. She wished now she hadn't come.

"A great deal of money is at stake," Kenna said.

The Deputy's well-manicured hands dismissed this. "I've known the Countess for decades. She's a friend of my husband's, and has assisted us many times over the years–with extremely sophisticated financial issues."

Andrea continued speaking in dry-as-dust tones. "We needn't argue the point. A private sale to the Countess is best for all concerned. As JAFA's attorney you're obliged to discuss any offer with its trustee. Deposit the bonds with me tomorrow, I'll see they're authenticated. The Countess can fax you her offer and you can present it to your client. All very efficient, leaving plenty of time to present them in Basel–if that's still your desire."

Kenna realized she was being dismissed. She returned the crisp tone.

"I'll discuss it with Michael Fein." Then, giving in to a courtesy she did not feel, she added, "Thank you, Andrea," and felt betrayed by her words.

## *19*

The man in high-topped sneakers and British topcoat watched from the shadows as Kenna's cab pulled up in front of the brownstone. He waited until she had paid the driver and stepped out of the car. She had barely inserted her key in the lock when Nicholas Chariot appeared at her side. "Let's go inside," he said in a low whisper, leaving out any trace of the brogue he had used in Aunt May's garden.

Kenna cursed the cab as it sped off, its driver oblivious to the man now forcing himself into her home. Why did she not accept Michael's offer to drop her off first?

Moving with the Irish agent into the foyer, a physical response of automatic tension locked down her upper body: arms, chest, sternum – a single unit. Stay aggressive, she had been told in the self-defense classes she had taken. Show him he's in for a fight. All that was fine – except it suddenly seemed a certainty that any scream she attempted would produce nothing more than a hoarse whimper.

He led her into the study and closed the door behind them, keeping a deceptively casual hold on her wrists. Striding with her to the desk, he reached for her grandfather's desk lamp with easy familiarity. He flicked it on. Then he released his grip and backed away from her into the room's shadows, leaning casually against the stonework mantle of the fireplace, keeping his distance, but not too great a distance, between them.

Kenna removed her coat and positioned herself warily behind her grandfather's desk. What would the man do if she picked up the telephone on the desk and dialed 911? His eyes read the question and he gave a slight smile: “Not a good idea.”

“What do you want?”

“If I were you, Lady Jane, I’d cancel your trip to Basel.”

“What do you know about it?”

"I'm expected to know," he said.

“All very mysterious, isn’t it? What’s your point?”

“You think you’re going to make it to Switzerland.”

She set her lips stubbornly.

"The lady lawyer disappears," he said. "Postcard from Greece. ‘Having a lovely time.’ Official view? She made a scarper with the bonds."

"What are you talking about?"

"You weigh –" He let his gaze slowly pass over her. “– one hundred and fifteen pounds?"

She let her eyes roam the desk surface as if something there could explain her grandfather’s connection to this intruder.

"A man and woman. Two men. I can't say what the gender makeup will be. But there will be two of them. Americans. Germans. Or some other interested party. Hustling you off the plane, out of the terminal. They'll meet you and they'll be your last best friends, and they'll see to it you never arrive."

“You're scaring me." She meant to throw it away with irony.

"That's how it is. Do you think the American government is going to let you put the touch on the German treasury for billions of dollars?"

"We must try,” she said. “The debt should be paid. It’s the international rule of law." She was aware how naive that sounded. Rule of law. Her grandfather had been murdered. She could find no one to confirm it. Or connect his death to the bonds. But she knew. And this man would say anything to hijack her fear.

"In your research, did you turn up the guy in Montreal? Walked into an Ontario bank last year to pledge an attaché of gold bonds. Who did the Canadian Mounties call first?"

Kenna refused to play.

"The FBI. Strange thing to do, isn't it? There's no reciprocity. America is Canada's 'sleeping elephant'–Pierre Trudeau's phrase. But the Mounties called the FBI." Nicholas paused for effect.

"Because they were afraid not to. Germany is an ally. The U.S. will look out for its interests. The debt is old. Europe is struggling. What does it matter if Jewish investors never see their money? On the other hand, if Germany loses its gold reserves, it will be kicked out of the EU – and that means instability for all the G-8 economies. This is not about justice, it's about money. Cold, hard cash. You of all people should know this."

"Are you suggesting a motive for my grandfather's murder?"

"Am I? Eighteen months ago. Man arrives at Dulles with a briefcase full of bonds. Former Army captain. Slumped in his seat. Collapsed on the plane, it seems. Rushed to the hospital. But he's DOA. Shot in flight with a small caliber pistol. Do you have any idea how reckless the murderer was? Could have shot a hole in the fuselage."

"Was she caught?"

"Was *she* caught?" He sniffed his disgust. "You think you know these people? You think you know anything about them?"

Kenna remained silent.

"What happens if Germany doesn't pay?" he insisted.

"We'll file a claim with the World Court. The time is right for that."

"Brilliant. Germany has avoided liability so far. How do you explain it?"

"Lack of State Department cooperation, I would say."

"You're catching on."

"It doesn't follow that my life is in danger."

"Follow this: someone sees you as a patsy. They're going to use you to discredit the bonds, to put an end once and for all to JAFA's claim. It could be Michael Fein. Or someone in JAFA itself. And after they've succeeded, you'll end up a CIA desaparecido."

Kenna clasped her bracelet with her left hand. Marshaling her fear into sarcasm, she said, "Isn't the CIA villain a bit trite for the piece? I don't see anyone from Langley in my rooms. But you're here. It's you that's keen on exploitation."

"How do you get that?"

She smiled, signaling wonder at his transparency. "I could be very useful to the people you work for, especially with my background in international law. I'm not blind to what you can get from me. You'll protect me all right, for a stake in the bonds. A nice bit of financing for your terrorism."

His watchful silence only stirred her to greater emotion. The evening's stresses had left her incapable of censorship, spilling every thought as it arrived for duty – with no time or inclination for diplomacy.

"For all I know, that's been your interest in my grandfather all along–" Her voice broke. She felt incapable of fighting any more battles–least of all with this opponent. "Is that what you wanted from him? A money pipeline? Or–it's votes you need right now, isn't it? Campaign funding to elect your thugs to Parliament. And all for the good of the Irish rebels. " She stopped speaking altogether and turned away.

"Not thugs," he said calmly. "Activists."

"Murderers."

"If you're referring to our candidate's activities in the 1980s, our aims were different then."

"The means to fit the times?"

"I won't attempt to justify murder," he said. "But this isn't about what you can do for us. I made a promise to your grandfather. I've gone to considerable trouble to warn you – twice now. You're the one who's going to need our help." His voice had grown dangerously soft. "Don't wait too long to ask for it."

## 20

Thursday morning broke fine and cold. Kenna returned to the brownstone from her three-mile jog, feeling refreshed and clear-headed. With less than forty-eight hours remaining before their departure for Basel, events moved quickly, everything seeming to happen at once.

As she showered and dressed she made mental note of the items she would need in Switzerland. To avoid the rush of last minute detail she packed a small bag and laid out her travel uniform: corduroy riding pants, quilted jacket, turtleneck, gray suede boots.

Inside the pocket of her jacket she placed Lara's photograph.

*Don't trifle with magical thinking, lass. The superstitions of the Irish will hold ye back.*

She couldn't agree more. But for now it was all she had of her grandfather's past. She loaded his trial briefcase with passport, laptop and research materials. Fastening the latches, she ran her hand over the faded gold initials on top. JFR. John Francis Rand. "Johnny" to his Irish relations. "Jack" in America.

*Ye'll get over it lass.*

She placed the bags near the door. Then she looked up the international code for Zurich, and dialed the U.S. Consulate there. Her request was ordinary enough: she and Michael needed a letter of introduction to Gunter Raskoff, director of the Bank for International Settlements. If Andrea would not smooth the way to redeem the bonds, she would ask the Swiss Consul to intervene.

The polite voice of the White Rabbit who answered her call, after several put-throughs, assured her that her inquiry would be relayed to the Consul's office. Consul would reply in due course. But when, exactly? Not sure. Not sure. Consul was very busy. Not available. Tied up in meetings. When her follow-up fax produced no reply within the hour, she put through a telephone call to Basel, the medieval Swiss banking center an hour's train ride from Zurich. She asked to speak with Raskoff directly.

It was four o'clock Swiss time.

"I'm sorry," the Director's secretary informed her in clipped English. "Herr Raskoff cannot receive you next week. We are a central bank. All appearances must come via proper channels."

"Such as –"

"An advance appointment must be approved."

"That's why I'm calling – to request an appointment," Kenna said just as formally.

"That is not the way it is done. All appointments, appearances, interviews, whatever English word you choose, must come from proper persons."

The woman's hostility was so palpable, she almost laughed.

"I'll start at the beginning," Kenna proposed. "I'm an attorney. My colleague is Michael Fein, a prominent New York attorney and scholar. We will be traveling to Basel from New York, arriving on Wednesday. Our client is a private fund with a large portfolio of German gold bonds. Germany's deadline for redemption of the bonds expires next Thursday."

"Yes, yes."

"These are bearer bonds. Like cash to anyone who has possession of them–"

"Do you think I don't know what bearer bonds are?"

"That's why we must see Herr Raskoff in person. We want to confirm with him the protocol for redemption."

"Not possible."

"Is the Director available now? I could speak with him myself."

"I repeat –"

"We've approached the U.S. Consul in Zurich," Kenna interposed. "I'm sure our Consul will have no objection to arranging the meeting, but time is short–his reply may not arrive in time."

"Then perhaps you should not come. You must be guided by your Consul," the woman said crisply.

Herr Raskoff is going to see me, Kenna told her silently, with or without your help.

"I'll call back tomorrow," she said, "May I make a note of your name?"

"Teni Huffman."

So much for advance planning. Kenna called Michael's office.

He wasn't in. She would have to tell him about the Countess, she decided. She had told Andrea she would. But the exercise could only distract them from preparing for the trip. She already knew the end result. 'Nada,' to use the Countess' vernacular. Even assuming the woman's access to South American banking interests, Countess would not pay anything near par for the bonds, let alone their value in gold.

"Time is too short," Kenna had told her hostess. Happy choice of words. Nothing against your friend the Countess. Nothing slanderous, or insulting. Simple lack of time. JAFA would have to proceed to Basel without the benefit of negotiating with the "richest woman in South America."

When Michael called back half an hour later, he sounded in high spirits. "Good thinking, about the Consulate," he remarked when she had brought him current on her morning's activities. "Although we may not need them.

Andrea called me this morning before nine. She offered to help us after all."

"Great." It sounded flat. But there was nothing she could do about it. Her thoughts were racing. She felt a dull premonition. Why had Andrea called Michael and not Kenna?

"You must have been persuasive last night. She offered a diplomatic introduction to BIS – provided her expert examines JAFA's bonds to confirm their validity."

"She didn't mention an expert last night. Why is that necessary?"

"Germany claims a large cache of bonds were stolen during the last days of the war. Stacks of certificates were kept in the Reichsbank to be canceled–so-called 'dead bonds.' If Andrea gets involved, she wants to be sure she's not backing something that's not on the up-and-up. She needs assurance that JAFA's bonds are not tainted by any suggestion of fraud. Anyway, she rang up a German bond expert who is in New York this week. Klaus Ernst. He's going to look at them right away. I delivered the bonds to her office this morning."

"Shouldn't we discuss it?" Her voice betrayed the unpleasantness of the surprise. What had happened to the easy camaraderie of the night before? Where was their "partnership?"

"We *are* discussing it. I thought you'd be pleased. I doubt if Andrea has ever read the fine print – or even seen a bond certificate. Maybe she'll appreciate the significance of what we've been fighting for."

It was not injured pride she felt. It was alarm. Wasn't it all too neat – the "bond expert" and promise of a blue-chip introduction falling into place just before the trip? *Don't like it,* a stubborn child-voice said within her.

"You'll meet the bond maven yourself at noon."

Before she could protest, he added, "I can't go. I'll be busy with appointments. But you can pick up this guy's report, and the bonds."

"Did Andrea sign for them?"

"Yes, counselor." Colleagues still–charming and light-hearted. "I have a receipt. And my law clerk kept a stern eye on her while she placed them in the State Department vault."

Kenna remained silent.

"She also mentioned she has an interested buyer for the portfolio. Countess Fabia Santiago, who we met last night."

Blast and damn. The South American banker and her kneecap-snuffling canine were still in New York. Nicholas had trotted her out as CIA-lackey, for no other reason than to put her guard up. Now, thanks to Andrea, the woman had insinuated herself close to the bonds.

"Not the best idea," she said, cursing her gift for understatement.

"Dicey, I agree. I harbor no illusions she'll pay the price we need, but presumably, Andrea intends this gesture as a favor–we have to hear her out."

"The Countess will be far more pliable with you. She referred to me as a 'debutante.'"

He gave a short bark of laughter, ever cheerful. "My c.v. is short on dealing with pretentious South American provocateurs. That's why I'm sloughing off the task on you. Andrea is glowing about her pal's connections. If the Countess has access to legitimate investors willing to act quickly, we can avoid the red tape of dealing with Germany. But if she can't guarantee immediate funds, or she's intent on bottom-fishing, I authorize you to kick her down the stairs."

Very funny. A confrontation with Andrea *and* the Countess – trial by fire, anyone?

"What happens if Andrea's bond expert trounces their value? I thought it was important to force Germany to acknowledge the debt to the world–that was the reason my grandfather signed on–"

The silence went on longer than she would have expected. "Nothing's changed," he said.

"Ok." She decided on non-committal. "I'd better move if I'm going to arrive at Andrea's offices before noon."

"Excellent. Call our security service when you're ready to leave Andrea's building to escort you to our offices. My money's on you over Andrea or the Countess. Now, relax."

Michael had recovered his high spirits. "And keep good thoughts."

Impossible, Kenna thought, feeling suddenly cross.

## *21*

Kenna's appointment with Andrea Reich-Hermann was confirmed for noon. She entered the Citicorp Center's spacious plaza from Lexington Avenue. A bracing chill from the fountain pool swept the open space like an Arctic breeze. Passing under the bronze sculpture that graced its center, she quickened her steps toward the entrance to the aluminum and glass tower occupied by the State Department.

In trouser suit and pumps, and only slightly strained by the travel briefcase she had brought for the bonds, she threaded her way among a crowd of suited professionals and through the revolving doors. Once inside the cavernous lobby, she stepped to one side to orient herself.

In front of her, three banks of elevators served the three vertical zones of the building. At the lobby's rear, a row of express cars whisked passengers to two sky lobbies at speeds of hundreds of feet per second.

Under the narrow-eyed scrutiny of a male security guard, she moved to take her place with other visitors queuing up before two metal detectors. The guard's partner, nearest to Kenna, was a heftily built African American woman. Her lapel badge read 'Nan Robinson.' A fierce one, Kenna decided, trying out an adjective used by her grandfather. Not one to crack a smile or exchange a casual comment on the weather.

Robinson watched as Kenna opened her grandfather's briefcase. She scanned its contents, items Kenna had already packed for her trip: Passport. Research file. Contact information.

She let her hand rest on her holstered pistol as she flipped open the passport. Her examination seemed to go on a shade too long. Kenna felt aware of the restiveness of the businessman behind her, shifting his briefcase from one hand to the other. Check your terrorist profile, why don't you? New lawyer in heels with almost empty briefcase– not a match. At last, Robinson directed Kenna to a row of yellow visitor's badges, watched as she clipped it to her jacket lapel, then waved her through.

Kenna found the elevators serving floors 1 through 20. She glanced at her watch. Eleven-forty and the lobby was already bustling with the early lunch crowd.

She switched her case to her other hand and shouldered forward against the tide of office workers balancing drinks and sandwiches from the plaza snack bars. She pressed the button for floor fifteen. There, in the reception area, she would be received and escorted up one flight to the offices of Andrea Reich-Hermann.

Kenna resisted the impulse to make sure the woman guard wasn't still watching her. So what if she was? She wasn't planning to stick around. She would reduce the exercise to its essence. Retrieve the bonds. Get the letter. Get out. Brevity, courtesy, tact. Nothing provocative. Nothing that could give offense or open way to argument. As Michael had said, hear the Countess out. Then, kick her down the stairs. An amusing image, but she didn't feel like laughing.

She was aware of the stuffiness of the car and the crush of humanity around her. This was not something she could do every day. Or very much at all. John Hermann had made it clear the firm's associates were expected to eat in the conference room, or at their desks. Get used to it.

The man behind her held his briefcase against the small of her knee. A handbag belonging to the woman on her right had the heft of a two year old, edging its contents deeper into

Kenna's ribs with every sip of the owner's latte. Everyone had their own floor it seemed. Only eleven more to go.

She steeled herself for the Countess' python charm. Her grandfather had performed just such high-wire acts of negotiation as would be required this morning. Listen courteously. Consider briefly – just long enough to give the impression she'd come with an open mind. Then, "I'm sorry. Our positions are too far apart. It's not possible for JAFA to entertain your offer at this time."

If she carried it off, there would be no hard feelings. No difficult or awkward exchanges. Ask politely for the letter and the bonds. Then–whoosh! Back to Kansas, Dorothy. And, she cautioned herself–however brief or vague Andrea's letter to Gunter Raskoff might be, just take it and get out of there, before Andrea could change her mind.

*"When the court rules in your favor, lass, don't tarry. Put the wind at y'er back."*

And so she would.

# 22

It seemed to Klaus Kessel, as he waited in Andrea Reich-Hermann's conference room that Thursday morning, that an act of terrorism was required. He was as familiar as anyone with the State Department definition – "An act of premeditated, politically motivated violence intended to influence a target audience."

Premeditated. Politically motivated. Check. Target audience? That would be JAFA and Kenna Rand. And he would expand the net to include anyone with the serious intention of redeeming the German gold bonds.

Violence? That would depend. He studied the photos he had shot outside Rand's apartment. The first was a close shot of the lawyer, taken with a telephoto lens. Her expression held that unique quality of awareness, as if she were scanning the field for her photographer.

She was a striking girl, with an expectant tilt to her chin, and strange, intelligent eyes. A quality of reserve made her seem older than her years. In her wary expression he saw the young lioness scenting the hunt. Not, he thought, the docile and unsuspecting gazelle on the open plain. Youth is arrogant, he told her image. Too sure of its own untried abilities. Did you really think you could manipulate two governments?

Kessel put the photos away with a sense of reluctance. He took pleasure in his private tete-a-tete with – what was the apt term? His "quarry." He drew from his briefcase pocket a sheet of lined note paper containing the notes he had made on the plane. He would have been the first to give lip service to the rule that it was ill advised to put anything in writing. But he enjoyed the process of putting pen to paper. With its square, chiseled edges, the geometric lettering he'd practiced since adolescence was pleasing. The look of the letters bespoke a writer whose world was in perfect order and under his control.

He reviewed his "mission statement" again, more irritated than amused at the stupidity of the anagram he'd unconsciously created as its conclusion:

1. <u>D</u>estroy the credibility of JAFA's bond claim.
2. <u>I</u>mpair the value of the gold bonds.
3. <u>E</u>liminate the principals who stand in the way.

# 23

The doors opened at the 15th floor. Kenna stepped into a spacious lobby of blond woods and tinted glass, dissected by a wide interior staircase.

The reception area of Andrea Reich-Hermann's offices lay hushed and vacant. Behind a low reception console, a young man in a rumpled white shirt and PBX headset accepted Kenna's hastily-made business card and prattled her name into the microphone that hovered at his lips. Andrea's secretary would be with her shortly.

She glanced at her watch again–ten minutes to kill. Andrea had once admonished Kenna to use her power as a professional. "Always keep people waiting," she'd counseled. "It's fatal for an attorney to imply her schedule is flexible."

The post-modern seating areas in the present space did nothing to entice her. Chrome and leather torture-rack. Was she really expected to brace herself in the posture of a downhill racer, and thumb through current issues on international finance? At least the Countess hadn't arrived. She would be spared making small talk for the next quarter hour–about Escada, no doubt.

A door drifted open from a conference room, and a crisp male voice rose and lowered into a portable handset, as if the man was walking around as he spoke. She found herself making an exercise out of trying to catch a few words. "Proceeding per schema. Waiting for her now. Details in an hour… expect my call…"

The minutes dragged, heightening the natural tension. Apparently Andrea's obligatory waiting period was still in vogue. No doubt the gambit served a psychological purpose. Kenna was beginning to feel the kind of tension she felt before a big race. Let's get on with it, can't we?

Across the lobby, the express elevators were partially hidden by the staircase. One car was stopped and the doors locked open. Curious. The bullet car shouldn't have stopped on floor fifteen, they were intended exclusively for direct access to the higher floors.

Yet there it was.

She sauntered to the other side of the reception desk for a better look. She recognized the ginger coiffure and cranberry Chanel suit of Andrea Reich-Hermann, standing before the open car. The Deputy appeared to be arguing with its occupant, whose hand restrained the elevator doors.

Kenna signaled and smiled for the receptionist–no problem, her demeanor assured him, back in a few.

Moving lightly across the plush carpeting, she was almost at Andrea's elbow when the older woman riveted with a quick, hare-like movement.

"You're early," Andrea said. Her eyes were bright, she cast a warning look toward the figure in the elevator.

Fabia Santiago stood not five feet from her. A gloved hand rested on the panel, as though to restrain it–which was superfluous because the doors were frozen open. With her other hand, she was shoving a thick pad of documents into one of two oversized duffel cases. The stack of German bonds had its wrapping intact, and though she moved to obscure them, the Countess could not hide JAFA's distinctive letterhead.

"Don't leave," Kenna said. "I need to take those bonds."

The Countess' sable-cuffed arm shot back inside to flick the key and press the "close" button. Kenna's eyes flew to the discreet arrow over the car. Lit up, flashing.

And then the ballet began.

Instinct took over. Kenna thrust her briefcase between the closing panels. The doors sprang apart with a sharp whine, then jerked closed again. Second time and the panels flew open. This time Kenna used the case to push her way inside. But the Countess had played this game before. She jerked the bag inside the car and Kenna fell backward. Her knee hit the edge of the door. She lost the tug-of-war for the briefcase and it spun back at her with the forceful kick of the Countess' boot.

She struck the up button, still hopeful, and the doors gave a fitful jerk. But Andrea's arm flew out to detain her and the doors closed. She watched, unbelieving, as the light above the car went out and the elevator started its descent.

"Call Security!" Kenna instructed the young man at reception, "Tell them to hold the express cars at the bottom."

She punched the summons for the other express car. It sped past the 15th floor on its way to 44. Not going to happen. With a dark glance at Andrea, she raced for the stairs.

She wrenched open the emergency exit-door and plunged down. Her shoes pounded on the metal risers. Like the other athletes in her college gym class, she'd jogged the concrete bleachers in the school's auditorium. But not in two inch heels. At the first landing she tore off her pumps in one motion and pushed them inside her skirt pockets, then flung herself down the airless shaft again.

All the while her thoughts raced like tandem cyclists, one stretching for the finish line, the other trying to make sense out of what she had seen. Why had Andrea released the bonds to the Countess? What would she tell Michael?

Kenna arrived at plaza level panting and clutching her side. The lobby door was unlocked, as she knew it would be for emergencies. Bursting through it into the main lobby, she faced a sea of heads. Every employee in the Citicorp Building, on their bleeping lunch break. Had the bullet car descended yet? Where was Security? As she forced her shoes on, she saw the building's guards move toward her. Careful what you wish for, she thought.

# 24

"What the hell?"

Klaus Kessel sprinted from the conference room. He had been waiting for Andrea Reich-Hermann to introduce him, her self-titled "bond expert," to Kenna Rand – phase one of a simple and straightforward plan to discredit the lawyer and her clients' gold bonds.

Unfortunately, Kessel had breakfasted late, arriving at Andrea's offices only half an hour before. Rudely, she kept him waiting – retribution, he supposed, for his own tardiness. She even accepted several phone calls in his presence, before leaving him alone in the conference room while she greeted another visitor. He hadn't had the chance to drill the Foreign Assets deputy on his detailed choreography for this morning's exercise. But he thought she understood the summary of the plan he had delivered in his tutorial style less than half an hour before.

"This morning, I am Klaus Ernst, German bond expert. You can remember that? When the lawyer arrives, I will inform her that JAFA's bonds, which she represents to be valid obligations of the German government are, in fact –" he paused for effect. "Illegal contraband, removed from the Reichsbank vaults by the Allies in the last days of World War II. In one stroke – the lawyer and the claim – dismissed. Who will attempt redemption of looted bonds?" He offered an eloquent shrug at the plan's logic.

"Unfortunately, her arrest as a conspirator in a scheme to defraud the Germans will detain her until after the deadline in Basel has passed."

Kessel, as Ernst, would seize the bonds. Two FBI agents were now stationed in the lobby, the African American woman named Nan Robinson – who looked like she could wrestle rattlesnakes with one hand while herding elephants with the other – and her subordinate, a man who posed as a fellow security guard.

Kessel had contacted the FBI before leaving Zurich, furnished them with a quickly conceived "file" on the lawyer, and secured their cooperation in carrying out a sting that would result in federal charges. Whether Rand would ever receive the stiff sentence the crime would bear – did it matter? He had only to summon Nan Robinson from the lobby and let the wheels of American justice grind to their ultimate conclusion.

But events had not followed Kessel's careful script. He did not know exactly what had gone wrong during the last ten minutes, but he had overheard enough to know Kenna Rand was racing down the stairwell in pursuit of the bonds.

"What the hell –" Kessel's green-lensed eyes were angry slits, and a vein in his temple throbbed with rage.

Andrea Reich-Hermann, her body ramrod stiff under her Chanel suit, faced a man possessed by fury.

"I worked it out myself," she said.

"What did you *work out*?"

"I'm sorry not to have consulted you, there wasn't time. I decided the bonds must be removed from circulation immediately. I saw an opportunity and seized it." She almost smiled. Not sorry. Bonds and Countess, hasta la vista.

"Wasn't time – for what? I explained to you my strategy."

"To be frank, I considered the idea you outlined this morning implausible and stupid. Like most men you tend to over-analyze things. How do you think I've achieved my position? Whoever controls the action controls the outcome…"

"Focking-A." Kessel's Euro-inflected American accent made the words both ludicrous and menacing. Andrea shivered in spite of herself at the force of his invective.

"What do you think I am here for? If you had not tried to *improvise*, the bonds would be removed from circulation. With their value tainted, the girl's credibility would be destroyed. The deadline would pass, no redemption. What the hell were you doing?"

Less than ten feet away the young man who handled the phones flicked them onto night service and fled up the interior stairs. Kessel let him go. "I am in charge," he said. "Not you."

"My husband has something to say about it."

"Your husband?"

"John Hermann is my husband."

Kessel shook his head in wordless anger. "All in your discretion," Hermann had said.

"But now there can't be any claim," Andrea went on in her most reasonable tone. "Rand can't litigate their value or provenance. The original bonds will disappear, and no one can prove their validity."

"Or *in*validity. Stupid woman. I leave you to explain the result to your husband." Kessel spun away from Andrea and flicked open his cell phone. He reached Agent Robinson in the lobby and spat his words into the line.

"Kessel here. Suspect is on her way downstairs. Cover the emergency exits."

He glared at Andrea. "Subject believed armed. Expect resistance. International fraud. Currency violations. Use of force is justified."

Kessel snapped the phone shut. "When I get back," he said, "We have something to talk about." He strode to the exit stair and plunged down after Kenna Rand.

# 25

*A moment's delay, lass, to gather y'er bearings.*

Kenna stooped to recover her breath and slow her heartbeat. Then she straightened, hands at her ribs, to survey the scene before her. With exits on three sides, a shopping concourse behind her, and six subterranean levels of shops and parking below, including subway access – the Countess could be anywhere.

More urgent now, the two guards making their way toward Kenna. To her left the male guard, checking faces. Friend – or foe, she queried him silently. On his heels, the African-American woman who had checked her in less than half an hour before. She remembered the name on the woman's badge – Robinson. The agent spoke into a transmitter on her sleeve, chin dipped low into her cuff, eyes searching the crowd. When her gaze met Kenna's, her mouth tightened and she moved forward, her hand reaching for her gun. No, this is not how it will end. You might mean well, but…

Still Kenna hesitated. Seconds were passing. Then through the sea of heads she glimpsed what she was looking for – a blond chignon. The Countess was proceeding to – now *through* – the handicapped exit on the plaza side of the building. She vanished into the crowd.

That's where I have to be.

Kenna merged into the mass of humanity, locking her arms to her sides and slipping between and among her unknowing compatriots.

Scouting for an opening, she found one and rushed the exit in a jog. She fell in behind one of the city's urban linebackers, a man who knew a thing or two about crowded lobbies and revolving doors, and was rewarded for it. Shoving his way into the moving panels, he spun them outward with a force the Incredible Hulk would have envied. She hurled herself through after him. *Owe you one.* But the unknown Galahad disappeared into the masses, unaware of his heroism.

Outside, on the plaza of white limestone, she barely halted. The wind had risen. The winter sun brought no warmth. The darkening shadow of the bronze sculpture revolved with menacing slowness.

She swept by a pod of smokers. Even in this weather they gathered, coat collars turned up, sneaking a furtive puff. "Hey, slow down. What's your rush?"

No rush. Just a pleasant stroll through the plaza. A quick survey behind her confirmed the two agents were caught in the human bottleneck. They could not stop her now without creating panic.

She kept her eyes on the Countess, proceeding as majestically as a yacht approaching the open sea. The woman's sable coat offered a kind of camouflage in the fountain's shadow and just for an instant she vanished, then materialized once more, sweeping toward the broad stairs that led to Lexington Avenue.

Weaving quickly behind her – gaining, running now – Kenna gathered hope. She had twenty years on her quarry. Not to mention a regular training schedule. She would overtake her on the stairs.

"Look out, we're taping!" She danced over the cables of a local television crew huddled around two men. One, the insipid local host, whose crinkly, made-up eyes were familiar to most New Yorkers. His guest – French diplomat? The cameraman side-stepped into her, tangling his cord in her feet and nearly knocking her down. "Watch where you're going, lady."

Lady. At the top of the stairs on Lexington, a line of private cars stood ready to whisk executives to their luncheon appointments. Halfway up the steps the Countess turned. *Cool customer, aren't you? I know you now. Thief.*

The Countess narrowed her eyes to scan the plaza. It was as Kenna had thought. The older woman needed to catch her breath. Kenna took the stairs two at a time. The Countess started upward again, pausing to acknowledge Kenna with her index finger, moving it back and forth slowly as if admonishing a naughty child.

Wedged in among the black sedans, a white limousine reposed, its engine running. She recalled seeing it upon her arrival – noting it, not thinking anything about it. The Countess moved toward it. The driver, in small cap and gray suit, stood ready to welcome his passenger. With one hand he held the door open, while in his other he held the dog's lead. Oh, yes, the Doberman was there. On his feet now. Sensitive, quivering, Mister A sensed his mistress. His ears flew back as he fastened his eyes upon Kenna.

Kenna slowed involuntarily. "If he attacks you," the Countess had said.

Her hesitation was brief, but it was enough for the Countess to reach the limo. One of the black Towncars was wedged in behind it. She didn't have to think about it. She signaled the Lincoln's driver. The red number on its windshield identified it as car No. 9035. Fine. With any luck No. 9035 could overtake the Countess. I'll find you, she promised.

With a practiced elegance the older woman ducked her head and swept into the limo, tossing the two satchels containing the bonds – JAFA's bonds – onto the seat.

She snapped her fingers once. Mister A, in one swift, graceful leap, floated into the vehicle. The Countess murmured something to the chauffeur that made him whip around to regard Kenna. The next instant the door was firmly shut and the driver was at the wheel.

Kenna reached the street in a run. The limousine driver hesitated before pulling into the heavy traffic. The Countess' sly glance found Kenna and she lowered the tinted window as the driver paused for a single second. And Kenna still hoped –

"Stop! Halt!" The guards were right behind her.

But the Countess' gaze moved beyond Kenna. Smiling now a strange unreadable smile, and giving the impression of having staged everything to her own satisfaction, she lifted her hand in a signal of triumph.

Kenna could not help turning back to meet the eyes of the man whose physical characteristics – tanned pate, fringe of pale hair meeting the collar of his leather jacket, and eyes the color of sea algae, seemed familiar.

"Freeze! You're under arrest."

But she did not freeze. There was the Lincoln. Tantalizing in its closeness.

"Stop or I'll shoot."

Even as she flinched, she was not alarmed. The police would never fire in a crowd, in Manhattan, in the middle of the day.

She heard the crack of the gun before the crowd did. In her peripheral vision she saw a few individuals lunge for cover or throw themselves to the ground. The chaos that she anticipated encouraged her to go for it. But it was too late. When at last the echo died and she watched the white limousine disappear down Lexington Avenue, Kenna stopped, defeated, next to Car No. 9035.

"Don't move, girlie – they're behind you." The Towncar driver's words held a note of regret. He gave a small shrug. Lost a fare. Again.

"FBI. You're under arrest."

The agent's fingers closed around Kenna's wrists in a rough grip. Her arms were wrenched behind her. She was spun rudely and pushed onto the Lincoln's hood. A sharp jab in her back, and she was eagle-spread against the car, helpless to turn her head, unable even to look at her assailants.

"You're making a mistake."

"Right."

"I'm an attorney, you've got the wrong person. The thief is getting away."

"Yeah? And I'm Princess Leia."

The female agent replaced her gun in her holster. She held Kenna fast while her partner went through the motions of patting her down. The lawyer heard the click of handcuffs and registered the unfamiliar awkwardness of her arms locked behind her. She felt her knees start to buckle though her mind was alert.

"I can't breathe," she said. She struggled to quash the panic that threatened to take over. "Let me go," she said with a command she did not feel.

"You have the right to remain silent," the woman intoned. " – the right to an attorney. If you can't afford an attorney one will be appointed for you –"

"Turn her around."

Kenna recognized the cruel educated voice of the man who had been waiting in Andrea's conference room. The man with the lizard green eyes.

"Let's look at our prize."

"Kenna Rand," the beefy African-American agent said in a voice thick with irony, "meet Klaus Kessel."

## 26

In the Vaud district of Switzerland near the tiny 10th century village of Valorbé, a private Cessna jet glided low over the walled estate of Prince Barron von Kadow, otherwise known as Miguel Santiago, and entered final approach for landing in a large clearing that had been made for that purpose. Sitting in a window seat was a slender dark-haired young man with an old world mustache.

The wind off Lake Geneva was strong and the plane rocked from side to side before touching down and skimming the tarmac surface of the clearing. The pilot applied the brakes immediately. He had landed there before and wasn't eager to reprise his tangle with the row of cypress trees at one end, where a white Bentley sat idling its motor.

Within ten minutes the single passenger found himself in the library of the chateau belonging to Prince von Kadow, whom he knew to be, notwithstanding the confusion of titles, the Countess' brother.

"Your sister promised the bonds to my government," the young man insisted over tea in the Prince's drawing room. His voice sounded a note of childish obstinacy. "I've just endured the grotesque experience of landing in a veritable wilderness – and you tell me she's still in Manhattan. Does she imagine I have time to sit around waiting for her like a lap dog?"

Meister, the junior minister of finance from Slovakia, had good reason to feel vexed. He was a member of Slovakia's "sperm bank," children of high officials who had come from the private sector to rule after the fall of Communism four years before. He knew there were those who resented his swift ascendancy to junior ministry, and he expected to silence them. His success in pulling off the Weimar bond transaction would demonstrate he was, indeed, worthy of his position.

"Time is short. Our debt to Germany is due in less than a week. I had intended to barter with the bonds. If we cannot satisfy Germany's demand, there is no hope for our plans to join the EU." He found himself speaking to the older man in short halting bursts as if his host did not comprehend English.

Receiving in reply only a politely raised brow, he reiterated his grievance in slightly different terms. "She gave me your name and insisted I meet her here. I've brought the money. I need the bonds."

"You'll get them." the Prince replied, pouring himself a sherry from a crystal decanter on the sideboard. "When Fabia says she will do something, it is a fait accompli." He returned to his chair, moving with a languor that made him seem older than he was.

"You don't know who I am," the young man insisted. "We have contacts from the old regime. It is not a good idea to play games with us."

"If I were you, I would get a room in Geneva for a day or two," the Prince replied calmly, apparently unimpressed with Meister's attempt at thuggery. He looked around with a vague smile. "I'd put you up here, but –"

"Why do I have the impression she never had them?" Meister's mouth twisted with disgust. A thin veil of sweat glistened on his mustache. "I should have known. I should have asked for proof that she had them in her possession."

The Prince covered his yawn with a polite hand. "Don't make your company so unattractive," he said in what for him was a burst of temper. "For all you know, she's already on her way here, with the portfolio you so tiresomely covet."

# 27

Only an hour had passed since Nan Robinson and Klaus Kessel rushed Kenna through the courtyard side of Manhattan's Federal courts building to a room where Kenna was fingerprinted and charged under the federal Securities Act with the unlawful attempt to pass stolen monetary instruments.

Kenna had endured fingerprinting once before. Only three months ago she had rolled thumb and fingers through the plastic slime of a live-scan machine to become a member of the New York bar. An intrusive process, she had thought then, but it had meant induction into her profession, a welcome rite of passage to a world of prestige and responsibility.

This time, under the coercive twist of Robinson's grip, her hand shook badly.

The ruthless efficiency of Robinson and the other officers afforded Kenna little time to consider the events that had just occurred, or to quell the alarm that threatened to surface. As Kenna submitted to the folding, stapling and spindling of the criminal justice system, the child-observer inside her showed up for duty.

Where are you going – what do you see? I am going to London to see the Queen. I am going to jail, she amended, and felt a shiver of fear. Focus on the present, she reminded herself. I see the hallways and the doors. I see the floors. Not funny. With her hands cuffed in front of her, forcing her shoulders to round forward, it was not an easy task to keep her gaze lifted.

The courthouse interior was unexpectedly clean, she noted, adopting the inner voice of a docent. The architecture, 1930s Federalism, evoked the setting for every New York cop show. And the surfaces – something the janitorial staff could be proud of. High-gloss walls of cream colored enamel. Large vinyl floor tiles buffed to a sheen. No graffiti. The elevator into which she was crowded in the close company of her keepers was faced in brown marble. Likewise the walls below the wainscoting. Never a cheerful choice, the somber shade further darkened the hallway. But at least it didn't show hand-prints.

Along the corridors, solid oak benches bore the patina of thousands of anxious litigants. It was late enough in the day, she supposed, that most of the court calendars had been handled. Only a few stragglers were seated now, hunched forward, waiting, and barely looking up at the young woman and her small entourage of handlers.

Her interview took place in a spartan room the color of yellow peas. A beige metal table separated Kenna from Deputy U.S. Attorney Wendy Vaughan, a forty-something military brat, Kenna decided, in crisp white blouse and khaki suit. She registered Kenna's reserve with polar-blue eyes that said "I'm the night owl, you're the field-mouse – welcome to the forest."

*Caution here, lass. Less said, less explained.*

How difficult it would be to refrain from offering a defense. The "mea culpa" approach, in which one blurted out one's version of the facts, then threw herself on the other side's mercy, was a a fool's game. But it was tempting nevertheless. Easy enough to practice taming the lion when it wasn't *your* head in the beast's mouth. Still, she summoned all of her will to hold her tongue, coaching herself to silence in the face of a string of hostile questions about herself, her grandfather and Michael Fein.

“You should consider hiring a criminal lawyer under the circumstances,” Vaughan goaded her. “Mr. Fein is likely to end up a co-defendant. His involvement can only prejudice your situation. We can help you. Obviously, you were just a pawn of JAFA. Selected for your youth and inexperience. I understand how that can happen. You had no personal knowledge these bonds were phony. You were just following orders from Michael Fein. You help us, we help you. No need for you to take the fall."

Kenna was shaking her head before Vaughan finished speaking. She smiled a dangerous little smile, but refused the bait.

“Just so you know, we're considering amending the charges to include Mr. Fein in a conspiracy charge."

It would be disaster if Michael were charged too. It would look like conspiracy and prevent either of them from meeting the deadline in Basel. She set her lips and studied the formica desktop in front of her. The only way to deflect intimidation was with silence.

At last Vaughan raised her eyes to the FBI agent Robinson. "What can you do?” She shrugged. “People don’t help themselves.”

Kenna did not move a muscle.

“This is a waste of time, I'm going to grab a quad soy latte. Take her upstairs to Division 9, Judge Tyra's courtroom. She can wait for her attorney there."

# 28

By the time Kenna arrived in Division 9 of the United States District Court, Manhattan, the two o'clock calendar had been cleared. The paneled courtroom was empty save for the Judge's clerk and female bailiff, who were engaged in languid speculation about the fate of an interstate child-abductor whose trial had concluded that morning. The jurist himself had retired to his chambers to await the arrival of Michael Fein, whom Kenna had called immediately upon reaching the Federal courts building.

Seated at counsel table were Nan Robinson and deputy Vaughan, with Kenna sandwiched between them. Bit of overkill, she thought, with the armed bailiff not more than ten feet away. The latter gave the high sign to Vaughan, who strode to the sidebar and checked in with the clerk. Then the Assistant DA returned to counsel table, seated herself in the oak swivel chair next to Kenna's and commenced rocking the seat restlessly with her foot.

Robinson hailed the bailiff in a jocular tone.

"What're you doing over there, Rosita--making odds? You know better than that. Gambling's illegal in the state of New York."

"You going to arrest me?"

Klaus Kessel entered the courtroom and flung himself into a seat at the back. With his briefcase open, he looked up a Manhattan listing on his PDA screen, tapped in the number on his Nokia 2100, and began speaking sub-audibly into the speaker, all the while drilling his neon-green eyes into the back of the defendant.

"I'll tell you why I'm calling," he said. "You might have told me your wife is the foreign assets deputy. She's made a cat's breakfast of everything. Was it your wife's brilliant idea to pass the bonds to a Latin American con artist? I've had dealings with Fabia Santiago before, by the way. The idea was to set up a sting, not a focking nine-ring circus."

The CIA man had plenty more that he intended to tell John Hermann. But the bank chairman responded aggressively, and Kessel found himself listening to Hermann telling him what he already knew – that it was imperative that Rand be retained in custody until Germany's deadline had passed.

"When we met in Zurich I told you I'm not a team player," Kessel cut in. "You went around me. Your wife is an amateur. She's not a professional in these matters. The situation is now totally – " he searched furiously for the perfect description. "Bogus." Damn. He meant botched. The word was botched.

"You proceed too slowly," Hermann charged. "Andrea saw a chance to remove the bonds from circulation, and she took it."

And passed them to an international thief. Idiot.

"You created sympathy for the Jews by stealing their bonds," Kessel said. "Did that occur to you? You weakened the case I set up against the lawyer."

"Bah! We made it easy for you, Kessel. You can't be timid in these matters. I trust Andrea's judgment. Boldness is strength."

Presumptuous asshole. The arrogance. Kessel knew he was over-reacting. But Christ! Would he never learn? Careful planning bungled by civilians. Saved only by the fact that Rand was in custody – sitting less than fifteen feet from him. He replaced his sunglasses, almost stabbing himself with the temple piece.

"What is happening now?" Hermann demanded. "Has she been arraigned? Has she –"

"I have to go. Something's happening. I'll get back to you," Kessel said crisply, cutting off the banking director in mid-sentence.

# 29

The bailiff picked up the handset and listened into it. She stood up and raised her hand in a signal to the clerk. Her message was clear even if Kenna had not been so acutely attuned to changes in her environment – the Judge would take the bench.

Bloody hell. Michael, where are you?

She could not resist glancing back to see if he had arrived. It caught her off guard to see Kessel in the third row from the back, obviously engaged with his Blackberry. What was he doing here? He raised his head and returned her stare. Chilling, behind those wrap-around sunglasses. She refused to look away, tensing as if to ward off a physical attack.

"Face front," Vaughan said, "the Judge is coming out in a minute."

Robinson drew her around. The agent's touch was light this time, but Kenna winced. Her shoulder could still attest to the officer's aggressiveness.

She had already made up her mind that she would have to represent herself when Michael pushed through the doors and rushed down the aisle toward the counsel table.

"Kenna, darling."

"You're late," Vaughan said, studying him critically. She passed him the government's statement of charges. "Enjoy."

"Good afternoon to you too," Michael replied. He threw a tense smile at the clerk and signaled to the bailiff. "Ten minutes. I need to speak with my client. Cuffs off, please."

As the bailiff picked up the phone to relay the fact of Michael's arrival to the Judge, Vaughan stalked out of the courtroom, looking at her watch. Nan Robinson released the handcuffs. Kenna shook her wrists, turning them to alleviate the pain.

The bailiff looked the newcomer over and turned back to the clerk. "What do you bet Vaughan fights like hell to keep her in custody over the weekend?" she said, without any attempt to avoid being heard.

*What do you bet?*

Michael guided Kenna to the jurors' box, up the steps and into the last seat in the third row where they would not be overheard. He set down his briefcase, and closed her hand in his warm one. "Now, are you all right?"

She gave him a brave smile. "Thank God you're here. I still can't believe it. Andrea simply handed the portfolio to the Countess. I almost caught her – I could have stopped her–"

"Tell me exactly what happened."

Kenna's account was brief and articulate. Michael listened attentively, his anger growing. But he did not interrupt her.

"That man at the back of the courtroom is an international currency agent named Klaus Kessel. The woman next to the prosecutor – FBI. They acted on Kessel's authority apparently. I was aware the FBI was involved last year in locating suspect bonds. But I have no idea how this guy Kessel links up with Andrea."

Michael turned his attention to the statement of charges Vaughan had handed him. He scanned the pages briefly. "Pretty sloppy indictment. Single count. 'Attempting to defraud another with respect to the sale, trade or exchange of securities.' The government alleges that you arrived at Andrea's offices with the intent to sell JAFA's bonds to a South American banker, one Fabia Santiago."

He raised his hand in a gesture of empathy. "I know."

He resumed reading. "The Countess met you at Andrea's apartment. You introduced yourself as an expert on German gold bonds and offered to sell her JAFA's portfolio, which you represented to be worth billions, mentioning nothing about the speculative nature of the instruments."

Kenna shook her head. "She's lying. Andrea mentioned the bonds when we were introduced at her cocktail party. The Countess suggested buying them for antique value. I did say we expected to get more in Basel, but I discouraged her."

Michael raised his hand again, still summarizing aloud for her benefit. "A meeting was set up to exchange the bonds this morning at the office of Andrea Reich-Hermann. Acting on information furnished by the Countess – that she suspected the bonds were part of war contraband looted from Germany at the end of World War II – the government obtained a letter from a banking director based in Basel, Switzerland – see Exhibit 1."

Michael folded back the pages to reveal a document bearing the name and crest of Prince Barron von Kadow, and a faxing legend: Vaud, Switzerland. He handed it to Kenna. She reviewed it quickly.

*"Responding to your fax of Thursday evening, we have referred your inquiry to the German minister of foreign debts. He confirms the serial numbers of the gold bonds listed in the portfolio are among those looted from the Reichsbank on May 14, 1945 by the Soviets. A declaration to this effect will follow from the minister himself."*

Kenna stiffened. She read the words a second time, acutely aware of the significance of von Kadow's letter. How did the Countess – or von Kadow – learn the serial numbers of JAFA's bonds? Michael had not delivered the bonds to Andrea until Thursday morning. Unless she and Michael could impugn that letter, the government had stated a prima facie case against her. *Intent to sell stolen securities.* Enough to hold her. Sufficient to put her in jail. She could feel the panic building again.

"Michael –"

"I know, darling. Keep your nerve."

She knew Michael urgently wished he had hired another lawyer to represent her. But Kenna had been adamant. You must come, she had said, sweeping away at once the issue of his being a corporate lawyer, when a criminal specialist was required. It has to be you, she had said. And now. Things were worse than he had expected. She could see it in his face. Even Michael could see they were vastly over-matched.

"Ready when you are," Vaughan's voice carried as she entered the court room. She set her empty latte container on the floor in the back row, and lifted her chin at Kessel, who ignored her. She resumed her seat at counsel table.

"Two minutes," Michael replied.

"What else do they have?" Kenna asked.

"Photos."

"Yes?"

"The evidence list refers to several photographs of you taken in front of your apartment, in the company of a man called Nicholas Chariot."

Michael's expression was impassive, but he could not hide his interest in her reaction. She reluctantly studied the evidence list, struck with a renewed sensation of unreality. Someone had obviously staked out her apartment building over the past few days. And it could not have been Nicholas – what reason would he have?

"They allege Chariot is a lieutenant in the Irish Loyalists, an extremist group that opposes detente between Sinn Fein and the North."

"What does Nicholas Chariot have to do with the bonds?"

Michael shrugged. "It demonstrates motive. The government alleges you're an Irish sympathizer who intends to use the bonds to buy arms for the underground."

"Spy fiction." She clasped the gold torque circling her wrist. "If anything, I long for an end to the violence. I could never align myself with a terrorist faction."

"Nevertheless –"

"Ten minutes are up, counselor," Vaughan settled herself forward in her chair. She caught the eye of the bailiff. "Showtime."

# 30

Judge Julius Tyra took the bench at two-thirty, appearing impatient and already irritable. He was a fierce looking man with a brusque burr in his voice and the scowl of someone with chronic indigestion. Counsel for each side stated their appearances, and the room fell silent for three minutes more as the judge reviewed the government's file.

He looked up and addressed Michael Fein.

"Counselor?"

"Before Ms. Rand enters her plea," Michael began, careful not to characterize Kenna as "the defendant." "It appears that crucial evidence cited in the papers – evidence that is integral to the government's case – has disappeared."

The Judge flipped through the information before him until he found the one-page indictment. "What evidence?" he asked.

"The bonds," Michael replied.

The Judge narrowed his eyes at the prosecutor. "Is this so? May I see the bonds?"

Vaughan exchanged a look with Robinson, raising a pale brow as if to say, "I told you so."

"They're not actually in court, your honor," Vaughan answered.

"Where are they?"

Vaughan cleared her throat. "The Deputy for the State Department turned them over to Countess Santiago to have them examined by her own experts."

“Isn’t she one of the government’s witnesses?” He flipped to another page. “She’s the one on whose opinion you relied in arresting the defendant, isn’t she?”

“That’s correct, your honor.” Vaughan poured herself a cup of water and took a quick sip.

"Where is this ‘Countess’?"

"We have our agents out looking for her, your honor. There was some misunderstanding with the witness. She was an innocent player in the sting the government set up, apparently assuming she could take the bonds temporarily for her own purposes. It's just a matter of hours until we recover them. Mr. Fein insisted on an immediate bail hearing. "

“That’s the defendant’s right, isn’t it?”

“Be assured, we don’t object to the timing of the hearing. However, we feel the absence of the bonds is not prejudicial at this stage.”

"What is your point about the bonds, Mr. Fein? If they are deemed to be fraudulent, and there are witnesses to the defendant's attempt to pass them off as authentic –" The judge turned his attention to Michael.

He was ready.

"The bonds are crucial evidence. True, the government offers a listing of their purported serial numbers. But we can’t actually compare the list with the bonds themselves. How do we know we’re talking about the same certificates? Without them, the defense is deprived of the opportunity to offer its own authenticating evidence."

"What do you propose to the court?"

"The charges should be dismissed at this time. If the evidence is recovered, the government can reassert its charges. For now, well, at a minimum I suggest the government has acted in haste–"

"And at a maximum?"

"They let the evidence get away."

"It would appear so."

A snapshot of Klaus Kessel at that moment would have caught his proud features working in a state of controlled fury.

*What did I tell you,* Kessel silently admonished the absent Andrea Reich-Hermann, *why couldn't you leave things to me?*

Vaughan spoke. "If I might direct the Court's attention to the file, there's a letter from Prince von Kadow of Switzerland, who avers that the bonds are in fact included on Germany's official list of stolen contraband."

Judge Tyra scanned the contents of the letter.

"It's not under oath," he said. He turned his interlocutory gaze toward Michael.

"As the Court astutely noted, the government's letter is a faxed copy, not an original," Michael said. "Incompetent under the Best Evidence rule. And its content is double hearsay. The author purports to summarize another's opinion – the alleged conclusions of Germany's finance minister. The minister isn't qualified as an expert, so his conclusions, even if they were offered first hand, are inadmissible."

"Isn't that a matter for trial?" the Judge asked, glancing at the clock.

"The point is, your honor, there is insufficient evidence to hold the defendant. Without examining the original bonds, no expert in the world can offer a credible opinion on their validity."

"Where do we go from here?" The Judge's mouth was set in a grim line.

Vaughan requested a brief recess to confer with Robinson. At Judge Tyra's brusque nod of assent, the two stepped out into the hall. Kessel followed them out.

"Well?" Vaughan fixed her cold gaze on Klaus Kessel.

Robinson spoke. "I assumed you had the bonds. We shouldn't have taken her into custody without them."

"Brilliant, Robinson," Kessel replied.

"Well?" Vaughan repeated the question. "The judge is ready to dismiss. What do you suggest?"

"It's all in the file I gave you," Kessel fumed. "The issue is not what evidence will be offered at trial. The question is whether we have enough evidence to hold her now. Today. And the answer is yes. The lawyer is a pawn for a terrorist group. She attempted to pass securities believed by the German government to be fraudulent. She's a high-flight risk. We had to act fast."

"I got that the first time around," Vaughan said stonily. "If we can't produce the bonds, or the Countess, we have no right to hold her."

"You must find a reason." Kessel drilled the lawyer under his electric gaze. "The German minister will provide his statement under oath. Witnesses will be found. The bonds will be recovered before trial. Just get the defendant bound over. Do your job."

Vaughan pushed her face closer to Kessel's. "I don't care who you are, Kessel. I don't care about your status in the mucking bureaucracy on high. I'm not going to jeopardize my credibility on a flaming inter-agency boondoggle."

Kessel turned dangerously cool. "You know what to say," he said. "Get in there and say it." He flung open the door to the courtroom.

"I apologize to the Court for the delay," Vaughan began when she and Robinson were again seated at counsel's table.

Kenna chafed at the hypocrisy in all this feigned courtesy and deference. The judge was clearly annoyed that his golf afternoon had been ruined by an unscheduled hearing. Vaughan's obsequiousness was a put-on. Kenna herself was torn between abject fear and outrage. Michael clearly had better control of his emotions. Why couldn't it just be over?

Vaughan continued smoothly. "When we were called into this matter to cooperate with an agent of the United States government, we were satisfied that the circumstances were sufficient to justify the charges. Our position has not changed. The situation was exigent. Urgent measures were required. The necessity to recover the bonds from Countess Santiago poses only a temporary problem which will be resolved in the next forty-eight hours."

Vaughan's demeanor suggested one whose earnest efforts at compromise qualified her for sainthood, at the very least. "Let the record show that we offer to continue this hearing until Monday morning. We expect to produce the bonds and other evidence at that time."

"Your honor -" Michael raised his palms upward.

"Is this Countess Santiago a reliable witness?" Judge Tyra asked.

"Are they checking the airports?" Michael interposed drily.

The Judge's frown deepened as he grasped the implication of Michael's remark.

"The Countess is a legitimate businesswoman from Argentina." Vaughan's hand clenched her papers. "As of this morning she was staying at the Plaza. We expect to recover those certificates within hours."

"They're bearer bonds, your honor," Michael said. "The Countess Santiago can immediately pledge them or sell them. She can even redeem them in the same Swiss bank that claims they're no good, if she wishes to. Possession is ownership."

Vaughan tossed Michael a tight smile. "The Countess is a reputable international financier. She is vouched for by Andrea Reich-Hermann, Deputy of Foreign Assets for the State Department. As an expert in German bonds, it was on the basis of her suspicions that the FBI was called in. She asserts that the bonds in question are the property of the German government."

"Is the defendant the owner of the bonds?" For the first time, the judge regarded Kenna as an interested party.

"No, your honor. The bonds are owned by a trust that–"

"Why isn't the trust joined as a defendant?" Judge Tyra demanded.

"We expect to amend the charges shortly," Vaughan said, with a superior smile in Michael's direction. "We had to act quickly, as we were informed the defendant was preparing to leave for Switzerland tomorrow morning."

Michael shrugged eloquently. "The government's case is a shambles. Ms. Vaughn admits her client failed to take proper precautions with crucial evidence and witnesses. Even if the bonds are produced on Monday, where is the proper chain of custody? Who is this 'Countess' and why should she be believed? In the government's dubious effort to appease a deputy in the State Department, it has rushed the doors of the court house. Having stumbled and fumbled all along the path, in the course of it, they've trampled the rights of this young lawyer. The showing must fail."

Judge Tyra glowered in silence for several seconds.

"The Court feels forced to accept the government's offer of a continuance. The charges will stand for now. The defense motion to dismiss is taken under submission pending a hearing on Monday."

"But your honor –" Michael rose to his feet.

"So ordered. Anything else?"

"The subject of bail," Michael said quickly.

"Yes. May I hear from the government?"

Vaughan tossed a sly smile of victory in Michael's direction. "The defendant is associated with a terrorist group sympathetic to the Irish underground. Photographs in the court's file reveal the defendant in conversation with one Nicholas Chariot of said terrorist group. The photographs were taken less than a week ago. As noted earlier the defendant is a strong flight risk. She is scheduled to leave for Switzerland tomorrow morning."

"I am not inclined to grant bail on a felony where the risk of flight is as great as this. Mr. Fein?" Judge Tyra glanced at his watch.

"Risk of flight is minimal to non-existent," Michael said easily. "Ms. Rand is a member of the New York bar, with no prior record. She graduated cum laude from Columbia Law School and earned a profile in Who's Who in American Universities for her research on the subject of German gold bonds. She has lived in the community all her life and is a partner in the law firm of Rand & Rand. Moreover, she's about to start a position as associate counsel with Hermann & Kroft."

Michael's slight smile seemed to regret the prosecution's excessive zeal in moving for bail in such circumstances.

He finished in a sober and confidential tone. "Given the inadequacies of the government's case against her, the court should release my client without bail."

Vaughan was on her feet. "This case is of international import. The German government quite naturally expects us to take every precaution."

"I've heard enough for one afternoon." Judge Tyra closed the file. "Defense counsel cites the inadequacies of the government's case, and I find his argument compelling. Don't press your luck, Ms. Vaughan. With Mr. Fein, I find myself wondering whether the case will even be viable on Monday. On the subject of bail, the court finds the defendant's position with Hermann & Kroft is sufficient evidence of defendant's integrity and ties to community."

Kessel nearly vaulted from his chair. The blood rushed to his face. He felt the vein in his temple swell like a python's lunch. Well, isn't that fantastic? Hermann's first-year associate!

"It is hereby ordered that the defendant Kenna Rand be released on her own recognizance, subject to relinquishment of her United States passport, if any. The matter is continued to ten o'clock Monday morning. The defendant is ordered to appear at that time. Defendant's failure to appear will result in issuance of a bench warrant for her arrest."

The jurist addressed Kenna for the first time since the proceedings began. "Ms. Rand, you'd better not have any thoughts of leaving Manhattan before Monday. Flight is evidence of guilt. If you ever want to practice law in this state–"

Judge Tyra passed the file to his clerk, stood up and strode from the bench. "Court is adjourned."

# *31*

The winter light was already fading into the headlamps of rush hour traffic as Kenna and Michael climbed into a hard-won cab that whisked them toward Michael's townhouse at Park and 80th. For a time there was silence among the car's three occupants, as Michael tapped up messages on his PDA and the driver scowled into the dusk. For her part, Kenna was thirteen again, riding in a taxi from the Nun's school after her grandfather's plane crashed in the Budapest countryside.

No one knew anything for certain, she was told. Except the pilot was dead. The nuns had thought she would be devastated. Ghastly news, they whispered among themselves, hands clasped with concern. Instead, Kenna felt a huge relief at the uncertainty. In the absence of knowledge, there was hope. When she had finally arrived at her aunt's residence and heard her grandfather's voice on the crackling phone line – well, it had all been all right, hadn't it? Until Monday, the Judge had said. Uncertainty again.

Michael brought her back to the present. "You're not speaking," he reminded her in his teasing tone, as if light heartedness were called for.

"I should go home."

"Agreed. But you're in no condition to think about dinner. I have a better idea. The post-arraignment supper at Chez Michael's is pretty good. I think I can get you in."

Kenna swept her hair back into a ponytail, just managing a smile.

"Supper first," he added with mock firmness. "I can't leave you tired and unfed."

Kenna forbore further protest. She knew she needed time alone to consider what had happened and what was to come. But Michael was right. In the present, food and comfort were called for. There would be chance enough to restore her defenses tomorrow when her mind was fresh.

At last the driver braked to a halt and the two lawyers stepped into the night air. While Michael settled the fare, she took a moment to study the fine old edifice before her. Some buildings could be like a welcoming friend. The solidity of form, the warmth of its greeting, nearly pulling you inside. She had expected Michael to reside in a sleek contemporary box, one of the gleaming high-rises that lit up the night with their numerous windows. But from the flax colored stone facade emanated a sense of calm that seemed to fit the man who had been her champion today.

A doorman buzzed them inside, returned Michael's greeting and held the elevator as they entered. They were comfortably silent on the ride up, with Michael watching her anxiously until she gave him another wan smile. From the street, faintly, the urgent wail of sirens. Going somewhere, apprehending someone. An involuntary trembling racked her. *Give yerself time, lass. The hours have spent ye. Y'er spirit will come back.*

At the 6th floor they stepped into a well lighted hallway offering two entrances. Michael unlocked one of them, then stood aside to admit Kenna to a commodious apartment overlooking the shadowy trails of Central Park. Here was the spare contemporary style she had expected, in a neat high-ceilinged living room of bold art and Mondrian colors.

"Don't talk, don't think," Michael said, when he had settled his guest in one of a pair of fireside armchairs. "Just keep me company."

He moved about her, adjusting ottoman and pillows, placing two coffee table books on the side table next to her.

She checked their titles, touched by the gesture: "*New York in Photographs*" and "*Rem Koolhaas – International Architecture for the Millennia.*" His choices amused her. After all she had been through, did he expect her to immerse herself in art for the next half hour?

"I'm a competent quick cook," he told her. "Smoked salmon and herb omelet is my specialty. If that's okay? I'll have supper for you in two minutes. Well – maybe not *two*." Michael took refuge in an outgoing manner even more extroverted than usual in a masculine effort to lift her spirits. She didn't mind, she decided. She felt all the free will of a kite at the shore in a March breeze, wafting close to the sand in a death dive, then suddenly buoyed by Michael's bursts of affability.

He started a log fire in the grate and set about uncorking a chilled bottle of Leon Beyer Riesling 1991. "A glass of Alsatian sunshine will bring the Irish bloom back to your cheeks," he said, filling two glasses with the crisp pale wine.

"Between France and Switzerland," he added, as if she hadn't heard of the Alsace region.

"You really don't have to wait on me." She sat very straight in the comfortable wing-backed chair.

He studied her with mock sadness.

"It's the least I can do," he said. "You're my broken sparrow tonight."

Michael tipped his glass to Kenna in silent toast, then left her, propping the door to the galley kitchen open. Through it, he spun brief, colorful stories of a seemingly eclectic career, cleverly narrated so as to require no response from her. She took a sip of the wine. Perhaps it was the image of the Alsace his words had evoked, but she did feel a surge back to the living. How lovely it would be to bike there, along the chain of 10th century villages she'd seen in photographs, like links in a bracelet. She let herself take in the room's spare contents and the few black and white photos. Michael's parents and family members, she guessed.

The rustling of her host's efficient preparations against a background of Willie Nelson songs cheered Kenna and, when he emerged with two trays of the supper he had prepared, and refilled their glasses, she realized she was ravenous for the simple feast.

"You once spoke of secret agendas," Kenna began when he had cleared their plates and poured two demitasse of espresso from a glass coffee press. "Is there something I should know about JAFA's portfolio – or JAFA itself?"

Michael brushed his thick hair from his temples, leaned forward in his chair and fixed sorrowful black eyes on Kenna. He hesitated as if he did not know how to begin. "What do you want to know?"

The strangeness started in her gut. She refused to drop her eyes. Tell me, she said, using only her body language and without uttering a word.

In a voice that had lost its customary cheerfulness, he said. "There exists some question about the portfolio's authenticity." He let it lay there. They both dreaded her picking it up. *Careful lass. Don't rush to find betrayal in a friend.*

"You lack papers for the bonds?"

"Yes."

"Then the government's charges may be proved right?"

He got up to stoke a fire that was merely embers. A calculated prodding brought it back to life. She let the minutes pass.

Finally he said. "The government managed to take advantage of a problem that I've been aware of. Your grandfather knew about it too. I don't believe the portfolio includes any of the bonds alleged to have been looted from the Reichsbank. But – basically, I can't prove JAFA's bonds are *not* on Germany's list of looted bonds."

"You let me believe their provenance was absolute."

"Yes."

So the extreme danger she had felt was real. No wonder he felt responsible for her. For the charges against her.

Michael set the poker back in its stand and stationed himself against the hearth, careful, even in his distraction, to avoid any surface that might have soot on it. The stiff Oxford blue of his dress shirt was still fresh after the long day. He ran a hand through his hair. It was the only clue that his composure might be under attack. "It's a long story. Will you hear me out?"

She shrugged coolly. Why not?

"JAFA was formed in 1946 to lobby the government's Finance Office. The war had been won in May of '45. The bond holders hadn't received any interest at all for thirteen years. The value of their investment had plummeted and something had to be done. We wanted the State Department to make a formal demand upon Germany to make good on the gold bonds. But they rebuffed our request. So we started our own effort.

"The Germans resisted, laying on like plum jam its 'poor little me' argument. The Third Reich was bust – kaput – with substantial war reparations to pay. All the Allies thrust out their hands for a share. The Jews, who had lost so much, didn't stand a chance. The Germans tried every game to avoid paying their pre-war debts. The bonds were the last thing they intended to make good on. They claimed Roosevelt, who, it's well known, had it in for Wall Street, shrugged off Hitler's default as a lesson to the bankers. The old Reich had ceased to exist. There were two post-war governments. West Germany insisted East Germany owed the debt. East Germany shrugged it off on Berlin. Game. Set. Match."

He lowered himself to the ottoman in front of her, reached out to take her wrists then thought better of it.

"Germany was allowed to set up a Validation Committee of Swiss and German members to evaluate every bond submitted for redemption. You know how JAFA would fare under *that* procedure."

Michael's brows gathered in disgust. "The Germans have yet to approve a single portfolio for payment."

"Was JAFA represented in the negotiations?" Kenna asked.

Michael rose and refilled her demitasse.

"The man sent by the U.S. to negotiate the accord was Tom Rane, John Hermann's predecessor." Michael nodded his head in reply to her silent question. "Yes. Hermann became his protegé. Rane had served on the board of J.Dalton & Company – the issuer – and JAFA had a lot of confidence in him. JAFA felt the bank owed an obligation to the bondholders which would be fulfilled by a vigorous campaign to force Germany to pay.

"Rane played right into the German committee's hands. In a show of support for the 'Validation Process,' he deposited our authenticating papers with the Germans as proof of JAFA's claim. They disappeared. A day or so later the entire portfolio was discredited by German officials claiming the serial numbers on the bonds were on a secret list of 'looted contraband.'"

"The Germans kept your records."

"Yes. We withdrew our claim. We had to. Fortunately, we were able to recover the bonds themselves. But the papers, documenting that the bonds were kept in this country, and therefore could *not* have been stored in the Reichsbank in May, 1945…"

Kenna regarded him steadily. That explained why Michael had jumped at Andrea's offer to authenticate the bonds through her "bond expert" – a current valuation would not raise any new issues and could overcome the old ones.

"When were you going to tell me?"

"On the flight to Basel. It sounds rotten. But I needed your help to track down the contacts your grandfather had made."

"What contacts?"

"Jack believed there was something about the bonds themselves that establish their validity. He said the Germans are the world's record keepers. He surmised that in the last days of the war, the Germans had marked the Reichsbank bonds in some way."

"Why would they have done that?"

"Hitler was scrambling for funds to continue the war. Jack believed the Germans intended to re-sell the cancelled bonds even though international law would have required them to destroy the cancelled certificates. Instead of destroying them under the usual custom with cancelled debt instruments, Jack believed they were re-marketed by the Reich's bankers."

"What country would have accepted them under those circumstances?"

"It was a question of who would have looked the other way. Jack wasn't sure."

"Marked in what way?"

"That I don't know. Before your grandfather died he'd received some confirmation of his theory. His inquiries led to Switzerland, and a small village near Geneva where he hoped to find the answer, the only name we have is Les Grottes."

She recalled the name among her grandfather's current files. "Why did you keep this from me?"

"I didn't want to impair the portfolio's value. Bonds without papers – the Germans would laugh up their sleeves." He shook his head in self-reproval. "I knew you would add credibility to the project. But you wouldn't sign on to a losing proposition. I thought once we got inside the settlements bank we'd have a chance to build world opinion in our favor. It might drag on for years but…"

"What about *my* credibility?"

Michael sat forward, fixing her with troubled eyes. "You trusted me. I betrayed that trust – for the worst possible motivations."

He sought redemption in the fire's blaze. "I told myself it was for your own good. That you'd never accept the commission if you knew the truth, that you'd be depriving yourself of the chance to launch a career in international law. Typical lawyer bullshit."

He laughed hollowly. "I launched your career all right."

He stood up and moved restlessly to the hearth.

"Why did grandfather agree to help you – if he knew the portfolio was questionable?"

"He'd tried to redeem them once before, in 1945. To save a child in Berlin. The attempt went nowhere, the bonds disappeared. He wanted to find out what had happened to the child he tried to save. I think he found what he was looking for – before he was killed."

The words hung between them.

Michael started across to her. The phone rang and it disoriented him. He changed direction and picked up the receiver on the desk near the window. But he turned his face to her and watched her with brooding eyes as he listened to the caller.

"I'll get back to you later. Give me the number there." He wrote down the digits on a pad beside the phone and said, "I'll remember," as he replaced the receiver.

"I can't tell you right now," Michael said in answer to her silent query. Again the expression of regret.

Kenna stood up and folded the comforter in the chair, walked her tray into the kitchen, aware that his words had banished the closeness of ten minutes before.

He met her in the doorway and searched her face wordlessly.

"And now?" Kenna said.

"And now," Michael said firmly, "I'm taking you home."

## *32*

Kenna awakened in fear, listening. Her night clothes were damp with sweat and her skin taut with gooseflesh. The antique travel clock on the desk across the room shone its green numerals – two o'clock. She had slept fitfully since Michael left her off around eleven. And now she scanned the silence for the sound that must have awakened her.

There it was again. The tiny metallic burp of a door handle being turned by a gloved hand. Someone was in the apartment.

Rising silently and placing her bare feet lightly on the rug, she prepared herself for the intruder. She pulled the covers over the bed-warmth that could betray her presence. Then she moved noiselessly to the closet, opened it and stepped inside, pulling the door closed behind her.

She huddled in the closet among her shoes, listening intently. Not more than thirty seconds passed and, through the narrow gap between closet door and frame, she saw the pin beam of a magna-light sweeping an arc. A figure moved like a shadow into the room and shone the light across the bed.

This is no thief then.

She was aware of the sound of her adversary, the swishing of someone accustomed to silent movement. Aware too of the wave of evening chill that swept in with him. A scent of night air that she now associated with terror.

In the first minutes in the closet she had fought to keep her accelerated breathing silent. But now she could not have breathed deeply if she wanted to, all of her functions had locked down into her chest as if restrained by armor.

The narrow beam of light swept the floor and shone in the cracks of her hiding place. Kenna's heart pounded violently. She recoiled further into the tiny space. Never had she been so aware of the terror of the hunted. He was on the other side of the door. Worse – much worse than confrontation. In the next instant the door would open and he would be there. With a knife, with a gun.

The wailing horn of an alarm went off across the alley and she flinched violently. "Shit!" Her neighbor's voice. She heard the sound of a window sash being raised, and the room was suddenly bathed in light. Chaos had erupted across the alley. She sensed the figure on the other side of the door, debating his next action. For a moment Kenna had the absurd fear he would join her in the closet.

The alarm continued. Her first thoughts had been joyous, welcoming the distraction and the possibilities it offered for rescue. Then it occurred to Kenna that the din would block out her cries for help. She was alone in the apartment with the intruder. Her neighbors had their own problems. If you want to kill me, now is the time.

He was there. She was here. How much distance separated them–a foot–two feet, maybe? The minutes seemed to have ceased their onward progression. She listened so intently her jaw started to numb. What – *what* could he be doing out there? Just when she felt driven almost mad by fear, the intruder retreated. Sweeping a penlight over the closet door once more, he moved into the hallway. She listened to the light tread descending the stairs, the easing open of the outer door and she could see, in her mind's eye, the figure pause on the front stoop before escaping down the street and into the night.

Kenna huddled in the closet, not daring to summon help. Five minutes turned into more. An uncontrollable shivering took her. She started counting and waited for the terror to dissolve.

# 33

Five minutes turned into twenty. Her neighbors' alarm had abated what seemed a long time ago, and they had moved to another part of their apartment. They left the window open a good four inches. Good. She could hear them moving about in there, and smell a lighted cigarette. It was satisfying to think she could call out at any rate, if he returned. Still she waited, breathing in short shallow intakes through her mouth.

When at last Kenna stole downstairs to the foyer, a street lamp shone through a hole in the outer door where the deadbolt had been. With great effort she moved the library furniture to the periphery of the room. She flung the carpet into a semi-roll and heaved it in front of the door. She checked the windows, still locked.

The entrance to her grandfather's study was ajar. Inside, the wall safe stood open, the desk chair swiveled round to face it. Jack Rand's small folio of bonds was gone. Along with his file.

## 34

At ten-thirty Michael rang. The bell of the study telephone woke her from a troubled sleep among a set of sofa pillows she had placed on the floor of the den. She had covered herself with the duvet from her bedroom, then lain wide awake until almost four o'clock in the morning, listening for the return of the intruder.

"Christ! A break-in? Are you all right?"

"I'm glad to hear your voice," she said. He sounded so – rational.

"What happened?"

"About two o'clock, a noise woke me downstairs. I thought of investigating. Then I heard someone coming up the stairs. I got out of bed, pulled up the sheets to make it seem it had not been slept in, and hid in the closet. Right away, I could see his penlight moving underneath the door…on the bed, along the carpet. Bloody terrifying. He must have known I was there. The bed was still warm. Michael, we were ten inches apart. If he had flung open the closet door…"

"Frocking Christ! What did you do?"

"An alarm went off in the building across the alley. It seemed to go on forever. It should have given him the cover he needed to come after me but…" She felt the first real sense of relief. "He left. I'll never know why. When I got up the courage to come downstairs, the chair was in front of the vault. Grandfather's bonds were gone."

"Why did he go upstairs?"

A lawyer's question. The immediate one.

"Terribly thorough, I guess – as midnight intruders go."

"Not funny." Michael sounded uncharacteristically stern. "Have you reported it?"

"Whom to? My pal Nan Robinson?"

There was a pause. "At least you should file this at the local level. You need to create an official record of the theft."

She waited, letting him think about that. , it had been her first instinct – to call the police. She had quickly dismissed the option.

"You're thinking it will harm your case on Monday," he said.

"Yes."

"It could help it…"

"Less than seven hours after being charged with attempting to pass stolen securities my office is broken into and personal portfolio taken."

Michael's tone was disappointed. "It sounds implausible."

"It sounds lunatic," she said. "I have no proof the intruder was even here. I seriously doubt there are any fingerprints or forensic evidence. Even if there were, there's nothing to prove he broke in *last night.* Vaughan will turn me into marmalade on the stand. My credibility will be shot if I offer up an obvious attempt to cast myself as victim."

"Not if Andrea backs you up. Let's conference her in right now."

"That would be a mistake." The force of her resistance restored her. "I don't want Andrea involved until the charges are dismissed on Monday. If they *are* dismissed."

"And the reason?"

"I've been thinking about those few minutes in Andrea's offices. Quite frankly, Michael, there are gaps in logic. It doesn't make sense. Countess didn't *steal* the bonds – not from where I was standing. Andrea voluntarily gave them to her. She allowed Countess to get away. As I ran for the stairs I caught her expression, and I couldn't read it. That's the problem, since you're asking. I'm not sure I like Andrea's role in this."

"Obviously, relinquishing the bonds to the Countess was unfathomable. She might have felt she was acting appropriately under the circumstances. Let's assume she was taken in. She can't admit her mistake. After all, Countess is an old friend of her husband's. Now she's had time to reflect on the serious spot you're in. I need her to show up on Monday, as character witness, if nothing else."

"But Michael, why didn't Andrea attend the arraignment – if she wanted to support me? And what was Kessel doing in her office? The so-called currency expert."

"Good question. Let's call her now."

"Absolutely not." The panic of last night started to rise again. "Promise me you won't contact her without telling me."

"Kenna, darling…"

Darling again. He sounded impatient. "You need all the help in high places you can get. I won't argue with you now. We can discuss this later. You need to report the break-in. I'll handle the fallout in court. I'll be there in less than thirty minutes to help you with your statement. And don't even think about going back to your apartment tonight. You're coming over here. Or -" he continued as if her silence had been an objection – "if that spooks you, there's a small hotel near my place… I won't leave you alone."

"It's gone beyond that, Michael."

She spun her grandfather's chair around and switched on the computer. A few taps on the keyboard brought up international flight information.

"I'm leaving for Mexico tonight." Her words surprised her. Until that moment, she hadn't really thought about what she was going to do next. Even as she spoke, she debated whether she would actually follow through on the spontaneous remark. But her spirit lightened with the prospect. Why not take back the self-command the last twenty-four hours had stolen from her? She couldn't stay here whiling away the hours until the court sealed her fate on Monday. And she wasn't going into seclusion in a hotel.

"Careyes, Mexico," she murmured, preoccupied now.

"Careyes? Where the hell is that?"

"Hermann keeps a villa there." She tapped up a search for "Careyes," paraphrasing aloud an archived story that appeared on the screen: "Careyes is a resort not far from Puerto Vallarta. A magnet for the international set..."

"So you imagine the Countess is in Mexico?"

"Yes. I do."

"Why?"

"She as much as told me she was going there. She and Hermann are lovers, by the way." She selected an itinerary and printed it out.

"I find *that* hard to believe," he said. "The Countess is long gone by now. Halfway between New York and Geneva. She knows what the portfolio is worth. What could be the point of linking up with Hermann in Mexico?"

"The prosecutors hadn't found her, had they?"

"What do you mean?"

"Vaughan and Kessel. They had no idea where she'd gone. If she was on her way to Geneva, they could easily have confirmed it."

"So it's Mexico – in your opinion."

"We have to start somewhere."

We? He hesitated, surprised. He kept his tone light. "I'm hardly an expert in criminal law, but there's no chance of your getting leave of court for a weekend trip to Mexico. "

"I agree," she said evenly. "Petitioning the court would be a waste of time. I'm going anyway."

"Have you forgotten, counselor? You're under subpoena to appear before Judge Tyra on Monday."

"I'll be back by then." Sunday evening in fact. She selected the return date and printed the revised itinerary.

"I don't need to remind you. If you're apprehended in Mexico, you'll go to prison. It will look worse than if you hadn't left. Flight is presumption of guilt."

"A Delta flight leaves for Puerto Vallarta this afternoon at five o'clock, there's a car to Careyes from there. I can be at the resort at ten o'clock tonight, local time." It might have been a long-anticipated holiday. She might have been planning it for weeks.

Michael was nothing if not calm and reasonable with her. "We can get the charges dismissed if the bonds aren't produced. The judge is with us so far. But you have to stay in New York. We can do our due diligence from here. It's crazy to act on impulse."

Instinct, not impulse. An athlete couldn't blow off the race because of fear. This *was* a race. She could not tell Michael – but it hit her that she did not trust the legal system. A lawyer, and she did not believe "Justice" would prevail. Too much riding on others. The judge. Vaughan. Andrea. Michael himself.

"By Monday, Vaughan's case will be stronger," she said. "Thanks to you, I'm not spending the weekend in jail. But if the prosecution beefs up von Kadow's letter, the evidence will be compelling enough to set the case for trial. All Vaughan has to do is fly him over here. With Andrea's statement that the sale was arranged, it's enough to keep me in Rikers. And the photos with Nicholas Chariot provide a motive. I'd prosecute the case myself if I were Vaughan."

"JAFA will put up whatever it takes to keep you free. I won't let you spend an hour in jail."

"You won't have a choice if Vaughan does her job. She has only to amend her charges to include you as co-conspirator to drastically change the game. The bonds have already caused my grandfather's death. I'm not letting them –" She steeled herself. *Trust yer judgment, lass, ye'll know what's right.*

She began again. "You said the original certificates may be marked in some way that proves their authenticity. The only chance we have is for us to recover them."

Michael hesitated. It was "us" again, as it should be. Some unconscious part of her still valued his support. He could not forget the way she had appeared at her grandfather's wake. Rebellious. Incautious. Last night he had seen a different side of her. Subdued, but apprehensive. The game had changed and she had been quick to appreciate it. She had needed his protection. She needed it now.

"You stay here," he said. "I'll go."

"I can't stay here."

"You're reacting to my words last night," Michael said.

"You didn't reveal anything I didn't already know. Grandfather was murdered for his knowledge about the gold bonds."

"We don't know that, Kenna."

She knew.

The line was silent with his frustration.

"Book *two* seats then – business class," he said.

# 35

Six hours had passed since Michael and Kenna shared a cab to JFK's Aero Mexico terminal and boarded flight 111 to Puerto Vallarta. At nine-thirty p.m., when they should have been departing for Zurich, Switzerland with JAFA's bond portfolio, Kenna and Michael were among the first passengers to lurch down the plane's ramp onto the narrow spit of tarmac that was the Mexican resort's arrival zone. A blast of tropical air hit them like a tsunami.

The circle of floodlights lighting the terminal threw the last twenty feet of pathway into darkness. Kenna plunged forward until she glimpsed a small door, and swerved inside. Not the most auspicious entry to an international airport. The interior's illumination was not much improved either. More than one of the ceiling lamps flickered indeterminately. Michael made a quick stop at the lavatories while Kenna strode ahead with her single bag and backpack. She passed through the small building to the curb, where she managed to flag the only jeep-taxi that had pulled up to greet arriving passengers.

"Do you speak English?" Kenna inquired in Spanish, flinging her bag into the vehicle's boot and taking a seat in the back.

"What else?" the driver answered in a crisp European accent that drew her head up in surprise.

Austrian, she recorded. The man's face and shoulders were in shadow, though as he leaned forward she saw deep patches of sweat at the armholes and spine that stained his linen shirt. Lifting his eyes to address her in the rear-view mirror, he added cheerfully, "Ran out of bread. Got to earn a living in this trucking place."

The American slang was outdated by a few decades and that, combined with his Germanic delivery, struck a bizarre note of dissonance in the jungle landscape.

"We're staying at Costa Careyes," Kenna said. "My companion will be along in a minute."

"Sorry, can't take you there" the driver said, shaking his head ruefully, and leaning back to swing the rear door open again from the inside. She placed her hand firmly on the handle.

"Why not?" Almost ten o'clock on a Friday evening was not, she thought, a good time to find transport for a one hour trip through the Mexican jungle. A quick scan of the curb confirmed that no new cabs had pulled up. The few hotel vans bore local addresses in Puerto Vallarta, not Careyes.

"Bianca," the driver shrugged, as if amused at his own bad luck. "She runs the hotel. A bad thing to get caught in her web tonight." He threw back his head in a gust of Bavarian mirth. "You won't see me as Bianca's pony-boy. Been-there, took the trek, bought the t-shirt."

Who was Bianca? Kenna hadn't time to explore the driver's meaning, for another passenger was heading toward them, wearing the determined expression of an experienced cab-sharer. Bloody hell. She could see the moment of conflict coming. She was about to lose the only transportation within ten miles. If this black sheep of the von Trapp family had a choice, she and Michael would be flung out to fend for themselves.

"We're terribly tired," she said, drawing a twenty-dollar bill from her backpack and offering it to the jeep's driver. "Just arrived from New York. Couldn't you drop us off near the hotel, without running into Bianca?"

The driver snatched the bill gracefully, tucking it into the pocket of his shirt with the air of one conferring a favor. "For an American Goldilocks I will do anything!"

His face moved into the light and he appraised her with frank regard. He was an attractive man of thirty or so with straight brown hair and high cheekbones. His features had an Aryan beauty that was almost feline, his expression lit now with sexual interest. "Do you like a spanking now and then, Goldilocks?" he asked.

Before she could answer he laughed decadently and started the jeep. "Do you like a spanking, little girl?"

Great. She had managed to attract a lecher *and* a sadist. "Just take my companion and me to Costa Careyes," she said firmly. "That's all we need for now." Michael arrived at last, a little out of breath. Offering an apologetic shrug to the hapless traveler who had tried to beat his arrival, he threw his bag in the back and slipped onto the seat beside Kenna.

"Good luck," he waved the man off cheerfully. "It'll be hell trying to get a car at this time of night."

Within a few minutes they had left behind the airport's phantom landscape and were flying through the decrepit urban gashole that was downtown Puerto Vallarta.

Here, 'decaying infrastructure' took on new meaning. The streets appeared to be in a state of permanent construction. There was not a square of roadway over ten meters that wasn't torn up. Even at this time of night, crews of jack-hammer junkies stood in the blitz of searchlights as if it were Mardi-Gras, offering Kenna their woozy, gap-toothed smiles as the open jeep passed by, and stopping work to hail her with leering shouts of approbation.

"They like you," Michael said, laughing at her attempt to avoid eye contact.

"I'm flattered." Catching his spirit, she waved and flashed the men a smile, inciting even greater swagger.

Ulrich Kuhlman – Kenna had made it her first objective to study his cab license – catapulted through the darkness undeterred, swerving round sinkholes like the telemarking skier he undoubtedly had been. Soon, the chipped stucco and broken windows of white-washed residence apartments gave way to a dense wall of luxury high-rise hotels, lining the famous beaches that drew thousands of winter sunbathers to the city.

Leaving the town behind at last, they entered a tropical landscape lit only by stars and a gray sliver of moon. The narrow road was no less rutted than the streets of Puerto Vallarta but at least it was not under construction. And the scents that filled the night air were of jasmine and passionflower, not human waste.

"Jews are not appreciated down here," Ulrich remarked conversationally to Michael in the rear view mirror.

"Oh yeah?" Michael said, amused by his candor. "What makes you think I'm Jewish?"

The Austrian shrugged as if it were self-evident.

"Not a big Jewish destination – Careyes," Ulrich continued.

"Why not?" Michael traded a look with Kenna.

"No infra-structure in this place."

"What do you mean?"

"Frontier law," Ulrich said. "The police can be bought. Ha! They expect to be. Part of their compensation. There's no accountability – no protocol. Everyone for himself." He yawned indulgently. "This place draws unwholesome types, people with a past." His tone confirmed his preference for such people.

"Does Bianca have a past?" Kenna asked.

"Italian aristocrat, so they say. But nobody's checking. Bianca runs the villas where you're staying. She won't be on the desk tonight, but if she were – well, you might not be staying there."

"Is the anti-Semitism here that strong?" Kenna asked, regretting immediately that she had played into his attempt to spook her. She tossed Michael a rueful smile.

"We don't call it anti-Semitism down here," Ulrich replied. "We're a closed circle you might say. Careyes has always been a community of expatriates. Austrians, Italians, Argentines, tax-dodging Brits, any European deadbeat with a need to lie low." He gave a big guffaw, clearly enjoying his self-appointed role as tour guide.

"Your hotel is thick with them," he went on, "right up your alley." He drove more sensibly now and Kenna had grown to like the man for his exuberance.

"You'll run into some characters tonight. The local crowd will be at the Sand Bar. That's Bianca's watering hole for her stud service."

"We'll seek them out," Michael said, dryly.

"But, really," Ulrich said. "Stay clear of Bianca. She's a bit crazy actually. She knows everyone down here, some you wouldn't want to know. And she's got her own Mexican Mafia. Lucky, at the bar, has big ears. Whatever you might think, he does what he's told. Be careful what you say." He turned to emphasize his point.

"We're looking up a friend here," Kenna said. "She may be staying with John Hermann. Do you know where his villa is located?"

"Ho-ho, Goldilocks. You don't want to go there."

"We were told she may be staying there."

Ulrich tipped his face upward into the mirror. His expression showed plainly that he was not fooled by her attempt at casualness. "Well then, you'll find Hermann at Villa Largo, Jimmy Goldsmith's old place."

"Sir James Goldsmith – the corporate raider?"

"Boots-up a few years ago, poor guy. Cancer. But his protegés are still around. Hermann bought the place. Keeps up the local tradition."

"What tradition?"

"We're a haven for international crooks, South American exiles. Hermann finds them colorful. Helps them out from time to time with favors from his influential friends. Charming collection if you like dangerous jet-set lowlifes."

His tone took on a taunting aspect as he went on.

"People like Lucan. Poor sap killed his nanny by accident. Meant to murder the wife to resolve a custody dispute. A *most* incompetent assassin. Not unusual in this place. But the real losers are the unlucky chumps who've failed financially. Or ruined others. Ran through their fortunes – like me." There was something in his laughter like regret. He stretched one arm against the steering wheel and ran the other hand through his hair.

"What draws them here?" Kenna asked.

"Affluent friends. One can live cheaply here." Ulrich flashed a mysterious smile. "In Careyes, we always say 'it's the *facade* of wealth that counts.'"

Out of the tropical brush Kenna glimpsed a gleam of light. And then another. Then through a clearing in the wilderness the hotel emerged, ablaze with lights. The jeep swept sharply onto a gravel drive and, barely slowing, pulled up to the hotel's entrance.

Michael and Kenna descended from the jeep. From the open lobby, two Mexicans in chino pants and white shirts shifted from their place near the bell captain's desk to the rear of the jeep. They lifted the travelers' bags from the back and placed them inside on the tiled floor. Michael drew a fifty-dollar bill from his billfold and passed it to Ulrich, who tossed back a mock salute. Instantly, the jeep was off in a crunch of gravel and spin of the wheels.

Kenna followed the Mexicans into the brightly lit lobby. "We reserved two suites," she told the desk clerk, deciding to take the natural awkwardness out of the situation.

The clerk let his eyes float from Kenna to Michael to Kenna again. "I hope this will not be a problem," he said in a soft voice. "We have only a two-suite casita." His tone implied it was the saddest thing in the world. He waited.

She and Michael exchanged a smile. The clerk's attempt was amusingly bold.

"It has two bathrooms," he said helpfully. "Two bedrooms. A large living room and terrace. More comfortable, I think, to share. I hope you will find it so," making it a question – Kenna's call – and sweeping his silky lashes against his cheek.

"You prefer separate apartments, don't you?" Michael asked her frankly.

She allowed her smile to cover the awkward moment, answering quite differently than she had intended. "The two-suite villa sounds fine," she said.

"Villa Torre," the clerk spoke firmly to the bellmen. Then to Kenna – "Are you hungry, señorita?"

"Yes." The half-thawed chile relleno and chocolate flan that was the plane's fare had not tempted her, and she was starving.

"The Sand Bar is still open. Follow the path upward from your villa. The view of the sea is spectacular. The drinks are strong and the menu is satisfactory." He consulted his watch. "The locals will keep it open until midnight at least."

As Kenna and Michael turned to follow the bellman to their casita, she caught the hotel clerk watching them thoughtfully before retreating into the shadows behind reception.

# 36

After a quick refreshing shower in her suite, Kenna changed into loose trousers, sleeveless bodysuit and sandals. Michael, too, appeared revived, with his hair slicked back, fresh shirt and khakis. "Nice digs," he said when they met in the shared living room that opened to a dining terrace and view of the sea and rocks below.

Michael opened the French doors to the terrace and a warm breeze swept the room. The scent of night-blooming jasmine was like a tonic and she almost regretted what she planned to say. She wet her lips before beginning.

“We should clear the air, I guess.”

“Should we?”

“Shouldn’t we?”

She looked down, laughing. “I meant–”

“I know what you meant.”

He stood mirroring her, his hands lightly circling each of her wrists. He checked her face and seemed to find his courage there. “A breakneck weekend in Mexico, in defiance of a court order is not the way to begin – what I want to begin."

She let her incipient awareness of his desire wash over her, feeling both resistance and attraction. For a moment she was afraid she needed to do something: to avoid events taking what her thoughts ludicrously labeled “a turn.” She decided to wait it out. See what happened. No words. Curious, she studied him. A man twenty years older than she. Secretive.

Possibly a liar. And obviously, exercise-averse. Almost surely he had something to do with her grandfather's death.

Michael's expression was equally impassive. He released her wrists, placing them at her sides, and finished with a silent gesture that said the matter was self-evident. Not the right thing. Not the right time. Yet.

"Okay," was all she said, though something about the patency of his emotions had touched her.

"Let's shake on it." Michael again offered the crooked smile and Kenna could not repress her own small laugh at the gravity of their exchange. She extended her hand, smiling, and he closed it in his, and pulled her toward him, playfully.

"Oh, hell," he said. "Why do I feel like a twenty-five year old?"

Kenna felt her face grow warm, but she continued to meet his eyes.

"Good," he said. "Great." He gently guided her face close to his. When their lips touched, she relaxed against him. She had never kissed a man with a beard, she thought. Incredibly soft. Incredibly sexy. She hadn't expected the softness. She wondered if they would reprise the kiss. But he stepped back half a step and regarded her happily. She felt her face smiling too. Two crazy idiots, she thought. So that's what flirtation with an older man was like. They remained close to each other, smiling mysteriously for several moments, after their hands had dropped to their sides. "Let's find the famous Bianca," Michael said at last. "And get some grub."

# 37

The scene that greeted Kenna as she and Michael approached the highest point of the hotel property above the sea was an indelible one.

The Sand-Bar, a thatched open-air structure of native palm fronds, stood in a clearing of tropical brush above the hotel.

At the crescent-shaped bar, a retro collection of men with mustaches, and women in jeans and scarf-tops, dangled like empty charms from the rattan stools, letting their fingers play with cigarettes, or rest on the colorful hand-blown glasses of martinis and margaritas that decorated the counter before them. On a vinyl dance stage, a couple danced to a '70s disco beat played from two speakers fixed precariously to the underside of the roof. The thumping bass sound of Donna Sommer blasted the tropical night, swinging back on them like a boomerang, while a breeze wafted up from the sea, lightly ruffling whatever it could catch and bearing a dense perfume.

The newcomers' arrival was watched with hungry interest. Kenna felt the tiniest hairs on her arm lift in apprehension. Michael moved closer to her, as if he could eclipse any risk of danger with his physical presence. His tone when he spoke was light.

"Ulrich's local color, I presume."

Two men parted a path and Kenna advanced to the bar, slipping onto one of the stools they had recently vacated. Michael stood at her side. He glanced around easily, taking a calculated stock of their environment, but playing the role of the easygoing turista.

It was not hard to identify Bianca, the only unescorted woman at the bar. She was provocatively posed, her derriére resting against one of the stools, her elbow crooked to maintain a lighted cigarette close to her shoulder, as she conversed expressively with the bartender.

She could have been the Countess' less fastidious double, a blond with dark roots whose ponytail was pulled back with a limp scarf. She wore a man's dress shirt loose over designer jeans, the sleeves of her shirt pushed up fashionably to the elbow. On her feet were leather thongs; from her wrists hung a collection of heavy bracelets of Mexican silver. She turned to assess their arrival, greeting them across the bar stools with a thick, rolling Italian speech.

"Welcome!" She flashed dark eyes and pristine teeth but Kenna missed the warmth behind the smile.

"Americans," Bianca said to the immediate company. "We needed a few to meet our quotas." The laughter was shallow and polite and shut off as briskly as a light switch.

Clearly the mistress of ceremonies, Bianca introduced herself and then the bartender 'Lucky,' an Englishman in his forties whose dashing good looks and dissolute charm would probably never desert him entirely, though dissipation had been underway for decades.

"Yanks," he said in drawing room English, looking them over shrewdly. There was nothing genuinely friendly about his interest. Part of the job description no doubt: sizing up new arrivals.

"What will you have?"

They gave their drinks order. For Kenna, plain tonic. Michael ordered a Margarita.

"Where in the States are you from?" Lucky asked, splashing tonic into a Scotch tumbler and squeezing a lime into it. His look, as he set the drink before her, stayed on Kenna a beat too long and she recalled Ulrich's warning about him. Chances were excellent that no secrets of any interest were kept for very long in Costa Careyes.

"New York," she replied, sticking to the truth. We're on a small holiday," she confided. "Just the weekend."

She watched his quick movements over the Margarita glass. Rubbing the used lime on the rim, inverting the glass onto a plate of coarse sea salt, setting it down with a shake. He tossed two shots of agave tequila and fresh lime juice into a chrome tumbler, and poured the Cointreau from the bottle without measuring. "I'm sure everyone asks – " she met his eyes. "The source of your nickname?"

He added shaved ice, put the lid on the tumbler, and gave it a few seconds of vigorous shaking. He poured the absinthe-colored liquid into the glass.

"Always scored at cricket, luv," Lucky replied, giving a successful attempt at cockney inflection. Then, to Michael, setting the Margarita before him. "And I always collect my bets."

"Lucky–" Bianca interposed with precise cruelty, "isn't lucky at *every*thing."

Kenna tried to puzzle out the malice that underlay the woman's remark. She could not fail to note the quick flash of anger that shot across the bartender's face like a comet before he busied himself with the rinsing of glasses.

"Fishing tomorrow?" Lucky asked after the awkward pause. "Just wander down to the boat ramp when you're ready. One of the Mexican boys will take you out. They know the best spots for snorkeling. Some rummy caves and what-not in these waters. Lovely. Chef will fry up whatever you catch tomorrow night. Something to talk about when you get back to New York."

This was supposed to pass for the instant chumminess that fostered good feelings between guest and staff. Why then did she decide she would not ever be alone with him? Kenna found his eyes uncomfortably on her again. "I like to jog," she said. "Are there any trails around here?"

"You're better off on a horse," Bianca put in. "This is not Central Park." She inhaled deeply on her cigarette, turning her head to release the plume of smoke into the night air. "We have a polo field." She appraised Kenna narrowly. "You look like you could handle a few chukkers. If you can ride. There's always the chance for a match. Just saddle up one of my ponies at the stables. Tell them I said it's all right."

"So you play?"

"We all play down here," Bianca answered. "Polo, that is."

"There must be a few regulars in the private villas then?"

"Not many," Lucky replied. "We're a smallish community."

"Sir James Goldsmith used to keep a place in Careyes, didn't he?"

"Used to." Lucky intercepted a look from Bianca and shifted his eyes to the bar. He picked up a glass and squinted at it against the light. Then he plunged it into a soapy dish, rinsed it and set it on the sideboard.

"You're interested in Jimmy's place?" Bianca asked gently and dangerously.

"I read of it once. It must be very beautiful." She wondered how convincing she was in her deliberate casualness.

"It's like a prison there."

"What do you mean?"

"High walls. Electric gates. Cruel dogs." Bianca's expression was still aggressive. "Comfy if it suits you. I like it."

"Hard to get in," Kenna said, giving an ingenue's smile.

"Harder to get out," Bianca corrected her, dousing her cigarette in an overfull ashtray. "What do you do – in New York?" she asked.

"Until recently I've been a student. But I have to start working soon." She affected the right tone of regret. "A last getaway before leaving the leisure class."

"Very amusing, I'm sure," Bianca replied shortly. She turned to Michael. "You're an attorney?"

He laughed easily. "It's that obvious?"

She lifted her shoulders, dismissing the observation as an easy parlor trick. "And you are interested in Villa Largo," she mused. "American groupies," she said mildly to Lucky.

"I wouldn't mind seeing the place," Michael replied.

Bianca used her cigarette as pointer, designating a hilltop a few miles north of them. "Then look for yourselves. You can see the villa from here, actually. John Hermann owns Villa Largo now, doesn't he Lucky?"

She addressed Kenna. "Your former Secretary of State. You will not remember his influence," she clipped the final word as if it were an insult. Then: "Maybe you have business with him."

It was the sudden brightness of her eyes and not her words that Kenna recorded. "Not unless he wants to offer me a job," she said lightly.

The music stopped and the dancers moved back to their table. All was silence except for the low murmur of cocktail talk and the throaty har-hars of a circle of British hold outs, who had reached the point in the evening, as suggested by the ring of empty bottles ornamenting their table, when every five minutes meant an increase in noise level.

Bianca dusted herself down and straightened the spread collar that fanned from her brown throat. She lit another cigarette, her bracelets jangling noisily. "Play the disco music, Lucky."

Lucky reached down below the bar and fiddled with a CD player. Another Donna Sommer song filled the night. He replenished Bianca's champagne glass. She turned purposefully to Michael. "Your friend is so beautiful – and so young," she said, all the time speaking to Michael in a tone implying something more. *I'm more to your liking*, her eyes seemed to say, *Why don't we spend some time together?*

Michael's smile was cool. He shrugged, letting her know it didn't work that way.

"I think you must dance very well," Bianca went on, her eyes still frank and suggestive. She indicated the small disc of warped sheet vinyl that served as dance floor.

Michael smiled. "It's tempting, Bianca. But we're hungry and tired. We'd like some sandwiches if you can arrange it." He nodded in the direction of a smoldering fire pit to one side of the bar that apparently served as grill for the plates of carne or pollo offered on the bar menu.

"No problem," Bianca said, giving a curt nod to Lucky. She lifted her champagne in a silent toast and turned away, preparing to circulate among the few tables that skirted the dance floor. "If you need a guide tomorrow to Villa Largo, let me know," she said before moving off. "I know your John Hermann very well."

Twenty minutes later Michael and Kenna had finished the grilled meat sandwiches produced under Lucky's supervision and moved to descend the steep jungle path to their casita. Michael offered a wave to Bianca who gave a brusque, unsmiling salute with her cigarette. Kenna felt Bianca's eyes upon their backs. She even fancied a whispered dialogue between the hotel manager and Lucky. The sound of lizards rustling in the brush startled her briefly. And she remembered that night creatures were not the only dangers here. Snakes and scorpions prefer the sun.

# 38

The morning turned out gray and overcast after a brief and brilliant dawn, which only Kenna had seen. Navy colored clouds wore ribbons of black that would soon become a heavy pelting rain, as a small tropical hurricane keened toward the peninsula from a roaring sea. All this Kenna could see below the wide balcony off their living room.

A small brown maid entered their kitchen at seven o'clock and a large pot of coffee was delivered to the terrace fifteen minutes later. This was followed by a plate of fresh fruits, pitcher of orange juice, cereals, scrambled eggs with jalapeño peppers and curiously, broiled steak and mashed potatoes glistening with starch.

Kenna poured herself a cup of strong black coffee with heavy cream and nibbled at the papaya and strawberries. Should she waken Michael? The telephone rang in the living room. She answered it before it rang a second time. A voice with a trace foreign accent, only a trace, said: "We have your modem line for you."

"Thank you," she said. Kenna snapped open the lap top on the rough table that served as a desk. She switched it on and plugged in the resort's phone line connection. Then she began the process of tapping into Columbia's Research Library, glad she had not relinquished her access code after law school. After a frustrating ten minutes she located the information she was looking for under the subject "European Titles."

*"Born Fabia Santiago Bucher, in Buenos Aires, June 1947 of Argentine mother, German father. Brother Miguel, born 1949. Parents married, 1951."*

Kenna could almost feel the editors' lifted brow – illegitimate.

*"Father's employment: Liaison, Argentine Bureau for German Relocation."*

The Countess' marriages were described, along with her divorces, the last from an Italian count: *"(Right to title disputed by spouse.)"*

Kenna scrolled to the back of the section titled "Notes."

*"Countess Fabia Santiago is currently sought by British intelligence for help with their inquiries in connection with the Isle of Man banking swindle (1991) and the suspicious death of a Barbados banking officer (1993) allegedly injected with a South American toxin called oleandrin (footnote). Anyone with knowledge of…"*

Kenna sat back and digested what she'd read, aware of the pickup in her heart rate. So the Countess was wanted for 'help with inquiries.' The phrase was typically British, a subtle way of saying that the Countess was a prime suspect in bank fraud and murder. It changed things. The impulse to pick up the phone was strong. She saw herself calling London blindly, asking to speak to someone in British intelligence, explaining that she knew the whereabouts of a woman sought in connection with certain events.

Impossible. Not only were the charges in question dated – off anyone's radar, next to the critical issue of the next London transit bomber. It would take many calls, many conversations to reach the correct party. My name, sir? Kenna Rand, alleged felon, illegally abroad. No, she could not afford such a risk.

She turned to the footnote: "Oleandrin, a toxic substance derived from a South American plant related to the common oleander, and developed into an injectable poison by the Russians during the cold war. Dried, ground into a powder and re-moistened, it can be injected readily." Yes. Readily enough all right.

She returned to the bedroom, located her backpack and searched her wallet for the card given her by Nicholas Chariot at her grandfather's wake. If he were associated with Irish intelligence as he implied, he could secure further details from his London counterparts without risking exposure. But – why would he do that for her? What could she offer him in return? Kenna studied the card, turning it over to read his private number.

Michael emerged from his room, appearing fresh and rested. She replaced Chariot's card in her wallet and restored the screen to the mild scandalousness of Countess' biography. He scanned the words quickly over Kenna's shoulder.

"Illegitimate," he observed. "In a Catholic country, that could explain a lot about our 'Countess.' A title, even a dubious one, tends to smooth over the rough edges of society's elbows. We now know the prosecution's key witness is a liar. Any reasonably prudent fraud suspect would go back to New York and turn this thing over to professionals."

"*We* are professionals," She joined him on the terrace.

"Oh, sure. The Hardy Boys in Careyes. Wouldn't you feel more comfortable preparing your defense from the security of my apartment – while Interpol or the FBI close in on the bonds?"

"It was our friends at the FBI who arrested me." Was it only yesterday? "They're hardly likely to believe me now, and turn their attentions to pursuing the Countess."

"I didn't like our friend Bianca," he said. "Or her pal Lucky. She's not the most savory character." He helped himself to coffee and a plate of fruit. "You know, don't you? She'll be on the phone to Hermann as soon as she's up and decent. It won't take her long to work out who you are and send for the Federales. It's all about picking the fleas off the back of the Alpha-male around here. And Hermann's the prime Silverback."

"Bianca is nothing more than the hired help. Hermann wouldn't have her as a 'friend.' I can't believe she can call Hermann and whisper rumors in his ear. Two visitors from New York – so what? He's hardly interested in salacious details of her nights at the Sand Bar."

She added: "Don't tell me Lucky caused you to lose your courage?"

He favored her with a look that said he was not going to fall for such a transparent assault on his manliness. But by the time Michael had finished a plate of fruit and his first cup of coffee, Kenna had persuaded him, over his objections, that they could not leave Careyes until they had at least verified whether the Countess was staying at Villa Largo. Only then, with information to trade, she said, would they have a real chance of getting the bonds back.

"For the *short* term –" Michael was careful to make his point by meeting her eyes. "You're in charge. I'm only the sous-chef. But," he said, firmly, "We leave tonight, no matter what we find out at Villa Largo." He turned to his plate of steak and eggs jalapeño, with a dollop of mashed potatoes. "Now, counselor, how do you want to proceed?"

Kenna considered. Last night she had been ready to jog the roads to Villa Largo. She hadn't even a real plan in mind. Just go there. Arrive. All she had to do was to confirm whether Countess was present. If she could show a connection between Hermann and the bonds…then Andrea would be forced to intercede. And she could do that on a morning run in the tropics. But that course appeared even less practical now. In the rain. In the dense brush. It would simply take too much time and expend too much energy. She looked dubiously at her companion.

"I'm in better shape than you think," Michael offered. "I treadmill two miles a day. Wolf down a low-fat Mediterranean diet. Salmon or cod twice a week, oatmeal every morning. I'm a very good boy."

Kenna surveyed him with open skepticism. "And this morning?"

"A well-rounded meal. Protein, carbs and fruit. It's only common courtesy to eat what's offered to you. I'm *trying* to be a good guest."

"A guest who's forty-five years old and at least fifteen pounds overweight."

"Ouch. Forty-seven," he corrected her. "And I'm not overweight. This is body mass. Muscle. What do you expect of a Jewish boy from the Bronx?"

"A little weight training?".

"Lovely girl. But naive. You can't defy genes or nature. I'll always be something of an urban bear."

"A mesomorph," she said, allowing him that.

"At your service."

"Ectomorph," she replied, with a slight bow.

"Obviously." He raised his eyes to her with an expression that was both amused and admiring. He reached out playfully for her hand.

"Mischief-maker," She turned away to hide the color she felt rising in her cheeks. Moving to the archway she looked out at the sea and the ever-darkening sky.

"I confess I thought I could recover the bonds," she said. "I really thought I could do it. But it seems so – unlikely. Am I crazy?"

"Probably." Michael said calmly refilling his coffee cup.

Restless again, she strode to the telephone and dialed the front desk. "I saw hotel jeeps when we pulled up, didn't you?" she asked Michael, cupping her hand over the phone. The clerk answered at the other end and she inquired in English about renting a jeep.

"It is *possible* to rent one of the hotel jeeps," the man conceded politely. "If they are not needed for hotel business. Bianca has not arrived yet, I cannot ask her. You won't be driving far?"

"Bianca mentioned a polo field nearby," Kenna improvised. “I realize we can’t play today, obviously, but we’d like to look it over.”

"Ah, yes." Relief sounded in the man's voice. "If it rains today, there won’t be any games," he said dubiously.

"We'll take a chance. We’ll be down shortly to pick up the jeep."

She swung the terrace telescope from the choppy gray surf below the hotel, in the direction that Bianca had indicated from the Sand Bar. At the edge of a cliff, she saw a Mediterranean style villa. At its wrought iron entrance, two men stood casually alert. Americans by the look of them. Attired in Dockers, golf shirts and boat shoes. The men scanned the road in front of the villa for several minutes. Then one looked at his watch, spoke something to the other, and they strolled back inside.

"Would John Hermann still enjoy Secret Service protection?" Kenna asked.

"I hadn't considered that."

"Neither had I," she said.

The maid discreetly entered to clean the breakfast dishes and make the beds. Michael relocated to the terrace with his mobile phone, as Kenna excused herself to complete her preparations. Over t-shirt, shorts and running shoes, she slipped into track pants and a light rain slicker. On her way through the living room, she grabbed her backpack and tossed a bottle of mineral water to Michael. With a last look around, she met Michael's eyes. "Shall we?"

## 39

The resort seemed deserted at nine o'clock in the morning. Under the threat of precipitation that had come up overnight, it would be a rare guest who would venture from their villa and the warmth of a cozy fire. The jeep was waiting when they reached the lobby.

A lone hotel man worked the phones behind the registration desk. Michael and Kenna lingered impatiently until he placed one of the callers on hold, left his station for a small room off reception, and returned with a single key.

On a map of the area beside the front desk Michael picked out the polo field south of the resort, in case they were asked about it. Then, he inquired casually: were any scenic drives on the north side?

"Well," came the hesitant reply, "the drive toward Villa Largo is a lovely one. About a mile and a half north of the hotel. You must take the road called Alcazar de la Mar. It is known for its views of the sea. But you will find the way narrow and very steep. It's a dangerous drive if you don't know it well," the man cautioned Michael. "And don't make the mistake of continuing past the villa, the road ends abruptly at the diving cliffs."

"Looks like that's the one we'll take," Kenna said when they were outside.

There was no one to watch as she shifted the Jeep into gear and pulled away from the curb. She turned north, returning along the course they had traveled with Ulrich, until she'd passed a tiny turn-off into deep vegetation. A barely legible wooden sign read “Alcazar de la Mar ” – if one imputed a letter here or there that was faint or missing. She put the jeep in reverse, backed up and turned in. The road led upward, winding above the resort. Below, they could see the few boats of Mexican fishermen trolling for local sea bass in the roiling waves. A light drizzle had begun.

They had driven for fifteen minutes when Kenna glimpsed Villa Largo through dense vines. They paced its serpentine wall another half a mile. She stopped the car fifty yards from the double iron gate.

She idled the motor, then stepped out to study the entrance.

"Cameras," she said in reply to Michael's unspoken question. "A small one attached to each of the gateposts. I have no idea about their range. Do you?"

“Not really. Logic would suggest they're meant to capture images at the gate. But I can't say for sure.”

She thought for a moment. "We passed a clearing off the road about two hundred yards back. Let's leave the car there."

She put the Jeep in reverse and backed up slowly until she reached a mere track of road, and turned onto it. A few hundred yards farther on, they reached a small landing strip. She pulled in as far as possible and parked the Jeep in the trees at the edge of a grassy lot. They got out and sauntered over to a corrugated hangar about twenty feet away. Kenna peered in the windows while Michael strolled around to the front. Except for a small Gulf Wing airplane, the hangar was empty.

"Nobody's around," Michael said when he returned.

"Do you think that's Hermann's private plane?" Kenna asked.

“I would think so. There are few other residents in this area.”

“Do you mind staying here?" she asked. "I'm going to jog back to Villa Largo." She tossed the vehicle's key into Michael's palm.

“Are you crazy? What happens if they arrest you – or worse?”

“If I’m not back in – say – forty minutes, you’ll get help from the resort. You’ll think up a perfectly plausible explanation as to what we’re doing here. Interest in Moorish architecture or something – and you’ll rescue me.”

“Moorish architecture is not going to cut it with Bianca,” Michael grumbled.

“Cliff diving, then.” She laughed nervously. “Please don’t make a fuss.” She hesitated, asking for his assent. “This is what I came for. If I catch a glimpse of the Countess, I’ll come back for you.”

"Twenty minutes," he said, finally. "And I'm coming after you."

"Agreed," she replied and left him looking worried.

## 40

Inside the white walls of Villa Largo, Countess Fabia Santiago reclined in the capacious marble bath that adjoined John Hermann's master suite.

"I rarely take a morning soak," she said into a portable telephone. "As you know darling, I prefer to bathe at night. But your villa is so lovely. So like my Amalfi childhood. The balconies and pergolas of my family's estate."

A long window gave a view of Careyes Bay, its waters growing darker and more turbulent every minute, in contrast to the still water in the glimmering sixty-five foot pool that floated upon a white limestone terrace and fell off visually into the sea. The Countess closed her eyes, enjoying the fantasy her words evoked. A childhood of heartbreaking perfection.

The silence from the other end went on too long.

"You are not saying anything, John."

"I am not interested in your past – a dubious one, if I'm to believe Kessel. We are discussing the gold bond portfolio. Why did you take it out of the country, Fabia? What were you thinking?"

The Countess lowered her eyes to the immediate foreground, where Mister A sat at attention, alert to every nuance in his mistress' volume and tone.

"Kessel?" she repeated. "I would not place my trust in him, darling, no matter what *strings* you pulled to engage him. We have a history you know. He has tried to interfere with me before. He is – " she searched the horizon for the appropriate term. "An autodidact. He will run things himself. Decide, *himself*, how things will be done. And you will find the situation out of control."

"You're the one who's out of control. What the hell goes through your head? Did you imagine you were going to rip off the bonds and turn them in without anyone noticing they were missing? You've put me in a very embarrassing situation. If a connection is found between you and me – I should not need to tell you the consequences. The prospect is nuclear."

As she listened she reached with her free hand for her cigarettes. He was speaking again, with what she had come to dismiss as his "Bold World Leader" voice. "I am sending a courier to pick up the bonds."

She lit a cigarette and inhaled deeply. Then she rested it upon an empty abalone shell beside the tub and glared out the window. He assumed she was going to turn the bonds in to Germany. For the good of the German State, no doubt. For nothing but a small reward. Some little bauble of recognition. What was the English phrase – a mere bagatelle? Just to be his little sweetheart.

"Yes, yes I see," she said, following the pool's horizon. "Send your courier. I don't promise to wait for him. I have commitments in Europe. I am leaving today. You can't believe the turn the weather has taken. The wind is like a tsunami. If I don't leave in the next half hour… .When I have turned in the bonds, you can join me."

"I'm not joining you anywhere. This has gone too far. Andrea suspects – "

"Andrea suspects! Who cares? We can live abroad now. No hiding and seeking. No playing games in and out of Mexico. We can live together always. In the hills of Cascais or on the Spanish coast. It will be wonderful, darling." She lifted her eyes to Mister A as if she were addressing him instead of her lover.

He was getting fed up with her whims and the airy-fairy voice she assumed. "Andrea is my wife. I love my wife. Is that simple enough for you? I don't believe she gave you the portfolio. I imagine you took it on some pretext or other. Well, you've bungled everything. You'll be lucky if the FBI doesn't turn its attention on you."

"They will not find me, John."

"You will wait there for my courier," he thundered through the crackle of Mexico's inadequate telephone system.

With great effort, the Countess gave her voice enormous charm and reasonableness. "I am doing this for us John. For you. If I have my own money... it is the only way you will leave Andrea. She is too strict. Too accomplished and too boring."

"You don't get it, do you? This is not a game, Fabia. You will wait there," he repeated.

She snapped the power off to disconnect the line. "Yes, darling."

She stepped from the tub and wrapped an oversized towel of Egyptian cotton around her, tucking the end into the cleave of her chest. She bent over from the waist to shake her breasts into the towel to give them lift, then re-examined her form in the mirror, satisfied. She tapped up an international number and spoke immediately into the telephone to the man's voice that answered.

"Miguel, it's me. Tell Meister I have the bonds. Tell him to immediately wire the deposit directly into my account. Unless the money is confirmed when I arrive tomorrow, I will sell them to someone else. I am leaving for Geneva tonight."

# 41

Kenna spent a boring forty minutes across the road from Villa Largo. It was not difficult avoiding detection by the two plainclothes guards. She was glad she had checked her watch at the hotel. The two men had appeared in the lens of the balcony telescope at eight twenty-five. It was nine-twenty now. She made a quick call to Michael's cell phone. But the transmission kept breaking up. She left a crackled message anyway, telling him she was okay, to give her another twenty minutes, and hoping at least some of the message was transmitted. The murmur of voices grew closer as she closed the phone. She would soon know whether they made the rounds according to a time table.

Kenna moved further into the tropical brush. The thin trousers over her running shorts clung to her skin. The constant rustle of wildlife around her recalled her to the fact that *she* was the interloper in this habitat. The sudden crackle of a branch made her snap her head around in alarm. But it was nothing. At least not for the moment. She shivered and blew into her hands.

She had no plan, having never studied the finer points – or indeed any points, of undercover work. She would not set herself up for disappointment by imagining that they could recover the portfolio and turn the Countess over to the authorities. She would now feel the trip was a success if she could simply confirm the Countess was in Careyes.

She was growing impatient when the crunch of gravel announced an automobile leaving the villa's grounds. A car swung toward her on the drive and stopped at the gates. The vehicle's fog lights were on, even in daylight. The idling motor told her the automobile would roll out of the drive at any second. As if she had planned it this way, she readied herself to dart inside the grounds, assessing the overgrown bird of paradise plants on the side of the drive closest to her for a potential waiting place. She visualized the moment, a few seconds only, when she could slip through. She would plunge immediately into the brush or behind the guard shack and wait until the guards made their rounds again. But she was not prepared for the car's passenger to speak. When the car's shaded rear window lowered and its occupant addressed one of the men who had run up from the house, Kenna recognized, in the few words that floated to her, the imperious tone of the Countess.

# 42

For the past ten minutes Michael had been crouched on a platform ten feet above the hangar floor. He'd moved inside upon the arrival of the Latino man in the vest, whom Michael had dubbed "'"the Mechanic." Now, he watched the mechanic roll the Gulf Wing out of the hangar and onto the tarmac in response to some crackled orders emanating from a two-way radio the man wore on his belt. Almost immediately the pilot arrived, boarded the plane and sparked the plane's engines into life. The Gulf Wing now idled on the runway, its ramp lowered, ready for its passenger.

Michael was feeling calm and curiously untried by his cloak-and-dagger response to the situation. He felt halfway amused by it. Lawyer. Intellectual. Confident in courtroom and boardroom. Hardly one to assume physical risk. Nevertheless, here he was crouched in the hangar in the middle of the Mexican tropics awaiting the arrival of a suspected murderess, in an enclave populated by anti-Semites. All for the love of a woman. A young woman. He smiled at the thought of Kenna. Impetuous, brave, smart – stubborn. All the things he wasn't. Well – maybe he was smart. He hadn't imagined falling in love with her. There was the moment when she led him across the grass to the gazebo in her aunt's garden… he had taken a seat on the swing where he could look at her. He had never considered the term "soul mate" in connection with himself. Could this be what they meant?

Two men burst through the side door, talking. "They called from the villa. She'll be here any minute." Their voices carried in the empty hangar.

"What's the rush?" the mechanic asked his companion, whom Michael pegged for the copilot, after his heart had stopped leapfrogging at their entry.

"Got to get to Mexico City to make an Air France flight, taking the nine-fifteen to Geneva tonight."

The first man swung into the small washroom, unzipped his trousers and stood pissing loudly into the toilet, leaving the door open. "I hope she knows the French at customs are going to slap that Doberman in quarantine," he observed. "I wouldn't like to be there when they try to take that dog."

"Scary biscuits all right," the copilot agreed. "As my kid would say. But she dopes the dog for travel. Sends him private. The dog arrives before she does and is delivered to her after she's landed. I doubt if it's legal. I don't look into it. She don't tell me and I don't want to know." He cocked an ear to the crunch of gravel outside. "She's baa-ck," he said under his breath.

## *43*

Kenna reached the airstrip ahead of the Countess, her lungs on fire with the effort of thrashing a shortcut through Careyes' soggy undergrowth. The borrowed jeep was still parked on the edge of the grassy parking lot but Michael was not in it. The light drizzle had let up but the sky was heavy with promise of more rain. Kenna positioned herself behind the hangar and waited. She was surprisingly unconcerned about Michael. Whatever his deficiencies in terms of physical fitness, he made up for them in resourcefulness. She allowed herself a millisecond's release of tension. Michael, at least, would know what to do.

It seemed only a matter of seconds before the Countess arrived. The car halted not fifteen feet from Kenna. The driver emerged and passed around the front of the car to the passenger side, held the door for the Countess, and she got out. A sharp smack of her hand against her left hip brought the Doberman from the back seat. He lifted his head and sniffed the air nervously. The Countess followed his scent, scanning the landscape with dark critical eyes.

"What is Bianca's jeep doing here?" she asked.

"Dunno," the driver replied, with the twang of England's North country. "Maybe she loaned it t'somebody." He looked around unconvincingly.

"If she loaned it to somebody, where are they?"

"Dunno, Countess." He shrugged. "Chartered a day-trip to Manzanillo?"

"The hotel could have dropped them off," the Countess replied. She moved her head like a watchful lizard. "The passengers do not need to leave the jeep here, do they?"

"If they want a ride back at night, they do," the driver insisted.

"Check out the hangar."

"We've already been in there," the mechanic interposed. "Used the toilet. Anybody in there, we would have seen him."

She favored the man with her ill will. "Check it out."

The mechanic lumbered insolently in the direction from which he had just come.

The driver released the trunk latch and the hood swung upward, exposing a set of vinylized canvas luggage. From behind the hangar, Kenna recognized the attaché she had last seen in the offices of Andrea Reich-Hermann. The bonds were here – not ten feet from her. Her attention fixed on them as if she could will them back into her possession.

The driver lit a cigarette and started on the bags. She could outrun him, she decided. He was a thin, seedy man with a small insidious paunch. The pilot had boarded already. The copilot was busy fueling the plane. That left only the mechanic, at present searching the hangar. She'd already made one headlong crash through the jungle. She could lose any of the Countess' present company if she had to. But what about the dog?

To her relief the Countess strode ahead with Mister A, the dog's lead around her wrist. The driver followed with a large bag in one hand and two smaller valises in the other.

Three, two, one. Her ears were full of a kind of waterfall, her heart was racing with the possibility of sweeping by the trunk, scooping up the attaché and disappearing into the brush.

"All clear," the mechanic announced, emerging from the hangar. The Countess turned at the sound of his voice and started back toward the car's open boot.

"I'll keep this with me," she said, snatching up the portfolio and giving a last inquiring look at the jeep.

Blast and damn!

Before Kenna could curse her bad luck with more vehemence the Countess boarded the Gulf Wing with Mister A. She took a seat by the window on Kenna's side of the plane.

The driver stumbled forward with the remaining bags, pushed them in and secured the luggage compartment. The copilot ran up the stairs to the cockpit, released the ramp and swung the door shut as the mechanic wheeled the servicing station from the runway. The smell of fuel stung Kenna's nostrils. The stutter of the small-craft motor grew deafening.

As the Gulf Wing's wheels started to move, Kenna stepped from her place of concealment, fully aware that she had nothing to gain by it. An impulsive move, she knew, and dangerous—but irresistible. I'm here, she said silently. I know who you are. For several seconds, she dared the Countess to meet her eyes. When at last she was rewarded, she caught an expression that revealed not so much shock as triumph. The Countess' malice was cool and taunting. So this was how it would be. As the plane commenced its screaming run toward lift-off, the Countess reached for the seatback phone.

# 44

"We've got to get you back to New York," Michael said, as they hurtled down the mountain road to the resort. They decided to take the jeep as far south as the small airport at Manzanillo, hire a plane to Mexico City and leave the vehicle for the hotel to recover. There had been no trouble with the mechanic. He had lifted his chin toward Michael in a silent expression of "Hi mate," not even curious as to how Michael and Kenna materialized so suddenly on the landing strip. Then he had indifferently watched them get into the jeep like any two hotel guests bound for Bianca's casitas. Not worth his concern.

When they reached the hotel, Michael parked discreetly down the drive from the motor court. Kenna made a shortcut dash to their rooms, collected their things and placed them in one of the guest carts.

She swung through the living room of the casita for a last look around. Lucky the bartender stood outlined against the doorway. Her first reaction was a sense of annoyance.

"What do you want?"

"You've been summoned by her royal highness."

"What does she want?"

"You'd have to ask her. I'm just the court's plaything."

"Summons delivered. You can go by-by, now," she said, in her sweetest little-girl voice. "I'll stop by the desk and see your boss on my way out."

"Me thinkest not, m'lady."

His almost girlish lips curled into a sleepy smile. How she had underestimated his muscular heft at the Sand-Bar last night. With his British accent, she had branded him a public school weakling. Well, she had been wrong.

She ran for the kitchen and a back exit. But he was swift too, with something on his mind. He followed her into the kitchen and banged the pass-through shut behind them. Then they played ring around the table until he beat her to the screened servant's door.

"Won't Bianca be jealous?" Kenna asked. "Or is it the Countess who pulls your chain?"

A smirk of menace crossed his decadent face. "Don't matter, luv," he replied in the passable Cockney he used to entertain the guests. "I'm going to enjoy this."

He was between Kenna and the door now. She faked a pass around the butcher block work table. He wasn't fooled. He grabbed the lip of the table and with one heave, pulled it closer to him. She could not get around the table without coming into range.

"My companion will be back any second."

"I daresay he won't. It takes a good while to check out of Careyes, especially if the bill's delayed." Lucky gave a sharp smile. He pushed the table over and made a dive for her. Kenna moved toward him rather than away, confusing his calculations. Before he could try again, Kenna grabbed the kitchen knife Maria had used to chop the potatoes. She held it before her and planted herself firmly, leaning slightly forward to give herself better leverage if he made her use it.

The weapon created an impasse. He could not chance passing too close to the knife in order to leave the way he had come. She would not allow him to get near enough to disarm her. She would stand there all night if that's what it took to wear him down.

"Just let me walk out of here," Lucky said, with a humility he could take off and put on again like a jacket. His eyes were cautious now. The bravado dissolved. She could see him measuring the distance between them, deciding that he could not reach her wrist from where he stood.

"Ain't going to happen," she said, enunciating clearly as if he were a foreigner. "Not until my friend arrives to show you out."

He flung the chair down to block her way. But she did not allow the movement to unsteady her.

"Self-defense is big in the States," she said. "Kick-boxing, fencing, karate. We find it useful where I come from."

He produced a surface smile. "Don't they tell you when to quit?" He cast his eyes downward as though he had come to a decision. With zen-like slowness, he lifted his hands above his shoulders with his palms open, stepping his feet backward toward the rear deck. "This how they do it in westerns?" he asked, with a comic lift to his mouth.

She allowed him to reach the door. Still facing her, he gripped the latch behind him with one hand. Instinct said he couldn't leave it alone. She made up her mind to use the knife if he tried anything.

He lunged at her and caught her hand. She found out she was wrong about using the knife. She held firm as he sought to wrest it from her. The blade flicked this way and that. The knife was now a thing in play. At the last instant she flung it sliding across the floor out of reach. One hand was free now. He was fighting for it. She grabbed up Maria's chrome potato-masher from the counter and rammed it into his forehead like a branding iron, knocking him backward. He fell heavily, his head snapped back against the paver tiles.

The barman did not move. She stepped on his chest and leaned down to check his pulse. You'll be fine, she told him silently. She rolled him over so he would not choke on his spit. Then, she was out the door in seconds, making her way quickly to the place on the road where Michael waited with the jeep.

# 45

A little more than ten minutes passed since Kenna and Michael descended the ramp of the single-engine plane they had hired in Manzanillo, and threaded their way quickly through the tour groups entering Mexico City's international terminal. Once inside, Michael strode to the Air France counter and purchased two first-class tickets. His own, for passage through Paris to Geneva. For Kenna, non-stop to New York.

"I have to go with you," Kenna insisted, reviving the debate that had occupied them during the past forty-five minutes. "You'll need me in Geneva."

"I'd rather you did come," Michael admitted. "But it's not possible. You'd only be arrested and returned to the States. I would too. Then where would we be?"

Michael moved his bag to his other hand and took Kenna's arm. "I'm going to make sure you get on that plane."

"Excuse me, but your departure time precedes mine by ten minutes. I'll see *you* off."

He scowled. "Don't even think of blowing off your appearance in Judge Tyra's courtroom on Monday," he said. "Not for a second. You have to show up on Monday. If you run into any trouble, call Ron Scott at Shea, Gould. Roommate at Harvard. He handles some of the largest white-collar defense cases in the city. Ron should have been your lawyer in the first place," he added, with his deprecating smile.

"This is not about me, Michael. Remember, I'm a lawyer too. All things being equal, I would comply with the court's order. But circumstances have changed. We're so close to the bonds. I can't go back now."

"You can and you will. At this point it's only conjecture that you violated the terms of your release. Based solely on a phone call from the Countess, who is hardly credible, I might add. There's no reason to give the prosecution a fait accompli. Trust me, Kenna. I'm not going to do this alone. I intend to barter a few chips from diplomatic circles. And I'll call you with updates. But I'll call you in New York."

She couldn't let Countess get away. She had come too far. If she was to seek dismissal of the charges, she had to produce the bonds and the Countess. And she had trouble seeing how anyone else could make it happen.

"I should have told you," she said. Her left hand sought the gold cuff on her right wrist. "I checked out some research on Countess. British intelligence is looking for her. MI6, to be precise – the UK's agency for economic espionage."

Kenna ignored his silent look of inquiry: why hadn't she shared the information earlier? "She killed a guy in Barbados. At least they want to question her about it – so you see, we both have to follow her to Europe. I have information the Brits need to know if an arrest is to be made. The woman is lethal. I have to watch out for you, and vice-versa."

"Nobody kills lawyers," Michael scoffed. "They just malign them. I can handle the Countess."

An unexpected thrust from behind sent Kenna spinning into the wall of the concourse, separating her from Michael for an instant.

When she found him again, he was slumped against a parked janitor's cart. He recovered his briefcase, and got up slowly.

"Michael – what is it?"

"Too much exertion for an old man. I got the wind knocked out of me - have to learn to look where I'm going."

He wasn't convincing. And she wasn't convinced. She scoured the area in front of them, packed so tightly it looked like an arriving subway platform. A family of very small people staggered ahead over-burdened with plastic bags and roller carts, while a pod of airline personnel casually trawled their under-seat luggage behind them.

The men's lavatory lay ahead on the right. Michael veered toward it. "I'll be right back," he said with a smile that didn't quite work. "Quick trip to the toilet."

"You're not all right. Let me get airport security." Again came the smile, weakly reassuring.

She scanned the crowded concourse for sight of the Countess. They had discussed the prospect of trying to apprehend her in the airport and turn her over to the Mexican police. But they agreed to do nothing unless circumstances were optimal. Let her proceed to Geneva. Let her believe the bonds were safe. Time enough to act when Interpol was on their side.

Kenna shifted her weight restlessly. She bent down to retie her bootlace, glancing at her watch. Time seemed to have slowed to a crawl. How long had Michael been in there? His collapse unnerved her, resembling, too closely, her last moments with her grandfather. Michael's self-assessment was true – he was woefully out of shape.

"Goldilocks!" The Austrian jeep driver loped toward her with a foolish smile.

"Ulrich, what are you doing here?"

"You *do* care." He gave a good-natured leer. "There's something 'Last Tango' about you today, little girl. Too bad we can't have a drink together. They've got me picking up a big-shot from the States."

"That's great," she said. The words were mere reflex. "Look, Ulrich. I need your help. Michael is in the men's room. I'm afraid something's wrong. He's going to miss his plane. Will you find him?"

"One of the more unusual requests of the afternoon," Ulrich said. "But not unwelcome. Wait for me, little girl." He swerved into the lavatory. Kenna stationed herself literally in the doorway, to the consternation of two Latin businessmen coming out. She ignored their raised brows of disapproval.

Almost immediately she heard Ulrich's hoarse shout. She raced into the tiled room. She knew, before he spoke, what she would find.

She dropped to her knees beside Michael. Ulrich rushed to the concourse. "Medicos! Urgencia!"

Kenna peeled off Michael's jacket and loosened his tie, coaxing him in a soft but urgent tone. "Michael. Stay with me. Stay here." *Don't bloody go anywhere.* She tucked his trench coat around him to keep his body temperature warm. She thought she saw a slight swelling above his collar like the puncture of a bee. She put her ear to his chest and listened, unsure whether the faint sound was her heart or his.

Scarcely breathing herself, without thinking, Kenna began CPR. She moved rapidly between short bursts of air into his mouth and cardiac pressure. She kept her eyes on Michael's face. Now she could distinguish her own chest pounding in fear as she drove the heel of her hand under Michael's breast. She wondered at the tangle of her thoughts, that she would bruise him, that they would be arrested. That he would die.

Ulrich returned, having roused the paramedics. "They're coming," he said. "Get out of the way." She ignored him.

"You'll tire," he said. "We have to take turns." He half-lifted her to one side, and crouched close to Michael.

"It's a toxin called oleandrin," she said. Her voice was low. For Ulrich's ears only. She formed the word carefully, as if the report on her grandfather were playing on a screen before her. She did not dare repeat it. The sooner the doctors knew what they were dealing with the better Michael's chances. "It was used by the U.S.S.R. during the Cold War. You've heard of it before." A South American poison that freezes the muscles, her inner commentator added. And: the heart is a muscle. But she did not say it. Could not say it.

Ulrich closed his eyes briefly, he understood. He worked quickly over Michael as Kenna brushed back the hair from Michael's temples with her sleeve.

She relieved Ulrich and felt Michael's chest give a monumental heave. His eyes flickered open. "Darling," he said with effort.

He did not even try to smile, as if he knew he could not hide the seriousness of his condition. "Don't stay here," he said in a voice that seemed to come with great effort. "Go back to New York."

"I will stay with you."

He struggled to shake his head. "No." And then, indistinctly: " — ".

"What did you say?"

One look at his face confirmed the effort the elusive speech had cost him. Her brain was alert with questions. But Michael's gaze had turned inward, seeking some inner landscape.

Ulrich touched her arm. "You have to go."

When she hesitated, he said, firmly, "Look, it's all over Careyes. You're wanted by the FBI. If you stay, we'll have pandemonium. The Federales. Papparazzi. We may not get him out of here in time." He handed her a card from his billfold. "Here's the number of the phone in my jeep." He added in a low voice, so intense tears rushed to her eyes. "I'm going to take care of this guy like he's my brother."

Gently, Kenna lifted Michael's ticket from his suit pocket and tucked it in her trousers. She gathered up his papers and put them in the attaché, which she tucked close to her side. She held his eyes. "I'm coming back to you, Michael," she said. "Don't go anywhere without me."

Kenna closed Michael's fingers over the Celtic bracelet on her wrist and closed her own hand over them. The white-coated medicos arrived with stretcher and oxygen, sweeping down around Michael.

"Stay lucky," she said. She kissed him and felt the warmth coming back into his lips. The medics clapped the oxygen cup over his mouth, plunged the syringe into his arm. The struggle for life would be Michael's alone now. Reluctantly, she moved out into the concourse.

# 46

Kenna was the last passenger waved through the boarding door for Air France's flight to Paris. It had been a narrow squeak at the gate, when the attendant shoved Michael's pass into the scanner. "Have a good flight, Mr. – uh, Ms. Fein. Wait a minute, may I see some ID?"

"No problem – I showed it to get my boarding pass."

She fumbled in her backpack with all the composure of someone really looking for her passport. Her mental clarity was such that she didn't protest or indulge in a pretext which would have aroused suspicion and given her away. Like a winning forward in a college game, she simply waited for the clock to run out. "It's in here. Sorry about this. And you can call me Michaela. My parents were hoping for a boy." Flash the apologetic smile. She hoped there was plenty of room in First Class, she said, reminding him of protocol. He wasn't a stupid man.

"Step through. But next time, keep your ID handy, Michaela." She gave the conciliatory smile that was expected, and moved easily toward the ramp. Will do, chief.

With relief, she saw the curtain already drawn on the First-Class compartment, signaling that in-flight service had begun. "That's okay," she said quickly to restrain the steward from admitting her to the cabin. "I'll find a seat upstairs until after takeoff." She had no desire to plunge head-on into a meeting with the Countess in the confines of a few seats. Too late, she realized the risk in choosing the airbus' second level.

If she had arrived earlier, she could have hidden among the masses in steerage. Having climbed the carpeted stairs to the lounge, she was now trapped. If the Countess came up to stretch her legs…

She traded away her First Class stub for a seat in the back of the lounge. Then she threw herself onto the cushion, buckled her seat belt and rested her head against the seat. She would have six hours to pray for Michael, contemplate what she would do upon arriving in Paris, and avoid the Countess.

## 47

At that very moment Klaus Kessel was selecting a three-hundred-dollar cigar from the excellent reserves of Prince von Kadow, whose chateau overlooked Lake Geneva.

"Fabia is an interesting woman," Kessel mused aloud. “And resourceful. I don't know how she manages it, but she moves quite effortlessly among various governments."

"Yes," the Prince agreed. He led his guest to a pair of leather armchairs before a marble hearth in the library. He made a small silly bow from the waist.

Kessel sat down in one of the armchairs. He snipped his cigar-end with the antique sterling cutters offered to him and settled down for a well-earned respite from the indignities he had suffered at the hands of Andrea Reich-Hermann and her posturing husband.

Kessel knew the Prince’s title was a fictional one. A little checking confirmed the so-called “Prince” was one Miguel Santiago from Argentina. But Kessel could afford to be generous. When he'd left New York Rand was mired in criminal proceedings. The bonds – he’d grown resigned to the fact – were in the possession of the Countess, who would no doubt soon pass them on to her Slovakian contacts. At least the portfolio was not available to embarrass the banking giant with a claim for payment. Despite all the chaos, he had been successful. The risk was contained.

"The Countess is attractive," Kessel conceded. "For her age. And sexually, well, still desirable to some. Always taking into account, she's hardly a debutante."

It amused him to juxtapose the image of the Countess with that of a debutante. God and Nietsche–could that sharp-toothed marmoset ever have been presented in high society as she claimed?

Perhaps another man would have discerned the variation that had taken place in the mood of his host, but Kessel remained occupied with his cigar. He was not entirely untruthful, he had thought her desirable – briefly.

"How did you meet Fabia?" the Prince asked.

"Barbados. 1991." Kessel spoke somewhat grandly. He was, after all, playing a role. He was in no hurry to be told why the Prince had asked him here, before returning to Zurich. Prince von Kadow served on the Board of Directors for BIS, the Bank for International Settlements. Undoubtedly he wanted to follow up on his communication to Andrea Reich-Hermann, to make sure the Jewish gold bonds would not find their way to Basel. Kessel wouldn't be surprised if the man wanted to express his gratitude and appreciation. He enjoyed a pleasant moment in contemplation of an appropriate offering.

He had never given too much thought to retirement. At forty-nine, he was still a young man with energy and drive for a second successful career. But his career-path with the Agency had not been untroubled – that business with the Countess in Barbados had started his descent. A future sinecure with the Bank in Basel would not be unwelcome.

"You remember the Barbados fiasco?" he asked his host.

"Barbados. The bank that disappeared." The Prince raised an amused brow. "All its deposits, including a large collection of bearer bonds in its vaults. Pfft!"

"And never a question asked." Kessel could not restrain the note of pride in his tone, forgetting for the moment, the incident had nearly cost him his career.

Another careless scheme of the Countess. While scavenging gold bonds for the Germans in 1991, she'd left a trail as bright as neon. To protect certain interests close to the U.S. he'd had to blow up the fucking bank. It hadn't gone well in Langley.

"An interesting phenomenon," the Prince agreed.

A short manservant padded silently behind the two men, placing a pair of Bavarian crystal goblets on a tray which held an already-decanted sixty year old port, Quinta de Malvedos, 1931, eight hundred dollars a bottle.

"The investors were well-insured," Kessel added.

"Were they?" the Prince asked. "Who were the investors?"

"Hasn't Fabia told you? Ah, well, just to finish the subject then." Kessel allowed himself to expand under the influence of his surroundings. "It is said –" He thought it best to give the illusion of discretion, although there was little chance the Prince would have any use for the anecdote. "– the money men were composed of various governments that owed debt to Germany. Though the bank's assets were destroyed, the governments involved recovered their losses by way of insurance. The bonds mysteriously found their way back to Germany, and Germany's finance minister marked the debts "PAID."

"Clever, yes?" Admittedly, he was putting the best face on the scheme. They were damn lucky some career-clawing business journalist had not pursued a line on it.

The Prince studied the ash of his cigar, a gesture Kessel accepted as encouragement.

"An interesting plan, wasn't it?"

"I don't really follow," the Prince replied.

"The Germans were able to honor the bonds in secret," Kessel explained. "They did not have to admit their validity, which would have encouraged a swarm of bond-holders like JAFA to come forward. Unfortunately, a scheme like that cannot be repeated. Even the dunces who watch international finance suspect that Germany engineered the bank's disappearance to remove a large cache of bonds from circulation."

"I see," the Prince murmured vaguely. "It appears you have a gift for enterprising solutions. But, this current business of yours. Tracking bonds for Fabia I understand."

"I work for the American government," Kessel answered stiffly. Didn't the imbecile know who he was talking to?

"A kind of securities shill, then."

Kessel studied the smooth face of his host. A slow cold rage had begun to build at the Prince's insult. "And you are a – banker."

The Prince made another playful bow from the waist. "I am a Director of the Validation Committee for BIS – Basel's settlements bank. As you know, we decide whether the various financial claims against Germany are 'kosher.'"

"As I understand it, my client has you to thank for a recent opinion letter that JAFA's portfolio is on a secret list of invalid bonds."

"Well, yes. I try to be helpful with such matters."

"Inasmuch as Germany has never released a list identifying the so-called 'stolen bonds,' how can you claim to know the Jewish bonds were among those stolen?"

It pleased Kessel to take up the counter-argument in conversation. And it pleased him even more to let the Prince know how transparent he found his attempt to side with the Germans.

"Obviously," the Prince offered a closet smile, "I must have seen Germany's list myself."

Kessel regarded the man coolly. Did this dunce seriously believe that anyone having the least sophistication in finance swallowed the notion of a "secret list?"

"Americans are too trusting of Swiss banking interests," he said.

The Prince's brow lifted. "Americans should keep their noses out of Europe," he replied. "We have our own ways of managing the past."

"Really?" He could now barely contain his revulsion for this preening neo-Nazi colleague of Fabia's. "I would imagine your position at BIS gives you a great deal of influence over European banking matters."

"That's true. Each year I lead a forum at Davos in discussion of world trends."

"Very elite. And who sets the agenda? Your Swiss colleagues, I expect. Lap-dogs, as usual, of any government whose currency dominates the world markets."

Kessel recognized the effect his words would have on his host, but he felt suddenly pissed off that he'd been intercepted by this poseur on his way back to Zurich. He meant to enjoy himself for as long as it took to finish his cigar. He took the bottle from the tray, topped off his glass of golden port and raised it to his host. "To your *position.*"

"Your health," the Prince replied, darkly.

The swallow of liquid gold did its work. Kessel drew his chin toward his throat, allowing his host the full effect of two glittering green eyes that hovered like blimps above his cheeks. "Do your banking colleagues know your father was an accommodator for the SS?"

The Prince said nothing, only half-turned with a sad, aristocratic smile.

"My father was associated with Austria's royal family. Unfortunately our titles were lost during the war and we've yet to be allowed to formally reclaim them."

"I see I'm misinformed." Kessel dismissed the subject with an exaggerated wave of his hand. "Your mother, I believe, is a Jewess from Argentina. That makes you half Jewish."

The Prince answered in the tone of one reproaching a child. "You are not terribly familiar with South America, are you? Argentina is a Catholic country. Mostly Europeans and Mestizos. There are few Jews there."

"An intriguing story, your father's," Kessel mused. "A German soldier, deserter really – anticipating Hitler's collapse, transforms himself into profiteer. A fine business, 'relocating' Nazi war criminals to Argentina. What a windfall! You must have inherited some gold yourself, from the thugs who hired your father."

"One inherits many things," the Prince replied, gesturing to indicate the room's objects. He let his gaze fall on the delicate old patterns of Herend china he had taken pains to collect.

"But the irony. Why would such a man, a former Nazi, marry an Argentine Jew?"

The Prince shrugged. "An interesting story, as you say, but it does not apply to me."

Kessel's insolent gaze drifted to a black and white photograph in a polished frame. Two children, a boy and a girl, regarded him with watchful eyes. Dressed in a manner almost comically formal, they posed together on the runway of a tropical airport.

"Your sister?" Kessel asked.

The Prince nodded. Then, savoring his pleasure in what he was about to reveal, he added softly. "Fabia."

Kessel reared back only slightly, his nostrils drawn together in displeasure. That was something he should have guessed. Prince von Kadow. Countess Santiago. European aristocrats, my ass.

He recovered quickly. "Let's get to the reason you invited me here."

"Fabia asked me to find you."

"Yes?"

"There was a complication in your plan. The lawyer is undoubtedly on her way to Switzerland."

The Prince rose suddenly to stoke the fire though it hardly needed his attention.

"What are you saying?" Kessel spoke to the man's back. "When I left New York she was scheduled to appear in federal court tomorrow for her bail hearing."

"And well done too." The Prince continued to prod the fire, speaking casually with his back to Kessel. "I'm sure your clients must have been pleased with your work. Fabia thought you'd like an 'update.'"

Infuriating imbecile. " Give me the rest of your *update*."

The Prince affected to ignore Kessel's compelling stare. "As you yourself know, the lawyer was free on bail. She followed Fabia to Careyes, thence to Mexico City where she boarded a plane for Geneva, by way of Paris. Fabia called me in-flight to ask me to get hold of you. She and her 'groupie' are in the air as we speak."

Thence? In the air 'as we speak?' Had these words ever before inspired their hearer with such fury?

Von Kadow went on as if reciting a catechism. "And her companion Michael Fein, well, Fabia…"

"What kind of pig's-breakfast is this?" Kessel shot forward and placed his glass softly – too softly – on the table. "The lawyer has no passport. How did she get on an international flight? How will she get through Customs?"

"She has an Irish passport it seems."

Of course she had. The rage that too often now threatened his self-control, focused on the Countess.

"Fabia allowed herself to be followed by a couple of attorneys?"

The Prince turned to face Kessel. "You wanted to know why I asked you here," he said, smiling again his deprecating smile. He turned his palms upward, " – an impulsive young woman."

"Impulsive?" Kessel rose from the armchair of sleek brown leather. He paced the room. Seeing the ashtray on the mantle he strode to it.

"Impulsive, maybe, in your lexicon, but Fabia's greed has taken things too far this time."

The blue vein that gorged with blood when Kessel's anger was most intense marked his brow. Seeing his reflection in such a state usually made him preen with admiration. His thoughts this time were fixed on an inner landscape. He recalled the series of interviews with his superiors that followed the incident in Barbados. And there was the Texan on his way to Basel last year. Someone shot him in the head on the plane – the woman was mad!

Clearly, she didn't give a damn about the girl tracking her. She only feared the Slovakians would use the girl to try to get the bonds themselves. That explained why he had been summoned to her brother's chalet as if he were her servant. He was nominated to clean up after her. Again.

Kessel stubbed out his cigar with a ferocity that left no doubt of his intention. "Fabia doesn't leave me any choice," he said grimly. "Thanks to her the girl has become redundant."

# 48

At 1:45 p.m., Monday afternoon, the lights went up in the cabin of the Air France flight to Paris. Kenna arched her back against the seat and massaged the stiffness from her neck. Despite a troubled sleep she felt surprisingly rested. She reached for the telephone tucked into the seat back in front of her. After half an hour, she still could not get through to Puerto Vallarta. She could not reach Ulrich, or check on Michael's condition. She did not realize how quickly she had come to rely on the charming, bearded man. It had been like a tonic to feel, briefly, important to someone. She touched her hand to her bracelet and sent a silent invocation, *don't leave me.*

By the time she had freshened herself in the toilet and returned to her seat, a respectable lunch of spinach crepe and strong tea appeared. Her second cup, heavy with milk, brought her fully into the present. She felt cautiously pleased with herself that she had avoided confrontation with the Countess so far. Within half an hour, however, they would land at Charles de Gaulle International Airport, and it would be nearly impossible to conceal herself on the second leg of the flight to Geneva. No solid plan occurred to her. She had not thought that far ahead. Keep the Countess in her sights. Wasn't that difficult enough?

At least she could proceed directly to Customs, having no bags to collect, and thereby avoid being observed by her fellow passenger until re-boarding. She considered the possibility that Customs might detain her, if for no other reason than she lacked a U.S. passport. She drew out her Irish passport. "Ireland's way of denying a negative population growth," she'd scoffed to Michael. She felt grateful for it now. It had posed no problem to Mexican security. While the French might not know exactly where Ireland was located, she doubted the passport would cause any trouble with customs officials.

Kenna was the last to descend the stair to the main cabin, reassured to see the empty seats of First Class. As she moved onto the concourse she had the eerie impression of being watched. With a mixture of relief and fear, she glimpsed the familiar blond chignon and full sable coat gliding along the corridor ahead of her. Why not overtake her, she asked herself. Do it here. Do it now. Pull her off the transitway, through one of the doors and wrest from her the Louis Vuitton satchel containing the bonds. She had the element of surprise and the gift of speed. She could disappear in the crowd before anyone knew where to look for her. Even dragging the heavy bag.

The older woman changed course at the public lavatory. Kenna dove into a news kiosk to wait for her. A copy of *USA Today* caught her eye with its summary of inside features: GERMAN BOND FRAUD, page 8. She scanned the article with instant understanding of its implications:

"*An attorney recently admitted to the New York bar has been charged in an international bond scheme. Kenna Rand, principal in Rand & Rand, a New York law firm, is alleged to have offered to sell worthless securities issued by the German government in the days before Hitler's ascendancy to power. Claiming to represent JAFA, an Israeli-American fund, Rand is alleged to have arranged a sale of the suspect bonds for millions of dollars to an Argentine banker. Michael Fein, Trustee and legal counsel for the fund, could not be reached for comment.*"

They had not included a photograph. But they had used her name. If she got into a scuffle with the Countess in the terminal, she'd be immediately apprehended and held for U.S. authorities. As it was, it would be a miracle if Kessel had not phoned ahead to have her picked up at Customs. Making sure the Countess had not exited ahead of her, she moved rapidly through the crowded concourse.

In the customs hall, Kenna joined the short line of non-French-nationals. She watched over her shoulder for the Countess, slouching into the mass of travelers rapidly filling the line behind her. Several international flights must have landed within minutes of each other. She had arrived before the crowds. When her turn came, she approached the customs officer, trying not to overdo the show of casualness.

The man glanced with little favor at the traveler before him. Always inclined to simplicity in her dress and makeup, she had left Careyes in travel clothes – a spare black uniform that appeared to arouse in the Customs man his distaste for “feminist” attire.

"Irlande?" he asked, peering at the photograph page in her Irish passport. When she did not reply immediately, he asked aggressively in English: "No bags?"

She smiled, shrugging off her backpack as though to offer it to him, all the while willing him to refrain from opening it. If he bothered to examine its contents, he would find a New York driver's license that established her country of origin as the United States. Where, then, he would demand to know, was her U.S. passport?

The man accepted the backpack and released its clasp. She held her breath as he drew out mirror and cosmetics pouch. He made quite a show of removing the few items from the pouch. Lip gloss, moisturizer, cleansing pads, mouthwash. She was prepared to smile demurely for him, acknowledging woman’s natural vanity. Then he retrieved her Filofax. Flipping through its pages, he asked, "You arrive from Mexico City?"

"Yes."

"What were you doing in Mexico?"

"Visiting a friend," she replied, emphasizing the crispness of her accent.

"And what is the purpose of your travel to France?"

"I am not staying in France, regrettably," Kenna replied with a smile. “I'm actually traveling to Geneva to visit a college friend.”

“Friends.” He took his time stuffing her belongings back into the pack and pushed it toward her. Several moments passed with his eyes fixed on her in a sullen scowl. Just to let her know he disapproved of the whole proposition, he rifled the passport pages several times. Debating, it seemed. He turned to a blank page at the back, picked up a hand-stamp and punched it downward with unnecessary force. The red circular imprint it left had gone out of style several years ago in support of the new and improved, borderless Europe. "Welcome to France," he said, flapping an impatient hand in the direction of the green-lighted exit.

Kenna hastened to the gate and checked in for the Geneva flight. From an unobtrusive seat along the wall, she scanned the trickle of passengers. A few European businessmen, a few families with children. She felt the tension of an almost certain confrontation with the Countess, unless she could board after her, and unseen.

There was that moment when she desperately wished she were just another traveler heading for a holiday along the placid banks of Lake Lucerne, studying her French tapes and finding charm in Air France’s blue and white plastic dinner service. She thought of calling Aunt May, regaling her with vivid stories of international travel, and promises to send Godiva chocolates. Boarding the plane, she resolutely banished the wistfulness, as she took Michael's seat in First Class.

# 49

At five minutes to departure, the Countess had not arrived. This worried Kenna. She snapped open Michael's attaché and flipped through the papers in Michael's file, something she should have done before now. Among them, she found the letter from the director of BIS. She scanned its faint faxing legend:

PRINCE BARRON VON KADOW, VALORBÉ, SWITZERLAND.

"Excuse me," Kenna detained the steward. "Is this city near Geneva?"

"Valorbé?" The steward's brow knit in concentration.

He turned to his partner. "Belle-Louise, come here. Prés de Genéve?" He pointed to the faxing legend.

"Twenty minutes north," came the answer. The woman displayed her watch-face. "If you are going there you would have done better to take the fast train. The airport is south of the city."

Minutes remained before the land crew would slap the plane's bolt into place and withdraw the ramp. Kenna snapped the briefcase closed. She felt an urgent need to get off the plane. Gathering her jacket and backpack, she fought the final boarders toward the exit.

"But you cannot go, mademoiselle," the steward cried. "We are leaving now!"

"Rain check," Kenna said, executing a short leap onto the boarding platform.

She raced up the ramp. Reaching the concourse, she broke into a run through the terminal, weaving her way against a tide of departing passengers. Almost immediately she was aware she had attracted not one, but two pursuers.

She had first noticed the American when she'd finally boarded the 747 on its second leg to Geneva. Every seat had been filled. Yet he sat alone in a coach seat just behind Business Class. Before the curtains were drawn, he had looked casually at her, concealing his interest. She had expected to see the Countess. When she did not, she knew she had to deplane. And she had known, without thinking too much about it, he would follow.

Dead eyes, buzz-cut hair. FBI? He carried an aluminum briefcase. His Burberry-lookalike overcoat was too new. And – didn't he know? One could always tell by the shoes. His were sturdy and reliable. Florsheims. He could have picked her up at Customs. But he hadn't. So it wasn't to do with Monday's court hearing.

Then who was the short, swarthy one, winner of best supporting actor in a foreign film? She recalled a stubble beard, weapon-bulge, and he was wearing a green suit. It was because of the suit that she'd noticed him in the news kiosk before boarding. His back was to her, browsing Duty-Free. And she had thought that one could hardly move in such form-fitting clothing. Well, she had been wrong. Frenchy would have beaten the American if he hadn't gotten stalled behind a baggage trolley. So the chunky little guy was – Interpol?

Don't like that, she thought. Don't like that at all.

She took the escalator leading to departure level as quickly as she dared. With any luck, she would lose her entourage. Bursting through the automatic doors to the street, she arrived breathless at the curb. To her right, a line of dour French citizens patiently waited in a taxi queue. A cab rolled forward and a small, neatly dressed Parisian at the head of the line moved forward to claim it. He opened the door and tossed his attaché on the seat.

Kenna stepped in front of him. She threw herself into the cab, tossing the attaché back to its owner. "Catch, monsieur." She could not repress a grin of mischief as the black Renault shifted into gear and spun from the curb. "Au revoir!"

It would have been impossible not to smile at the expression of startled dismay on the man's face as he turned, disbelieving, to his compatriots. "L'Americaine," he said, scowling. Purely for the benefit of his compatriots, he raised his palms to the heavens as if that explained everything.

# 50

"Vite! Vite! LeTGV."

The cab responded immediately. Hurling forward like a whirling toy, it soon left concourse Charles de Gaulle far behind. Kenna had no idea which of Paris' four terminals formed the debarking point for the fast train to Geneva. She sketched her dilemma to the driver in high-speed French, the words tumbling rapidly as the Renault darted and weaved through the streets of Paris.

"Le TGV?" The driver, a large African with glittering white teeth and a single gold earring, seemed perfectly at ease steering with one hand, while addressing Kenna in the rearview mirror with his brisk, sly manner.

"Yes, Geneva." Kenna spoke quickly too.

"Ah, the North station."

The man pointed to a small clock fixed to the dashboard. "Forty minutes," he said in French. He grinned. "Do you have your running shoes?"

Kenna bit her lip. They would set a world record if they had to. She studied the driver's face. A few short hairs sprouted on his chin. His eyes were lit with a fierce energy. The effect was slightly manic. Like it or not, he was her only ally.

"Hurry, monsieur!"

She had lost sight of the Countess after Customs. She could only hope the flight attendant had been correct, and that the Countess intended to take the Paris-Geneva fast train.

As they reached Boulevard Peripherique, the ring road circling the inner city, her view through the Renault's rear window raised her alarm. A pair of cabs, one black, one yellow, threaded in and out of the thick Paris traffic. The driver met her eyes in the mirror, grinning. They were being followed. Not a very propitious beginning to her visit to the City of Light. It would take only minutes before the first of the two cabs would overtake them.

Another rapid exchange with the driver established the route, twelve or so minutes on foot, to la Gare du Nord. But if she were forced to leave the cab, it would be better to cut over to Rue Rivoli, he insisted, where several large hotels offered the chance to hail another. He pounded the wheel once with excitement as he grasped the reason for her contingency plan. "You are the fox, aren't you?"

Was she? Well, she had better outrun the hounds, whoever they might be.

Kenna positioned herself to observe her pursuers in the taxi's side mirror.

The black car was in the lead, three vehicles behind Kenna's. Weaving between lanes, its driver tailgated first one car then another in an attempt to force his way through. The yellow cab followed, hemmed in behind a tourist minivan and a motorcycle she thought she had seen leaving the airport. She strained to make out the driver's face under his helmet.

She flinched as the yellow taxi lunged sharply, forcing the motorcycle to fall back or be crushed by entering traffic. The bike swerved to avoid the cab, almost plunging into a swarm of pedestrians at the curb. The yellow car leapt forward, pacing its black counterpart. Kenna could only just make out the form of its passenger hovering intently at the driver's shoulder.

"Merde!" Kenna's driver unloosed a torrent of speech, his words flying back at her like daggers in a knife-throwing competition.

"Shit! Who are those guys? What do they want? Those bastards! Those dogs cannot chase down George Bouvier. I will pull by the Hotel Meurice, you must get out, cross the lobby to the rear door."

Are you crazy?

Kenna struggled to protest, but her attempt was lost in the man's torrent of speech. It was one thing to parry phrases with Sister Katherine in the classroom at Marymount Middle School. Quite another to crack the code of a Paris stranger, whose words meant survival.

"To the left of the toilets and telephones is a flower kiosk. Tell the owner, Rosa, to stand at the rear entrance to the hotel, the one on Rue Strasbourg. Can you remember that? Ah, she will know. She will signal when I am there, and you come out quickly – I will be waiting."

"No!" But even as she spoke, the Renault lurched to a halt before an arcade of fashionable shops attached to the Hotel Meurice. The driver, Bouvier, clearly had his own ideas.

"Allez! Allez!"

Bloody hell! Kenna sprang from the cab to the brass doors of the Escada boutique and swept through its plush interior into the adjacent lobby of the Hotel Meurice.

The hotel was one of two classic Paris hotels known to Kenna – the Ritz being the other. The Meurice, she knew, was celebrated. From his apartment on the fifth floor, the Duke of Windsor had leaked Allied secrets to Hitler, enabling troops of the Third Reich to breach the Forest of Ardennes and seize Paris. It seemed strange that the intrigue in which Kenna had become a central figure should bring her here.

As she entered the hotel, the doorman moved toward her with a frown of disapproval at the black Nikes she'd put on in the cab.

Kenna brushed by him with a purposeful smile.

"Bonjour, monsieur." She hastened through the lobby, with the air of a young woman who knew exactly where she was headed. He had started after her, but his advance became tentative as she veered off into the corridor to the left with its discreet signs announcing the telephones. You don't need to be quite so obvious, she told him silently. He stood poised uncertainly, keeping his eyes upon her, dominating the space with bulldog ferocity. Why don't you stay where you are, she told him silently, I'll just saunter along here. Out of sight, out of mind.

At the gift shop opposite the flower kiosk she brought herself up quickly.

The impression of Rosa as a plump motherly figure that had unconsciously formed in Kenna's thoughts was completely undone by the restless Scandinavian beauty who scowled into the corridor like a dominatrix.

"Rosa?" Kenna inquired.

Her rescuer's raised brow was not the friendliest of greetings. "Oui?"

"Monsieur – " Kenna retrieved the driver's name with effort. "Bouvier –"

"Oui, oui. C'est ca." Rosa dismissed Kenna's attempt with a wave of her hand. "I know."

Rosa moved with big-boned grace toward the revolving doors at the end of a long corridor that led to the rear motorcourt. Turning once, she admonished Kenna with a large, blood-red nail.

"Wait here." And then, twisting her mouth into a droll smile. "Make a sale while I am gone."

Very funny. Rosa's shop was crowded with tropical flowers and exotic leaves: scarlet Anthurium, pink-minks, purple bottle-brush; giant yellow sun flowers, white African daisies. Lovely, but no fragrance. A vase on the floor held staffs of fresh lavender as tall as wheat. The scent was haunting. Kenna positioned herself behind them, with a straight sightline to Rue Strasbourg, a narrow, crowded boulevard where Rosa now impatiently paced with a streetwalker's roll. At the sound of a man's steps coming from the direction of the lobby, she prepared herself to run for it,

Bouvier or not. Rosa appeared at the rear door, raising her finger sharply. Kenna was at her side at once. "Merci," Kenna whispered, slipping past her collaborator to the curb.

But the imposing Rosa had already returned to her exotic flowers.

"Bien, eh?" Bouvier lit up appreciatively, as Kenna plunged into the back seat of the Renault. He applied himself to the task at hand, whipping in and out of the dense traffic. But his glory was brief. The plan had depended upon Kenna's pursuers falling off in confusion. The drivers had simply maintained their pace, which brought them to Rue Strasbourg within three car lengths of Kenna.

"Merde! Merde!" The Moroccan was inconsolable. The two cabs had picked up the scent again and were moving rapidly between lanes, when a new dark blue Mercedes entered from a side alley, forcing its way in front of the black cab, whose driver slammed on its brakes. As if in slow motion, the yellow taxi, in transit of changing lanes, careened into the black cab, spinning across both lanes and creating a screaming pileup of crushed metal that left four cars disabled.

"Fantastic!" The Moroccan grinned. Suddenly the lanes were empty, the Renault shot forward.

Kenna watched the blue sedan in disbelief.

The Mercedes did not stop. Its sudden acceleration moved it out of range of the harrowing incident. It drew alongside and Kenna wondered briefly if she were going to be killed. She threw herself flat against the seat and tried to make out the driver.

The Mercedes held its speed, pacing the cab, as if taunting Kenna, its interior hidden behind darkly tinted glass. Unexpectedly, Bouvier threw open his door and Kenna heard the unmistakable crunch of creased metal.

"I mark it for you!" he cheered in French.

Abruptly, the blue car swerved, then quickly accelerated again and disappeared. It had all taken seconds. Someone very reckless and very cool had been at the wheel of the Mercedes.

Was it the driver's negligence – or skill – that aborted her pursuers? She wasn't entirely sure she hadn't met a new and dangerous adversary.

Bouvier brought his taxi to a squealing halt inside the Napoleonic arches of la Gare du Nord. Kenna shot out one last question.

"Which track?"

"Douze! Twelve, mademoiselle. And forget the fare. We are cowboys you and me, we will meet again. Now, quickly!"

So he *could* speak English. Bloody French. She tossed two bills on the seat, and plunged into the swarm of travelers entering the station.

## *51*

"Cut off!"

The French Interpol officer spoke excitedly into a cellular phone he'd taken from the breast pocket of a rather too-snug double-breasted jacket the color of peas. He seemed uncaring that blood was flowing freely from a gash in his forehead onto his suit, and his conversation was eagerly attended by the still-shaken cab driver whom he'd instructed to, “get on the radio, idiot, find me another ride!”

"Freak-ing Mercedes. American, no doubt. Ass-hole. Drives like an anti-terrorist." The man spoke with the blend of clipped precision and American slang that characterizes Europeans whose knowledge of English has been acquired in government training.

"I don't know who it was. I don't know what's going on. And quite frankly I don't give a damn. Interpol doesn't get involved in this way. We wait to be told where to pick her up. We're not getting in the middle of some inter agency free-for-all," he said, his voice rising.

"Yes, I have tried to intercept Kessel. He's on his way back to Zurich, I am told. He's working for the American government. Though they don't say so. Whatever he does, he will be protected. If the Americans want her, let Klaus find her.

He added, pausing to scowl. “We never get any credit anyway."

The man lifted an arm and, with a swipe at the communicating glass, slammed it closed. "Merde yes, I know what I am doing. He's the professional. Let him take the heat. He knows how to get in, do what he needs to do and get out. If he has a 'rage problem' as you say, then we don't want to be involved. That will be a problem for the Americans."

## 52

Kenna raced through the Gare du Nord and onto track 12. There were other trains boarding, but none was pulling out. A running leap landed her on the metal stair as the doors folded closed.

The conductor extended his hand, whether in warning or assistance Kenna could not tell, but Kenna clasped the rail with both hands and swung herself through the narrow opening, barely missing collision with the man.

She would be remembered. That could not be helped. It was not every day that a passenger propelled herself from the platform onto a moving second-class carriage, then fumbled to pay the fare with American dollars.

She needed francs, didn't she know? Or at least old francs, which could be traded at national banks. The man could not suppress his disgust at her ignorance. Michael had tried to change several hundred dollars in Mexico City but the airport exchange had been closed. The conductor scowled at the bills. One could not force dollars on the French – she could not get along in this way. His nostrils flared in irritation. He continued to grumble in the face of her composure. But Kenna's accent was impeccable, and her demeanor said it was not important, cash was cash. And in the end, the man accepted the bills and proffered the ticket, letting her off with a chilly stare to ensure she was informed of his disapproval. As she turned away, she could not suppress a grin of exultation.

## *53*

The Grand Vitesse TGV bullet train from Paris to Geneva takes three and a half hours. Time enough for Kenna to sit back in her second class compartment and assess what had happened and what would come next.

Her skin was still clammy from the exertions of the past half hour. She put up her collar to avoid getting a chill. If not for the blue Mercedes she would be in custody at this moment. Thanks to its driver she was free to pursue the Countess and try to recover the bonds. But she shivered to consider the obvious – how narrowly she had escaped being flung into a French jail.

The second class compartment seated six comfortably, three facing front and three facing rear, with chrome luggage racks overhead, and a glass partition on the aisle that ran along the left side of the train, enabling train personnel to see inside as they passed.

The young couple across from her had practically ignored her when they burst into the car as the train was pulling away. The man's once-over, that's all. Now it seemed they had been building to a spat. Lover's quarrel. And she did not exist. Or, rather, existed solely as interested observer to their petite domestic vignette. The girl, perhaps a decade younger than the man, professed to be "trés trés jaloux" of the attention her companion had lavished on the guide at the Musée d'Orsay. The young man protested. One must see the treasures of Paris. They would begin a family soon. Perhaps they would not travel for many years. He placed his arm awkwardly around the girl's shoulders. It was important to build memories…

*Forget the memories. It's important to stay alive.*

Kenna focused her attention on the landscape, a blur of lakes and woodland that resembled the northeastern United States, except for glimpses of stone chateaus and shuttered farmhouses. Occasionally the lacy spire of a church steeple confirmed the presence of a village among the hills. She lowered her window. The bracing air smelled of nature and wood smoke and she allowed the thrill of it to overtake her. She was under the leaves in Aunt May's garden, listening to her grandfather with his students outside his teaching office at Columbia, or returning home from the YMCA's autumn kick-boxing class – flush with adrenaline and competition.

Reluctantly, she drew her face away from the glass and raised the window. Wouldn't do to attract attention as the keeper of the brisk air. She glanced at her watch. Departure had been prompt at four o'clock. They had been traveling twenty minutes. Arrival in Geneva – seven thirty. Sometime between then and now she had to confirm that the Countess was on the train.

She drew a notebook from her backpack and pretended to study her notes while she considered what to do. Assuming Countess had boarded the Geneva train, there would be the difficulty of finding the Countess' compartment. Kenna had noted only two first-class coaches, on the other side of the dining car. She would have to pass through the dining car to reach first-class. And she must be prepared with a lie for the steward, who would ask for her first-class ticket. At all costs, she would have to avoid the smiling Gaul who welcomed her on board.

She calculated the number of compartments in first class. She had glimpsed a lowered shade in car No. 5, the first coach beyond the dining car. A shade had been pulled, too, on the flight to Paris. She realized it did not mean anything. But it was a beginning.

Kenna consulted her watch again in what she knew was a nod to tension. Dinner would be served between five-thirty and seven o'clock. That would be the natural time for her explorations. And just to be thorough about it, assuming she found the Countess – or the Countess found her, she knew she would have to try to recover the bonds, even though she would then have the additional task of concealing herself until the train reached its destination.

She pulled a Eurail schedule from the pocket beside her seat. The train stopped briefly at Valorbé, just outside Geneva, as the Air France steward had said. It troubled her that she'd seen a reference to the village in her grandfather's papers. He intended to contact someone there, but she could not pull the name from memory.

The conductor entered the car and the lovers' spat grew more intense. Whether the scene was for their own pleasure or for her benefit she still could not tell. And it did not matter, for it suited her agenda. If the train man recalled the occupants of the coach at all, it would be the lovers who claimed his attention.

"Les billets, s'il vous plais."

Handing her pass to the collector, Kenna said nothing, grateful to avoid a second confrontation. The train had reached its full velocity. She allowed herself a view out of the window. But this time there was no pleasure in it. Her inner landscape was a terrifying one.

Michael had lain so pale against the red tiles of Mexico City's airport lavatory.

"His pulse is strong," Ulrich had said. And Kenna had seized the hope implied in his remark – until the first medic spoke: "This is a bad one."

She studied Michael's phone with a sense of its futility. If she used it, the signal could define her location for those who wanted to know. Interpol, she supposed, could stop the train and board it any time. At the very least, Frenchy and the G-man would then be waiting for her at Valorbé.

The smooth rails of the fastest train in Europe made very little noise. The conductor moved on. There remained a little more than an hour until first dinner service. Soon there would be a lot to do. She rested her head against the seat and closed her eyes. She wondered if, at the end of the journey, she would have the bonds – and whether Klaus Kessel and the man in the green suit would be waiting for her.

# 54

When Kenna awoke she was alone. The lovers had gone. No one had come to take their places. The landscape outside the window was dark. A light from the vestibule cast shadows over the compartment. Kenna found her watch, tipped its face toward the illumination. Six forty-five. The dinner interval was almost over, in less than an hour they would arrive in Geneva. Time to go to work.

She checked her backpack, removing each item and replacing it to make sure the essentials, passport and documents, had not been trifled with. Then she moved lightly down the empty corridor toward the dining car.

When she reached the platform she fought the door open and stepped into a bleak, fitful wind. The thunder of the tracks hit her like a wall and the chill air bit through her light clothing. A second door acted as insulation between the two cars, but Kenna remained on the platform to avoid discovery, and peered in through the glass panels.

The dining car glowed from sconces along its walls. They cast a theatrical light upon the tables set with pale linens. The atmosphere seemed almost prescient. Few diners remained. Most would have returned to their compartments to collect their hand luggage. But a lone figure caught Kenna's attention, her hair like meringue in a confectioner's window. There you are. As easy as that.

The Countess sipped espresso before a plate of biscotti while a bored waiter hovered with a silver coffeepot. The two figures raised their eyes as though sensing that they were observed. She withdrew quickly, holding her breath, then realized, just as quickly that she was invisible to the occupants of the lighted car. When she moved to the door again, the Countess was drawing a cigarette from a gold case. The waiter bowed slightly to light it for her and she said something flirtatious to him. Was she inviting the man back to her compartment? Don't accept, she urged him silently – as much for your sake as for mine. He actually hesitated and his eyes skirted the almost-empty dining car. But the Countess' penetrating gaze must have warned him and he gave the charming smile, the look of polite regret that said: "If only circumstances permitted–"

*You dodged a bullet, cowboy.* An impromptu liaison would have spoiled her plans, too. The Countess was a kettle of snakes on her own. No need to take on a protector as well. The Doberman – where was she keeping him? Normal quarantine would be four to six weeks. She hadn't seen the dog in Mexico City or Paris. She had no doubt the Countess had worked out the means to avoid the usual technicalities for her pet. Even so, would the canine be with her on the train, or shipped separately?

Kenna moved again to the freezing platform and allowed the door to whoosh shut. Pressing her back hard against the car to avoid being beaten by the wind, she considered what to do.

A train was not the likeliest of places to conceal herself. One aisle up, one aisle back. The bonds were so close. The Countess, so close.

She thought of Michael and her spirit faltered. She wished she could reach Ulrich.

There was no time for reflection, but she forced herself to make time, to think through what had happened and the course of action she was about to undertake. If Michael did not recover, what difference would it make if she succeeded in getting the bonds back? If anything happened to Michael, she would cease to care. Her grandfather gone. Michael gone. Would it matter then, what happened to the Countess?

There were moments in the past week when she did not feel the least motivated by vengeance. She could act to save herself or someone she loved, she had thought, but she could not pursue the Countess out of vengeance alone. But she had been wrong. Her commitment to find and punish the Countess was as strong as on the morning after her grandfather's death. It was not hatred that she felt, but recognition of evil. Every sensibility that had made her take up law, and which had created the strong bond of understanding between her grandfather and herself, was awakened. More than money was at issue. It was simple arithmetic. There was no one else.

Kenna fought the wind for the third time to survey the dining salon. This time the car was empty of other diners. The Countess had vanished, her waiter and one other stood chatting at the bar. What's next? This would be her mantra to keep her focused on each step. She forced open the inner door. Neither waiter looked up as she strode through the coach to first class.

No one stopped her between cars. She paused at the head of the long corridor, which was deserted. The Countess had disappeared into one of the compartments. Kenna stopped before the third door on her right and placed her ear against it. Silence. Without any hope of entry, she closed her hand around the handle. Locked.

She ran through the possibilities. She would discreetly knock on all the doors in the two cars, starting with this one. If the occupant was a stranger, she would give an excuse. She summoned the phrases in French that she would need. If the Countess answered the door, she would... well, that would be determined by circumstances.

She had been a decent athlete in college: soccer, squash, tennis, golf. She had taken kick-boxing at the local gym, and a year of fencing. Her defensive skills were strong, she thought.

Yet she had not been trained in martial arts. And it would be wrong to underestimate the Countess. A skilled rider, who undoubtedly played polo with the locals in Careyes. As long as she doesn't answer the door with a polo mallet…

Kenna's head flew up, startled, as a conductor entered the coach. She watched him approach, checking his features against those of the dour ticket agent who had issued her second class ticket. She tensed, ready with some excuse – which would get her nowhere, except an escorted march back to her second-class compartment.

As the man drew closer, she exhaled deeply. She had never seen him before.

She approached him, forcing a bold tone. "My key," she said in French.

To embellish or not to embellish. She stood very erect and gave a Mona Lisa smile. This is my compartment, she said silently. Please let me in without further delay. The man raised a brow in irritation. He gave her the benefit of a narrow, suspicious glance. Then, approaching the door to her left, he inserted a long key from a ring of fifty and tried the handle. To her astonishment it opened, and she stepped cautiously into an empty sleeping compartment filled with Vuitton travel cases in the brown and cream pattern familiar to her.

A mirrored door connected the sleeping room with another. As Kenna entered, the connecting-door drifted ajar with a gust from the passageway. In its mirrored panel she glimpsed a vacant sitting room with another small door, closed tightly, that must open to the toilet.

Kenna listened. If indeed this was the Countess' suite, she had stepped out.

She surveyed the room. Louis Vuitton in every possible shape. Hat box, attaché, passport folio. Manicure set on the bed. The bond certificates were numerous, of thick vellum. They would make a bulky package. She supposed they could have been checked. But it seemed far more likely that the

Countess would keep them with her. Yet the briefcase, when she unlatched it, was empty.

Her attention was caught by a duffle bag, partially visible under the sleeper. She drew out the bag of stiff canvas and read the engraved tag: *Mister A.* She opened the zipper and noted its contents: Dog biscuits, muzzle, vitamins, blanket, freeze-dried steak, silver dish. So where are you Mister A?

When she opened the narrow closet, she heard the sound of running water from the lavatory next door. She examined the sable coat the Countess had worn in Andrea Reich-Hermann's apartment. The coat felt heavy. Removing a nail file from the manicure set on the bed, she slipped the sharp end of the file under the coat's hem and slashed the silk lining. Sorry about your fur.

Reaching into the coat's silk-lined pocket, she found a slip of paper, a claim check for 500 francs, on which was printed the word "chenil." She puzzled over the word until it connected. Chien. Kennel. So the dog *was* on board.

The sudden rush of a flushing toilet snapped her to attention. Kenna froze, listening. The zip of a cosmetics bag and the click of small containers on a steel counter meant the Countess was in the suite – freshening her makeup in the toilet.

The toilet door flew open. There was a flash of fabric and the strong fragrance of perfume as the Countess swept into the sitting room next door. Kenna's sensation of power was immediate. The murderess had no idea her pursuer was there, with her, in the suite. Kenna's mouth felt dry. Her pulse beat fast; she fancied she could feel it in her wrist.

Any minute now the Countess would fling open the mirrored connecting door to catch the mixture of fear and determination in Kenna's reflection. She played the next moments through in her mind. But it was foolish to stick around, there was no need to be a hero. The prize could be claimed without confronting the Countess. Kenna tucked the kennel-claim into her trouser pocket and stepped silently to the exit. She eased the outer door open.

There was one more thing to be gained here, she decided. As the Countess moved toward the sleeper, Kenna let her hand float to the luggage shelf near the door. Silently, Kenna snatched up the Vuitton passport folio, before soundlessly slipping into the corridor.

# 55

Kenna hastened through the dining car to second class. A single waiter was closing the bar. She could feel the train slowing. She had lost track of time in the Countess' compartment. She threw herself into an empty seat and checked her watch. After seven o'clock. The train would arrive in Valorbé in ten minutes.

She studied the claim check. A small key was attached. All right then. Back to the Doberman. Reaching into the purse belted around her waist she drew out a hand mirror. Tilting it toward the light from the car she surveyed herself. She pulled out a pale lipstick and applied it with a hand trembling badly. With both hands she caught her hair and pinned it up, allowing a few tendrils to trail around her face. Then she slipped on her backpack and moved swiftly along the corridor toward the back of the train.

There was nothing as silent as the corridors of a train at night in the countryside. She strode quickly through second and third-class carriages. Few passengers were about and even fewer conductors.

At the back of the train was a door marked Train Personnel Only. She turned the knob and entered the car.

"Oh, no, Mademoiselle, you cannot be here." The small man rose from his seat upon a trunk where he'd been reading *Le Figaro*. He seemed a kindly man, and he moved toward Kenna as if to guide her back through the door she'd entered.

"I am sorry, sir," Kenna said in French, "but my dog, he's ill. I must walk him on the platform."

"Oui, oui," the man began excitedly. "Yes. After the train has arrived."

"I have to take him now. It's urgent."

As she spoke she took in the contents of the car. On the left were stacks of checked and over-sized luggage, while the right contained myriad cages and kennels of cats, small dogs, and even a brilliant colored parrot. Kenna recognized at once the large steel-mesh travel kennel in which Mister A reclined. The Doberman rose, tense and snarling.

# *56*

The carrier was just under three feet long and not quite two feet wide. Its height, twenty-five inches or so, was adequate for the dog to stand. Yet he seemed to expand himself to fill his confinement. As Kenna approached, his frenzy began. He commenced whipping his lean body against its sides.

"The dog knows you?" the guard asked doubtfully.

"He is my dog!"

Kenna exhibited the claim ticket.

He didn't bother to look at the receipt, it would have meant switching his attention from Mister A, whose bared teeth shone like ivory spikes through the mesh door.

"I cannot help you," he said. "You can visit your dog, but the regulations do not permit you to take him." As if to punctuate this remark, the man stepped to the exit and folded his arms.

The dog paced up and back tearing at the wire panel of his cage, pushing his snout through the grid and tilting his head to gnash his teeth at the wire. Kenna swallowed hard. She had come this far.

“Do you have a bowl for some water?” she asked, her eyes sympathetic and hopeful. “I need to give him his pill or he will be very bad.”

She waited. Silence could be very effective . . .you had to have time for it.

He indicated a bulk water container on the counter. "I bring you a dish," he said. "I leave you for one minute. Don't take your dog from here." Giving her a frown that left no doubt of his reluctance, he stepped outside, closing the door firmly behind him.

She squatted down to study the kennel's clasp, a bar with two springs that, when pressed together, allowed the door to swing free. On the outside a leather muzzle swung from a brass clip.

At the back of the cage was the valise, a duplicate of the one she'd seen in the Countess' compartment. She drew the muzzle from the clip. It was made of belt leather with an open cup that fit over the snout and a strap over the ears.

She fumbled futilely in her pack for a leather glove. She had thought the Countess' gloves an affectation. But now she knew their purpose: protection, a necessity that she would have to do without.

The dog showed a keen intuition. He knew what Kenna intended, and he proclaimed himself ready, standing poised and quivering at the wire door for the moment of release.

The skin along his snout was drawn up in malice, his eyes had narrowed into slits of hostility. But Kenna kept her focus on the choke chain he wore, a thick collar of chrome links with an engraved bar for his name. Grab and twist. That was all.

Gingerly, Kenna adjusted her position. She held the muzzle in one hand, as she pressed the latch with the other. The heft of the Doberman's body was greater than she'd anticipated. Almost immediately her hand fell away.

The dog lunged forward, forcing the door free. His head whipped around to tear her wrist. She fumbled for the choke chain around his neck.

The Doberman lunged again, snapping his jaws into her leg before she could dodge away. A near miss of the bone. But he'd broken the skin. Blood surged onto her trousers.

She banged his snout hard against the floor of the car with her forearm. Crooking her leg awkwardly in front of her, she stepped on his throat with her foot. Now she gripped the choke chain, and listened to horrible hoarse sounds of the dog choking. At any moment, the guard would return.

At last she clamped the muzzle on, her fingers awkward and trembling. Somehow she managed to latch the belt over his skull. The dog was wild. She couldn't hold him. He knocked his way out of the cage. As she leaned in for the satchel, he flew onto her back. She went down. She felt her knee snap. Now she was in the pen, aware of a sharp pain where her kidneys began.

Dragging the case behind her by one strap, Kenna knocked her way free of the cage. She rolled toward the exit, hugging the bag to her chest. When she felt the door with her foot, she reeled to standing. The dog was there too. He rose on his hind legs and pinned her to the wall, mauling her sleeves. But he would not be contented with her limbs. He wanted her face.

Kenna turned her side to him keeping her body tight and hugging the wall toward the door. The case was heavy with bonds and she moved clumsily.

The dog renewed his attacks, lunging at her face with his full weight against her. Using all her reserves she thrust the valise at him. It caught the dog off-guard. He torqued to the right. Before he could recover, she opened the door and placed her wounded leg outside, attempting to conceal the blood from the porter. She eased the rest of her body into the corridor, leaving the Doberman thrashing furiously inside.

The porter approached with a saucer, frowning. Kenna gave a wan smile and tried to hide her limp as she retreated as quickly as she could along the corridor. "He's better now," she said, in what had to be the darkest irony. Her knee was swelling rapidly.

She lurched and almost fell with the train's motion. When she reached the platform between second and third class she met the man and woman who had shared her car. The man studied her and she tensed with the realization he was going to summon one of the porters. Then, with an expression of regret, he indicated the steep bank that ran beside the tracks.

He spoke to her in English. "Valorbé, good little town. I wouldn't hesitate to stop here."

The woman too gave her a sorrowful look.

What are you trying to say? Kenna's thoughts were disorganized now – with the impulse to speak, and the need to act.

The pair moved past her and preceded her into the coach. Her heart was beating wildly. Beyond them she could see the Countess advancing toward her with a scowling train man. Standing now between the Countess and Kenna, the lovers created an interlocking structure of arms and bodies in an impassioned embrace.

Kenna watched the bank speed by below her. The train was slowing, but not quickly enough. She gauged its deceleration. Every second's delay was in her favor. Feeling sick with fear, she rested against the orange exit doors. Above them, a yellow button with a red lever. A sign, in four languages, forbade pressing the button or pulling the lever.

"Do not open door whilst train is moving." What antiquated grammarian had been here before her?

Kenna hesitated. She estimated the ground was seven or eight feet below her. Still the train sped on. The Countess would enter the platform any second. Exhaling deeply, Kenna depressed the button and dropped the lever. The orange doors sprang apart. A shrill alarm sounded as she plunged into the darkness of a moving landscape.

# 57

Kenna landed on her injured leg and cried out in pain, crumpling to the ground with the roar of the train in her ears. She rose quickly on instinct, to reassure herself that she could walk. Then she limped along the track as fast as she could in the darkness.

Valorbé's small station seemed a dimly lit oasis. She stumbled toward it, concealed by the last of the coaches, until the train ground to a halt. She threw herself on the embankment and peered through a break in the cars to observe the proceedings.

The few passengers who disembarked at Valorbé dispersed quickly. The Countess stepped down and was greeted by a tall blond man with thinning hair, whose white Bentley automobile hovered in the background, its engine running.

The Countess spoke rapidly to the porter. No doubt the older woman's demands included an immediate search of the train. What surprised Kenna as she watched was the porter's resistance, his vigorously shaking head, and his words, equally insistent–that the train would be searched on arrival in Geneva, and not before.

The man Kenna guessed to be Prince von Kadow studied the landscape in an absent manner. His glance turned in her direction, and several seconds passed before Kenna became aware that he had picked out her position on the embankment. The man's eyes glittered like a night creature's, locking Kenna's gaze in his own.

In the next second the Prince would expose her, his summons would send the porters racing to apprehend her. She readied herself for flight. Still, he allowed his gaze to rest upon hers with that curious detachment. After seconds that seemed like hours, the Prince turned calmly to the Countess, manifesting no more interest in Kenna than if she had been an abandoned wheel-axle. As if he had all the time in the world, he gestured his companion to the Bentley. Within minutes they had collected Mister A and the full complement of the Countess' patterned luggage.

The Countess was the last figure to move toward the waiting car, turning to deliver a final imperative to the hapless train officials. "Idiots! Find her, arrest her!" she demanded, with a fierceness that drove the men back into the train.

From her hiding place, Kenna watched the Prince's automobile issue smoothly from the station. *"Ye'll be all right now, lass."*

She clasped the gold cuff at her wrist and spoke an involuntary prayer of thanks as the train resumed its journey to Geneva.

## 58

Kenna hungrily regarded the warm light from a small wine-growing estate on the hill above vineyards. Her knee was throbbing, the blood sticking to her pant leg. More than half an hour had passed since she started her trek toward what she hoped was a village, proceeding slowly, painfully, and hugging the shadows of the narrow country lane.

Cautiously coming out of the clearing that surrounded Valorbé's railway station, she'd found herself in what she thought to be farmland. But as she made her way along, the twisted vines of grape fields revealed themselves, ambling for miles along the gentle hills above Lake Geneva, which shone below her, a silent black pool.

She'd caught a ride part of the way. An old man in a truck. Not a curious man at all. She didn't have to speak more than a few words. And she gave thanks to her sixth-grade tutor for her fluency in French, a language, in southern Switzerland, less remarkable than English. At her bidding, he left her off some ways outside the village. A mistake probably, as she'd already made three attempts to find shelter from the night's chill without success.

None of the doors of the lower bungalows had yielded to her summons. And she doubted her luck would improve at the end of the long uphill climb leading to the lighted house that now attracted her.

Outside the first bungalow, hardly more than a tumble of old stones, she'd noticed a water connection, and turned the faucet to splash water on her face. She drank deeply, having overlooked how thirsty she was, and tied up her trousers to wash the gash in her leg.

The bleeding had stopped and she was able to cleanse it gently without reviving it. But the pain had grown more insistent. She thought for a moment, as she leaned down close to the water, that she would pass out, but she forced herself to move on.

Kenna wearily focused her thoughts on her options: a few kilometers up the road, there was the village. Or – her eyes drifted to the hill's summit – there was the small estate.

She felt so fatigued she didn't remember resuming her climb until she found herself before a door of weathered pear wood. A sigh of weariness escaped her as she raised the heavy brass knocker. Please let someone be home.

She let it fall with a thud that startled in the stillness. Then she leaned against the door, listening.

The door was pulled inward by a youthful man in his early forties. His attempt to add maturity with trimmed goatee and un-rimmed lenses only made him appear younger. He observed her with the precision of a camera's lens, taking an impression that omitted nothing – damp hair, damp clothing. Sweat and pallor of exertion, though the night air was brisk. Her trouser leg shone with the dark stain of blood.

"Bonjour, Monsieur," Kenna spoke haltingly. "Do you have a room for the night?"

"No," he responded irritably. He spoke formally, in Swiss-accented French. "Does this look like a hotel?"

She looked beyond him into the foyer where a child's jacket hung upon a peg along the wall. He followed her glance, and the longing in it, but his face hardened, and he prepared to shut the door.

What could she say to win him?

"I arrived from New York today," she began.

"Vous etes Américaine?" he interposed quickly.

"Yes."

He regarded her sternly, his consternation that of one who finds himself followed home by a stray. He seemed to debate between several courses of action, neither of which overwhelmingly appealed to him. At last making up his mind, he turned to call to someone in the rooms beyond.

"Ginger! Voilá Américaine."

Ginger? Kenna's hopes rose immediately. From within came a woman's voice in which Kenna discerned the soft speech of Texas.

"American? Wonderful. Who is it, darlin'?"

The man moved to one side in a gesture of resignation and Kenna stumbled inside. Stepping into the foyer, the warmth and good cheer hit her like a wave. Home, she thought, in the seconds before sinking, unconscious, to the stones of the entry hall. Though it wasn't.

## 59

Kenna awoke in the center of a domed bed, rising like a loaf of country bread on a mattress of goose-down.

Her ribs felt like kindling. The bruising of her organs made them tender to the touch. The wound in her calf pulsated violently. She recorded every symptom, then dismissed them with an intention to ignore the pain.

She would not even look at the torn flesh where the canine's fangs had broken the skin. Certainly it was no good exploring the possibility of rabies, with their painful shots, taken in the stomach over several days. Given the care the Countess lavished on the beast, she thought dryly – she could assume the dog was inoculated.

Light poured in through a wall of French doors. Kenna struggled to sit up.

Except for the thin bodysuit she wore, her clothes were gone – along with her backpack and Countess' duffel bag containing the gold bonds.

She rose gingerly, easing her bare feet into a pair of clogs. A cotton robe had been laid out for her. She put it on. Pausing to steady herself, she took note of her tiny room.

A graceful vanity and chair claimed one wall beneath a pair of village scenes. Through the French doors she could see acres of vines sloping to the road. Beyond lay the dark jewel of Lake Geneva, glinting in the morning sun.

Somewhere a cock was crowing. It should have added to the impression of rustic tranquility that had been artfully helped along by human hands. But the quiet seemed all wrong. Someone had gone to a lot of trouble to make her comfortable, removing her soiled clothes, her backpack and–duffle bag of bonds. And there was the thoughtful provision of robe and clogs.

The thought consoled her that she at least knew what she wanted from her hosts. That would be an advantage. For she had need of this respite. There were things she must do that were more easily accomplished from a settled place. For one thing, she needed to reach Michael.

She didn't allow herself to consider what that communication might mean. Favoring her good leg, she moved to the terrace that ran along the outside of the house, pleased that it afforded her an exit should she need one. The air, cool and fresh, swept around her like an exuberant ghost. She breathed in deeply.

The design was not grand, a rustic country home of plaster and fieldstone, with roof tiles of red slate. On several acres, its broad grassy yard sloped to an old pergola on the banks of a small pond, where a pair of geese fluttered restively among domestic ducks.

Kenna watched the birds zig-zag wildly as a child, no more than five years old, vigorously pursued them. "Come here ducks," he cried. "Ici! Ici!"

She limped toward the pond, feeling an unexpected surge of pleasure in the child's antics. "Ici, ducks!" she said by way of introducing herself.

The little boy paused to study her, a stranger in his mother's cover-up. She returned the gaze without speaking. Apparently finding her satisfactory, he led her to a stone bench. With a child's practicality, she was accepted at once. She was to be his audience of one.

"Where is your mother?" Kenna asked him in French.

The boy shrugged. Irrelevant question, his manner told her. Pascal Lebecque- he offered his name – had no time for anything but ducks. Under Kenna's attention, the child became a tiny Napoleon, striving to impress her with his authority over them.

She watched him from her throne, occasionally responding to his commentary, which came rapidly. Pascal developed an immediate fascination with the sound of her name, concluding his updates in French on the epic chase of the canards, with the exotic word "Kenna."

As she watched Pascal, she recalled the strange connection that had passed between her and the man she thought of as Prince von Kadow. She had no doubt he and the Countess were partners and that she was in immediate danger. She could not estimate the distance between this house and the tiny station. Six miles? Seven? This was von Kadow's neighborhood too.

Her watch showed eight fifteen. She must find her possessions, rinse the blood out of her clothes. Perhaps that had already been undertaken by her hosts. And dry her clothing. No easy matter in Europe, where clothes dryers were markedly inferior to the infernos of the United States.

A computer would be handy too, the Lebecques must have one. She would mock up a letter of introduction to the director of BIS. Could she master French software?

Glancing back toward the silent house, her anxiety returned. She raised herself to standing, the sharp pain forcing her eyes closed. She felt a stab of disappointment. Given her physical weakness, and the uncertainty of train runs between Geneva and Basel, it was looking less likely that she could arrive before the bank's closing hour of four o'clock. She would have to leave by nightfall.

Pascal's childish summons interrupted her thoughts. "Look, Kenna! All the ducks are swimming!"

"Trés bien, Pascal," Kenna said. At least she could conceal from a five year old her pain and fear.

# 60

Kenna excused herself from Pascal, with solemn promises of return, and made her way back to her room. She took a bath and put up her hair. Painfully, she washed her wound, careful to avoid re-opening it.

In a wooden cupboard she found a bottle of hydrogen peroxide. She poured it over the ragged tear and watched it foam, repeating the process until half the contents were gone. It was no good saying the wound was not infected. Kenna knew better. She blotted it with a towel and almost cried out. She had to close her eyes. Lying back on the bed, her whole body ached. She closed her hand round the Celtic bracelet.

*Ye'r part of a strong tribe. 'Tis the McCarthy women that ruled Kerry, lass.*

She didn't feel very strong. When she forced herself to sitting, every movement was effort. Moving to the vanity, she resumed her toilette with the quaint European products she found there.The process consumed another thirty minutes.

In the closet a pair of couture jeans and Swiss-eyelet blouse were hanging. Why couldn't her hosts have returned her trousers at least, she thought unreasonably. She had heard a French designer once remark that a woman's clothing must serve as armor for daily life. Kenna's austere attire, Lycra turtleneck, boots and narrow pants, insulated her from the vulnerability of being female. Without her uniform, she felt exposed and oddly feminine. A sense of her own fragility overtook her.

She found a man's Irish-knit sweater in a drawer and put it over the blouse so just the collar tips were sticking out. When she'd dressed, she opened her bedroom door and listened into the hallway. Still the silence. She moved again to the terrace to assess the position of the estate from the road. Then she proceeded toward the main part of the house.

As she reached the kitchen, a woman emerged carrying a tray of coffee and brioche with homemade jam. "Bonjour Mademoiselle," the woman said. She indicated a place that had been set for her on the patio outside.

"Merci."

Pascal ran up to examine the contents of her tray. His exchange with the woman named Dominique revealed that she was his mother's helper from the village. He boasted to Dominique about his new acquaintance, trying on various identities for her. Kenna was, according to one account, a friend of his from America, she lived with Spiderman. And she was a friend of Superman, it seemed. Pascal related the high points of his campaign against the ducks, which in this new version, had been undertaken to protect Kenna from them.

Though Dominique's gap-toothed grin appeared friendly enough , her quick eyes held too much interest in the mysterious visitor. The lawyer in Kenna would get right to the point. "May I have my things?" she asked in French.

The woman narrowed her eyes as if straining to understand.

"My bags," Kenna said.

The friendly squint was repeated, embellished with an apologetic shrug.

Very well. She could be stubborn too.

At that moment Ginger Lebecque appeared, a Texas blond whose easy American manner seemed surreal in the Swiss countryside.

"Good morning. Sleep well?"

"Yes. Thank you. I've asked Dominique for my things," Kenna replied, trying for cheerful reasonableness.

"Dominique, our guest's bags, s'il vous plait."

"You look very pretty in our local fashion," Ginger said, smiling. "After breakfast Dominique can help you with your laundry."

"I don't intend to stay the morning. I need to get going." She did not return the smile. While Kenna the guest might seem polite and detached, she would not betray the professional inside her who, even in this rustic haven, needed to act with caution.

Madame Lebecque seated herself across from Kenna. She lifted the small pot. "May I pour you a café Américain? The usual stuff they import here is bitter and thin, a far cry from the coffee we get in the States."

The sun warmed Kenna's skin. The sweet air and fragrant scent of the coffee swept over her. And the warm brioche could not have been more delicious had it been baked by Julia Child. Was this what coming home would feel like?

"Beautiful here, isn't it?" Ginger asked.

"Yes." The moment was coming, she reminded herself. She had prepared her script: *My friend and I became separated yesterday in Paris. When I got off at Valorbé to phone him, I found myself stranded.*

But she did not have to trot out the simple lie, for Madame Lebecque seemed anxious to talk about herself.

"It's so good to have a visitor from the States. I'm from Houston, Kenna. A little town outside, actually." She poured herself a half cup of the coffee, and added almost as much cream.

"How did you come here?" Kenna asked politely.

"A circuitous path," she laughed. "I was the little girl who always dreamed of becoming Miss America and representing the United States in foreign lands."

There were special classes for child beauty-contestants–did Kenna know? Kenna had never thought about it, her own childhood being so utterly different. Unlike Ginger, she had attended a girl's school and roamed streetwise through the Bronx until age 11, when she and her grandfather had moved to Manhattan's westside. Evenings were spent in her grandfather's library among his books.

"I was eighteen when I won the crown," Ginger said. "All that tutoring paid off. My 'reign,' world travel with a chaperone, was all I could have hoped for."

*Why tell me? Is this fairy-tale for my benefit?*

"I met André in Brussels," Ginger said, refilling her guest's coffee cup. "He was getting his doctorate in 20th Century European history. We moved to this village where André was raised and started a school – L'Ecole Anglais. Grades six through twelve. We cater to the children of American diplomats employed in Geneva."

Good, Kenna thought. Excellent. But where was the bloody housekeeper? The woman was certainly taking her time returning Kenna's possessions.

She looked at her watch. "If I could have my things–"

"Dominique," Ginger Lebecque called to the servant in the kitchen, where an infant's laughter could be heard.

"We have a new baby," Madame Lebecque explained with a blend of pride and apology. "She's a love. Different from this little Texas tornado."

Pascal had drawn into his mother like a dinghy to a yacht. He stood observing Kenna with a child's fascination for the exotic. Here was a woman – like his mother – who spoke in an American accent. Here was a woman, unlike his mother, who exhibited an appreciation for the challenges of subduing waterfowl.

Dominique emerged at last with Kenna's backpack and duffel bag. The backpack was just as she remembered it but Countess' satchel containing the bonds had been opened. The latch was undone and the belt hung limply along the patterned leather. A glance inside confirmed the bonds were gone.

## *61*

Ginger spoke. "Your papers looked terribly important, so André put them in his vault. They're perfectly safe."

Kenna's sense of alarm escalated. What kind of people would examine her possessions and remove them to their "vault?" Everyone so courteous, so thoughtful and polite. Dare one inquire, she thought – have I been robbed?

"Madame –" Dominique interrupted, speaking rapidly in French. "Here! This must have fallen out."

The woman extended her hand toward Ginger. In it, she held the passport Kenna had taken from the Countess. Ginger read the name inside. "You know this woman?" she asked, the tension returning to her mouth.

"Oh that. Found it on the train," Kenna said. She lifted it lightly from her hostess' open hand, and tucked the folio inside her backpack. "No problem, I'm going to leave it with the station lost and found desk. They'll take care of it." She rose before there could be further discussion. "Now, please show me how to dry my clothing. And get my papers from your safe."

## *62*

Less than twenty kilometers from the terrace where Kenna reposed with Madame Lebecque, the young man known as Meister sat in a lakeview chateau in the presence of both the Countess and her brother Prince von Kadow.

"You promised the bonds to my government," Meister stubbornly replied to the Prince's summary of recent events.

"We do not need a history lesson Meister," the Countess spoke with crisp sarcasm. "That was last week. As of last night the bonds are with the girl."

"A lawyer," the Prince offered drily.

"A lawyer? She will take them to BIS."

"Yes. Yes. We know all that." The Countess stalked a rectangle around the men with Mister A clicking at her heels. She was dressed too warmly for the room, in which a fire glowed behind the 18th-century screen. She wore a full length sable coat and rose-tinted glasses. Though she couldn't have said why, the silk lining of her coat billowed as she walked, adding to her growing irritability.

"We thought you should be told," she said.

"You know where she is I suppose." Meister let his eyes follow Mister A. "Can you sit down?"

The Prince answered his guest from his seat on the sofa. "We don't know where the lawyer is. When Fabia left the train, the girl and the bonds were gone. But she can't have gotten far. There was a – contretemps – with Mister A."

The younger man could not restrain his expression of fear. "How?" he asked.

"It was nothing," the Countess replied. "A flesh wound apparently. I gather this from the fact that she eluded us. The dog could have killed her. But he has been so well trained, he restrained himself."

The memory seemed to enrage her. "How Miguel? When could she have left the train?"

The Countess increased her pace. Passing a music table, she swept a plate of cheese biscuits onto the floor with the sleeve of her coat. The plate shattered.

"This is insufferable," she said ambiguously.

The Prince closed his eyes, briefly irritated. "Don't derange yourself Fabia."

He turned back to their guest. "The Swiss authorities refused to search the train until it arrived in Geneva. Too lazy I expect." He spoke mildly as if the indolence of the authorities was a matter for humor. "They wouldn't disturb the passengers."

The Prince reached forward and picked up the hearth brush. Then he knelt by the remains of the cheese biscuits. For a moment the room was silent save for the sound of china and cracker filings being brushed onto a silver tray.

"Anyway, the problem is not as serious as Fabia suggests," the Prince rose from the floor and placed the tray on the table. "I have alerted the security firm at the Bank. They will be watching for her. If she is foolish enough to try there, Interpol will scoop her up at once and the bonds will be recovered."

"Excuse me for disagreeing with you." The young man inclined his slender frame, not toward von Kadow, but toward the Countess. "Let's not delude ourselves. She will go there. She will 'try' as you say. Interpol will identify the bonds as belonging to the Americans. They won't hand them over to you simply on your saying please and thank you. The plan is finished. We want our advance back."

The Countess halted before a trail of cracker residue.

"Sit!" The Doberman lowered his haunches to the floor, and sat quivering before the inviting fragments.

"Stay!"

The two men were silent during this display.

After several moments she snapped the dog's leash. The dog lowered his fine skull and commenced licking up what remained of the crumbs with a delicate tongue, cleverly avoiding a few slivers of glass from the plate.

"Oh, please, Fabia," the Prince said. "There are still bits of china on the floor."

"The girl will not get to BIS," the Countess said. "Klaus will not allow it. Even now, Kessel is on his way here, to Valorbé. Klaus will find her." The Countess turned toward the young man and mouthed her words as if speaking to a child. "She will not get to BIS."

"Then why do you bother me with this? I've done my part. The advance has been deposited in your account. If we don't have the bonds in twenty-four hours our need for them is finished. We must withdraw the money."

The Countess snapped the leash again to end the feast, and gave a curt nod in the direction of her brother.

"Kessel will need backup in Basel, just in case," the Prince said. "Fabia wants the Slovakian government to send support there at once."

"You intend to *occupy* the city of Basel? That's fatuous."

"A few men," the Countess answered. "To assist Klaus – he will supervise them. It is an insurance policy only, to prevent an embarrassment at the Bank."

Meister's eyes narrowed. "You were to deliver the bonds to my government. We have our own sources to find the money, but you promised to deliver them before next week when Germany calls due Slovakia's loans. That's why we're paying you a $50 million commission."

"$75 million. Things have become more complicated." The Countess drew up to the young minister. Mister A commenced a low growl. If he wasn't terrified, the young man would have thought the whole scene comical.

"I insist on your cooperation," she said.

"But Slovakia's central bank is one of BIS' voting banks!"

"So?"

"Our minister is on its revolving Board."

"And?"

"If it is found out Slovakia used hired thugs to discourage payment to American bondholders –"

"This young woman is traveling alone. She's a fugitive, wanted in the U. S. for theft and embezzlement. You will be doing Interpol a favor. No one will know the soldiers are associated with the Slovakian government. As a way of doing business in the former Soviet Union, I would have thought it would come naturally to you. I am sure it did to your father. I'm sure he wouldn't have run home crying. With your help the girl will be detained. The bonds recovered. The next day your soldiers will be gone."

"You said she will not get to BIS."

Whether the Countess' loosening of the leash was voluntary or accidental could not be discerned, but its effect, bringing Mister A's incisors in very close proximity to the delicate hands of the young man, was immediate.

"All right," Meister said, turning his eyes from the tan daggers along the Doberman's snout. "I will ask the government to act immediately on your request. We can provide three men only, but they are trained with Slovakian intelligence. Tode can be here this afternoon. He has worked with Kessel before. The other two will join Kessel at the Bank tomorrow."

He allowed a crease of irritation to cross his brow. "Now will you please stop snapping that leash? And take that damn dog out of here while I have something to eat."

The Prince, who had stepped out of the room to take a telephone call, re-entered at this moment, repressing a look of mild concern. "That was Dominique at the Lebecque wine estate. It seems they have a visitor."

## *63*

It was past noon when Kenna changed into her things and prepared to leave the Lebecque estate. She had spent the better part of the morning laundering her clothing with the housekeeper's help, all the time feeling the woman's sharp eyes upon her – as if she, Kenna, were a captive and the gap-toothed servant her keeper.

When at last she'd prevailed upon Dominique to toil over her trousers with a hair dryer they succeeded in drying them ninety percent. Kenna put them on and gathered her things.

After a brief introduction to the kitchen computer, she tapped out a letter to BIS, managing to print it in the absence of prying eyes. She placed a call to the number she had for Ulrich's jeep. Her inability to get through felt frustrating and she finally gave up, more than ready to move on. But Ginger Lebecque put her off about fetching the bonds until André returned for lunch.

"That doesn't work for me," Kenna said to her smiling hostess. "I have to be in Basel by nightfall."

With polite insistence, she asked Ginger to telephone André at the school so she could speak with him. Ginger insisted politely that André would be back at noon and could not be interrupted until then. The three of them would have a quiet lunch together, after which they could drive her to the train station, thereby making up for any delay in her schedule. As she, Ginger, did not have access to the vault, it really was useless to further discuss the matter.

The term "stone wall" took on fresh meaning in the tirelessly feminine manner of Ginger Lebecque. Kenna nearly struck out toward the village on her own to find the school and confront André. In the end, however, she accepted the postponement with little grace.

André Lebecque arrived home about twelve-thirty and the three of them sat down to a meal of fresh trout and new potatoes. M. Lebecque poured three glasses of pale wine from a bottle with a lizard on its label.

"Aigle wine," he said, holding the small fluted glass to the light. "Estate bottled. Our Canton produces all of Switzerland's most reputed growths. We do not export this wine, even to the United States. It is the best in all of Switzerland." He placed the glass before Kenna.

"Wine has been produced on this land since Roman times," he continued. "Too bad you haven't time to tour our vineyard."

Kenna gave a chilly smile. She had no intention of sticking around any longer than she had to.

"Les Grottes – " she mused, reading the estate's name on the label. She recognized the name from her grandfather's research file, which she had failed to study thoroughly before its theft from his office.

She recovered quickly. Grottes, grottoes. "Are there caves here?"

André hesitated. "Beneath the vineyard. For centuries they've been used for storing wine. Now we age the wines there."

"Really." Swiss wines don't require aging, Michael had told her in his rambling effort to distract her the evening of her arrest. They're drunk young.

The superficiality of André's conversation disturbed her. Where were his questions concerning the Countess' passport? Wasn't he curious about the bonds?

His eyes followed Dominique casually as she returned to the kitchen. When the pass-through had closed behind her, he spoke. "My wife tells me you found a woman's passport on the train."

"Do you know Fabia Santiago?" Kenna asked.

André studied her keenly. "Yes. We do know her." He met his wife's eyes, as if a decision had been made. "She was interviewed in connection with a mysterious series of events here several years ago, but no charges were filed." He spoke carefully. "There was a death. Never solved. The locals believe it is because of connections to her brother, who is associated with large banking interests." He gestured toward the kitchen. "We don't speak about such things in front of Dominique, even in English."

The air felt changed by André's candor. The tension of the moments before had dissolved and she felt an instinct to respond in kind. Instead, she laid her fork down and let her lawyer's caution take over.

"You must travel in interesting circles," André said.

"I don't understand."

"You know the Countess, don't you?"

"I met her only once, at a party in New York."

"And you run into her again in a village of two hundred people."

"This wasn't my destination," Kenna reminded him. "I'm going to Basel, actually."

"Bal," André remarked with dry correctness.

"Sorry?"

"In the south we use the French pronunciation. In the north you will hear them say 'Baa-sel.'"

They were silent as Dominique swung into the dining room with a platter of pears and cheese. She placed it on the sideboard, presumably for serving after the meal. When she had returned to the kitchen, André addressed Kenna in a tone of polite irony.

"Now, leaving aside the fairytales – we have told you what we know of the Countess. How does an American lawyer come to possess this woman's passport?"

Kenna took a moment with her wine.

"I'd better explain from the beginning," she said.

"You better had."

# *64*

Choosing her words carefully at first, Kenna related the story of the gold bonds, keeping it as spare of detail as possible. She described the theft by the Countess, Kenna's arrest, Michael's intervention and their foolish pursuit of the Countess to Mexico. Of Michael, she said only that he'd left her at Paris and she'd been forced to continue alone.

When no reaction seemed to be forthcoming from her host, she spoke at last. "I hope you understand my American way of speaking."

"We are taught English over here as if our lives depend upon it."

André continued the wry tone. "Now, it seems, you want to get on to Bal and turn in these bonds for payment."

"Yes."

"Why?"

The last question was shot at her like a dart.

"I would have thought it was evident."

She had no desire to bring up her personal motives. She realized for the first time that the project had become personal. Turning in the bonds seemed intimately connected to her grandfather's death and finding Lara. She had no desire to share with strangers the emotions that drove her.

He put his fork down, waiting for her.

"It's the right thing," she said.

"The right thing for whom?"

"I had the impression you would support JAFA."

"We don't support spurious claims."

"What are you suggesting?"

"What proofs do you have that these bonds were held by American investors? How do you know they were not stolen by the Russian Army as your State Department claims?"

"The bonds belong to clients of my grandfather's. The portfolio is represented by a man I trust."

André seemed unimpressed. He drew a cigarette from a silver cup on the table and dropped it in his shirt pocket. "Jews can do no wrong, is that it?"

He wasn't going to give back the bonds.

"How do we know this fund you represent isn't engaged in a gigantic fraud?" he asked. "Jewish sympathy runs high right now. Poor Israel – the target of Arab hostility. Switzerland and Germany discussing war reparations. Everyone weeping on their shoulders over the past. Even your major art collections turn back the art they have paid millions for. Maybe JAFA hopes to cash in on public support for restoring the lost wealth of the Jews."

"The point is –" Kenna kept her eyes upon him straight and unblinking. "My grandfather believed there was evidence here, at Les Grottes, that supports our client's claim."

André was silent for a few moments before a strange smile flashed through his goatee. "Your grandfather sounds rather astute."

"Something that would refute Germany's claims that they are contraband." That was what her grandfather had believed, wasn't it?

"What would that be?"

She fixed him with her most direct gaze. "Records of the Reichsbank, I would assume, wouldn't you?"

"I'm sure I don't know." He pushed his chair back from the table and stood up. "Now I'm going back to work," he said shortly.

Kenna stood too. "I don't give a damn what you plan for your afternoon," she said. "I need you to return my bonds and documents right now."

“Not just yet,” André said with a sardonic lift to his brow. “You'll forgive me if I do some checking on your story first. We will talk about your bonds when I return at six o'clock."

# 65

Pascal was at school and the infant taking her nap. When Ginger retired to her room and André returned to his work, the only sound was the rustle of Dominique in the kitchen.

Kenna returned to her room briefly. The conversation at lunch had heightened her sense of unease. She couldn't count on André's returning the bonds. How did she know he hadn't already called the Swiss police – or Interpol?

She lay back on the bed to rest. Through the pain and fatigue, she suddenly wondered if André was right. What did she really know about Michael or JAFA?

Kenna touched Michael's attaché that he had brought with him to Costa Careyes. Five days could seem very long ago. She opened the case and went over his papers once more, looking for some reference to Valorbé or the Lebecques.

The wine at lunch made a poor companion to rational thought. She had been through the pages twice when she found a slip of yellow ruled paper written in Michael's hand: "Lara – Valorbé." It seemed to be a scrap from a telephone message. So the village did have a connection to the child, or at least, her bonds.

After five minutes, she had made no further progress. "Keep your nerve," the bearded man had told her. He had meant it lightly, thinking only of the frustration of dealing with Swiss authorities. The phrase seemed to apply more than ever. It was like running in the forest in the dark.

Kenna struggled to standing. Movement and action were the only things to banish such thoughts. Proceeding cautiously into the hallway, she commenced a silent tour of the first floor.

She stopped outside the room that Ginger had referred to as André's study. She turned the knob silently. The door swung in, and she stepped inside.

A simple decor and high ceilings recalled her grandfather's library. The scent of old leather brought forth an impression of academic life. A computer hummed at one end. At the other, a table before a pair of windows held two leather albums. They were as large as the illustrated books she had seen in the museums of Dublin, and capacious enough to hold the bonds.

She drew back the window curtain to study them. Each volume was secured with its own lock. She moved swiftly around the room, looking for a set of keys. The Austrian desk offered a possibility. Or the silver box on the mantle. The desk was locked, while the box contained only cigarettes.

She heard a sound and turned quickly. Then she heard nothing more.

André's vault, Ginger had said.

She moved to the bookcases and studied the panels at length, running her hands along them to feel for a seam, removing two volumes at a time to scan for a keypad. A tiresome task, she thought, even under the best of conditions. She examined the walls and floor, lifting the rugs and glancing behind paintings for signs of a door.

She had just decided to abandon the search in frustration when she felt someone behind her. She jumped, her heart racing.

"I offered to show you the cellars. But you declined."

André Lebecque had entered the room almost stealthily. "Are you working for the Countess?" he demanded before she could speak.

"I told you everything," she said.

He dismissed this with a wave. "You've told me nothing. A child's tale, with a few goblins and faeries. But I have ways of checking on these things."

He paused. "As for the entrance to the caverns that you were looking for just now – it is here."

André swept past her and released a latch in the floor with his boot. The entire bookcase swung in and a cold draft swept into the room.

"I advise you not to continue your investigations. Or to think of leaving on your own. If you do, I assure you the police will be involved."

He kicked the bookcase shut and turned abruptly. Striding in two steps to the desk, he unlocked its drawer and took from it a key, which he displayed to her before placing it in his pocket. His formality was chilling. "Excuse me, I return to my work now."

## 66

It was as if the watcher had waited until André's gray Golf turned out of the drive and proceeded slowly in the direction of L'Ecole Anglaise. He had moved quickly then, leaving the military jeep camouflaged among rows of olive trees and making his way along the side of the house. In less than a minute he had subdued Ginger Lebecque in her bedroom. He trussed her with fishing line and silenced her with duct tape. Now the man in the ski mask moved softly down the hall, past the kitchen where Dominique worked quietly. He stopped at the library door, pausing to listen. Kenna had already unlatched the door leading to the caves and pulled the wall shut behind her.

# 67

Kenna entered the passage leading to the caverns, knowing that André had not meant for her to do so. He had intended to shame her for imposing on his family under a false pretext. He hadn't believed her account. That was clear. But rather than feeling any regret, she was aware of a rising resoluteness inside her. It did not matter what he thought. Her grandfather had believed some secret about the bonds could be discovered here. Now, through personal decisions of her own, she had come to Les Grottes.

*'Tis the Fates, lass. We don't know the patterns, but the Fates do.* She did not believe in such things. Even in her weakened state, she had chosen the small estate over the sure thing of the village. The power of suggestion, perhaps, arising from Michael's mention of the Lebecques and their small wine estate in Valorbé. But whether she had come here through choice or destiny, it would be unacceptable to leave without finding out more.

The caves were damp. The moan of the wind made her shiver with cold. Every ten feet or so, a wall sconce glowed with dim illumination. After a shallow foyer that was roughly level, the limestone floor sloped to the road below the vineyards, and she was compelled downhill faster than she could comfortably walk without pain. Kenna took note of the chambers along the corridor, but she kept to the main path.

She felt glad she had checked her watch when she stepped inside. At the end of only four minutes, she was beginning to feel like Alice trapped in Wonderland, and considered retracing her steps. She recognized the fact that in all likelihood the study door locked itself after her. Considerations of pain or fear were useless. She had to keep moving.

After another twenty feet or so, she passed a chamber in which metal cabinets were stacked almost ceiling high. There were large sealed crates, too. Art, perhaps? She shook the strong chain-linked door and jiggled the lock. But it held, and she went on, mentally storing numbers, sizes and shapes in her memory.

Another door of thick wire cables presented itself. She stopped before it. This time the Yale-style lock yielded when she gave it a yank. Whoever preceded her had failed to close it with a click. Kenna stepped inside. She tried the large crates but they too were locked. Peering between the slats, she could see what looked like bulky objects wrapped in cloth.

The archives along the walls were locked too, in gray metal drawers, neatly labeled with family names followed by dates: 1933-39; 1940-45; 1946-51. Crouching to study them, she recognized common Jewish surnames. She moved immediately to those under the letter "D." Davel, David, Davos, Derain, Dirken. Lara D. Lara – what? She tried the child's given name with the various surnames. Davel. David. An exercise in futility. Unless she could go through the records, there was little chance of achieving a brilliant breakthrough.

The sconces flickered and went out. She was in darkness. A brief wave of panic surged up before they flickered on again, though the illumination was weaker. She realized with a sinking spirit that the lamps were on a timer. They would eventually go out altogether.

Reluctantly, she edged back into the passage, leaving the door's lock un-done in case she should want to return. She pushed on, faster now. It had been a mistake to enter these cellars without a flashlight. She was starting to fight panic when she glimpsed a series of oak casks on wooden transepts. The smell of old wine reached her nostrils, and small diaries on each cask confirmed in a faded hand that wines had been vatted here in the past. The cave's entrance had to be near at hand. By now Kenna felt light-headed. She moved quickly. She stumbled and nearly fell in her anxiety to reach the light and air of the hillside.

# 68

"Very pretty," the man in the ski mask said. "A beauty queen, aren't you? We should spare the beauty queens. They produce pretty children."

The Slovakian smashed the glass of the photograph casually against the bed leg. He lifted Pascal's photo from the frame and raised it before Ginger Lebecque's horrified eyes.

"You don't know where the lawyer has gone it seems. Too bad."

He tore off the ski mask. He did not worry that she would describe the taut features accentuated by his shaven head.

"Tode," he had been called by his classmates in grammar school. The German word for skull. Yes. It had bothered him then. Particularly when the word had come from the lips of the little girl with dark hair. Tode – a term of dread since ancient times.

He didn't worry about Ginger Lebecque seeing his face. The Lebecques had reason to keep silent. He knew their reasons, having studied Meister's intelligence before coming here. And Ginger Lebecque knew that he knew.

The Slovakian paced the room with his languid dancer's step, consulting the photograph. "He rides a bike already. They grow so quickly. One minute nursing his mother's breast, the next doing 'wheelies' in the street." He issued a harsh bark of pleasure at his mastery of North American slang.

He spun a chair around to straddle it from the front. "I'm impressed by your loyalty to your American guest. But I know someone who will tell me everything. Children are too innocent for games like these."

He raised his chiseled head, listening. "The village bell. Two o'clock. Time for all the school children to return home. Time for Uncle Tode to pick up his little charge. Gentle Uncle Tode."

The Slovakian mercenary remained seated on the chair, his hands resting casually over the wooden rail of its back. He glanced idly at the photograph still in his hands, before tearing it in two. He held the larger image toward Ginger Lebecque.

"Interesting, isn't it – how a photo can be cropped? This image is amusing. How does a boy ride a bike without his legs? Ha!" The harsh bark erupted again. "Special Olympics for him, I suppose."

The man lifted his graceful frame from the chair and moved out into the hallway. Ginger moaned, writhing to get free of her bonds. After a long silence the front door slammed and she stiffened, listening intently. She felt herself almost faint with terror when she heard the noise of the jeep starting.

## 69

Tode knew, as he sat at the wheel and started the ignition, that Kessel would be angry. Not just angry. Over the top. He knew that he'd blown it back there. And way down deep inside he suspected that his plan, such as it was, to kidnap the child and barter him for the lawyer, was a mistake.

He debated calling Kessel, making his report and taking the abuse that he knew was coming. He felt pretty sure he knew what Kessel's instructions would be. Comb the area, track the girl. Easy enough. But he would have to admit that he failed. And something else – he'd have to admit to exceeding Kessel's directions. He'd left quite a mess to be reckoned with. And if he came back without the young woman, well…

That is why Tode had no desire to call Kessel. The man who was Tode's temporary superior had a rage problem. Tode had known the CIA man to turn insane at times, using the occasion of a subordinate's report to hurl abuse in a manner so unrelenting that even those who'd been trained to carry out the most brutal acts of violence could not endure such episodes without suffering a depression.

He'd experienced Kessel's rage first hand. The last time was over four years ago. Yet he could still feel his chest constrict. Afterwards the emotional fallout had surfaced. He had felt shaken and feeble like an old man, with an impotent rage of his own. Tode was only thirty-two. The last time it had taken several days before he recovered. It was not an experience he would voluntarily repeat. Thus it was that Tode decided to proceed according to his own judgment.

# 70

The village kindergarten at 2:05 p.m. exuded the chaotic air of a village fair. Cotia Huffman, Pascal Lebecque's favorite teacher, stood in the playground waving good-bye to several of her young charges, her left hand resting firmly on the handlebars of Pascal's red bike. "Until tomorrow," she called in her musical voice.

For the small boy with the dark cap of Beatles-cut hair, the indignity of being detained, even by one he loved so well, seemed intolerable.

"I am going now, Cotia," he said in French, with a trace of exasperation. Indeed in his entire life, he'd known no one who spoke English except his mother. And now, Kenna!

"Are you certain, Pascal?" Cotia asked, her hand still resting firmly on his bicycle. "Can you find your way home all alone? Shall I call your mother?"

"No-o." He drew out the word in a scowling objection. "I am big enough now. I can go home by myself. Besides, Kenna is there. Mama is busy."

"And who is Kenna, your mother's sister?"

"She is from America. She is Batman's girlfriend."

"I think you are spinning tales again, Pascal."

"No. She is Batman's girlfriend." Pascal's voice rose. He had to get going. The idea was to surprise Mama and show Kenna how grown up he was by riding right up to the terrace before they could meet him on the road.

"Now when you get home, you will call me – yes?"

"Bien sur, Cotia. I will."

The boy pushed off before she could change her mind. He gave a last wave, more to demonstrate his one-handed agility on the red bicycle than from social courtesy.

"Au revoir, Pascal. Take care."

## *71*

Kenna stepped outside the cave into strong sunlight. The wind had increased in intensity with the afternoon clouds moving in. European skies, she thought, breathing fully for the first time in twenty minutes, Botticelli-blue one minute, El Greco gray the next. It occurred to her that she might have to return here after Basel, to unlock the secrets she did not have time to explore.

She shielded her eyes to study the house, fifty yards away. Almost at once she caught a glint of metal among the olive trees and the stealthy movement of a man running toward it.

Her heart began to race. For two days and two nights she had been steeling herself for this moment. One minute, fearing confrontation with the CIA man, the next minute, planning it. If Kessel found her, she would do this. If Kessel is here, she will move there. She had always believed the conflict would arise between her and Kessel, or her and the Countess. But her foresight had been limited.

A vineyard tractor for hauling grapes stood at the cave's entrance. Kenna mounted it and turned the key. Then she proceeded toward the house at a pace that was frustrating in its lethargy.

By the time Kenna reached the terrace, the jeep had disappeared. Her brow was damp with perspiration, her heart beat wildly. But she didn't notice any of this. Cautiously, she entered the French doors at the back of the house.

The door into the hallway stood open. Kenna felt suddenly, acutely aware of the silence. Blood was everywhere. On the walls, on the floorboards, streaked like polish on the surfaces of tables.

In the kitchen, Dominique, the Lebecque's servant from the village, lay sprawled, half crawling toward the French windows leading to the terrace. Kenna knew immediately that this was not the work of a madman. It was very careful, very neat. Almost, one might say, artistic. A study in retaliation. The intruder had not found what he came for, and this was his response.

She cradled Dominique, the bright liquid staining her clothing for the second time in two days. This time it was Dominique's blood that soaked her trouser leg. An hour before, she'd feared the woman's almost malevolent curiosity. But now, she was dying – or dead. Gently, she placed the woman's head upon a stack of clean linens and closed the lids. Almost stumbling from revulsion, she moved into the hallway.

The sacking of the house had been carried out with casual violence. She had no doubt that the impulse to murder had come upon the killer during his final sweep through, when the frustration of failure had overtaken him. As though to omit evidence of his presence would only magnify his failure.

Kenna's eye was drawn to the fragment lying on the floor. A torn photograph. She turned it over. The image made her draw in her breath sharply: Pascal, on his red bicycle. Pascal, who was now on his way home.

Kenna reached for the telephone. No dial tone.

Without waiting, Kenna was out of the house and running through the fields toward the school.

She moved fast, adopting a strange swift canter that favored her good leg. She had become again the athlete, one whose awareness of pain dissolved in the face of crisis. She paused once to listen, for the roads in this part of Switzerland were not well traveled. Except for the slow rumble of an occasional farm truck the air was silent. She imagined that she heard, up ahead, the distinctive hum of a jeep's motor.

Before lunch she had changed into her uniform and running shoes. But she hadn't paused for her jacket. Now she shivered involuntarily in the wind.

Dominique. The thought of the woman lying in a pool of blood was more than she could bear. Yes, she had mistrusted the Lebecques – justifiably so. But if she had been candid with them about what had happened to Michael–or if she had never stopped here–Kessel would not have come. She had brought tragedy to this village.

# 72

Tode pulled over to the shoulder, with the engine running. He considered reversing his decision and calling Kessel at the contact point a few miles from Valorbé. As he decided against it for the second time, he felt his cell phone pulse against his thigh. It was Kessel.

The CIA man acted domineering and irritable. It was long past the time when he should have heard confirmation that the lawyer was apprehended and Tode himself on his way to Kessel's location with her and the bonds. But as Kessel listened to his colleague on the other end of the telephone, the blue vein swelled in his temple.

"You did what? You stupid cretin. Do you know what's going to happen if that lawyer gets to the bank?"

The conversation descended into a diatribe of personal abuse. Then Kessel ordered Tode to report to his superior immediately, they would track the subject together. Kessel would wait half an hour, no more, so Tode had better get his ass on the road.

Alone on the small farm road, Tode replaced the portable phone on his belt after Kessel's last sentences died in the handset. He had not offered his plan to kidnap the Lebecque child and barter him for information about the lawyer, though he had planned to. But, as in most instances of working for the Zurich bureau chief, what Tode intended to say fell away in the force of the man's fury. He wished there was a way to redeem himself. But just then, Tode could see something coming toward him on the road. Was it, could it be, a small child on a red bicycle?

# *73*

Kenna came to a point where the path dog-eared and stopped. One fork cut away sharply toward the road and she followed it. This would take her close to a point just below the village.

Kenna ran full-out. Ragged in her breathing, trembling in her limbs, she had hit the wall some time ago. But that did not matter. She kept moving, weaving between the plane trees that lined the road until she heard the squeal of the jeep's brakes. The killer had passed the boy too fast, then shoved the jeep into reverse.

She slipped to the side of the road, advancing through the trees. Then she saw them and stopped. Tode was talking to the little boy, taking his time, nervously looking to the right and left, as if *he* were the one pursued.

Unwatched, she studied the scene, trying to quiet her breathing. A series of possibilities played through her mind. She had harnessed some of her first terror at Dominique's murder. With the physical exertion of the long run, self-discipline, more or less, was once more hers. But she hadn't reckoned with her feelings for Pascal.

She clenched her palms on her trousers. As she did so, she heard the change in Pascal's voice. He'd made the transition from friendly child to frightened child. For Kenna, it was the sound of her own childhood, with its vulnerability and fear of darkness. She needed to act.

*Don't rush it, lass.*

The man stooped to take hold of Pascal, the child's voice rising again in fear.

"Non, non! Mama!" Pascal wriggled violently. His jacket caught on the handlebar of his bike. Now he was shouting. She waited until the man's attention was wholly on the boy. Seizing the moment's confusion, she moved from behind the trees at a dead run and hit the hired killer square in the small of his back. The force of her blow was a surprise to them both. Immediately, they were on the ground.

Kenna had never had occasion to use the techniques practiced in her gym's self-defense class two years before. The class had been billed provocatively: "Girls! learn techniques while you tone." She'd felt more confident immediately after taking the class. But she had never put her training to the test. She was completely uncertain how effective such techniques could be in violent conflict.

Get him down, the instructor had said. Keep him there.

Now her opponent reacted quickly, struggling to roll over her. In that instant she found herself looking into the eyes of a hired killer. An expression of incredulity mixed with amusement as if any moment the joke would be revealed. But in the next second she caught him in the groin with her knee and used his contractions of pain to force him down, locking his arms beneath him with her knees against his trunk.

She straddled him, riding the small of his back, and held his head against the cobbled road with both hands. She kept his arms pinned with her feet. It couldn't last.

"Run, Pascal!"

The little boy appeared frozen, biting his lip, as if making up his mind. She repeated the words in a hoarse bark. Finally, he righted his bike, struggled onto it, and took off toward home, a blur in a navy suit and cap.

Tode tried to rise. He lay on the road choking, with his neck arched and Kenna's thumbs in the knob of his throat. His face was the color of violets, his eyes narrowed with strain. The hired killer outweighed her by sixty pounds, she could not hold him for long.

The Slovakian bucked once with his hips, and she was off him. She felt something hard against her thigh, and put her hand around his cell phone, strapped to his belt. He made a strike for her with his left hand forcing the heel of it, like a bit, into her mouth. He grabbed for her wrist and missed. Her head flew back. He torqued hard to grab her other hand. She fumbled for the phone with both hands, tearing it from his belt. He got one hand around her throat. Now she clasped the phone like a dumb-bell and struck him with it. Hard over the eye. Again. Again. He put up his hand. When you think it's done, keep doing it, the instructor had said. Don't stop. Don't stop until you're free.

Tode seized her wrist but he could not see. She struck him again with the phone. Again. It had to be hard. Kenna was out of strength, out of breath and close to losing consciousness. She knew he had a gun and she wondered distantly where it was. Mental telepathy, it seemed. He swung to his feet and staggered toward the jeep. She got there ahead of him, seizing the weapon from where he had laid it on the gear box. Gripping it in both hands, she whipped around and struck him in the face. He fell to his knees, with the blood spurting from his eye. She made a series of two-handed blows like a woodsman chopping a tree.

She didn't stop striking him until she saw his head go limp and fall of its own weight onto the stones. Blood began to flow like a gentle creek onto the road, turning the pale stubble of his skull a brilliant rust.

Kenna collapsed beside him, panting with terror and fatigue, and holding the gun to his throat. Her hand was trembling. She realized she should leave. He did not seem to be breathing. She pinned him with her legs, listening for his breath. But she heard nothing. She thought how strange it must appear to anyone coming upon them. A woman astride a spent man. An erotic scene, no doubt, but appearances could be deceptive. In this case it was only life and death.

## 74

"Stay in the jeep. I'll be right back for you," Kenna admonished Pascal when they reached the Lebecque residence. Then she was out the door and across the gravel driveway to the house. The killer was gone now. She had rolled him to the side of the road into a shallow ditch, taken his keys, then returned with Pascal in his jeep.

After the first few moments of panic when Kenna had comforted him, pressing the child's face in her hands, the incident receded, leaving no apparent mark on the boy.

He exhibited a sturdy curiosity on the ride back, testing Kenna's knowledge of the vehicle's instrument panel, yet she felt keenly his relief at her presence. She looked back once more at the child in the jeep and waved to him. Pascal sat quietly, watching the house. His return wave was hesitant, as if knowing that whatever lay inside could breach his childhood forever.

Kenna rushed to the bedroom wing of Mr. and Mrs. LaBecque, instinctively pausing at the closed door. She realized she was holding her breath. She swung the door wide and stepped inside.

Ginger Lebecque lay contorted on the bed, bound to the headboard and gagged. The nylon line Tode used had left deep cuts in her legs. Her wrists were bleeding. Her head hung limply against her shirt like a decorative bauble.

But Kenna quickly confirmed the only thing that mattered. Ginger was unhurt. Terrified, but alive.

## 75

She had not expected André and Ginger Lebecque to react in quite this way to the afternoon's events. If she had any doubts that Les Grottes was something more than the idyllic wine-estate it appeared, they were eradicated by her hosts' immediate actions.

Ginger closed the children in Pascal's room and locked it. Then she changed into a long-sleeved sweat suit which hid the slashes of red on her wrists and ankles, and handed Kenna a pair of gloves.

"You were never here," she said, sweeping the light switch and door knob with a towel. "We spent the afternoon in Geneva, shopping for the children, we returned to find *this*."

Gone was the Texas beauty queen, Kenna thought. In her place, she saw a woman of fierce efficiency.

"A thief," Ginger continued, "interrupted by Dominique. Tragic, but nothing to do with us."

In less than an hour the gloom of dusk had fallen. Like some professional crew of janitors, the three of them wiped down the walls and surfaces, pulled out the drawers and emptied the chests. Ginger's jewels had been transferred to butcher wrappings and placed in the freezer, leaving her jewel-case on the floor. The idea was to tailor the story to the simple minds of the local police. A transient, finding a lonely house, enters to rob and is surprised by the housekeeper.

When the kitchen still-life included only the dead woman on the floor, they were ready to set out for Geneva and the train station. The curtain would rise when they returned.

While Ginger bundled the children into the car André led Kenna to his study. He moved to the desk and withdrew a small ring of keys. "I have something to show you."

He lifted the massive volumes from the table by the windows and placed them upon the coffee table. He snapped the first one open, placing the heavy cover to one side.

"My father," he explained, "was employed as archivist for the University of Geneva. He was drafted into the Swiss Army in 1941 and assigned to record political events in Europe. His mother, my grandmother, was a Jew. She left Switzerland when my father was fifteen, he never saw her again. But he used his position to document what he saw. Ginger and I have continued his work, in a different way. Those records in the caves have been gathered over decades to try to authenticate property that was lost or taken in the war."

As he spoke, he flipped through pages of black and white photos. "These are rare," he said. "No one knows they exist. The Swiss destroyed my father's records after the war. But he was very meticulous. I restored the negatives from work copies."

The images were eight by ten inches, composed with a beautiful starkness. It was clear André's father had possessed an instinctive gift. She studied each one, touched by this compelling record of a place and time so different from her own. She knew she must be on her way. But the photographs re-created for her the urgent environment of her grandfather's first effort to redeem the bonds. She turned page after page, aware of André beside her, strangely gratified by the effect the images had upon her. Suddenly, she stopped.

"This one – tell me about it."

"You have seen this picture before?" She had caught him by surprise. This was not the disclosure he had planned.

"This picture is one of the reasons I came here." She pulled from her knapsack the photo she had found in her grandfather's study and held it alongside the page in the book. They were not exact copies, but it was clear the photographer had taken one after another in a series. "Is there any way I could find out what happened to this young girl?"

"She would be almost seventy by now."

"I realize that. How can I find her or – what may have happened to her?"

"André, we have to go." Ginger's approach had been silent. "The children are already in the Sport-U. We'll wait for you."

"We're coming." He slipped the photo from its sleeve and handed it to Kenna. On the back were words written in German, in what must have been his father's hand.

"What does it say?"

*'Lara, Berlin, 1945. I saw this girl in front of a grand house. All the furniture, rugs and tapestries had been removed by the German police. She had only her dog, she had tied a handkerchief around the dog's snout and evaded the police by hiding under the stairs. She told me she was waiting to be sent for by her sister in America. I planned to return to Switzerland that night and told her I would come back that evening to take her with me. I thought I could get her across the border as my assistant, then send her to my sister in England. She said when I returned she would be gone. She was expecting her papers to come through at any time. The dog's name was Max.'*

"Did your father return? Did he take Lara with him?"

"That," he said, with an air of regret. "I do not know."

She could not hide her disappointment. No surname. No fresh leads. Only the phrase, "her sister in America." She tucked the photo into her backpack. "What were you going to show me?"

"Ah," he withdrew an envelope from the pocket of the back cover and turned to her with a curious expression.

"I've done some checking on your bonds. Your State Department claims JAFA's' bonds include those looted from the Reichsbank in May, 1945 by the Russian Army – "

He extracted a photograph from the envelope.

"Here is the Reichsbank in February, 1945, three months *before* the Russians entered Berlin."

The Berlin street scene showed a city in chaos. Men and women were running, some with children. Curbs and street lamps had been destroyed, the latter transformed into sculptures of twisted iron that lurched from the sidewalks like so many drunken swabbies. Her attention was caught by the remnants of an imposing stone edifice in the background, surrounded by rubble. Its letters however, were still intact: *Hausam Werderschen markt* – the Reichsbank.

"This was taken on the fourth day of Allied bombing in February, 1945. The date is easily confirmed by the records of the Allied Command, although no one has bothered to confirm it. Look at the devastation. Do you think there was anything in the vaults by the time the Russians arrived in May?"

A sense of jubilation swept her. She wished Michael could be here. It was as if she had known all along that Germany's tale of Russian looting was nothing more than a convenient ruse to avoid payment. Now there could be no impediments in Basel – assuming she could get inside the bank.

"What happened to the money and securities that were kept there?"

"The gold bonds?" he asked, smiling.

"Yes."

"Himmler ordered everything transferred to the caves at Meissen, 110 kilometers south of the city. Check your war journals. The Russians arrived from the north in May. They never had a chance to pillage the Reichsbank."

André drew another photo from the envelope. "In April, the Allies advanced from the south in a plan to meet the Russians in Berlin. They came from the Italian front, my father was ordered to join them to record the final triumphant events."

A strange excitement lit André's face. "At Meissen it was a small group of Americans who 'liberated' the caves. Here is your record of the Allied victory."

She felt her breathing quicken at the sight of the young soldiers loading crates from limestone caverns onto military jeeps. She took her time studying the sequence of photos, not willing to make assumptions from which she would be forced to retreat. In the background, the company of GIs cracked open wooden crates with a tire-iron, while in the foreground a young soldier with a crew cut had speared a stack of bond certificates on his bayonet and lofted it in the air.

A shocking comprehension grew upon her. "Is this what you wanted to show me?"

"Yes."

Kenna seized the magnifying glass from the coffee table and held it to the letters on the canvas sacks, into which his fellow officers were stuffing stacks of German bonds:

PROPERTY OF THE UNITED STATES GOVERNMENT.

## 76

It is less than an hour's drive from Valorbé to Geneva's Bainhof. Kenna spoke little on the way there. She clasped firmly Michael's attaché containing the bonds, which André had returned to her.

André drove separately in the jeep, abandoning it among the trees near Tode's body. Kenna clearly grasped why André did not attempt to conceal the dead assassin. To do so would only implicate the Lebecques. Instead the police would assume Tode had an accomplice who turned on him and killed him. And the accomplice? Once the jeep and body were found, it would only be a matter of time before the local authorities initiated their search for Kenna.

They passed no one until the autobahn, for which they shared a sigh of relief.

"Who was he?" Kenna asked, when the children slept in their mother's lap.

André found her eyes in the mirror. "Fabia Santiago is a scavenger. She finds assets of the Jews and turns them over to certain interests in Germany. She has contacts within the Slovakian government. That man back there – he is Slovakian intelligence. I am almost sure of it."

"Did he come for me?"

"It's not so simple." André gestured impatiently. "Do you think the lost assets of the Jews turn up spontaneously? That suddenly, after fifty years, people say: 'We have this art, this manor house, they were owned by a Jewish family before they were gassed. May we give them back?

"Not exactly." André spat the words. "Ginger and I are part of an organization that scours Europe for Nazi contraband. We search the records. When we find art, sculpture, deeds, insurance policies, whatever it might be, we trace the chain of title. We make sure before we speak. Then we grab hold like a pitting-bull.

"The Countess works too, grabbing up assets as fast as we can locate them and turning them in to Germany to 'repatriate' them before we can lodge our claim."

"What's in the caves?" Kenna asked.

"Les grottes holds records going back to the 1920s. They are valuable to those who would barter with Germany. I suspect the man who killed Dominique came for our papers as well as –" He left the thought unfinished.

"How did they learn I was staying with you?"

"The man you describe as von Kadow is Fabia's brother. Dominique used to work for him."

She recalled the housekeeper's sly manner.

"This is a Swiss village," Ginger said. "There's no love lost between the Swiss people and the Jews. And there's hostility for the work we do, though no one knows the extent of our involvement. We were working out how to let Dominique go. It was very sensitive, we didn't want her spreading rumors about us."

André's mouth twisted in a wry smile. "Even if they were true."

They'd reached the station. André's comments explained a lot. They had feared her as much as she'd feared them. Ironic, she thought, they presumed she was an agent of the Countess.

She slipped on her backpack. "I'm getting out here. You shouldn't be observed helping me, I've caused enough trouble for you."

"We will see you off," André insisted.

As they drew into the parking lot of Geneva's modern train station, he handed her a card bearing a name and street address.

"There is an expert on bonds and currencies in Basel. His name is Marten Bolls. He has a shop off the lobby of the Hotel Three Kings. Don't worry, it's easy to find. Follow the Rhine to the central district. The inn is centuries old, with a three-star restaurant and a doorman. Here is Bolls' residence address if you need a place to stay. He started his career working for Switzerland's finance minister. He knows the secrets of the bankers. Just mention André Lebecque. He will know me."

The train was already on the track. André started the ignition. Pascal jumped out after Kenna and stood gallantly before her. His eyes were soft from sleep. He seemed on the verge of collapse from the stimulations of the day. Yet he was determined to stay with his new friend until the last.

"Come away now, Pascal," Ginger said. "It's time to leave."

Stubbornly, the child remained beside Kenna until she knelt down to him.

"Je t'aime, Kenna," he said and buried himself in her jacket.

She lifted his chin to meet her eyes. "Au revoir, Pascal. I'll see you in New York. We have ducks there in Central Park, you know."

Strong emotions rushed up against her will as she hoisted her bag onto the platform. She felt aware of being alone, in the dark and headed to a strange city. Chilled to the marrow by the biting wind off Lake Geneva, longing for hot tea and a warm bed, Kenna boarded the night train to Basel.

## 77

Kessel sat and gazed in something close to dread at the scene before him. The highly trained Slovakian agent called Tode lay smashed in a ditch along the tiny village road forty or so kilometers outside Geneva.

The CIA man would not have been able to carry off his role as European bureau head if he had panicked easily. He had been in too many tight spots before. If anything, the latest snafu only stiffened his resolve to bring the matter to an efficient conclusion.

Now Kessel stepped out of the bottle-green Lotus and approached his battered subordinate. He cursed the man who had recruited him for this assignment. Shining his penlight on the Slovakian's face, he saw a goulash of blood and dirt. A grotesque swelling hovered over Tode's right eye. Kessel thought he heard a soft moan, and checked the injured man's pulse. It was weak but he could be brought around. As Kessel knelt down, he heard the moan again. He snapped his Glock thirty-two caliber into position. Tode's eyes snapped open, then fluttered closed. Kessel waited until the eyes flew open again, then fired straight into the soft cavity beneath the man's ear lobe. Tode's head jerked and fell into the dirt. Kessel rose and returned to the Lotus.

Once inside he started the car, then spun it around sharply and sped toward the autobahn. He would be in Basel in three hours.

# *78*

When it is midnight in Switzerland, it is six o'clock the same evening in New York. The cocktail hour. Thanks to direct dialing and a phone card, Kenna would be able to place the call from her Basel hotel room without disturbing the man at the front desk.

The Hotel Leipzig was a bleak establishment on the edge of the Old City, a brief taxi ride from the train station, and the only accommodation Kenna's driver could suggest at that hour.

She had arrived only a few moments before the concierge closed up for the night, and the scowl that marked his clean features conveyed clearly enough that he cursed her timing. She decided to make it easy for him.

“Can you check my passport tomorrow morning? It's in here somewhere–"

She mimed a search through her backpack, taking her time with it. She could not afford to leave her passport at the front desk overnight where it could be reviewed by others. And if she had to leave suddenly…

The young man, a student apparently, for he had been reading Ibsen’s *A Doll House*, wordlessly tossed the key to room 112 on the counter and dismissed the subject of the passport, pointing toward the narrow stair.

"Breakfast at eight o'clock," he said.

Climbing the stair to the first floor, she let herself into the stark room of chrome and plastic modernism. In contrast to the building’s dingy exterior, the room felt clean and spacious.

She sat on the edge of the bed, aware of a kind of homesickness for Les Grottes. It seemed like a lifetime ago she had encouraged Pascal with his ducks. In his memory she was a principal player. He would miss her. She missed him.

Over the next forty-eight hours she would not have time for yearnings or melancholy. Her phone card and the beige telephone beckoned to her. She would try to reach Ulrich in Careyes. Her other attempts had been hurried, distracted. Tonight she had all the time in the world. She tapped up the access code, followed by the Mexican phone number.

A welcoming sound, the carrier's chime, confirming the international call was going through. God bless American technology. And English-speaking operators.

The line rang in short bursts. She listened, tracing a thread in the quilted duvet-cover. It took her by surprise when the bursts cut off abruptly and a man answered.

"Ulrich?"

"Ye-es?" The playful Austrian sounded like a villainous Claude Rains.

"It's Kenna."

"The *fugitive*? You cannot believe the excitement you've brought to our little expatriate haven. Careyes hasn't enjoyed such a plague of journalists and international G-men since Lucan swam ashore from Goldsmith's yacht in the late 1970s. What a lark. Even Bianca is out-classed. And Lucky the bartender, disappeared. We all figure he must be on some FBI 'most-wanted' list somewhere."

"Please. Be serious. It's Michael I'm calling about. The circuits aren't very reliable there – your line may not be secure. Is Michael okay?"

"Believe it or not, the doctors have been hoarding anti-toxin supplies here since the 1950s. I've been declared a local hero! Jeep-driver saves tourist. I'll have a book contract in no time. All I have to do is finish writing my account of the last two weeks. 'Intrigue in Careyes.' What do you think of the title?"

The line was breaking up. "Can I speak with him? Where is he?"

"He's weak, Goldilocks. That's the truth. I'm looking after him. Keeping him 'under wraps.' Incommunicado. Sent for a doctor from the States. A Yankee-Doodle-medico. Don't think he should be moved. We're great pals, I'm going to – "

"Ulrich. Tell Michael I'll call again. I'm okay. Please tell him."

The line was suddenly empty of human voice.

She should have been relieved. Michael was alive. But in what condition. Shouldn't he be in an urban U.S. hospital with sophisticated equipment and medical care? She sat for some moments clutching her Celtic bracelet, feeling the cool resistance of the heavy gold. She longed to crawl under the tidy sheets and lose herself until the chaos could be over.

Instead, she got up and moved to the bathroom. The thick terry towels that graced every European hotel, regardless of the price of its rooms, sat folded on the chrome rack. She took a wash cloth and ran it under the water in the sink. Placing it over her face, she stood over the basin for several minutes, letting the fear and tension dissolve. Then she dried her cheeks and drew the combs from her hair, re-fastening it loosely with a covered band.

With fresh determination, she returned to the side of the bed, picked up the telephone, and connected once more to the international operator. She gave a number she knew well. For several seconds, she listened to the eerie sound of a transatlantic call connecting her to New York.

"Andrea Reich-Hermann speaking." The arch, over-educated tone of the Foreign Assets Secretary had a quickening effect on Kenna's pulse rate. She drew in a sharp breath.

"You're still in the office," she said into the echo.

There was a pause, and then. "*This* is a surprise. I hope you're calling to turn yourself in."

"I need your help actually. There isn't much time."

"I'm listening."

"I need you to call off the FBI. Klaus Kessel. Interpol. I'll give myself up voluntarily, *after* I've returned to New York."

"Why should I help you?"

"The charges are false. According to the indictment, a large cache of un-canceled bonds were in the Reichsbank vaults when the Red Army marched into Berlin in May, 1945. The prosecutor claims JAFA's bonds were stolen by Russian troops along with the rest of the bank's deposits. But the bonds couldn't have been in the vaults when the Russians arrived."

It took her a moment to realize Andrea was speaking over her, their words overlapping. The echo gave her a second chance to catch Andrea's sarcasm.

"Are you denying you're in possession of stolen bonds?"

"The contents of the vaults were moved to secret caves south of Berlin before the Allies' strike in February. The Russians never had the opportunity to liberate those caves. They never reached Berlin until May. I have a photograph – "

"Where are you?"

"Aren't you listening? I'll turn myself in, but I need your promise –"

" JAFA'S bonds are on Germany's list."

"There is no 'list.' Von Kadow is the Countess' brother – but you know that."

"Where'd you get this photograph?"

"Private archives. I can have it scanned and faxed tomorrow morning."

"You're near a scanner?"

*Careful, lass.*

"Tell the prosecutor to withdraw the arrest warrant immediately, I'll call you back for confirmation that it's been done." She would be free then to enter the settlements bank with the bonds.

"This photo," Andrea said. "What do you expect it to prove?"

"It's a dated war image of the Reichsbank from February, 1945. The bonds were not there. The bank was destroyed."

A sudden instinct for survival swept over her. It was not necessary to reveal all of the information André had given her. "Your records will confirm this, and the date of the Russians' arrival in Berlin. You have access to them."

"Nonsense, Kenna. Either you're very naive or your manner conceals a clever criminal mind. In any case, you're hip-deep in a scheme to trade illegal contraband. Did you ever wonder why Michael Fein would seek out a neophyte to represent JAFA? These so-called 'innocent' investors know the securities are worthless. The Jews want their day of retribution against Germany. And you're their 'drummer girl.' You personally mean nothing to Fein."

Kenna considered putting the phone down, walking into the bathroom and shutting the door until the ranting stopped.

"You could be working on Wall Street today, with a solid career path to the State Department. Instead, you're an accused felon. A fugitive. And now, murder. How do you look in prison-blue?"

Murder? The man who tried to kidnap Pascal.

"What exactly are you referring to?" Kenna asked.

The line was silent.

"JAFA has been very cooperative," Andrea said at last. "I've spoken with their new interim counsel. They're dismayed, naturally, by the fact that you attempted to murder their trustee and left him for dead in the Mexican airport. But they've very kindly thought to track your cell phone signal for us, something I didn't think of. I have JAFA's report of your itinerary right here. All they want is the return of their portfolio. Dubious though their bonds may be, they want them back. They have no desire to be part of an international financial scandal. I've promised to refrain from filing any formal charges against JAFA for the time being – provided you give yourself up by noon tomorrow. I can have a U.S. agent meet you in Zurich. Dufourstrasse 101, 3rd floor."

Zurich. One hour away. Andrea knew where she was.

Kenna would not let her voice betray the blow she had taken. "I'm leaving the phone now. I'm hanging up."

She replaced the telephone handset on its hook in the narrow room. Her right hand clasped her Celtic bracelet and she sat for several moments, trembling with an emotion she told herself was anger.

## 79

In the early hours the same morning, a green Lotus pulled up to an apartment building in the Kleinhuningen district of Basel, Switzerland. It was a good district, with old but imposing homes set back generously along broad, quiet boulevards, and having the advantage of immediate proximity to France on the west and Germany on the east.

No one came out to look at the man who emerged from the car. There was no one on the street, many of its residents working in the City's banking or government offices. A sudden burst of sun over-lit his pale face. With its broad flat planes it looked like a cracker that had not been quite baked enough.

His hair was the color of corn threads and clung sinuously to his scalp. He wore a dark turtleneck and dark scarf knotted at the throat of his Burberry which flapped away from his lean body as if accustomed to his impatient movements. Despite the expected warmth of the day, he wore a pair of shiny black gloves that fit him like a surgeon's.

The doorman admitted Klaus Kessel, greeting him with a perfunctory cheerfulness meant to disguise some wariness in his voice. The response he received in return was that usually reserved for a beetle one is too preoccupied to squash. The service man quickly averted his eyes toward the street.

Kessel strode to the elevator, got in and using a key, transported himself to the fifth floor which opened into the living room of a luxury apartment. He had forsworn staying at the apartment when he arrived at midnight in favor of a suite at the Hotel Three Kings, unwilling to risk arousing the apartment building's resident busybody Frau Grenat and her tirelessly vigilant Jack Russell terriers.

With a grim smile, the CIA man seated himself at the desk overlooking the street. He pulled at the fingers of his gloves in abrupt, angry movements. Somewhere in this strategic port city of three hundred thousand people, the lawyer was making her plans to redeem the bonds.

He had yet to make sense of Andrea Reich's hysterical phone message. "Rand is in Switzerland. She could be in Basel already. She plans to scan a photograph to send to me. Find her and pick her up immediately. Station yourself at the Bank around the clock if you need to."

Dear Andrea. Rand in Basel already. An infant could have told him that. What photograph? What did it matter. Did the hysterical woman expect him to careen around Basel in a dented Fiat interrogating innkeepers? The cinematic approach, no doubt, but useless.

Simpler to arrange surveillance of the Bank, as he had already done. The lawyer would have to show up there. That's what she was here for. Would she show up today or tomorrow? Would she arrive in the morning or afternoon? When she arrived, not if, how would he prevent her getting inside the bank?

With his left hand free of his glove, he checked the time, pulled the desk phone closer to him, and tapped a number that connected him to von Kadow's chateau.

After perhaps thirty seconds, he spoke into the desk speaker, punctuating his words by clicking the fingers of his gloveless hand in a fast angry pattern.

For his "telephone voice," Kessel had cultivated the accent, if not the lovable warmth, of the Austrian film star from California.

'Such a long time in America,' people said, 'and you still speak with an accent, especially on the telephone.' Yes? So what? If his voice was part of his artifice, it served his purposes. And lacking that effusive and telegenic quality of the California actor, it was a very scary voice.

"Have you called Raskoff at BIS?" he demanded when von Kadow had been summoned to the phone.

"Do you have any idea what time it is? I don't take my coffee until nine o'clock."

"Raskoff, you idiot."

"I really cannot get involved, Kessel."

"You should have thought of that before."

"If I must review my position for you," the Prince said, "I submitted the letter to your Foreign Assets Secretary based upon reliable information provided to me. The letter speaks for itself. I have no problem explaining its contents at this point. There's no need for me to take the extra step of attempting to quash JAFA's bond tender. That would be excessive. People will question my motives. Look into my relationships. And you know where that leads. I – I have a life here. Reputation and influence… Anyway, Raskoff is probably still sleeping. Or dandling his children on his knee over news of the DAX."

"I need your help," Kessel said in a tone that was anything but conciliatory.

"Must I say it again? This is a matter for you and Fabia. I am a banker, after all. I'm on the Board."

"That's why I'm calling you, you pretentious moron. This was supposed to be a manageable exercise. Young woman. Folio of bonds. A number of lugubrious mistakes have been made, all by others. Your sister seems to feel it's my obligation to retrieve the bonds for her. That's secondary now. In my judgment, it's absolutely necessary that I apprehend this lawyer before she delivers the bonds to your cretin-cohorts at the bank."

"You speak so formally Kessel! What's stopping you for heaven's sake? You have two assistants now, don't you?"

“Nothing is ‘stopping’ me. I can detain her outside. That’s not the issue. I want Raskoff’s cooperation in authorizing an arrest on Bank premises.”

Von Kadow issued a mirthless laugh. "It seems to me you might make the contest interesting."

"What are you talking about?"

"Blood sport. Don't you want a fair game? Give the hare a few yards start over the hounds? Let her get inside, Kessel. Let her submit the bonds for payment. Then let's see what you're made of. He, he!” He gave an annoying Austrian bleat that suggested a dirty little joke had been made. “Let's see what you do when the odds are equal."

Kessel’s ungloved hand started to systematically prick the blotter with the letter opener, creating an ugly pattern in the leather surface. How had things come to this? The subject he had so elegantly dispatched to a Manhattan jail cell would shortly be on her way to BIS with bearer bonds worth billions of dollars. Once accepted, the demand would be subject to international scrutiny. Germany’s denial of liability would not be the end of it. Not by any means. Greedy, stupid mistakes – by others. But it did not change the fact that it was his professional reputation on the line. He could not simply assail his superiors with a litany of excuses: “But she… and they… then Tode…” Ludicrous. All his careful planning – crashed, burned, descent into flaming hell.

"Don't you want a true contest?" von Kadow said, goading him. The banker gave an amused sniff. "No finesse with you, Kessel. No sense of fair play."

"You refuse to call Raskoff?"

"He wouldn't get involved anyway. Much too late in the game for the Swiss to openly take Germany's side. World opinion, against it. That’s why I can’t get involved. How would it look? How could I explain my own knowledge of things?"

That was it then.

"I'll call him myself. He should be informed of what's on his plate for today. Give me his direct line to his home."

"No. God no, Kessel. Don't do anything like that. Raskoff will only panic. He'll show her every courtesy if he thinks she's associated with JAFA. No sane man wants to oppose Jewish interests at this point. Are you mad? The last thing Raskoff wants is to be linked to some German conspiracy to avoid Nazi liability. Go there yourself. Don't be so spineless. Pick her up outside. Solve the problem. My God, man, it's not up to me to tell you your business."

Unfortunately, the idiot's assessment was correct. Gunter Raskoff, the director of BIS, was a scared rabbit of a Eurocrat. Switzerland had come under criticism for its so-called "neutrality," which turned out, under history's long-view, to be merely a slightly passive, and highly mercenary, face of Fascism. The Swiss would not be drawn into any dispute that affected Germany and the United States. That was where von Kadow was right. No. You could not rely on Raskoff, squirrel that he was. Though Kessel would have preferred to have the bank's management in on his plans, it was useless, even risky, to call BIS at this point.

"Good luck," von Kadow said cheerfully and then added, "My francs are on the lawyer."

Kessel put down the phone, aware of the vein that had started to pulsate in his left temple. The imbecile had hung up before Kessel could terminate the conversation. He felt a childish impulse to call the man back in order to hang up on him, and made a concerted effort to remain calm as he considered the situation.

So what if she arrived at the bank today? She wouldn't get inside. He'd already taken care of that contingency. In place of the bank's private security firm Securitas, he had installed Meister's two Slovakians. He did not like dealing with agents whom he did not know. Tode had been an example of what can happen when you hire subordinates whose tendencies you cannot predict. Slovakian agents were known for sadism.

What could you expect? They'd recently come from a police state, where violence and torture were de rigeur. With the fall of Communism, you had thousands of trained assassins out of a job. Kessel himself had changed with the times. Less violence, more brains.

Not much of a choice, though, was there? When he had called the agents last night, they'd seemed reasonably competent to accomplish what they were told. They were to call him as soon as she arrived and detain her until he got there. At nine o'clock he would check in with them to make sure they were at their posts. Then, he could do nothing until she arrived. In the meantime, he would have a fine, if overdue breakfast, make some calls, and rendez-vous at the bank in the afternoon. Assuming all went as planned, he would transport the girl back to New York tonight. If something happened to her on the way…

# 80

It was two forty-five that afternoon when Kenna stepped off the tram at Basel's Central-Bahn and proceeded toward the imposing glass and gold structure overlooking the Rhine. The Bank for International Settlements was less than a block away. That gave her more than an hour to work with, as the bank closed at four o'clock.

It was a cool day but clear, with dramatic skies. A good day for photographs, she thought. She'd lifted a postcard of the bank from the reception desk at her hotel. The building had been erected in 1971, as Switzerland was enjoying the euphoria of market expansion. It resembled a series of spinning plates set on top of one another. The entrance was set back perhaps ten meters from the street under a low eave that formed the first platter. Shallow steps of unpolished marble led to a central revolving door.

She'd felt extremely nervous when she'd started out and now felt incredibly calm. This had to do with her decision to fine-tune her simple plan, refining her "script" during the swift tram ride through the old section of Basel.

She would present herself as the Countess. It was a risky masquerade, but necessary. After her conversation with Andrea, she could take no chances on being recognized. The blue Givenchy suit and short suede gloves she had borrowed from Ginger Lebecque's wardrobe were elegant, but definitely retro. Donning them, she felt like Audrey Hepburn in 'Sabrina.'

The hat seemed excessive, but its half-veil appeared an affectation the Countess would assume. A speed-tour of the shops around her hotel had been worthwhile. The pharmacy offered hair lightener and a heavy pancake make-up two shades darker than her facial skin. And lucky find, a millinery store. It was a surprise how the combination of hat and foundation added ten years to her appearance.

Before she'd left her room in the Hotel Leipzig, she'd checked her mirror reflection against the photo of Countess' passport, and found a passing resemblance. Thanks to two peroxide applications and a card of hairpins, hair color and coiffure were now reasonably similar to the Argentine woman's. Kenna's eyes were gray, Countess' were brown. But their color hardly mattered behind the tinted lenses the Countess wore. She lifted the half-veil and put the dark glasses on. The effect would not withstand serious scrutiny. But it could get her inside the bank.

Mentally she checked all: passport; letter of introduction from "Prince von Kadow;" attaché containing the bonds. Her posture had always been good. Now she pulled her shoulders back even more dramatically.

Across the street from the bank was the Euler hotel bar. She entered the terrace. Choosing a table that afforded a clear view of the street, she sat down to wait and watch, to make sure she was not walking into a trap.

Only a dull throb remained of the pain in her knee. The Basel physician recommended by Ginger Lebecque had seen Kenna promptly at nine o'clock and treated her injured leg without question, all the while knowing her new patient was wanted by Interpol and the doctor was jeopardizing herself by helping Kenna.

Dr. Milan had cleaned the wound thoroughly, and it hurt like blazes, even more than Ginger's cleansing. Then Dr. Milan had started to apply a clean bandage, but Kenna declined any treatment that would call attention to the wound.

She was able to walk without limping. She had demanded an injection of steroid-cortisone, in the dosage given athletes who must play despite their injury. Dr. Milan did not recommend it. "You will injure it further. Such things take time to heal. Permanent damage could result."

These were the same admonitions that Kenna would have given were she in the doctor's place. But she was not in her place. There was only the single moment in time to turn in the bonds. She needed all of her physical strength to play the game to the end.

Kenna had tried to pay Dr. Milan for treating her. Two hundred Swiss francs had been forced into her hand by André Lebecque the evening before as the train stood ready to depart the small station. But the doctor wouldn't hear of it.

"When I am visiting New York and hunted by the police, you will take me in," the doctor said lightly. "It will be extremely helpful to have the favor of your friendship."

Manhattan was going to be well-populated with eccentrics Kenna thought, recalling the African in whose cab she had hurtled through the streets of Paris. She could not repress a smile at the thought of Bouvier and the good doctor as her house guests. Perhaps Rosa the hotel florist could schedule a visit as well.

In the end, Dr. Milan had kissed her on both cheeks and wished her "safe journée." It was little enough. But Kenna's heightened emotions were such that tears came at the woman's kindness.

It was time to begin. She hesitated. Why did she not cross the street and enter the bank? She recognized an acute case of stage fright. Once begun, there would be no turning back. Once inside, there would be only one way out.

Kenna drew forward and lifted the half-veil again. A beefy young man in quilted windbreaker and navy beret had moved to straddle the shallow steps leading to the bank, placing himself in the best position to stop anyone approaching the revolving doors.

A guard. Was that usual? He would watch her approach. What would he say when she entered, what would *she* say to him?

The thought of proceeding under his hostile eyes brought on her nervousness again. She felt her pulse pounding. This was no good. She resumed her seat and touched the passport in the pocket of her suit. I have a right to be here. I have business with the bank.

The waiter arrived. He spoke French and German and she curtly agreed on French. She ordered an Orangina and pretended to look at the menu. That was all right with him. It was after the lunch hour and well before dinner. He could not have cared less if the over-dressed patron who regarded him through dark lenses idled at her terrace table, waiting for some assignation.

The waiter moved to the bar, returning swiftly with her drink. He stood close to her table as he transferred the orange liquid from bottle to glass.

Kenna looked up to find his attention focused on the attaché. She instinctively tightened her fingers on the leather grip. The waiter met her eyes. His smile was not a pleasant one. She took a swallow of the cool drink.

"L'account, s'il vous plait," she said sharply.

As he moved away, Kenna started. Across the street a police car had pulled up. A Swiss policeman got out and approached the guard. There occurred then gesturing by the police officer and shrugging by the guard and, to her alarm, the officer turned and started across the street toward the café. The second policeman emerged from the police car and moved to follow his partner.

She surveyed the terrace for escape possibilities. Inside, a lobby stairway led to rooms that looked out over the café. Past the kitchen lay a dark hallway that likely gave onto the strasse behind the Central Bahn. She rejected the idea, afraid of getting lost so close to her prize.

Instead she rose, prepared to exit as she'd come. She would fall in behind the well-dressed Italian businessman who was also leaving the café.

Then she caught the action on the street. Perhaps ten feet from her a vagrant, weathered and wary-eyed, had attracted the officers' attention.

The vagrant, dressed in ragged high-top sneakers and a soiled jogging suit, had encamped in a flower bed next to the café, and now occupied herself in organizing her possessions on a torn quilt.

At BIS the guard stood absorbed in the distraction produced by the gendarmerie. Excellent. She would proceed toward the Bainhof, cross the street several meters down and approach from the side. Then, up the steps and through the bronze revolving doors. She visualized it all. Perfect.

The waiter appeared out of nowhere, presenting a bill for three francs fifty. Absently, she placed one of André's hundred franc notes on the tray and moved to leave.

"Attendez, Madame." The waiter moved to detain her. "This bill is too large."

"I have nothing smaller," Kenna said, proceeding briskly toward the steps.

The waiter followed, weaving among the empty chairs and tables. What was he doing?

"Something smaller, if you please."

Kenna continued toward the street.

He came abreast of her and barred her way, releasing a volley of French. Did she intend to leave without paying? It was not fair. She took advantage. To change the note would require all of the small bills from the bar. None would be available for the patrons who came at five o'clock.

The irony did not escape her. The attaché contained a fortune in bearer bonds. What did a hundred francs matter?

"Keep it," she said fiercely, her eyes on the action below. The police, having bullied the homeless woman for several minutes, had tired of the game. Satisfied that she would not produce any papers of identification or, more likely hadn't any, they bundled her across the street and into the back of the police car.

Kenna watched in panic. The guard's attention was still on the scuffle. Soon the moment would be lost.

At that instant the woman commenced a horrible whimpering sound like a wounded beast. Clawing for her possessions, her hands flailed toward the sky. A struggle ensued to restrain her.

There was something odd about the woman – beyond her disoriented manner. Kenna felt an instinct to rush from the terrace, gather up the tattered mementos and deliver them to her. Yet she remained frozen on the steps.

The prisoner was wrestled into handcuffs efficiently enough, but the moaning continued even after the car's doors were closed. The woman began lobbing her head against the glass as the vehicle pulled away.

That's how quickly it could happen. That's how quickly freedom could be lost.

She tore her eyes away from the drama and consulted her watch. Nearly three-thirty. She must start now. She drew a deep breath and, with a last glance at the stone letters on the building across the street from her that spelled out Bank for International Settlements – she descended the terrace steps to the street.

# 81

Bridget McNey was the twenty-year old cab driver who, half an hour before, had deposited the female vagrant in front of the Euler Terrace. She wondered if the doltish sod guarding the Bank, in beret and parka–not to mention a small handgun and holster visible when he moved–remembered her. She doubted it very much. She wondered where his book-end from this morning had gone–the one with a small sub-machine gun strapped under his parka. There had been two of them. Now there was one. Extended pit-stop probably. Or enjoying a quick brew and sausages across the street.

Now she pulled the empty cab around the corner and parked.

She got out and smoked a cigarette, a Marlboro. She'd bought several packs of them on her single visit to the United States. She liked the flying stallions and cowboys featured in the adverts. Somewhere, she had been told, there was a Marlboro Ranch, and Marlboro General Store. The adverts were all about Nature and the American West. Marlboro Country.

She was a Marlboro woman, she reflected. Tough, by nature. Like the young women she knew from the States. Witness Madonna. Bridget was tough too, thanks to the harsh training of her father and brothers. Bridget drew from her jacket the disposable cell phone and tapped in the numbers she'd been given.

“She’s here already. You’ll be surprised at her get-up.” She listened, taking a long satisfying drag on her smoke before responding to the voice at the other end.

"Yeah – I'll stick it ‘til you get here."

Bridget snapped the phone shut. As she did so, she looked up to find the young woman approaching her.

# 82

"Is your cab free?" Kenna asked in German.

The driver who, with her bare-arm tattoo and glittering nose-stud, looked like one of the city's young toughs, lifted her chin in assent. She made a silent, sardonic invitation for the lawyer to enter the cab.

Across the street from the Euler Terrace, the guard was still absorbed in his self-importance. He had not noticed the taxi on the side street.

Kenna got into the back seat.

The young woman closed the door, stubbed out her cigarette and climbed into the driver's seat.

"Do you speak any English?" Kenna asked her.

"It's okay," the driver replied.

"I have a request," Kenna said, speaking carefully. "I need you to circle the block and drop me at the entrance to the bank across the street. I have a hundred francs. That's all I have. But it's yours. Just go around the block and drop me there in front." She watched the woman as she spoke, expecting to repeat herself.

The driver started the car immediately. She proceeded steadily up the street to the strasse behind the Euler bar, turned right, then u-turned through oncoming traffic, sped into the left lane and turned left, and left again, in order to ensure that her passenger would step from the cab in front of the guard. Clever girl.

Kenna had considered crossing the street some ways down, near the train station, in order to limit the time the guard would have to confront her. However, without any street drama to distract him, he would have had all the time in the world to notice her and wonder why she had not simply crossed the street from the Euler bar, or why she had been in the Euler bar at all if she had urgent business with the bank.

The lawyer disembarked from the taxi, handing the driver her last franc note. To her surprise, the girl laid in her palm the proper change, snatching up five francs tip with a grin at the last minute. Kenna leaned into the cab, taking her time to retrieve the attaché.

In truth, she was bracing herself for the performance, her level of tension the same as if the starting gun was about to go off and the race would begin. She shut the door and turned quickly, gave a little run up the steps and swept by the guard with just the right amount of confidence. He started forward as if to detain her. His hand slipped behind his open jacket and rested lightly in the area where his gun butt must be. Soldier he was, she was sure of it, or ex-soldier. And he was armed. That was not easy to be sure of, not something readily confirmed from where she stood. But – yes, the bulge of a holster could be glimpsed beneath his jacket. She tilted her head, slightly frowning. The young man thought better of it, tipped his chin, and smiled. Swinging through the bank's revolving doors, she smiled back.

# 83

Two men in dark blue suits and vests watched with mild eyes as Kenna entered the vast lobby and approached their glass cage marked "Reception."

The echo of her footsteps felt disquieting. The steroids had not kicked in one hundred percent. It took all of her control to avoid the impulse to favor her good leg. Summoning the image of the Countess one last time, she stepped to the window.

"Good afternoon," she said, imitating the educated British Isles accent of her Irish relations, and waiting, as though she knew what was to follow.

The shorter man swung a stemmed microphone toward himself and spoke through the glass.

"May I help you?"

She withdrew from her attaché the letter she'd prepared on Ginger Lebecque's computer. It was addressed to "*Herr Gunter Raskoff, Direktor*" with, she had to admit, a pretty good semblance of von Kadow's crest and signature. She slid it under the glass.

Nothing in the man's manner spelled hesitation or concern. Nothing from the other one either, who scanned the letter with indifference . He was a supervisor apparently, stone-faced and gut-heavy. Too many sausages, she thought.

The supervisor seemed bored. The other man relieved – that she knew the procedures, that she gave the name of the bank's director, that the letter mentioned an appointment.

He ran his finger along a list of names highlighted in yellow, dialed a number, then spoke in a low voice to the person on the other end of the line, his hand over the microphone. She watched him turn to the supervisor with a question, then respond crisply into the open line.

He indicated an area of chrome and leather chairs, set around a huge low table of tobacco-colored marble. "Please to wait," he said. "You take coffee also?"

"That would be lovely," she said, trying for the right note of hauteur. She could not mimic the Countess' thick Argentine accent, but a touch of trans-Atlantic formality could fill in nicely.

She took a seat where she could observe both the lobby and the street outside. The imposing young man in windbreaker and navy beret who had watched her enter the bank had been joined by another similarly dressed.

*Two* menacing clones. And it was too late to dwell on the question they posed – with escape by the front doors barred, how would she get out if things went south?

Five long minutes went by. Then a smartly dressed blond clicked toward her from a door off the lobby, carrying a small tray with a demitasse and silver bowl. The bowl's hallmark, a winged eagle, stirred her memory.

The woman spoke with sly civility. "I am sorry. We have checked our records. There is no appointment. But perhaps you knew that."

"There must be some mistake," Kenna replied evenly. "An appointment was arranged. I'm sure of it. In any case, I must see Herr Raskoff this afternoon."

"Herr Direktor is busy."

"I'll wait."

"We can perhaps accommodate you tomorrow?"

"I need to see him today."

The secretary needled one of her shoes into the floor, flicking her bracelets as she did so. "I will tell him of your preference," she said darkly.

The espresso was too strong for Kenna, especially under the circumstances. Every sip increased her anxiety. Yet she felt she must pretend to drink it under the subtle observation of the two men behind the reception glass.

She had been only mildly surprised at the vast empty lobby. Her research had confirmed that BIS was a central bank, serving only other banks of Europe. There were no tellers, no teller's cages, notaries, or any of the retail characteristics denoting a consumer banking institution. So discreet were its workings, she could almost believe she had trespassed upon the offices of a government think-tank.

Five minutes more passed before the impatient young woman returned. "Herr Raskoff will see you. I explained your visit will be brief."

# 84

Herr Raskoff pressed von Kadow's letter between his thumb and forefinger as if he held a counterfeit franc.

As the blighted woman who sat across from him suggested, the bank's failure to process the bonds would mean hell to pay in the international press. Swiss bankers cheat the Jews – again!

He had no compunction about keeping her waiting in silence before him, like an entreating subject before her sovereign. It was she who had come to cause trouble at the end of a perfectly routine day. He rifled the papers she'd brought with growing irritation. She had the correct papers. Proper documentation.

Tall and correct, with gray hair brushed back from his temples, the bank director asked for her identification card.

"Is that really necessary?"

"You carry I.D. with you, don't you?" He was proud of using the English term.

She had not let herself consider this moment. To rely on the Countess' photo would be disastrous. The obvious differences, aquiline nose where Kenna's was small; full lips in contrast to Kenna's restrained mouth – were easily noticeable, although the photo had been taken at least a decade ago. And the passport raised other obvious questions, such as date of birth, country of origin.

He tried an indulgent smile, meeting the eyes of his secretary Teni, who hovered in the doorway like a sergeant at arms. "Come now, I have never known photography to improve upon an attractive subject."

He extended his palm to receive the document.

Kenna produced the passport, holding the page with the photograph toward him.

He moved her hand firmly to expose the passport number, tipping his head to one side to regard briefly the Countess' image. Kenna held her breath, certain that, while the general appearance might be similar, the older woman's features would not withstand comparison with the young woman before him. After a pause, he copied the number onto his tablet in a neat and legible hand. Without looking up, he asked: "You speak English in Argentina?"

"I learned it abroad," she said. "Boarding school."

"So." He closed the passport and passed it back to her. Much as he wished to consider the situation more fully, to call von Kadow, or check with another bank director at the very least, he knew it was down to him. All she asked was that he accept tender of registration today. As she had intimated, if he failed even to allow registration of the bonds, Germany's debt could become the bank's liability.

Rotten Americans! What a mare's nest. Raskoff rose abruptly. In a strangely formal gesture of dismissal, he bowed to Kenna.

"You will be comfortable in the lobby, Countess," he said. And then, to his secretary:

"Teni, take the portfolio to Heinrich. Tell him to compare the serial numbers to our records and make a copy. Get on with it. It is almost four o'clock."

Kenna followed the blond from the office, almost weak with relief.

## 85

She had performed well so far. She had tried not to appear nervous, though the air felt heavy with tension.

The man introduced to her as Heinrich, the bank's foreign securities director, continued to smile at his desk off the lobby, and lift his countenance reassuringly, as though the bonds she'd left with him for copying would be brought to her any second.

The lobby had grown stuffy. Kenna missed the white noise of the air conditioning system that had shut down a few minutes ago. She realized it could mean only one thing. The work day was over, the bank would be closing soon.

She had chosen a seat where she could watch the street unobtrusively. For the last fifteen minutes the two guards had not changed from their position, though one had taken a call on his cellular phone. She could see his lips moving and the nervous twitch of his shoulders.

Without turning her head she remained aware of movement around her. Maybe it was just the time of day. It seemed to Kenna that the lobby was filling with people. Sometime within the last ten minutes the number of male occupants had doubled.

She felt almost hypnotized, partly from fear, partly from the stifling air. She massaged her knee. The sharp stabbing pain had returned as the drugs wore off. And she felt uncomfortably warm. Wretched Swiss. Saving a few francs on energy. When would the bonds be registered? When could she walk out of here?

A large chrome clock dominated the wall to her left. The long hand jerked forward, bringing the time to five minutes until four o'clock.

Now Heinrich picked up his telephone. She could remain still no longer. She approached the reception island. The men who had greeted her twenty minutes before refused to meet her eyes.

"Could you call Herr Raskoff's secretary?"

"Hasn't she finished with you?"

"No."

A pause. "Very well."

Once again the shorter one swung the microphone toward his chin and spoke into it. Once again he gestured for Kenna to wait. Thin-lipped he added, "She is coming."

Kenna remained standing by reception. Time was wasting, her posture seemed to say, and he would pay dearly for it.

The snap of the blond's heels across the floor conveyed her irritation at being summoned from her desk.

"What is it now Countess?" she asked.

"It's almost four o'clock. I'm concerned Heinrich is taking too long to register the bonds. And now –" Kenna's impatience at this new development could not be concealed, "he's on the phone."

"What can I do – intercept his calls?"

"Herr Raskoff agreed the bonds would be registered today."

"Heinrich won't be long. It's a call within the building."

How did she know that? "The bank closes in five minutes. We have to finish right now."

"We may need you to come back tomorrow."

"That's impossible."

"It would be best."

For who?

Kenna spoke with the precision of one speaking to a child. "Is the German government willing to extend the deadline? If Herr Raskoff will personally confirm the extension..."

The woman's lips pursed with the unexpected challenge to her authority.

"Deadline? I know nothing about that. The German Secretary-General is the only one who can decide such a thing. He arrives tomorrow at ten o'clock. You can ask him yourself.

"There. You see? Heinrich is off the phone now."

Heinrich raised a finger of reassurance – any minute now.

The man wearing a black leather jacket and black jeans stood impatiently just outside the bronze street doors. His eyes were hidden behind wraparound ski lenses. The shadow cast by the overhanging canopy obscured his face. But she recognized his movement, the way he had of looking without stirring, the habit of one accustomed to the hunt.

## 86

Five minutes earlier, the green Lotus had pulled up in front of the Bank for International Settlements. Its occupant strode to the first guard and addressed him in German. He had tired of waiting for their call and knew instinctively that something had gone wrong. Either they had left their posts or – he could scarcely hope – the lawyer had decided to abort.

Something the guard conveyed to Kessel caused the CIA man's body to tense and reel back, only slightly, but enough so that the guard felt compelled to hasten his account, gesturing with one hand to suggest the upswept coiffure of a stylish woman.

The gesture set off some alarm in Kessel that turned swiftly to fury. "Idiot." He removed from his pocket a leather folio containing a photograph, and presented it for study by the guard. The latter placed his two index fingers to his lips, then slowly moved his head up and down.

"This *is* her? Is she inside?"

The big, baby-faced guard took a step back as if he feared being struck.

For an instant Kessel's self-control appeared to be touch and go. In fact, he appeared to be on the brink of a physical episode.

"Well?"

The soldier answered tentatively that he did not think it was the girl in the photograph, the girl with dark hair and intense slate colored eyes. But if Kessel was looking for a streaked blond with an upswept hairdo and oversized dark glasses, such a woman had, in fact, entered the building almost a half hour before. Then, as if his own words had managed to reverse his decision, he stumbled onward, developing the idea that, indeed, she *had* appeared somewhat youthful beneath the heavy pancake makeup, about the right size and build. He remembered an athletic quickness in her step and . . .

By this time Kessel had lost all patience. He jerked his head to see inside, unable to make out what he wanted due to the dark filtering of the glass. He did, however, catch his reflection and for a moment, he seemed transfixed by it. Admiring his manicured and perfect baldness, just a fringe of pale hair, with eyes the color of new leaves and skin shining with health. The vein across his forehead showed strength. When, as now, his temper flared it became engorged with blood, blue and pulsating with fury.

*Exkrement.* He deserved better than this. With a quick movement of his hand he summoned both guards. The three men entered the bank.

# 87

The female cab driver whom Kessel had brushed by rudely as he ran up the steps of the bank stubbed out her cigarette. He had looked at her briefly and she wondered if he would remember her. She doubted it.

For the second time that afternoon, she drew from her jacket the cell phone and pressed redial. She listened and then spoke just as quickly as the voice at the other end.

"He just went in. Nose out of joint actually. Our girl got here before he did. She's inside now." Bridget gave a quick sniff of admiration. "Got by the bloody thugs at the door. And, yeah – " She peered inside the bank. “It’s show time.”

# 88

Get out. *Get out.* Without waiting for a second glance at Klaus Kessel who was pushing his way through the revolving entrance doors, Kenna picked up the attaché and started moving.

Swinging by the desk of the Foreign Securities Director only briefly, she swept the documents into her portfolio, stuffing the bonds inside with rough accuracy.

"I'll take them now," she said, moving past a surprised Heinrich – who had risen in protest. She continued in the direction of a passage behind reception, where she'd observed a thin stream of visitors exiting a few minutes before.

The practical Swiss. The bank had been planned in the early 1970s, a time of commercial optimism. What could be more efficient than a private corridor linking the international bank to the central train station? A discreet directional sign confirmed it:

*"Bainhof."*

She had only to make it through that door at the rear of the lobby, then a three hundred meter sprint to the tracks. Board the train, any train. At this time of day the express to Zurich Airport ran every ten minutes. Just get to the tracks.

# 89

Kessel had not seen her. Seconds passed as his eyes adjusted to the gloom of the vast space. Then he observed the woman, dressed to the nines, and making for the rear exit with swift composure.

Couture suit, elegant pumps. He wasn't expecting to see her in such formal attire, despite the guard's report. For an instant, he was startled. But he recovered quickly as his glance lighted upon her attaché. He issued a low bark in German that sent the two Slovakian guards fanning out along the walls to meet her at the exit.

He could not alarm the dunces at reception, or any of the bank visitors now leaving through the front doors. Raskoff would not countenance a skirmish on the lobby floor. Anyway, it was too dangerous. For all Kessel knew, she'd already tendered the bonds. The game had to be played with precision from this point onward. He had to take her quietly.

The CIA man knew something that Kenna did not. At exactly four o'clock the exits would be sealed. With the perfection of Swiss watchmaking, steel bars concealed in the door-frames were timed to descend. Very soon, the open lobby would become a fortress.

Glancing behind her, Kenna's heart began to race. Kessel moved fast, leather jacket flapping sinuously. There was something so determined in the man. So relentless. She considered giving herself up. Here, inside the bank, she would be assured of some protection. Or would she? She thought of

Dominique's blood on the floor of the Lebecque kitchen. No. Giving up was not an option.

"Countess –" Raskoff's secretary appeared from nowhere. "Come back, please," she said as a command. "You must sign this book before leaving."

In her peripheral vision, Kenna saw the two guards advancing with grim deliberation. They would not run, she thought. That would be an unacceptable breach of bank protocol. She knew with certainty now, Kessel hadn't planned for her to get this far.

She took in the large hand of the big clock as it lurched forward, and divined what Kessel had known all along. Already, a series of gleaming steel spikes protruded from panels over the exits, commencing their slow, resolute journey to a track in the floor. Very soon, the bars would close off the entrance to the Bainhof tunnel. Unless she got there first, there would be no way out.

"Stop! You will be hurt. Stop immediately." The shouts from the men at reception reached her faintly like the roar of the crowd at the finish line. She did not need to look back to feel the blond, Teni, closing the distance between them. The pace of the guards, too, had quickened. And still no drama. Everyone observing the rules. No alarm, no threats, no guns. Why should there be?

Only Kessel could break the rules. After all, he had the U.S. government behind him, the stature of the United States, while she was wanted by Interpol. She felt the guards move for their guns. She knew then how it would be. They would take her at gunpoint, despite the presence of civilians. A terrible memory swept over her. She saw again the vagrant, moaning and lobbing her head against the windows of the police car. But she, Kenna, was not a helpless tramp.

She halted within six feet of the exit, conscious of the panic behind her as her pursuers realized what she had planned for the finish of this event. Keep your nerve, Michael had told her. With the agility of a dancer who had trained for just this performance, she folded her body into the low bend of a downhill racer. Clasping the case to her chest, she made a short, running approach and flung herself under the bars with four inches to spare.

Adios, Cowboys.

Elation was brief. When she tried to stand, she couldn't. Her jacket had caught. In this moment, she was helpless, dragged toward the floor by the moving spikes. She twisted violently to free herself, forcing her fingers up her back to explore the problem. Sensing weakness in the fabric, she gave a last violent tug and tore free.

But Teni the terror was right behind her. The blond clawed for Kenna's shoulder and missed, catching a ball of fabric in her fist. She held Kenna fast, wringing the jacket through the bars. "You must come back. Now!"

Bloody pit bull. Let go! Kenna had no time to reason with the woman. She could hear the guards shouting in German. She tore at the buttons on her suit jacket, shrugging it from her shoulders. Transferring the bond folio to her right hand, she slipped out of first one sleeve, then the other, passing the attaché hand to hand.

In an instant she was free, racing down the corridor to the trains. Behind her Teni was red-faced and furious. The guards drew their guns, giving a half-hearted shout for Kenna to stop. So that's how it worked. First, the perfunctory warning – then the bullet in the back. She could hear the sound of the bars going up, as the gears reversed. An over-ride system. It was only a matter of seconds before the soldiers would scramble through. But it was Teni who appeared most agitated, Kenna couldn't help thinking, especially for one holding a Givenchy couture jacket, circa 1984.

## 90

"Stop her!" Kessel roared in German at the two soldiers. "Don't let her get to the trains."

He turned and ran toward the entrance. From the street he would cross the plaza to the station, out the rear doors and down the steps to the tracks. He noted the time on the station clock as he emerged from the bank. He had to reach her before she boarded the commuter for Zurich. A million thoughts consumed him. The chase through the bank had raised eyebrows. In a small city like Basel there would be questions. He wondered if his first instinct, to take her back alive, was not unrealistic. A vision of Gabriela scorched his memory for an instant. Would he never be free of that? But he would not have to kill the lawyer in that way. It was not unheard of for a fugitive to fall in front of a train.

## *91*

The corridor connecting the bank to the bainhof was long and narrow and curved. At this time of day it was well lit by lamps that threw Kenna's shadow on the wall behind her, tall and menacing, like the shadows in a Hitchcock film. The guards' excited voices reached her, enough to confirm the steel bars had been raised and the soldiers were on the point of scrambling through.

An artery from another government building fed into the tunnel and a few fellow passengers trickled in. She felt reasonably sure she could elude her pursuers until she reached the tracks. But the voice inside her that knew about such things saw there would be more trouble upon reaching the station. Kessel was not a fool. He would have gone the long way around in order to catch her coming out of the tunnel. He would be looking for her, with his two thugs arriving from behind.

Now she heard steps approaching from the quay, a crowd by the sounds of it.

Kenna felt a spasm in her calf. Her knee wanted to lock up. She babied it with a speed-limp that must have looked painful. It was.

Not here. Not now.

The guards' footsteps raced along the corridor behind her, terminating all hopes of retreat. Ahead, a man and two women surged into the passageway, filling it. The man wore a billowing trench coat and flowing scarf. He was flanked by two women armed with barely-concealed submachine guns. What the bloody hell was this?

Moving like boxers – or dancers – the trio swept toward Kenna. She jogged to one side, trying not to slow her own pace. To her shock, they surged around her, sweeping her into their circle and back along the corridor to the tracks. She nearly fell several times, determined to use their momentum to propel herself out and away. Like a grunion caught in a rip tide, she burst with them from the tunnel into an iron and concrete landscape, where Klaus Kessel waited, adrenaline-pumped, clenching and unclenching a gloved fist.

"Shit!" Kessel's instant comprehension translated into shouted epithets at the two guards who emerged into view behind Kenna and forced their way through throngs of business commuters making for the trains.

Kessel drew his handgun.

"Don't get me started, lad," the male reveler pushed Kenna roughly behind him.

"T'would be a bloody shame to waste the innocents."

The words were hardly finished when one of the young women around Kenna let loose a volley of gunfire into the stones behind Kessel. She quickly turned her weapon on the two guards, who dropped to the ground.

Screams and pandemonium followed. Frightened commuters rushed to the safety of the terminal or threw themselves onto the platform. Station guards came out of nowhere and surged into the tunnel, almost colliding with the Slovakians who had risen hastily to their feet.

Kenna was swept through the chaos up a series of steps, up again on the escalator to the main floor of the station and out into the Centralstrasse, where the number fourteen tram, packed with polite Swiss office workers, stood ready to depart for Basel's old city. Like a rowdy group of celebrants, Kenna's captors swung onto the car, forcing her aboard as the doors closed.

Kessel emerged from the station at a run and ran alongside the moving tram, shouting threats at the driver. The polite but stubborn tram-operator averted his eyes, unwilling to stop to admit yet another passenger – especially one whose face was contorted with some emotion the driver had no desire to experience.

In that moment when Kessel's eyes met hers, she drew back as though he had struck her. As the tram moved down Centralstrasse she watched with dreadful fascination. In the diminishing figure of Klaus Kessel, she observed a man transformed by rage.

When she broke her gaze away at last, she turned to her companions, who stood crushed against her. One of the women was her cab driver. Back there in the tunnel, she had not been able to believe her ears when the man in the dark mustache had spoken, for she'd known him immediately by his voice. She looked into his amused green eyes.

"Kenna, me lass," he said. "Can ye say ye don't know me, old friend?"

"Nicholas. What are you doing here?"

# 92

Klaus Kessel sat alone on the terrace of the Euler bar, sipping a Pernod with a Cardinal chaser. Strangely, the air at five o'clock was warmer than it had been two hours earlier when Kenna Rand had stopped in the same chair at the same table. Even so, only one hand was bare of the gloves he had worn, the hand that Kessel used to lift the bottle to his lips.

Outwardly, Kessel exhibited no sign of his fury. But his anger, as palpable as a toxic fume, brought to the outdoor café an impression of something so intense and disturbing that the waiter sought to move away as soon as he had finished clearing the next table.

"You! Come here."

The waiter considered retreating to the bar, as if he had not heard.

"I said get over here."

Too late.

"There was a woman here earlier. A blond in a suit. Large glasses." The CIA man confirmed his facts in the server's countenance. "Was she with anyone?"

Ach! He remembered her. The nerve! She had tried to get away without paying, offering a hundred franc note. Where did she think she was? The waiter indicated the half-empty tables and chairs and swelled with indignation. How could he give change with the bar-crowd coming in at five o'clock to wait for their trains?

"What do you mean, tried to avoid paying?" The inquisitor's liquid green eyes bored uncharitably into the waiter's.

"You accepted her money, didn't you?" He forced the man's gaze down to the flagstone floor. "You accepted the large bill. She didn't wait for change. So you pocketed it yourself – without telling your employer."

Kessel turned away with a sneer. He had no time for petty theft, but it galled him to let the waiter think he'd gotten away with it. Not in the mood he was in. If he'd only arrived earlier. She had been alone at the café. He could have taken her there. Or the two dunces from Slovakia, those grotesque excuses for trained intelligence, why hadn't they observed her here? Directly across the street from the bank! Why didn't they stop her on the street, as he told them to. Before the Irish got there. The Irish. He recalled now the young cab driver lolling around the bank steps.

He threw back a quick shot of the Pernod, followed by a splash of beer. He went over the events since his arrival. Was there anything he could have done, or anticipated, to prevent this debacle? He did not want to dwell on his failure to properly surveil the bank. Leaving it to subordinates whom he suspected were little more than cretins. Overlooking the Irish. What brought them to Basel? What the hell was their interest in the bonds?

Like most disasters, the failure could be traced to bad judgments early on. It rankled him to realize that he doubtless would have attended the bank earlier if Andrea had not called him. Deprecating him, treating him like her personal servant. He was vaguely aware that his reluctance to oversee every detail of the day's proceedings at the settlements bank, delegating to the guards what should have been taken on himself, must be chalked up to rebellion. Pure antagonism to the she-harpie's dictating to him from her window office in Manhattan. His decision to keep away was a tactical one, he reminded himself. If Rand had seen him at the bank, she would have gone underground.

Now at least, he knew the company she kept. He would find her through the Irish. In the end his plan had been sound. He had to go back to that. The only error he could be charged with was failing to bow out of the whole exercise. But that had not been an option, had it?

His rage began to subside. It came down to a collection of stumbles and bad plays by others, he told himself. Easy mistakes that he, Kessel, would not have made. Meddling civilians. He took another sip of the liqueur, then the chaser. The alcohol had a calming effect. What *about* the Irish? Most people would mistake them for IRA. But he knew who they were.

Suddenly things had become easier. Simple now to label her a terrorist, one of the Irish Republicans. Went down a lot smoother with the American media, and it would not require the same cautious planning.

To kill a lawyer who had not been convicted of a crime was one thing – to kill a "terrorist," quite another. The world was better off without terrorists. Given the fracas in the station, there would be plenty of press involved. A word in the ear of the idiot Raskoff, and all would be golden. A terrorist in his bank! As he tapped up the bank's number, he felt calmer. There was always that silver lining.

After terminating his call with Raskoff, who had listened stonily and committed to nothing, suspicious that anything Kessel told him would get him further into hot water, Kessel reviewed his phone messages. The Slovakian mercenaries hadn't checked in yet. He had sent them scouring for her in the old city, where there were several safe houses used by the various groups who preferred to stay under the local radar.

Before too long, he would have to inform John Hermann that Rand had eluded them. It was not a chore he looked forward to. What would the banker's harridan of a wife say?

He wished he could tell Hermann the lawyer was under lock and key.

Kessel pushed away from the table and stood up, almost knocking over the chair. He hadn't eaten all day, and the drinks had gone to his head.

The waiter hadn't wanted to meet the man's eyes again but feeling Kessel's hostile presence, he was forced to lift his gaze warily.

"Don't look at me for the bill," Kessel sneered. "Take it from the 'tip' the woman gave you. The least she can do is buy me a drink."

Leaving the waiter trembling with fresh outrage over the treatment he had to put up with from his customers, Kessel moved quickly down the steps and plunged into the crowd of businessmen moving toward the station.

## 93

Not ten minutes by tram from the Euler Bar, the Slovakian junior minister of finance checked into Basel's Hotel Three Kings, the only five-star hotel in the city. When he was shown his room he moved directly to the French windows that opened onto the terrace over the Rhine. He stepped through them and scowled indifferently at a view that had captured travelers for centuries.

Meister was an incautious young man who believed that the laws pertaining to other mortals did not apply to him. Though he had been briefed on the necessity for covertness he didn't concern himself with the presence of the bellman setting out a terry robe on the bed.

From the terrace he watched a luxury cruise-boat glide toward the hotel dock from beneath Basel's Bridge of Flags. He punched up the numbers on his cell phone, almost forgetting, in his impatience, the five-digit scrambling code. Then he waited, drumming a beat on the terrace railing while the numbers connected him to the secret intelligence service of the Slovakian government.

"Yes. I'll wait," he said in German into the receiver. He ordered a beer from the bellman, who observed the guest carefully, noting a lanky young man whose attire – belted military-style jacket, tight jeans and boots, gave the appearance of a costume.

"And a plate of rosti," Meister added. And then, unnecessarily, "I'm starving."

The bellman merely nodded, holding up the room key with a question mark for an expression.

"Here, leave it on the desk."

The young man had not thought to pack a pair of binoculars. Thus, he was unaware that he himself was being observed through a pair of high-powered lenses from the deck of a castle ruin that lay across the Rhine.

When the head of Slovakian intelligence came on the line, Meister spoke immediately in a tone of self-importance. "Just checked in. Everything's okay. We should have the bonds within the hour. The Countess lost the bonds, the lawyer has them. But I've instructed the two you sent to pick up the girl and bring her to me. Almost five o'clock now? They should be here any minute."

The respectful formality of the man on the other end of the line was due, Meister knew, to his father's position. But that realization did not lessen his sense of importance. He lapsed into English. He enjoyed displaying his knowledge of American slang, confident that most of his superiors understood the language even if their fluency was dubious.

"It's not in the cards," he said, replying to his colleague's question about the Countess' commission. "We'll have the unpleasant chore of recovering the advance. But whatever I save the government remains in the Treasury. We don't need the Countess any more. Now that the lawyer has reached Basel with the bonds, Germany will pay a lot to get them out of circulation. Lose the bonds, lose the claim."

It was not only greed that spurred the young Slovakian to terminate his alliance with the spurious 'Countess.' His eyes narrowed as he thought of the incident at von Kadow's the day before. That stinking mongrel of hers nearly took his kneecaps off. False imprisonment, the Americans called such incidents, with their compulsion to assign a legal cause of action to everything. As for Klaus Kessel, the CIA man had been marginalized. Or soon would be. He could not help

Meister, who was part of the new guard in Europe. It was every dog for himself.

The Slovakian intelligence officer's voice brought Meister sharply back to the present.

"Kessel? What do I care? A shiv in his gut if they feel like it. Once we have the bonds, it's goodbye Kessel. As for the lovely Countess, if you find her, I do believe she's dispensable."

His colleague's reply must have pleased him for he smiled through his thin, boy's mustache that stretched like lace across his petal mouth. He resumed speaking in German.

"There's a dock outside for cruise ships. Once we have the lawyer, we can leave directly from the Hotel. In ten minutes, we can be in French waters."

Meister issued a cruel yelp of amusement. "Those currents are rough. She had better know how to swim."

The door closed softly behind the bellman. The young man rang off. He removed his suit jacket and loosened his tie. Then he threw himself into the pillowed chair on the terrace and narrowed his eyes sleepily at the Rhine River flowing briskly past the hotel.

At five-fifteen Meister was still relishing his beer when the room telephone rang. The news was not calculated to please the young minister. "Lost her? How could you have *lost* her?"

# 94

Keeping his voice low, Kessel placed the call to John Hermann in New York. He had decided to use the public telephones in the train station.

Kessel had not spoken with his client since his arrival in Switzerland forty-eight hours before, and he dreaded making the call.

He inserted the phone card into the box, well aware of the reception that his news deserved. The muscles in his jaw clenched involuntarily. His own earlier rage had dissipated, and he felt weary, almost as weary as Kenna Rand must be, somewhere in Basel's old city with her Irish friends. How would he get through this? What could he say in defense of this pathetic failure?

One word, he thought grimly: Fabia. Had it not been for her earlier fiascos, Kessel's reputation would have been spotless. Pristine. For years he had been the consummate professional. When the mission required the best, to plan and execute without a hitch, call Kessel. His superiors counted on him. Precise and efficient. Discreet and intelligent. The problems that led to his Zurich assignment had been put behind him.

And now. An A+ mission? Hardly. The bonds were still in the lawyer's possession. From the little that Raskoff admitted, she'd forced BIS to register the certificates. And a dedicated Slovakian intelligence agent lay dead in a ditch with a smashed skull and bullet through his head.

Good news first, bad news last. Fuck-all, there *was* no good news.

"Tode is dead," Kessel said when Hermann came on the line from his New York office. He realized Hermann probably had no desire for details, but he was grimly determined the director should share responsibility for the disaster. "I took him out on the road to Geneva."

"That is not something I needed to know," Hermann said stiffly. "Anyway, I've already been told about that." His glance traveled from the gray, leafless birches of Central Park to his sophisticated timepiece that told the time in four time zones. It was so high-tech he could practically pilot a car with it.

In the darkness of the New York afternoon, he could see how his face had aged in only a week. In his long lifetime, he had known prestige and power. His name was destined for the history books, despite the conflict-of-interest charges that had dogged him since the 1970s. Now, all was in shambles. Andrea had announced she was leaving him. Wasn't that like her? The first rat to leave the ship. Crumbling under that news alone, he had almost ceased to care about his directorship and the bank's exposure to JAFA's billion-dollar claims. But there were other risks too, which, with this latest news from Europe, posed more serious threats to his future. Kessel and the German gold bonds seemed almost trivial now – in light of the ruin Hermann faced in his personal life. Yet, the lawyer had to be stopped, in a way that could not be traced to him.

"It's after five now in Zurich. The settlements bank must be closed. Can I assume you are phoning to tell me you have the portfolio?"

"She registered the bonds," Kessel replied, with equal stiffness.

Silence. "But you did apprehend her?"

"We tried. She slipped through the rear exit to the trains."

"Where are the bonds?"

Kessel felt the sweat glistening over his sunlamp tan. He had not anticipated how difficult this would be. "She got away with the portfolio. The Slovakians are looking for her now."

Hermann vented a catalogue of Teutonic cruelty into the transcontinental phone line at his hired assassin. That's really all he needed just now.

"That is exactly what you were hired to prevent. It makes sense you would show up to intercept a known fugitive. But why did you involve the Slovakians?"

"Your friend the Countess arranged for them 'to help me.'"

A spasm of insults followed, directed both at the Countess and the man who prided himself on never making a mistake. It took several seconds for J. Dalton's director to control himself. "I don't want to hear her name again," he finished, coldly.

"Nicholas Chariot showed up," Kessel said, when he was allowed to speak. "You know who he is. I was ten feet from her, in the train yard, "He spoke bitterly at the recollection. How could he have anticipated the Irish? They'd come from nowhere.

"The Slovaks covered the rear. I covered the street. We had her, I tell you. Scum-sucking Irish started firing. The platform was in chaos. A flaming circus."

Hermann emitted a sharp snort of disgust. "Let me understand you. You were supposed to stop the lawyer from registering the bonds. That is what we discussed in Zurich. Last week everything was fine. Yes? She'd been arrested in New York, passport seized, charged with international fraud. Now, she's in Basel, a town of *minuscule* population. She's managed to register the bonds with BIS – and she is nowhere to be found."

Hermann's voice rose again in a symphony of fury.

Rotting brisket of worms. Kessel's vein began to throb. His own rancor was beginning to build. He debated interrupting the enraged Director to remind him that, at least,

Kenna Rand had no idea of the link between himself and J. Dalton & Company, but he restrained himself.

"What – just what do you expect me to say, Kessel – good job? Why didn't you alert BIS' director, what's-his-name, Raskopf –"

"Raskoff." Ah, yes, *there* was a question.

"It wouldn't have mattered," Kessel said bitterly. "She wore a disguise. A costume. Her manner…"

He realized how stupid it sounded. "She disguised herself as Fabia Santiago."

"Are you trying to tell me Fabia is responsible for her escape?"

"She had the Countess' passport. She'd done something to her hair. Wearing a veil, dark glasses – the guards were fooled. I only saw her from the back. Then I knew immediately." Almost immediately.

"I see."

"I'm not offering excuses," Kessel said briskly. "But this situation is the product of civilian interference. If, for example, your wife had not passed the bonds to the Countess, and if the Countess had not run off to Mexico, the matter would have ended a week ago in New York." Every frogging time civilians blundered into matters of intelligence –

"Fabia was trying to assist," the banker lied. "To get rid of the bonds and retire them for good."

Kessel sniffed contemptuously into the phone line.

"Fabia has been known to be precipitous." Hermann's voice took on a tired, distant tone that should have warned Kessel, but he was too busy feeling aggrieved. He would show the man in whose lap the responsibility lay.

"Precipitous? She eats her young, if she had any. In the first place, she's not an aristocrat, she's an incestuous Argentine con artist given to impulsive acts of homicide. A Fascist-spouting, self-hating Jewish Nazi, who conducts herself with all the finesse of a sow at the trough."

The Umlaut's silence was not a good thing.

"That's hardly the way I would expect you to describe my former mistress."

"Your mistress." That's the problem, then, is it?

There was a silence, then. "Now, what do you plan to do?"

I intend to sail to the Ilia Islands off Capri. He let himself imagine the satisfaction of making such a statement. I intend to go back to Zurich and leave this catastrophe for you and your "mistress" to clean up. Instead, he spoke decisively. "I expect to hear from the Slovakians at any moment."

"And what do you expect them to tell you?"

"They're to find her and bring her to me. On the way back to New York, she will be mortally injured in her attempt to escape. Because of her association with the Irish – " Ah, here was something positive he could hold out. "She will be cast as a terrorist. There will be very little sympathy if – "

"Forget the Slovakians! They want the bonds for themselves. They intend to trade them to Germany. The portfolio is enormously valuable to them. They will do anything to get it."

"What are you suggesting?"

"They will kill the girl! Most of them are frothing dogs, trained in torture by the old Soviet regime. If you had thought about it at all, you would know this. After they get through with her, there will be no question of making it look as if she tried to escape. All attention will be on the bonds. The media will make a martyr out of her."

"She must be found alive then," Kessel said, trying to keep up with Hermann's logic.

"Something new has surfaced. She's stumbled onto several photographs which are extremely embarrassing to the United States. Who knows where she got them. They were taken during the war and give rise to the implication that American interests are behind Germany's failure to honor the gold bonds."

"Do these photos have anything to do with you or Andrea?" The director's silence confirmed the sudden shrewdness of his guess.

"Just find her. Bring the photographs to me – or destroy them."

"Where are these photos?"

"That's what you must find out." The banker's tone turned icy. "You can't expect her to carry the evidence on her. Find her, get the photos, recover the bonds. And rein in those two idiots you hired."

Kessel's single-word assent was compliant enough, though the muscles of his jowl contracted with such ferocity he narrowly avoided a painful bite on the inside of his mouth. So the stakes had been raised. He had better check with his superiors. Was this still a matter for the CIA's economic intelligence division – or had it become the private concern of John Hermann and his difficult wife?

In New York, the CIA man's sullen single syllable was already fading into Hermann's earpiece. He put the phone down and stared at his reflection in the dying light of the afternoon. His cheeks were deeply lined with care and hard living. He brushed his palm over the top of his crew cut. Hermann had secretly enjoyed the edge of intimidation the unusual haircut had afforded. But the style was unpleasantly reminiscent of the haircuts given to prisoners. If he made it through this crisis, he would re-style himself, he pledged. He would re-create himself once more.

# 95

It was evening the same day and Kenna was still alive. Nicholas and Bridget had taken Kenna to a hotel on Freie Strasse in the old city. The numbers on her Swiss Army watch shone green in the darkened hotel room. She moved to the window and parted the curtains. It was eight-thirty and lamp light streamed in from the square.

She could hear the even breathing of her companion Bridget, the girl who, with Derek, another of Nicholas' colleagues, had been on the train to Geneva. It wasn't entirely true that they were following Kenna, Nicholas explained. They were tracking the Countess for the British government, Kenna happened to be part of the Countess' entourage.

"We picked her up in Manhattan in October. We had her under surveillance when she initiated contact with your grandfather with that story about being in the market for antique bonds. That's her modus," Nicholas said, sweeping a kitchen chair around and resting his arms on its back.

"She offers to buy an investor's bonds, takes them to be 'authenticated' and disappears with them," Nicholas continued. "If she encounters any resistance, she resorts to murder."

"You could have saved my grandfather's life."

A frown creased the intelligence man's features. "Don't think I haven't suffered the guilt of it," he said softly. "But we were too late. Jack knew the risks. He wanted to expose the game and Fabia Santiago's part in it. I did all I could. And I promised Jack I would look after you."

She took her time evaluating his comments, recalling the Mercedes in Paris, the couple on the train. It had been a shock to see Nicholas at BIS. With sable hair and dark mustache she hadn't known him. Only by his thick Irish speech, an affect he adopted as self-parody, had she been sure. His arrival had saved her life.

"We've got a faint image of her on camera – for all the bloody good it did us." He shook his head with genuine regret. "She used a plant toxin that immobilizes the muscles. It was developed by the Russians during the cold war. Ground into a powder and moistened, it can be injected readily. Respiratory failure follows quickly."

Pray, not always, Kenna said silently, thinking of Michael.

She studied him a long time before speaking. "You saved my life today. Grandfather would have been grateful." She stopped short of saying *she* was grateful. She did not know how she felt about Nicholas. He had his own agenda, of that she could be sure. If the intelligence man rescued her today, would he demand payback tomorrow?

Nicholas rose to leave them. But before doing so he moved close to her, unembarrassed by Bridget's presence. He drew her to face him with a light pressure on her shoulders and spoke softly without any trace of the phoney accent.

"I'm glad you're safe, Kenna Rand. But you're not out of danger."

He stepped back and donned the leather jacket that was almost a uniform in western Europe. "I'll be back at ten o'clock. Don't leave this room. And don't answer the door. I have a key." Then he stepped from the room into the hallway, a proper Swiss businessman.

## 96

That night a fair was held in the old city. Basel, respected center for banking and navigation, had never abandoned its identity as a European village. Once a month, the villagers set up bars and discos on the cobbled streets. Hauling sofas, coffee tables and bar stools to the Marketplatz, they arranged them into cocktail lounges under the stars. French champagne, four francs a glass. There was beer, and sausages, grilled on large outdoor spits.

A home-grown band played rock music, the distinctive post-Beatles sound Europe had never given up. Dance lessons were offered and young women, Kenna's contemporaries, partnered one another in classic blazers and kick-your-ass boots.

Bridget insisted on going out. "Just need a smoke in the open air. Ten minutes. We won't go very far. We'll stick it around here."

Nicholas was right. The prudent course was to lie low, play checkers or watch television in the small hotel room. But the adrenaline that had shot through her had not completely dissolved; a nervous energy had taken its place. She'd been dead tired at six o'clock and dropped off to sleep as soon as her head touched the pillow, but she had awakened quickly at the first chords of the rock band and lain in the darkness reliving – not the frightening events of the day, but the brief encounter with Nicholas, reviving, as it had, her concerns about Michael. She flipped open her cell phone and struggled with the impulse to power it on and place a call to Mexico. She closed it again. No point in confirming her location for Kessel.

Kenna splashed water on herself, put her hair up under a cowboy hat provided by Bridget, and the two young women slipped out of the hotel, to move briefly among the crowds, the music, the tantalizing smells.

The gabled rooftops and colorful turrets of the old city were charming. Bright geraniums and flags festooned each balcony and street lamp. And guarding every stone fountain was a bronze winged dragon, the city's symbol of its medieval past.

And yet Kenna searched every face, scanned briefly every eye. She could not afford to lose herself completely like the joyful Swiss, whose only cares – a tired economy and swollen welfare claims – seemed forgotten in the bracing air.

Kenna had changed into borrowed jeans and a soft chambray shirt over her turtleneck. Her lush hair, now blond, was tucked up under the hat. Even so, she felt exposed, targeted, as if Kessel could find her anywhere.

They stopped to watch a young Spaniard with wild eyes playing flamenco guitar. Taking in the young women, he began a set of Celtic aires. The simple plaintive ballads worked their effect on her. As the musician performed, she relaxed against the wall of the lighted square and listened to lyrics she'd heard in childhood.

*Oh, I wish I was in Derry, I wish I was in Derry, again.*

The haunting, repetitive ballad brought tears to Kenna's eyes. Bridget too fell under the night's spell, remembering, perhaps, Dublin life and her large family of macho terrorists.

Yes. She wouldn't mind being in Derry. Her thoughts turned to the times she had visited Ireland with her grandfather. It had been so welcoming there. The people, the landscape, as if she belonged. Under the bright moon on the cobbled streets, Kenna suppressed the emotion that came with sudden force. She'd done all she could for JAFA. All was in the hands of the Swiss bankers. She would have liked nothing more than to turn herself in and go home.

Kenna stiffened suddenly as a man behind her panned the scene with a camcorder. She turned her face away to avoid the lens, as the camera glided past her and over the young musician. A tourist after all.

The Marketplatz had become a sea of bodies. "I think we should go back now," Kenna said, leading Bridget into a quiet alley to get her bearings. "Any idea of the shortest route to Freie-strasse?"

But it was not Bridget who stood behind her.

# 97

The man wore a baseball cap low over his face. Out of the dark crevice between an inn and a stone wall he came. The heel of his hand gripped her mouth and her warning cry to Bridget became the moan of a deaf-mute. He twisted her arm behind her until her shoulder felt like fire.

He spoke in German. "Where are they?" At least that's what Kenna could make out.

She tried to break free and her shoulder resisted. He dragged her toward a dark passageway, twisting her body up against him.

"Where are they?" the man insisted in German. "Where are da bonds?" This time in English.

Kenna almost cried out to see Bridget behind him. Her companion was only five feet four inches, one hundred and five pounds. Run for it. Go for help. Don't try to –

Bridget lunged for the man's back, clawing at his eyes with her fingers and clinging to him like a tree monkey. The surprise attack forced him free of Kenna. His mask came off and his expression of surprise was not a good thing. The face was blond, Nordic. Kenna had seen him before. It was Kessel's young baby-faced soldier from BIS.

He swung around fast and knocked Bridget to the ground with the full power of his torso. Kenna kicked at him savagely but missed her target. He reeled away from her and she saw the knife. Before she could move again, he'd plunged the blade into Bridget with a savage thrust.

Kenna kicked the knife from his hand. But it was too late. Bridget was down, writhing toward the street. The man lunged toward Kenna. A second rapid kick caught his crotch, he doubled over gasping. She kicked him again and the blood left his face. He lurched into a collection of metal trash bins. The lids clanged loudly on the cobblestones.

Kenna ran to Bridget. "It's okay. You're going to be all right."

The man struggled to standing, holding his crotch. She had to get Bridget on her feet.

Suddenly, Nicholas was there. He gripped the man's head between his hands and battered it with his own. The thug went down, and Nicholas kicked him hard in the soft part of the back where his kidneys should be. Then he twisted the killer's arm behind him and in a savage wrench tore it from his shoulder.

"Let's go," he said, hoarsely.

A cluster of children gathered at the entrance and gaped wide-eyed. It wouldn't be long before their parents joined them.

In a swift movement, Nicholas lifted Bridget onto one shoulder. The bleeding had stopped. Not a good sign, was it? It could mean internal hemorrhaging.

"Take her other side. Let's get out of here."

Nicholas gave the knife a savage kick into the lighted circle where the young singer had been. Then they ran together, supporting Bridget between them. They kept to the alleyways behind the Marketplatz. Five long blocks from the old city to the Rhine. At the Bridge of Flags, they split up.

"Go back to the hotel," Nicholas said. "Clean out the bonds and Bridget's things. Don't leave anything in the room."

Kenna hesitated. "I have to stay with her," she said.

"I'll be takin' her now. I won't let her down. Now get on to the hotel. That's the first place they'll go."

He issued an urgent précis of the route to the castle-ruin where they would meet. Cross the Rhine, turn left at the park. Look for the turrets directly across the river from the Three Kings. Make sure you're not followed.

Kenna lingered. Her thoughts flew to Dr. Milan, Ginger Lebecque's friend. "Shall I bring the doctor?"

"The name, then. Give me the name."

"Doctor Anna Milan, 10 Friedrichstrasse."

"All right," he said. And Nicholas disappeared into the darkness with Bridget.

Kenna raced back to the hotel and up the stairs.

She paused outside the door and listened. Then she entered the room warily, locking the door with the key. Gathering the bonds and Bridget's few possessions consumed only a few minutes. As she was slipping out she heard the sound of heavy boots trying to be silent on the stair. She raced across the hall into the maid's closet. It was black as pitch inside.

She locked herself in, leaving the metal key turned in the lock. She listened, crouching against the door. Through the floor crack came the grunts and mutters of two men and the shuffle of their boots. She identified the smack of the bathroom door being flung back and the shatter of glass in the shower.

When they moved to the stair again, she held her breath. They paused on the landing for a last look around, just inches from Kenna on the other side of the unmarked door.

One cursed in a language that was not German. Then, "Should we wait?" in English.

"No way."

"Where will she go?" Czech-German again.

Kenna was aware of the brief silence that was the equivalent of a shrug. "Marten Bolls?"

"At the Three Kings?"

"Sure."

"You think she will try to sell them?"

"Sure. Where else?"

Kenna waited a long time in the dark with the clean fragrance of hotel soap and freshly laundered towels. Ten minutes had passed before she stole from the closet into the foyer and paused at the stairs. She decided on ascent this time, to the roof.

# *98*

Kenna exited the hotel roof via a fire stair at the back of the building, then hastened on foot in the opposite direction of Basel's old town, to the other side of the Rhine. A dark serenity lay there, dotted with vast unkempt lots and shuttered buildings.

Rising up before her in shabby dignity was the ruin of a medieval castle with deep-set windows, directly across the river from the Hotel Three Kings. At one time, the compound had been a wayfarer's inn and public house. Now, a Catholic day-school occupied its park-like grounds, enclosed by a wall of ancient wrought iron. She scaled the iron spikes easily enough and dropped onto the lawns. Then she limped to the back entrance as Nicholas had insisted. A priest immediately answered her summons and she nearly fell inside.

She was led to a large room that apparently served as the school's computer classroom, and instructed to wait. Nicholas was nowhere to be found. Her questions about Bridget's condition received little acknowledgment, the priest replying simply in German, "God will provide."

Not bloody good enough.

The priest withdrew and she waited alone. It was in crisis that ideas she would otherwise dismiss as magical thinking, reared like wild ponies, and refused to be contained. The strong conviction came over her that there was a time in any life or death struggle when events could be altered, before the Fates had stamped their seal upon them, and the sheer force of her will could change destiny. She had prayed, fervently, to change the outcome for her grandfather. But her attempt had come too late. She would focus fiercely upon Bridget. And hope to God she was in time.

Ten minutes later, Kenna hadn't stirred from the windows of the large paneled room that looked out over the Rhine. Moonlight still shone on the rushing current as though illuminating the power of her will.

When Nicholas moved to the window beside her, something reassuring in his presence made her turn to him quickly.

"Aye," he said, with suppressed emotion. "Missed her organs – just. Father Riordan says she should pull through all right. Twenty seven bloomin' stitches. But she'll be with us. Most likely."

It was then she allowed the doubts to surface. "I thought –"

"Me too."

She lingered in the room for several minutes, feeling a joyous relief. In her fragmented state she'd only thought of it now–she still possessed JAFA's bonds. What was she going to do with them?

# 99

Waiting for a call from the two Slovakian soldiers, Klaus Kessel was on the verge of an explosion. He'd spent two intense hours tracking his elusive subordinates through Slovakian intelligence. Finally, he reached Meister at the Three Kings.

"Where are they?"

"Who are you talking about?"

"You know fucking well who I mean, you wimpish dunce."

"I'm not going to continue this conversation if you – "

"Shut up." Kessel could make his fury eviscerate when he wanted to.

It was time. Meister had it coming. Kessel had held it in so long. Now Kessel indulged himself. "You pathetic wimp. Prancing choir boy. Sputtering Nancy. Imbecile." The line was silent when he stopped abruptly.

"I have your attention Meister. Good."

"I presume you got my location from intelligence."

"Where are those cretins you sent me?"

"Didn't intelligence tell you?"

"Tell me what?" It was back there all the time, waiting on the boil.

"We withdraw."

"You what?"

"Slovakia withdraws. We do not wish to continue with the idea."

"The idea."

"Yes. The – the arrangement."

Meister was beginning to stutter from the assault. "We do not wish to trade the bonds."

"You gutless buffoon. You're going after the bonds yourself. You'll pay for this you insipid weasel. I'm coming over there now to slice your balls off and throw them in the Rhine for the carp to nibble on, you pimping –"

But the line was dead. The Slovakian junior minister was busy checking out of the elegant Hotel Three Kings.

# 100

Kenna rose at five the following morning, unable to sleep with images of the Slovakian soldiers present in her mind. She stole into the school's infirmary and noted with relief that Bridget's color had returned. The girl looked small and delicate, nothing like the brash young tough from the day before. In the half-light that crept in on them from the school's deep-set windows, Kenna sent the girl a fierce command: *Just hold on.*

She had lain awake, turning over in her mind the question her grandfather had sought to answer, were the bonds marked in some way that might prove their value?

The issue had surfaced again in light of the Slovakians' attack last night. She had no doubt she'd been their target. But they had demanded the bonds, even knowing it was likely the bank had a record of them. The portfolio was still important to someone.

Her interest had once been aroused by an art concept called 'negative value,' in which the shapes drawn on the canvas were less significant than the empty space around them. It struck her that the bonds' value as currency might now be surpassed by their value to Germany if they simply ceased to exist. She had examined the instruments herself and noted nothing out of the ordinary. Perhaps there was something *missing* from the certificates that secured their value.

It was just before six that Kenna found the house of Herr Bolls in a quiet residential street near the museums. She would have liked to let Nicholas know where she was going, but he was gone when she had arisen, and she wanted to get the man before he left for his shop in the Hotel Three Kings.

Marten Bolls himself answered the ring at the door, an attractive man in his late forties, wearing a blue checked shirt and solid navy tie.

Kenna introduced herself and the man smiled slightly, lifting his brow in a skeptical manner.

"Come now," he said. "I'm sure you know my shop is not far from here. You could see me at nine-thirty when it opens."

“André Lebecque suggested I call on you here.”

The man took André's handwritten scrap without a word, casting his eyes quickly over it, before inviting her to step inside. Neither could resist an anxious scanning of the still-slumbering street.

"You will take coffee?" Herr Bolls inquired. "I'll just tell my man Roland to bring some." From the kitchen at the rear of the house, came the sound of CNN's financial news in English.

"I'm interrupting you," Kenna said.

"Just watching my portfolio go down the tubes. "He added with a quick disarming smile, "Any distraction is welcome, believe me."

The man had a direct and friendly affect. A slight European formality, that was to be expected. But she must be careful. She knew nothing of Marten Bolls, only that he'd run, for two decades, the antique currency shop off the lobby of the Hotel Three Kings.

The light of a fire drew Kenna into a small library off the foyer. The morning had been grey and overcast when Kenna set out from the castle-ruin and she had not felt the chill of her brisk walk across the Rhine until now. She seated herself on a bench in front of the hearth and waited for the warmth to penetrate her.

"Now, Fraulein," Herr Bolls moved as economically as he spoke. "Ah, good, you have found the fire. Let us have a coffee and hear why it is so urgent that you see me."

Kenna counted on her youth and the directness of her request to win him. She had resorted again to Ginger's bits of wardrobe, though not so elaborate as yesterday's. No hat, no gloves. And, thanks to the bank's exit grid, no jacket. But she looked professional enough and that was the impression she strove for.

She waited until Herr Boll's manservant arranged the elaborate service of Russian silver and Dresden china, and waited one moment more as he poured out two thick cups of espresso and steamed milk, using the continental style of pouring from two pots simultaneously. When he removed himself from the room, she spoke.

"May I call you Marten?"

"Why not?"

"I understand you deal in antique currencies and bonds. And that you're well-connected in these matters. I'm an attorney from New York. My grandfather and I were in practice together there. Recently he – passed away and I've taken over a matter for one of his clients. Perhaps you've heard about an issue of German gold bonds sold to U.S. investors in the years before Hitler came to power?"

A second assent, equally economical.

"Our client possesses a large collection of these bonds. As you may know, many believed the proceeds would help their families who remained in Germany. Almost immediately, Hitler put the issue into default. As a result their value plunged. And the families who purchased them were unable to get anything for them. But even after the war, Germany has refused to repay the debt or make any settlement, based upon its claim that our client's bonds were among those stolen from the Reichsbank during the last days of the war. My grandfather believed there was something about the bonds themselves that would prove they were not among those allegedly stolen. That's why I came to see you."

"So you have brought a certificate for me to examine – is that it? And you want to know: Is it a legitimate claim on the German government, or fool's gold?"

The way he put it made her smile. "Yes. That's exactly what I need to know."

"Have we met?" he asked unexpectedly. "Your face is familiar to me."

"I don't think so." She spoke cautiously. "I just arrived in Basel yesterday."

"Just as you say." He became business-like once more. "Then let me see this portfolio of yours."

She drew out a single bond and passed it to him, observing the man carefully.

He ran his fingers over the surface and reviewed both sides with a magnifying glass before he spoke.

"These are very rare," he said. "The parchment, the typeface. The terms are interesting. German on one side, English on the other. It's a great artifact. And payable in gold coin. *If* Germany would honor them, they would be extremely valuable."

He estimated the number of bonds from the list of serial numbers and issued a soft whistle. "You have a very important client."

Kenna felt his mind working, registering things about her.

"And the party you represent?" he asked.

"I'm sorry. That's confidential."

"Really?"

Again, the cryptic smile, acknowledging the fact that Kenna was not sorry at all. "I only ask for your sake. As I'm quite sure you know, "he said, "the value of your client's portfolio is dubious. The deadline for registration has passed."

He paused. "Even if you had registered the bonds at the settlements bank, it is doubtful Germany would pay."

He watched her face. "You presented them already."

"Yes."

"Who did you meet with there?"

"Herr Raskoff."

"Raskoff," he spoke with contempt. "His sole job is to be a brick wall."

"Why do you say the Germans will not pay?"

"You know all this. But when a woman is charming one can't fail to indulge her questions."

Charming she might seem, for the moment. But she would not leave without obtaining his help. She waited.

"Germany passed an internal law decades ago," he continued. "If your bonds are on their list of those they claim to have been in the Reichsbank at the war's end, they won't be redeemed. The 'list' is a non-list. Oh yes, they ask for your serial numbers. Then, presto, your numbers appear on their 'list'. In this way, all are declined."

"In your opinion then, my client's claim is worthless?"

"Not at all," he said, enjoying the game. "Things have changed. In the past, Germany relied on the bankers in such matters. Your bonds might be 'lost', or substituted for others that had already been redeemed. The certificates might be returned with holes in them, making them valueless. That is unlikely to happen this time. By registering the bonds yesterday it is possible – yes – quite possible that you will be able to press your client's claim. It may take decades. However, the Swiss are cautious just now about world scrutiny. It is unlikely that the record of your visit will be 'lost.' But that only makes the situation more dangerous for you."

"Because I did not turn in the bonds."

"Correct."

"If I had turned them in, then, based upon what you have said, there is a good chance the bonds themselves would have disappeared and their serial numbers would have turned out to be on the 'list.' But since I did not leave them with Raskoff, the bank is in a check-mate. If the bonds are produced, Germany's claim that they are 'stolen' could be proved to be a lie. Which brings us back to my question. Is there something about the instruments themselves that could rebut Germany's position?"

"Yes," he said slowly, passing the bond back to her. It was as if he was forced to recount the details of a grisly murder. "Yes. I think so."

She replaced the bond carefully in the largest compartment of her backpack.

"The Germans will pay to remove the bonds from circulation?"

Herr Bolls shrugged. "The Russians have scavenged for them in the past. They are not particular about such things."

"The Russians? But Germany claims it was the Red Army that stole them."

"Rubbish! The Russians are desperate to buy them. So how can they have stolen them?" He offered her a piece of toast.

"Why do they want them?" she asked, accepting a slice of thick rustic bread and spreading currant jam on it.

"Reparations. Germany demands compensation for Russia's plunder of the Reich in the last days of the war. Billions in German Marks, mostly for art held at the Hermitage in St. Petersburg. The Winter Palace alone holds trophy art valued at billions of dollars."

"So Russia intends to –"

"Russia would pay your client a small percentage of the portfolio's value, then tender it to Germany in lieu of its Manets, Degas', Matisses."

Nicholas had been sure that the men in the square were Slovakian.

Answering her thoughts, Marten Bolls continued.

"Russians are not the only ones seeking these bonds."

"Would the Slovakians be in the game?"

"Now? I can only guess. Slovakia is Germany's old war-time ally. The country is just now emerging from the sleep of Communism. There is a race to modernism, to join the

European Union and create parity to the United States. We even have our own currency in mind. The Euro is a powerless infant now, but one day…If the Slovakians are to compete in Europe they must be relieved of the monstrous debt they incurred in support of Hitler's war."

"Given that the bonds could be traced to my client, will Germany still accept them?"

"The people in this game will stop at nothing to remove the gold bonds from circulation." He put up a hand as if to warn her. "This is about gold, Kenna. Billions of dollars in gold. Still the most valuable currency in the world. That is why the Germans insist the bonds are worthless, while to the Russians and the Slovakians, they are very valuable indeed."

She decided to test him. "Perhaps then, you could arrange to sell my client's portfolio to Slovakia."

"I might have, yesterday." An enigmatic smile passed over Herr Bolls' attractive features. "You have seen today's newspaper?"

"I'm afraid I don't read German."

"This one is in English." Marten passed her the folded copy of *USA Today*, German edition, casually spreading the front page so that the headline and its corresponding photograph were immediately visible.

*"AMERICAN LAWYER SOUGHT BY INTERPOL*

*Sources have learned that Interpol has joined with the FBI in pursuit of an American lawyer suspected of trying to redeem German bearer bonds looted by the Russians in the last days of World War II. In a dramatic chase across continents . .* "

The photograph was a blurred one, the dismal product of an FBI shutter-bug. Meeting Marten's eyes she saw that he had known who she was from the moment he opened the door.

## 101

Herr Bolls poured them each a second cup of the espresso, manipulating the two pots of steamed milk and coffee with finesse equal to his servant's.

"So, are you Red Riding Hood," he asked slyly. "Or a thief on the lam?"

" I left a few details out of my account," Kenna replied with deliberate understatement.

"I am listening."

She succinctly recounted the facts surrounding her arrest, pursuit of the Countess and her harrowing visit to the Lebecques. In a few words she described the incident concerning Bridget.

"You see why we could not meet at your shop this morning? You're in danger if these people find me here."

He gave a shrug of disdain. "Do you think I haven't faced these threats before? Currency dealing is a hazardous profession. There is always some petty thief who would take me out. After the last mugging, I almost lost an eye. Luckily, the gun jammed. Now, I employ a bodyguard."

Herr Bolls smiled. "That deters only the amateurs. One day I will be killed. Whether they get what they came for or not, that will be the challenge. Now, where were we?"

"If the bonds held in the Reichsbank in 1945 were already redeemed, why were they not marked 'canceled,'" she asked.

Marten Bolls drew a cigarette from a silver box. He studied it, turning it this way and that. He finally lay it on his saucer, unlit.

"What do you think?" he asked.

"The Nazis must have intended to re-sell them."

His head shot up in a look that said she'd hit the mark. "It has been speculated," he said bitterly. "That Switzerland's exchange continued to accept trades on redeemed bonds in order to help Germany finance its war."

He let his eyes drift to his saucer again, twirling the cigarette as if it were a conductor's baton.

"Bond investors paid twice for the Nazis' genocide."

"Sadly, that is true."

He watched her, his expression one of regret for what he was about to say.

"It is not only the Swiss who are to blame. It was, you recall, a New York bank that sold the bonds to U.S. investors in the first place. Neither the issuing bank nor your government spoke up against Hitler when he almost immediately declared a default. One can only imagine the constraint upon Germany if the powers had insisted the country honor its debt. Did Roosevelt so hate the Jews?"

She hadn't considered that. In recent times, economic sanctions were imposed for such actions. What penalty had been imposed against Berlin?

"How did the bankers know which bonds were scheduled for sale through Switzerland," she asked.

He shook his head.

"I wish I knew. Perhaps some secret is encoded on the Reichsbank bonds, as your grandfather believed. If you find out what it is, your client's bonds may be authenticated. Either way, Slovakia loses its leverage to reduce its debt. It is now a race of time. They must get possession of your bonds *before* you can establish with certainty whether or not they are valid."

"Will you help me?"

His voice was suddenly mild, detached. "You have your answer already. It is too dangerous. Go back to New York. Conduct your investigation by post." She saw in his coldness an attempt to discourage her.

"You have no idea of the realities," he said, in a softer tone. "The stakes are too high. The gold bonds are a death warrant. They put Germany at risk. The Swiss too. Yes, this story is a poignant one. The betrayal of millions by the governments that should have been protecting them. But when you force attention on the gold bonds you are talking about a debt worth billions of dollars. While you are alive these stories live. But if you are gone – " he shrugged. "Records can be altered, papers lost."

His lips set in a grim smile. "Go back to New York."

She hesitated. Then she reached into her backpack. Drawing out Lara's photograph, she handed it to him.

"And who is this?"

"In February, 1945 my grandfather tendered a series of gold bonds to the Reichsbank for payment. They were offered in return for travel papers for this young girl. The bonds were never returned to him. The child disappeared."

He turned the photograph over. "Lara? Lara – what?"

"I don't know her last name."

"You intend to try to find her, I suppose."

"That may be too difficult. What I am looking for is a record of her bonds. An inquiry from an American lawyer would be placed in a file somewhere, even if my grandfather's request were declined. If I can trace what happened to her bonds – " Suddenly the careful enunciation of each word was required to keep her composure.

Marten Bolls toyed with the cigarette again and put it down.

Roland's entrance into the room had gone unnoticed until he appeared behind his employer holding a portable phone.

"Bruno is calling," he announced.

"My chauffeur," Marten explained, accepting the telephone.

"Yes Bruno?"

"Two?" Marten said after listening for a moment. "How are they dressed?"

Marten regarded Kenna with an expression of mild amusement. "Ah, the terminators are in front of the house." He sketched a quick plan of diversion to his driver.

"Now," Marten Bolls said when he had hung up, "You seem to have a gift for prophecy. If you won't listen to uncle Marten, then I must see what I can do for you."

For the next few minutes he led Kenna through a series of computer tasks to access the confidential files contained in the BIS databank.

He typed in the word "GULDENBUND."

"I set up the program," he said proudly. "When I worked for the Minister of Banking. It has proven useful, as you can imagine."

Marten tapped a key and a table materialized on the screen. Her heart began to race as she scanned the data.

He tapped "PRINT" and handed Kenna six pages of columns – the bank's listing of gold bonds secretly traded to Germany through BIS over six decades.

She raced to catch up. "What can I do with this?"

"At least some of these must have been among those kept in the Reichsbank. It is the evidence you need to force Germany to pay."

"How?"

"You will think of a way. Remember what I told you. These men who tried to kill you last night will try again."

"Is this then Germany's 'list'?"

"Unfortunately, I don't know the answer. There is only one person in Basel who can confirm that such a list exists. He worked at the Reichsbank, he might know something about the marking of the certificates."

Marten took a slip of paper from a pad next to the computer and wrote a name on it. “He is employed as a guard at the Kunstmuseum.”

Boll's man came to claim him and he stood to go, describing, hurriedly, the way to the museum. Before Marten Bolls slipped into the passageway that led to his rooftop and the helicopter waiting for him, he turned to Kenna. "Keep your nerve," he said, tossing off a smile.

Michael's words.

# 102

The door to the currency shop, next door to the Hotel Three Kings, was still bolted. Kessel glanced at his watch automatically. It was nine-forty. He had known something was wrong from the moment he approached the curb. He tried the door anyway, giving it a good jerk. But the place was dark, with chain links fastened on the inside.

It had seemed extraordinary good luck that the phone pad in the room vacated by Meister had surrendered an imprint made by his childish hand, *Herr Bolls, Bonds and Currency.* The note was Kessel's unexpected reward for sacking Meister's room last night. Unfortunately, Meister's dunces, Kessel was growing fond of that term, must have raised the alarm, for Herr Bolls declined to open for business today.

Kessel considered the idea of trashing the small shop, but he'd exhausted his physical rage the night before. Besides, it was broad daylight. Hermann's words had sobered him. If he did not want to cede control to the Slovakians, and endure the humiliation of returning to Hermann empty-handed, he must lose no time in finding Kenna Rand before they did.

## *103*

Marten Bolls had been gone for five minutes when Kenna slipped out into the street and hurried six blocks to the Kunstmuseum. The doors would not open for another half an hour or so. Kenna entered a small hotel dining room where a few art students were gathered, and ordered a large breakfast. Except for the bite of toast she'd practically inhaled in Marten Bolls' library, she had not eaten since noon the day before. The typical Swiss buffet, a plate of cheeses, delicate braunschweiger, followed by a bowl of meuslix and fruit with yogurt, was satisfying.

At ten o'clock Kenna paid the fee and entered the echoing rooms. She was given a gallery plan with her ticket, and immediately ascended the marble stairs to the second floor where the Picassos were located, reasoning that her greatest chance of running into Herr Fromm would be in the museum's most valuable collection.

"How will I know him?" she had asked Marten Bolls.

"He is a small man, with angry steel gray eyes. You won't underestimate his intelligence."

She moved through the second floor galleries swiftly, completing a quick tour of those on the third floor before returning to the Picasso rooms.

She had not asked for Herr Fromm at the entrance, declining to draw attention to her errand. Now she wished she had at least confirmed he was working today.

Kenna moved to the deep-sashed windows overlooking the street. The neighborhood was quiet. There was no sign of Kessel or the Slovakians. She had no reason to believe they would be able to find her here. But she was beginning to realize that Basel was practically a village compared to New York.

She considered running downstairs to the gift shop for a sketch pad, a prop that would label her as art student, and dismissed the idea just as quickly, recognizing it for what it was, an excuse for her restless energy. Surreptitiously reviewing the schedules she'd taken from Marten Bolls her thoughts quickened. Most who had redeemed the bonds were associated with foreign governments. What was the link, if any, between the American soldiers who had stolen the bonds at Meissen, and the governments which had redeemed them?

A party of French tourists entered the room in a swarm, led by a woman whose commentary, delivered in high-velocity French, had the wearing effect of a blue jay at four in the morning. Rat-a-tat-tat. How she had under-appreciated the soft lisp of her art-history teacher. She listened with half-attention, translating the art lesson automatically.

"Most viewers are drawn to the French Impressionists. They are superb. But we must not forget this museum's extraordinary collection of Pablo Picasso's works. Picasso was a Spaniard who studied principally in Barcelona, though his creativity found its greatest expression in France."

Where else? Impatience was getting the better of her.

"Though he worked in Paris at one time in his long life, at the time of his death his home was in the hills outside Aix…the light there… though untouched by Fauvism, he was inspired by Cezanne's empirical motifs which led to the evolution of Cubism. The French influence is clearly recognizable in… He later associated himself with the Spanish Republican cause with works like 'the Dream' and 'Guernica' . ."

She began to move about the room avoiding the students, aware that her impatience had more to do with the pressure of meeting the guard than the grating voice of the Parisian guide. A pair of bored stragglers sauntered in, herded towards their party by a man in the museum's blue guard's uniform. He was a small man, with angry steel gray eyes.

## 104

The appearance of Klaus Kessel was not a matter of surprise to the man who answered the door. In a town of 300,000 people it could not have been hard to track down the residence of his employer, whose shop had stood off the lobby of the Hotel Three Kings for decades. Marten Bolls' hired man Roland had been with the currency dealer for almost two decades. In that time, he had learned to anticipate what would be needed in any given situation and to react only to the extent required by the circumstances.

Bolls would have said the man was reliably discreet. Such was the case on the morning in question. Notwithstanding all the unusual events that had already taken place, to all appearances, Bolls' valet could have been greeting an electrician hired to repair a wall switch.

"It would seem you have no jurisdiction here," he observed with an air of regret, acknowledging the identity card Kessel flashed at him.

Kessel actually smiled. "That doesn't mean very much. I can get what I want very easily."

The CIA man slid his hand beneath his coat to expose the small pistol strapped under his armpit. Then he pushed the valet aside and forced his way in.

"Now suppose you tell me what your boss has been up to," Kessel said. He kept his hand within inches of his gun, as he surveyed the contents of the library through its open door.

He noted two coffee cups. A cigarette lay on the saucer of one, unlit. There was a fire dying in the library grate. It was easy enough to see Herr Bolls had entertained a visitor, and to deduce she'd departed on foot. Bolls' domestic offered a different account –almost apologetically – it seemed the visitor had completed her business and was leaving the city. She had left with his employer by way of the roof. "I expect they are on their way to Zurich," the man-servant added.

Kessel returned a wise smile. He knew better than to trust any "facts" that were volunteered. His pager buzzed and he answered the call, saying little and maintaining a cold eye on Bolls' manservant.

"Directive unchanged." The two words were relayed to him by Williams, the CIA lackey who worked for him in his Zurich office. Finally, his superiors had deemed it worth their while to respond to his inquiry about John Hermann. Irrespective of Kessel's concerns about Hermann, he was to complete the assignment as planned. The young woman must be intercepted and, in his discretion, returned to the United States.

No new intelligence was available regarding the subject photographs mentioned by Hermann. But if Kessel acquired any information about same, he should act on such information immediately, recover said materials and turn them over to his superiors. He must not bother himself about Hermann, whom Williams, with his overwrought sense of spy-speak, referred to as "the firm's principal." But proceed unchanged.

Typical, Kessel thought, snapping the pager case shut without bothering to reply. Status-quo at all costs. No one willing to review what had been a stupid blunder to have taken on in the first place. The single question to which he'd sought an answer, posing it in the carefully veiled jargon of his trade, had received a reply that was typically evasive. Assuming he recovered the photographs Hermann alluded to – and assuming the scenes they depicted were prejudicial to the interests of the United States – was he still to bring her back *alive*?

He turned back to Marten Bolls' valet. His mood had changed. All tolerance for cat-and-mouse parrying had fully dissipated. He needed to know where she had gone. And he needed to know now.

# *105*

Kenna waited impatiently for the chirruping French guide to lead her flock into the second gallery. She felt like barking at their heels like an Irish collie herding sheep, the result of Marten Bolls' high-octane espresso.

Under pretense of interest in Picasso's sketches for Guernica, the Spanish town used as a Nazi weapons test with Franco's blessing, she studied the old man who had entered.

His hair was clipped close to his skull. His face wore the soft coloring of age, his eyes were cold. An air of intimidation expressed itself in his ramrod posture and the impeccable fit and starch of his dark uniform. Though his build was slender, almost frail, it was a frailty of stature, not spirit. The total effect conveyed to her the fact that she could not expect a warm reception.

The tour finally moved on. It seemed to take forever for every straggler to pass through the archway into the next room.

When she was quite sure no one was looking she approached the guard.

"Excuse me, Herr Fromm. "

Nothing in his expression confirmed he had been addressed.

"I've been told to ask you about the German gold bonds."

She assessed the effect her words had upon him. His eyes exhibited stony interest, nothing more.

"And the Meissen caves."

"So you know about that do you?"

She placed her hands at the pocket of her jacket, touching only the outline of the photographs André had given her. Now that she'd engaged the man's attention, her fear left her. She waited.

The guard abruptly turned, and she followed him.

In a dark hallway that led to what looked like an elevator for large art works, she offered the envelope containing André's photographs, taken at Meissen. He slit it open, and cast his eyes quickly over the scene of American soldiers looting the bonds. He stiffened slightly, and looked at the back, before passing it back to her.

"I cannot help you."

"Marten Bolls suggested you would."

He shrugged impatiently. "The name means nothing to me."

"JAFA then."

"Ah, the Jews." His voice was low and mocking. He half-closed his eyes as though she bored him.

Kenna drew from her backpack Herr Bolls' copy of USA Today and held the grainy likeness of the Reuter's photograph before his eyes. He glanced from the image to Kenna.

"You are this thief?" The possibility seemed to amuse him.

"The details aren't true, but I am the person named in this account."

"A 'fraudulent attempt' to sell German gold bonds?"

She moved her head slightly in assent.

"They've turned you into a fugitive?"

"They?" Kenna asked, momentarily confused.

"Your government?"

"I hadn't thought of it that way, but yes, I'm wanted by the FBI. A man named Klaus Kessel is working for them."

"You have identification?"

She produced her passport.

He narrowed his eyes at her critically. "Why do you bother with me?"

"I need to know what you know," Kenna said. "A half hour of your time."

"I don't think I can help you." he said firmly.

"You're the only one who can."

He rose in a curt manner.

"I take coffee in twenty minutes. I will meet you in the sculpture garden at the stone fountain."

He disappeared deeper into the passageway, pressed a keypad next to the freight elevator and stepped through its silently parting doors.

# *106*

Surprisingly, Marten Boll's servant did not put up much resistance. A lifted brow, followed by a frown of concentration as if he was giving Kessel's inquiry its due consideration, and that was all. Six minutes after he'd entered the house, Kessel emerged onto the street with the relevant information: Bolls alone was on his way to Zurich. The girl had set out on foot, determined to elude two men Bolls had referred to, amusingly no doubt, as the "terminators."

Reference had been made to Felix Fromm. Kessel knew the name, but he could not place it. Who was Fromm? What could she want with him?

The spleen started to build up in him again. Kessel was self-aware enough to question whether what he felt was really anger – or fear. The panic a child might feel upon realizing the world is beyond his control. Right now, he needed to know about Fromm. It would drive him insane if the association would not come back to him. He resented the only idea that presented itself: telephoning that idiot von Kadow to jog his memory. Kadow alone would know the name. He would know, or be able to ascertain more quickly than Kessel, where the man Fromm could be found.

## 107

Few visitors to the museum ventured into its sculpture gardens. For one thing, the gallery windows were mostly on the street side. To observe its statuary of stone and bronze, one had to go through the rear exits and down rows of dwarf cypress and carefully tended rose bushes.

Inside a low wall, the views were restful. From the steps surrounding the fountain, or stone benches along its paths. For Kenna, the atmosphere was spoiled by fear and unease.

Three people, no four – had been brutally attacked since she began her journey. Grandfather was dead. Dominique too. Bridget, on the road to recovery. Michael – who really knew his condition?

She found a relatively hidden place on the fountain steps, and began automatically assessing escape options. Even in her present condition, she could scale the wall. Once on the street, she would run, or hobble or limp. She ran the plays over again in her mind. With her senses alert to every sound or movement, she waited for Herr Fromm.

Exactly twenty minutes had passed when the museum guard entered the garden from the rear of the museum, carrying a vending machine container of hot coffee. He strolled over to the stone step on which Kenna was seated and sat down.

"A lawyer," he remarked as if continuing their conversation. "All the way from New York. She asks the secret of the Meissen caves. She wants justice for the Jews."

He spoke coldly, pausing to raise the coffee to his lips. "I thought of becoming a lawyer. I was accepted into studies at Stuttgart. I would have made a good one, even exemplary. But then, I was a patriot first."

"You joined Hitler's SS," Kenna said.

"I am almost eighty. Whether I die today or next year, it is the same. I am not afraid of death. I no longer fear the self-righteous, or the Allies' tribunals."

"I haven't come here to make trouble for you."

"It's too late for that."

She held her silence. The outcome of their meeting lay in his control not hers.

"You need a record of the bonds taken at Meissen," he said shrewdly. "To save yourself, to prove your innocence."

"Yes."

"If such a record exists, don't you think it is extremely valuable?"

"You don't need it any longer," Kenna said.

He pursed his lips in anger. "Do you have any idea what it is like to live every minute of your life trapped like a dog in an alley? My records are my protection. They can buy my freedom."

"You still feel hunted?" Kenna asked.

"Maybe not," he conceded. "Now. But in the first years after the war... Knowing they intended to shoot us like pigs, or drag us in chains to the war courts. I avoided the Allies' snares, that's true. But ask, what is such a life?"

The sun slipped behind a cloud, casting a long shadow on the ivy-covered walls around them.

"Some of your -" She searched for a neutral term, "*colleagues* – moved to Argentina."

He gave a grunt of disgust. "Do they prize their lives any better? At least I can speak German here. And occasionally meet my old compatriots."

"I'm hunted too, Herr Fromm. You have no idea what I've lost. If I'm ever to know security again, I need proof of what was taken from the caves. I need to know how to identify the bonds that were in the Reichsbank vaults in 1945."

"You need to know." His tone was meant to deride her. "This information is valuable. I could have sold it many times."

As if he found encouragement in her silence he continued.

"I waited for the letter that would offer my pension. With private income, I could have lived pleasantly – in a manor house or country farm." He glowered at Kenna as if admitting a humiliation. "I served my country for nothing."

"You've been betrayed?" She tried to repress her surprise.

"That is a good English word. The cowards that govern now, they deserve everything they get. You should have seen their predecessors slither like whimpering dogs to the Allies. How quickly these weaklings betrayed their friends."

Kenna repressed an instinct to remind the man he had committed crimes against humankind. That he was, in fact and law, a criminal.

"Something else brought me here," she said.

The wind picked up, rushing the leaves along the paths like marching soldiers. Time was marching forward too.

She handed him the photograph of Lara she'd taken from her grandfather's safe. Was it only two weeks ago?

The old man stared hard at the girl and her dog. "How will you use this information – if it is available."

"I intend to prove the claim is sound. I'll ask for the Jewish fund to be paid according to the bond terms. And for Lara – or her heirs to be found, and paid what they're owed."

"In gold?" he said.

"Or its equivalent."

An expression of cunning briefly crossed his features.

"What will you give me for my records?"

She felt sorry she'd come. The man's bitterness surpassed what she'd unexpected. She'd imagined she could prevail upon his guilt and the human impulse for atonement. How wrong she had been.

"I'm sorry. I have nothing."

"You have something of value to me," he said carefully, watching her.

## *108*

"You aren't afraid of being followed," Herr Fromm observed when they met again in the café of the small hotel next to the Museum at nine o'clock the same evening as agreed.

"Not really," Kenna said. "I've been careful."

No one was on the streets at this hour, the museum quarter was deserted. In contrast to the color and confusion of last night's fair in the old city, the area seemed empty, except for the presence of the wind, pushing litter before it like a janitor with his broom.

An unusual restraint had come over her in the last twenty-four hours, an impulse to preserve her energies, and protect her physical resources. She had fought her way through everything, it seemed: the attack on Michael, the Countess on the train, Pascal's assailant, Kessel's pursuit of her through the bank, Bridget's rescue from the Slovakians. And now, for better or worse, she recognized that her options were limited. Whatever this man offered her, it must be good enough. She could go no further. There was no further to go. She straightened her posture, looking into his eyes expectantly.

"Here," the old man said, pushing a package toward her. She let it lie there, afraid to show the elation she felt.

"What can I do to help you?" she asked.

"A demand upon Germany's gold reserves would be catastrophic," he mused, letting the comment end in a question.

She nodded.

"It will spoil the cozy game of the G-8."

"That's true."

"Germany cannot remain in the European Union with its reserves depleted."

"Obviously not."

"An intolerable humiliation for the strongman of Europe."

She shrugged her assent to his conclusion, uncertain whether he welcomed the outcome or feared it.

He added, "The dog's name was Max."

She was suddenly aware of her heart beating fast. "What happened to Lara?"

He sighed, and casually looked toward the street. "My commandant asked me what we should do with her. A letter had come, an inquiry. You will probably find a notation of it in the Allied files. A lawyer in New York – another one, demanded to buy her freedom with the bonds. They asked me to take care of it. Clerks that we were. We were nothing. But I was determined to end the war in a way that would put me beyond any retribution. I put the letter with the others, in the vaults. They ordered me to send her with the others – on the train for the camp. At that time, the only transport we had fuel for went to Sachsenhausen," he said. "Half an hour from Berlin.

"But the photographer came along that day. I knew it was the end of the war, that his photos would be found. Children would be the first ones searched for. He asked me what would happen to her."

The former SS man spread his palms as if he'd had no choice.

"I let her go."

"The bonds, then, in the Reichsbank vaults, were they awaiting cancellation?" she asked.

He grunted his contempt and turned away. "Is that what they say?"

"Yes."

"More lies," he said, his eyes bright with hatred for the government that had ignored him. "The certificates should have been cancelled. Having been sold once, and turned in for payment. Instead, they were marked in lots, to be traded for gold on the Swiss exchanges."

"How are they marked?" Kenna asked.

"Those that remained in the United States presumably still bear an eagle on the underleaf. Those transported to the Meissen caves were re-bound with new facings for the Swiss bond market – "

"The swastika," Kenna finished.

It was Herr Fromm who first rose from their table. He gave a tight-lipped salute and moved off, shambling his way slowly down the Museumstrasse. As his figure grew smaller, Kenna watched, assailed by a fusion of emotions. She longed to hate this man, who had caused so much death. Only caprice had prevented his carrying out a child's death sentence. But it was more complicated than that. In the end, she threw some coins on the table for the server, clasped the package thankfully to her, and moved swiftly in the direction of the river, and the safety of the castle-ruin.

## 109

"Pick him up," Kessel said into the phone in the living room of his Basel apartment the same evening, glad to have a reason to give a directive that would be obeyed. The old museum guard Felix Fromm had met with the girl, given her a package. That much Kessel could piece together now, based upon his inquiries at the Kunstmuseum and the restaurant in the museum quarter. The contents of the package he did not know, but he could guess.

Fromm's history was known to Kessel. It had come back to him as he thrashed the streets around Marten Bolls' apartment building, intent upon finding the lawyer. He had remembered, but not before enduring the degradation of being forced to parry von Kadow's witless sarcasm from the phone booth off the lobby of the Three Kings.

"Where would she go?" he had asked the bank director.

"She?"

"The girl, idiot. She interviewed Marten Bolls, the currency dealer. She was just there this morning. He obviously sent her to someone else. Someone with knowledge of the bonds. Who would that be? Who is it likely to be?" He could tell from the furtive expressions of passers-by that he was now shouting into the handset.

"Oh. Well, have you tried to find Fromm? The Reichsbank guard. You know him. He tried to shake some money from our side a few years back when he realized the stakes. But someone told him we put a price on his head. Haven't heard his name in years."

So then he had remembered. Former SS officer assigned to the Reichsbank Treasury in the last days of the war. Fromm must certainly have information germane to the gold-clause bonds. Or believed he had. Information John Hermann wanted to conceal.

"Where is your sister?" Kessel cursed himself for raising the subject.

"On her way to Basel, didn't she call you? The Slovakian government wants her to return the bond advance. I don't think that will happen." Von Kadow smiled with private amusement.

Cursed woman. "I'll have her arrested. Or turn her over to Meister and his goons."

"Fabia is not at all pleased with your handling of the bank fiasco. According to Meister's version of things, the bonds are still at large, the lawyer has apparently gone underground, and now, thanks to you, it seems she intends to make an alliance with Fromm, who has nothing but ill will for Germany."

"It's not as bad as you think," Kessel found himself saying. "Even if Raskoff registered the bonds, you can guide the bank's decision. No need for an immediate tender to Germany. There are administrative obstacles you can propose to prevent any imminent decision on the bonds. You've used protocol before to block payments."

"Oh, that. Are you so sure?" von Kadow's false, hollow laughter crackled through the phone line. "I am considering recusing myself from BIS' directors' meeting on Friday."

"Christ! You're the only one who *can* influence things at this point. You have to recommend a special proceeding to determine the bonds' validity. Give the German government time to work something out or produce evidence the bonds are stolen. BIS could tie up the issue for years. Until…"

"Yes?"

"Until the bond-holders die off."

Von Kadow's languidly patronizing sigh infuriated Kessel. "Such an optimist, Kessel. Each day you become more of an American. Really, I don't see how I can put my reputation on the line. Not after the trail of breadcrumbs you've left for Swiss-conspiracy theorists. "

"Well, you had better put your glasses on."

"Is phone-intimidation the best Zurich's top CIA man can do?"

This time it was Kessel who hung up.

It had taken some time in following leads to locate Fromm at the museum. By that time, it was after four o'clock and the guard had gone home. But someone there remembered his lengthy morning break. Someone else had found his coffee container in the litter can at the rear entrance from the garden. And a randy young guard taking a few beers at a restaurant in the museum district had noticed a striking American taking leave of an old man, with a brown parcel under her arm.

Others might doubt that Fromm would share his knowledge, and risk serving a war criminal's sentence for the rest of his life. But Kessel knew otherwise. He could well understand the motivations that might turn loyalty to treason.

"Pick him up, bring him in," he ordered his underling in the Zurich office, though he knew the exercise was futile. The old man would be dead before they arrived.

# 110

Kenna concealed the brown paper parcel Herr Fromm had given her until she reached the walls of the old castle. She arrived there just after nine-thirty. No one was about. She placed the package on the kitchen table and went to make a large pot of tea before sitting down to open it.

Seated at the table with a cup of Earl Gray at her elbow, she opened the package. The contents consisted of about ten pages of typewritten script, apparently banged out on an old machine, for some of the letters were faint or distorted and some set too closely to others, making the words appear crowded.

The pages bore the unmistakable yellowed tone of age except for the cover page, a brief prologue dated that very day. Its message surprised her, for she had found its author embittered and self-pitying:

*I, Felix Fromm, give these notes to the American lawyer, for the first time to admit my knowledge of the lies that have been perpetuated for greed and to avoid retribution for shameful acts.*

*As one grows older one sees there is no point to avoiding the truth. We give few gifts during our lives, and confer much pain and suffering. This is my moment to offer a gift of truth that may help someone, while chastening those whom I have come to disdain.*

Kenna felt touched with some emotion she could not easily name. She put down the stack of papers and moved restlessly into the kitchen for fresh hot water before continuing.

She flipped through the pages of the list Fromm had given her. Until she compared the gold bonds on the list with JAFA's certificates, the numbers meant nothing to her. She drew from her backpack the spreadsheet Marten Bolls the currency dealer, had printed for her and began to compare the list of bonds taken from the caves with the bonds tendered to Germany after the war. She focused on a series of transactions taking place in the first post-war decades.

In 1953, 1954 and 1961, large portfolios had been tendered for payment through BIS. All of the trades had been brokered through J. Dalton & Company. It did not take very long to confirm that the bonds involved in the J. Dalton post-war trades to BIS had come from the caverns at Meissen. How did Germany's so-called "stolen" instruments get from the U.S. Army to J. Dalton's international currencies department?

## *111*

Forty minutes had passed since Kenna brewed her cup of tea and settled in her chair in the sitting room of the safe house to review the package from Felix Fromm. It was midnight, the city around her should have been sleeping, but the street sounds came to her faintly from across the river, muffled further still by thick panes of old glass and heavy draperies.

She'd compared the inventory of bonds taken from the Meissen caves with those brokered to Germany by J. Dalton & Company. Roughly eighty percent of the brokered bonds came from the Meissen caves. Now Kenna put the list down and opened the leather attaché containing JAFA's portfolio. What symbol would she find on them? Eagle – or swastika?

For the last seven days every movement, every thought had been guided by the urgent need to redeem the gold bonds and prove their authenticity. Here was the moment she had risked everything for. A chance to prove JAFA's claim genuine, and her grandfather's commitment justified.

Suddenly she froze, listening. She could hear footsteps trying to be silent on the stair outside. The priests had retired. Nicholas planned to stay in the old town. So they had found her. The Slovakians would know about the castle and the use to which it could be put. Perhaps they'd even followed her there. They would find Bridget. They would kill the priests.

She heard a step on the bare tiles outside the door. She heard a second one. Someone was standing on the other side of the door.

Kenna swept the parcel into the leather portfolio, and slipped the belt over her head. Then she stole toward the window and raised the sash. The heavy iron sign that bore the name of the old hostelry that had once occupied the site protruded just below her window. The crown and letters spelling KRONE HAUS were securely affixed to a cross-bar, the whole of which formed a support for her escape. She prepared herself to crawl onto the cross-bar and drop down to the gravel below.

# *112*

Kenna raised herself onto the window ledge as soundlessly as she could and slipped off her shoes. There was a moment of silence. The intruder on one side of the door, she obscured by darkness on her precarious perch. It felt as if her ears were straining to shut out everything but the sounds from the hallway. Then she heard a European key tumbling in the lock. Nicholas stepped into the room.

"I approve your escape plan," he said, smiling at the open window sash, as she lifted herself back through its opening. He swung a chair around backward and seated himself with his arms on the laddered back, looking up expectantly. Without further prompting, Kenna summarized succinctly Felix Fromm's account of the German gold bonds.

When she'd finished, he moved to the kitchen and brewed himself a cup of tea.

"This swastika – if it doesn't appear on JAFA's bonds?"

"It proves they were not in Germany in 1945."

"Legit, then."

"Yes."

"Due and payable."

"Yes." She couldn't help a small smile escaping.

"And how do we know Fromm tells the truth?"

"Here." She handed him the prologue. He read it quickly, then met her eyes.

"Let's get to it then," he said.

She wiped her hands on her trousers, drew out the top certificate and lifted the binding. The faded glue shone amber with age. Using her thumb, she raised the manila-colored backing carefully, studying the entire length of its underleaf. Quickly, she examined two or three other bonds in the same fashion.

No American eagle ever looked more imposing.

An hour passed before they had examined all of the bonds in JAFA's portfolio. Kenna restrained an impulse to cheer out loud. She smiled widely at Nicholas, who smiled back.

This was what she needed to refute Germany's “list.” Yet she was almost out of time. The BIS Directors would meet the next afternoon to vote on JAFA’s claim, a finding from which there was little chance on appeal. If Kenna failed to put before them this compelling evidence, Raskoff and the other directors would rely on von Kadow's letter. Germany would evade payment forever.

"You can't get inside BIS, Kenna. Kessel will pick you up before you're through the revolving doors."

"There *is* someone the Swiss bankers will listen to," Kenna replied.

# *113*

After Nicholas had freshened their tea, he seated himself at the table and rested his feet upon a chair. "Have at it. Let's hear your hypothesis."

"Hitler came to power in the fall of 1933," she began. "In early 1934 he instructed his finance minister to default on the bond issue, creating panic-selling. Through J. Dalton & Company, Schacht bought the bonds back from panicked investors for cents on the dollar, avoiding hundreds of millions of dollars in obligations. If the United States had enforced the debt, it's doubtful Hitler could have financed his war on Europe.

"But avoiding liability was only half the scheme. By arrangement between the Berlin Börse and SWX, the Swiss agreed to trade the worthless bonds on behalf of the German government. Germany continued to make interest payments to Swiss buyers, so it could keep a market in Europe. Bond manipulation schemes like this are illegal. But the Swiss looked the other way, allowing Hitler to profit from his own default.

"BIS is not a neutral party, then," Nicholas said.

"Correct. If the truth came out, strict monetary sanctions could be imposed against the Swiss for conspiring with Germany to sell worthless bonds. The damage to Switzerland's reputation would be monumental."

"So far, so good."

"But I haven't time to negotiate with BIS. I have another idea in mind. Going back to the Reichsbank in early 1945.

Germany couldn't flood the marketplace with the gold bonds, a large influx would have depressed their value. So the German Treasury stored the bonds, feeding them to the Swiss exchange a little at a time. When the Allies leveled the Reichsbank, everything was moved to the caves south of Berlin. There the bonds were liberated by a rogue company in the Office of Strategic Services. At that time, the unit served as European intelligence for the United States."

Kenna rose and began pacing the room, holding her cup in both hands. "Fast forward to 1947, two years after the war, when Congress created the CIA–successor to the OSS. What follows now is speculation."

"So noted," Nicholas said, with mock solemnity.

" J. Dalton & Company was approached by an officer of the OSS. He probably wanted an evaluation of the bonds that had been seized at Meissen. But John Hermann, on J. Dalton's board, realized the opportunity presented by the situation. Here were 'worthless' German bonds that could be traded in secret to earn huge commissions."

"If they were worthless why would Germany accept them?"

"That's what Hermann asked himself. And he came up with a very creative answer. Germany could only avoid the greater liability represented by legitimate portfolios like JAFA's, if all German gold bonds were removed from circulation. Otherwise, the swastika on the Reichsbank certificates could easily confirm which bonds were valid and which were supposed to have been canceled. Thus, Hermann induced the Germans to accept the Reichsbank bonds in trade."

"For guns," Nicholas said. "For tanks."

"Exactly. And to relieve the debts of governments the CIA wanted to control. Remember, JAFA's claim would have to be paid in gold. Even in the early 1950s, an enormous liability. If Hermann's scheme could evade payment of the gold-bond debt, the Germans saved billions of dollars that could be used to rebuild its economy."

"Sounds logical," Nicholas mused. "What happens next?"

"The year is 1953. JAFA and the other investors ask J. Dalton's directors to represent them at the London Debt Accord. The agenda was to forge a compromise of the debt. It was there, seven years after the war, that Germany came up with its 'stolen bond' defense. With J. Dalton's help, the member nations allowed Germany to set up a Validation Committee that would reject JAFA's portfolio as worthless contraband if it were ever tendered for payment."

"J. Dalton sold its American investors down the river Thames," Nicholas summarized.

She gave a mock salute. "Bull's-eye."

"But isn't this mere supposition, Kenna? Is there any evidence linking Hermann to the OSS-CIA bond trades?"

Kenna paused by the table and rifled her backpack. "Here," she said, producing Marten Bolls' spreadsheet of bond transactions.

"1953, the CIA's Operation Ajax succeeds in returning the pro-U.S. Shah Mohammed Pahlavi to power. 1954, the CIA orchestrates the overthrow of Guatemala's president. January, 1961, four months prior to the CIA-backed Bay of Pigs Invasion in Cuba. It continues through the early 1980s."

Nicholas fell silent. Kenna moved a chair to face him and seated herself in it, searching his face.

"Well thought out," he said, finally. "The bond transactions brokered by J. Dalton correspond to CIA-financed events."

She allowed herself a cat's smile. "Guess who took over J. Dalton's government bond portfolio in 1968?"

Nicholas stood up and placed his hands at his hips as if the time had come for action. "I buy the whole bleeping package, as you've sketched it out. But you're not going to get anyone to admit it."

"I don't need to."

## 114

John Hermann was still at his desk in the New York offices of J. Dalton & Company when Kenna telephoned. The four clocks that adorned his office wall kept him mindful of time differences: Zurich, 1:15 a.m., London, 12:15 a.m., Hong Kong, 7:15 a.m., New York, 7:15 p.m.

"I realize my employment date hasn't technically arrived," Kenna said when Hermann picked up the line himself. "But I'm ready to negotiate my first transaction with your firm. Sadly, our interests are not aligned."

"Where are you?"

She was not at all surprised that he recognized her voice instantly. Since her conversation with Andrea, in which she told her about the photos at Meissen, he must have been thinking of nothing else. But he sounded older. There was something querulous and tired in his tone. She had overlooked the fact that he was just an old man really. It had been easy to forget, under the force of his personality and his intimidating appearance. Had it been only ten days since she'd introduced him to Michael and been subjected to his insults? Now she wondered if it was pity that she felt.

"You know I registered the gold bonds?"

"So I have heard. But that means nothing. JAFA's bonds are worthless. I'm preparing as we speak a letter to BIS informing them that in our opinion the bonds are not valid."

"You should be an expert on worthless bonds," she said. "The CIA trades you executed for Germany involved billions of dollars."

"What are you talking about?"

"The evidence is sitting in your fax tray, with a photograph from May, 1945. Captain Randolph Forrest of the OSS, special intelligence branch of the United States Army, in the act of spearing a stack of gold bonds with his bayonet. A list of their serial numbers corresponds to those which found their way back to Germany in certain bond trades brokered by you. The sellers were various governments supported by the CIA during 1953 through 1961. If the whole scheme weren't illegal, you could be proud – it sounds prestigious to be responsible for arranging the CIA's first financing."

"My dear little girl, nothing you say has any credibility anymore."

"Are you sure?"

She let the minutes pass in silence. If he hung up on her, there was nothing more to be done.

"Let me check my fax tray," he said unexpectedly.

"I'll wait."

"What's your claim?" Hermann said cautiously when he returned to the phone. Gone was the arrogance, the boldness, which had intimidated her.

"Shall we start with the investors' general allegations?"

She took pleasure in summarizing them for him: *Fraud, Breach of fiduciary duty, Conversion. Criminal charges under banking and securities laws. Treason for unlawful ratification of the London Debt Accord, Conflict of interest, extortion, abuse of process.*

She added. "Do I need to continue?"

"All very fine legal concepts," Hermann said. "But where do you get your facts?"

"Marten Bolls. Felix Fromm. André Lebecque. The photos, you know about. There are records in Basel –"

"That's enough."

"I have more," Kenna said.

"I know what you want," Hermann said. "But even if my firm was motivated to save face on JAFA's claim, we cannot pay what the bonds are worth in today's dollars. The sums involved would precipitate a global crisis. No one can pay the value of JAFA's bonds."

He sounded almost sorrowful. The man was hardly younger than her grandfather had been when he died. But he sounded like a petulant child. What had happened in the last two weeks to eviscerate him? Was he really so afraid of public shame at the end of his life?

"What can I do?" he said. "Why do you come to me?"

"I need your expertise," she told him truthfully.

His firm was known for its influence. Hermann's reputation for negotiating global business settlements was unparalleled. Hermann alone could resolve the bond claim. His brilliance and acumen were qualities she'd admired – once.

"You flatter me," he said in a mocking tone. "What are you asking?"

"I'm not asking," Kenna said.

## *115*

The silence went on a long time. Kenna could hear the ticking of the three clocks in Hermann's office.

"What if I decline to do anything?" Hermann asked.

"I'll be very disappointed."

"Let me think about it."

"No time," she said, feigning regret. "The New York Times has a fax tray too."

"What's your demand?"

"I've thought about what would be reasonable," she said. "I've read your book on structuring settlements."

"Well?"

"The full face amount calculated at the price of gold in 1953 at the time of the London Accord, plus interest at seven percent."

She was aware of his deliberation, briefly tapping up the numbers on his calculator. When the machine stopped, he asked. "Is that all?"

"The settlement will be made public."

"Is that necessary?"

"Isn't it time that all who profited from Hitler's acts face their past?"

"Apparently," Hermann said bitterly, and hung up the phone.

# 116

Just after dawn, in the basement of the Bank for International Settlements, a night guard looked on as an attractive blond in sweater and skirt of fine Italian wool labored over a stack of files, tearing the pages from their brackets and forcing the fat paper stacks through the shredder.

The machine that dominated the stone floor of one of the basement vaults was industrial quality, the size of a floor furnace, yet it performed its work heatedly and with great laborious grunts.

"I can smell it," the building guard offered. "The shredder, it's too hot."

"It's not," she said.

"Turn it off for awhile."

His tone was brusque enough that she halted her procedures briefly, snapping a stack of papers on the worktable to straighten them.

"I've got to get these shredded before eleven o'clock," she said in a transparent attempt to appease him.

She pushed a stack of papers through the machine defiantly.

"What are they?" The guard drew closer.

"Papers. You can see that," the blond retorted.

"Anything to do with the Jewish accounts?"

"How would I know?"

The guard walked over to the box of files, flipped through their contents casually.

"Records," he murmured. "The Weimar gold-clause bonds." And then, "Is the Direktor so afraid of the American lawyer?"

"What do you know about it?"

"I know what the Americans and the British will say if we are caught shredding evidence of war debts."

"I am protecting the Bank," she said.

"Wait a minute – these are not marked for destruction."

She pursed her lips stubbornly.

"Halt, then. Halt this immediately – I will call Herr Raskoff."

The blond continued as if he had not spoken.

The guard pulled the cord from the wall socket and the machine issued a sharp burp as the pages lodged in the blades. He moved to the wall alarm and pressed it. Then he put his hand on his gun. Only tear gas. Yet -

"This is not right," he said.

The blond stood still. Her hands dropped to her sides and she scowled at him defiantly. "If they find these papers, they'll blame the Swiss. Do you like being Europe's whipping boy? Time and again we're punished for our neutrality. What can we do? Our geography is our destiny."

Replacing the files and sealing the boxes, he continued his reprimand. "Whatever it is, we should not be caught hiding."

He drew a stack of canvas currency sacks from a box and began stuffing the paper worms that filled the shredder bin into the sacks.

Steps sounded on the stone stair leading to the basement vaults, the combination lock turned and the vault door opened. The bank manager stepped inside.

"Herr Direktor!" the blond said.

"Teni? What are you doing down here? I need your help preparing for the Directors' meeting."

"I'm sorry, Herr Raskoff," Teni replied.

The guard stepped forward. "These boxes were not marked for destruction. They should be kept in a safe place." He scowled defensively as if he expected resistance.

The Director steepled his hands before him and studied his assistant. "Berger's right, this is not the way." Then softly. "Too late for this."

Raskoff turned to leave the vault. "Berger, put those papers in the locked room. Mark them "Confidential," and bring the keys to me."

"Yes, Herr Direktor."

The guard could not resist a smile of triumph at the administrator. Her eyes were fierce with tears, whether from fury or shame, the guard could not tell.

As if in afterthought, Raskoff addressed his assistant.

"The German Direktor is here. He brings surprising news. Germany is prepared to formally recognize the American bond debt. A demand has gone out to the German Treasurer for immediate payment of a compromise sum. J. Dalton bank will pay half the settlement to avoid claims of malfeasance. Too bad for them – the end, no doubt."

He shrugged. "But at least we," he added grimly, "will not be blamed."

## 117

Kessel read once again the written report that had been faxed to him in response to his inquiries. He was not surprised at the suspected location of Kenna Rand and her Irish compatriots. He could easily find them. But she would not be alone. How many Irish were there? He certainly had no intention of reprising the scene outside BIS and the train station.

While he debated what was to be done to apprehend the young woman, the phone rang in his Basel apartment. This time, the caller was someone other than Kessel's Zurich underling. In fact, it was not an underling at all. He knew the voice, he knew the name, but he did not use the caller's name in the conversation. In fact, there was no "conversation." Only a brief instruction and a phrase that virtually robbed him of discretion or control in completing his assignment.

His shoulders slumped ever so slightly as he listened to the crisp, incisive tone informing him that intelligence had been received regarding Kenna Rand's point and time of departure from Basel. He was to be there. He was to arrange for another to be there. A woman posing as a South American banker, who constituted a present and immediate economic threat to German-American banking interests. And he was to undertake there "a permanent solution" to the annoying problem of this individual. That's the way the caller chose to express himself. And Kessel knew what the words meant. There could be no doubt.

## *118*

There is a monument in Basel where Europe's strongmen, France and Germany, meet Switzerland. After Kenna completed her telephone call to BIS to confirm that the checks and settlement papers had been drawn, she made her way to Three Countries Corner. There, she would meet Nicholas and be transported to France. From Paris, she would find a flight home.

It would be good to get back to New York, she thought. It was November now. The weather would be turning cold. Although their latitudes were virtually the same, New York, in her slight melancholy, seemed sunnier than Paris. It would be good to leave Europe behind.

It was a cloudless day of high wind. Kenna took the No. 1 tram to the No.14, then followed the river on foot. On the outskirts of the old city were shaded parks of birches and dragon-spouting fountains. Save for the occasional pre-school child with his nanny, the parks were empty.

Gradually, the quiet residential streets gave way to abandoned docks and naval yards. Weeds grew tall along the banks, and the city's 16th century Guild houses were replaced by storage facilities of the Swiss Navigation Company.

Kenna paused once to stare out over an empty field, where the heavy European beat of a ghetto blaster issued from an empty warehouse, and a workman scrubbed a wall of racial slurs. She would not see Basel again for many years, if ever, no matter how events played out in the final settlement. And if she did return, the old city would not be the same.

Things had moved on. Expectations for the European Union had imbued a sense of Euro-pride and confidence. That would lead to renewed business vigor. Get out of the way charming village-culture, make way for the new industrial mega-Europe.

She quickened her pace. Five minutes later the path left the road, leading her down two flights of metal stairs to river level. Here began Drellanderecke, the Three Countries Monument, a man-made peninsula that jutted into the Rhine.

To her left a harbor of small craft docked on the peninsula's seaward side. Kenna studied the boats carefully but Nicholas' motor launch, the "Hey Joe," was not among them.

She proceeded uncertainly along the riverbank until a sign in German brought her to a long concrete terrace that floated on the Rhine like the deck of an aircraft carrier.

The terrace was set with café tables and aqua-colored plastic chairs on chrome legs. The lunch crowd had dispersed, the tables were empty save for one, its canvas umbrella folded against the wind.

Two waitress-coeds in sailor shorts, white berets and lace-up skates, hustled beer and chips to a large table of German tourists. Kenna strode the length of the deck to the bow, aware of the men drilling their curiosity into her back.

The Rhine narrowed here where the Swiss, German and French borders all converged in mid-river. The place was marked by a sleek metal sculpture that rose from the deck like a stealth bomber up-ended for launching. Each of its three curving wings bore a decal of horizontal bars in red, white and blue. A shallow pool at its base finished an effect that was pristine, neat, restrained. Like the Swiss themselves.

She felt lifted by the solitary moment, surrounded by the turbulent river. Its fast sweeping current was more like the open sea here, hurling its choppy waves at the banks of France on her left, Germany and Switzerland on her right.

She longed for the United States, for home. The wind that relentlessly whipped her clothes and hair, swept through her soul as well. The ending had come. At last the long, strange odyssey would be over. She had spoken, once, too briefly, to Michael. His words had been tender and tentative. He was still with Ulrich in Mexico, a good place for convalescing, he had joked, and he'd filled her in on Bianca and doings at the resort. She'd told him about Lara and he had been glad. He had things to tell her, he said in a serious tone. She would see him very soon, he promised.

She retraced her steps to the café section of the terrace and positioned herself near a tall silo staircase that offered protection from the wind. From there she could watch for Nicholas.

The strains of a melody drifted from the upper deck. Sadness came, unwanted. Could she go home? The charges would be dropped. And her grandfather's bonds would share in the settlement. Yet she'd violated a court order. She could face disbarment. And there was little chance of getting a position like the one she'd been offered at Hermann & Kroft. There was always the State Department. She smiled grimly to herself. The career path she and her grandfather had charted for her had lost its luster.

She did not see the Countess immediately. But her senses, so acutely tuned to her environment, scented danger. She raised her eyes to the river's bank where the older woman, having emerged from a black Mercedes, regarded her through dark glasses.

Beside her, Mister A strained at his lead – ears raised in two points, black eyes fixed on Kenna. She felt her heart race. What are *you* doing here? Her first thought was to stand her ground. To confront the woman who had murdered her grandfather.

*Move lass, leave it.*

Kenna met the eyes of the Countess and held them.

*No, lass. Move on.*

She did not need to see Klaus Kessel to feel his presence. The CIA man appeared less than twenty yards in front of her. Dressed in black leather leggings, his top-coat whipping round his legs in the wind, and a wool scarf flapping at his throat. When he saw the Countess, the snakelike vein crazed his temple like the mark of Zorro. He descended the steps to the quay two at a time.

"Take her Klaus!"

The Countess' commanding voice carried in the wind. She swept onto the terrace and hastened toward Kenna, stiff-gaited with fury, her sable coat billowing behind her.

"Stop where you are," Kenna said. "Don't come any closer." She held her attaché over her head ready to pitch it into the current. The case held only a few papers, but her pursuers couldn't know that. If that's what they were after, let them bloody swim for it.

The Countess froze in her place like a figure on an old music box whose tune has run down. Kessel too. The nautical waitress skated between them with a plate of rosti, while the table of Germans watched in unexpected silence.

"You," the Countess said, ten feet from Kenna. She released a latch in the handle of the short black crop she carried to discipline the dog and dropped a pellet into its compartment. Another 'click' and the crop became a projectile.

"There is a New Reich," the Countess spat each word. "It's *our* wealth you have taken. You'll pay for this."

Michael. Grandfather. She already had.

Two Germans rose from their table and started toward the Countess. Not tourists after all, Kenna recorded. Kessel, too, started forward, coming up cautiously behind Kenna. But she did not move. She waited. With a sense of shock, she realized that if she needed a rescuer it would be Kessel. He had come for her, to take her back. Those were his orders. But this . . . There would be witnesses! No, this was Countess' impulsive scheme.

Countess flicked something toward the dog's head. "Attack!"

The Doberman's nails clicked like daggers as he raced along the deck, his lead flapping behind him. This was the cue Kenna had been waiting for. Kessel moved too.

At her shoulder, she heard the hiss of the lethal pellet as the Countess fired. The Doberman roared in surprise and pain. Mister A had been hit. The dart dropped to the deck.

The dog spun around. Wild now, he lunged for Kenna, but missed. It was Kessel who caught her shoulder and brought her down.

Suddenly it was she and Kessel with the dog barking madly. She felt the Doberman's breath on her face. Kessel threw up his arms to defend the attack. Mister A locked his jaws onto Kessel's arm and tore through the jacket. The warm blood soaked through at once and Kessel bellowed hoarsely, registering fury as much as pain.

"Fucking beast – call him off!"

Kenna spun herself free and rolled down the ramp to dockside.

At the foot of the ramp a chain link fence and gangplank led to the water. The sign in German read *DOC GANG VERBOTEN.*

Kenna gained her feet and ran toward it. She heard steps behind her. She half-turned to face the Countess. The older woman swung at her, striking her with a force that knocked her to her knees. She grabbed hold of the Countess' sable coat with both hands, trying to drag her down. The Countess drew back her boot and launched it, connecting hard with Kenna's chest.

Kenna seized the boot with both hands and shoved it upward with all her strength. The Countess gave a sharp yelp. Teetering for balance, the Countess veered backward. Kenna gave her foot a mighty heave. The Countess struggled for her footing and lost, plunging off the deck into the rabid waters of the Rhine. Kenna leapt to the railing. Carried in the strong current with the heft of her fur coat dragging her under the swells, the Countess flailed like a drowning grouse.

The dog transferred his rage to Kenna, racing after her, white foam issuing from his jowls like lace. *Don't get sloppy, Mister A.*

In one leap, Kenna cleared the chain link fence and dropped onto the private gangplank, her heels inches ahead of the dog's tearing jaws. Then she was up and sprinting to the 'Hey Joe,' there at dockside, idling its motor in the choppy river. The Doberman hurled himself against the metal fence, baring his incisors through the wire.

"Good timing lass!" Nicholas' cheerful voice. "Get in the damn boat!"

Nicholas clasped her roughly with one hand while he steadied the wheel with the other. Within seconds Kenna found herself speeding toward the shores of another country. She looked back once. On the terrace she'd so recently vacated the two beer-swilling "Germans" hauled the dripping Countess onto the deck and wrestled her into handcuffs.

Nicholas grinned. "Got the bleeping witch at last."

The glint of sun on a watch face drew Kenna's attention to the quay, where the figure of Klaus Kessel was receding from her view, limping toward the old city of Basel. The cell phone rang in her belt and she answered it. Yes–she was informed by a rather efficient caller from BIS–Germany had approved the bond settlement.

## *119*

The Aran Islands, where the rough seas of the Atlantic roll westerly off Ireland's rugged coast, form three bronze pendants strung across the mouth of Galway Bay. The islands are timeless landscapes where little has changed for centuries and only Irish is spoken.

On the smallest of the islands, Inisheen, a stone-washed cottage stands on a knoll above the sea. Not long after Kenna Rand left Basel, the residents of Inisheen were heard to inquire of each other – when they met at the island's grocery the size of a coat closet, or over a pub supper of mutton stew and brown bread: "Did `ya see the light in McCarthy cottage? Now, who could be livin' there?"

It was here that Kenna Rand had come after Basel – not as her grandfather would have intended, to serve the cause of Irish peace, but in exile from betrayal. She had learned that all governments can betray their trust, if their citizens are rewarded for deceit.

On a quiet Tuesday afternoon, in a pasture of wild grass and black and white cows, only the occasional, officious barking of the cows' minder, a brown and white spaniel named Queenie, broke the silence.

The hired car remained hidden on the road – the way to the stone cottage being little more than a herder's path, with banks that rose nearly eight feet above the road on both sides. Thus, until the car pulled up to the white rough-washed cottage, Kenna stood transfixed by Queenie snapping at the cows' heels, causing them to jostle their bells and hurry to the barn for milking by Crissie, the local girl.

The car stopped and an attractive bearded man got out and shaded his eyes. Kenna mirrored the gesture, lifting her hand to push back her thick dark hair and visor her grey eyes. She started as if she knew him, and waved joyfully at the stranger on the road. She knew the man with his shining black beard and imposing presence, though he had lost considerable weight. She raced up the road to meet him, even as he moved toward her with a newly acquired limp. Michael.

THE END

## *ABOUT THE AUTHOR*

Kia McInerny is an author and attorney whose special knowledge of the history of German gold bonds led to *Bond Hunter*. The novel is based upon little known facts Kia uncovered concerning Wall Street's role in financing Germany's war on Europe.

Kia's other novels include *Max in Filmland*, a stylish tale of misadventure set in 1970s Euro-Hollywood and *Murder in Malibu,* a contemporary LA-noir tale of betrayal and murder, both soon to be available on Amazon. Kia's short fiction has been featured on public radio and in literary magazines.

In non-fiction, Kia's wine and travel essays have appeared internationally in Singapore, Ireland and the U.K, as well as in the United States. She currently lives in Santa Barbara and Los Angeles with her attorney husband.

*For historical facts and images regarding Kia's books, please check out the Author's page on Amazon.*